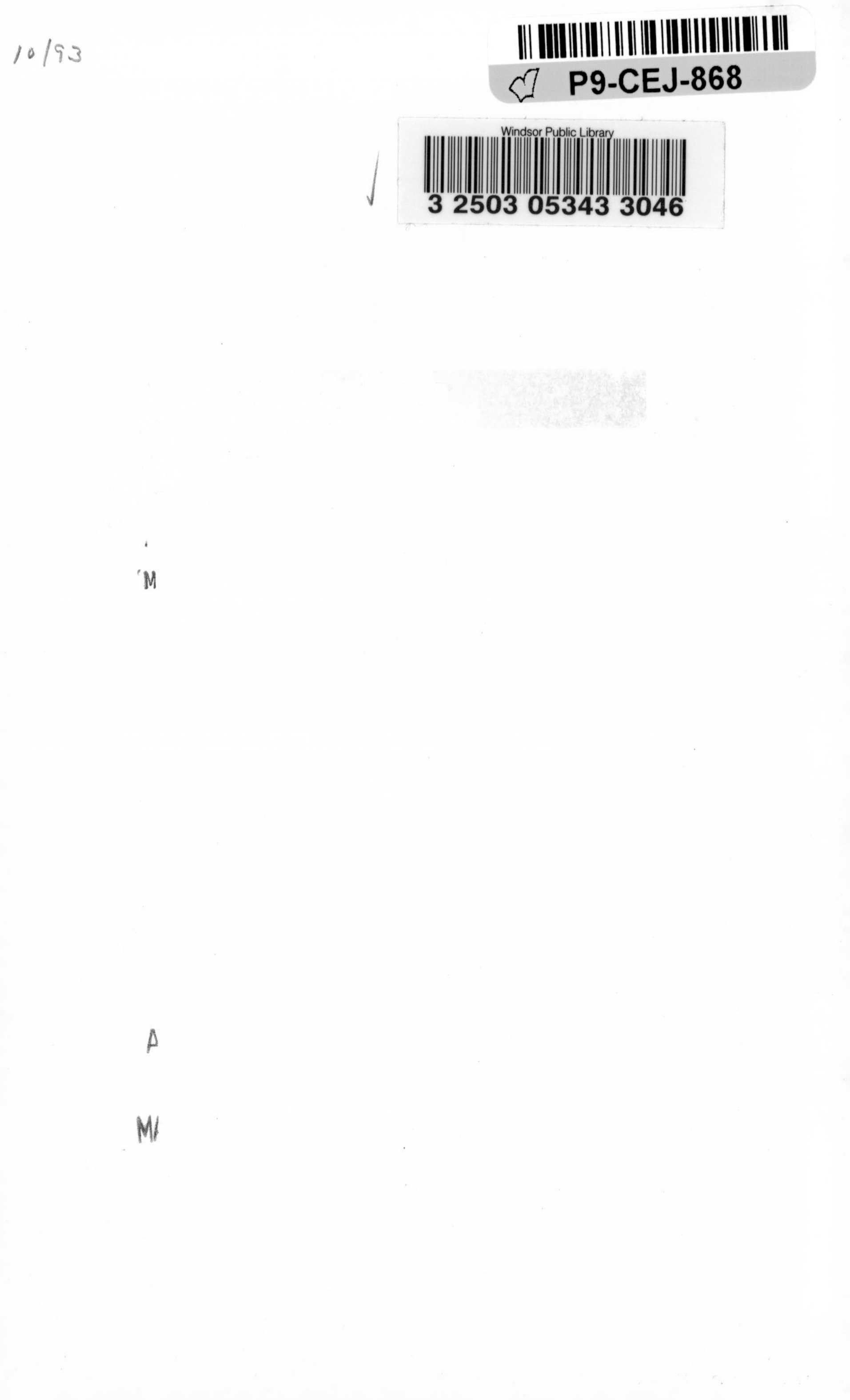

ARROWS
OF THE
SUN

Tor Books by Judith Tarr

The Hound and the Falcon

AVARYAN RISING:

The Hall of the Mountain King
The Lady of Han-Gilen
A Fall of Princes
Arrows of the Sun

Lord of the Two Lands

Throne of Isis (forthcoming)

Arrows of the Sun

Judith Tarr

A Tom Doherty Associates Book
New York

ARROWS OF THE SUN

This book is printed on acid-free paper.

A Tor Book
Published by Tom Doherty Associates, Inc.
175 Fifth Avenue
New York, N.Y. 10010

Map by Ellisa Mitchell

Design by Lynn Newmark

Library of Congress Cataloging-in-Publication Data

Tarr, Judith.
Arrows of the sun / Judith Tarr.
p. cm.
ISBN 0-312-85263-0
I. Title.
PS3570.A655A89 1993
813′.54—dc20 93-21617
CIP

First edition: September 1993

Printed in the United States of America

0 9 8 7 6 5 4 3 2 1

To Susan Shwartz, for the idea,

and

To the regulars of GEnie's Science Fiction Round Table,
who preferred a finished novel to the usual social niceties

With special thanks to
Jeanne Zimmerman and Harry Turtledove

KUNZERAN
ANJIV
R. Shahriz'uan (Great Flood)
VEYADZAN
ISHRAN
Kundri'j Asan
EMPIRE
MARKAD
Lakes of the Moon
Induwerran
KOVRUEN
ASANIAN
Karghaz
Shon'ai
Imuryaz
KARMANLIOS
SHENDI
Pri'nai
Magrin
R. Oroz'uan
R. Anz'uan
USADI
ANSAVAAR
VARESH
IGRAN
THE
INDERAN
UVARESH
KHARAG'UN
Burning Sea
GREAT DESERT
ELISA MITCHELL 93

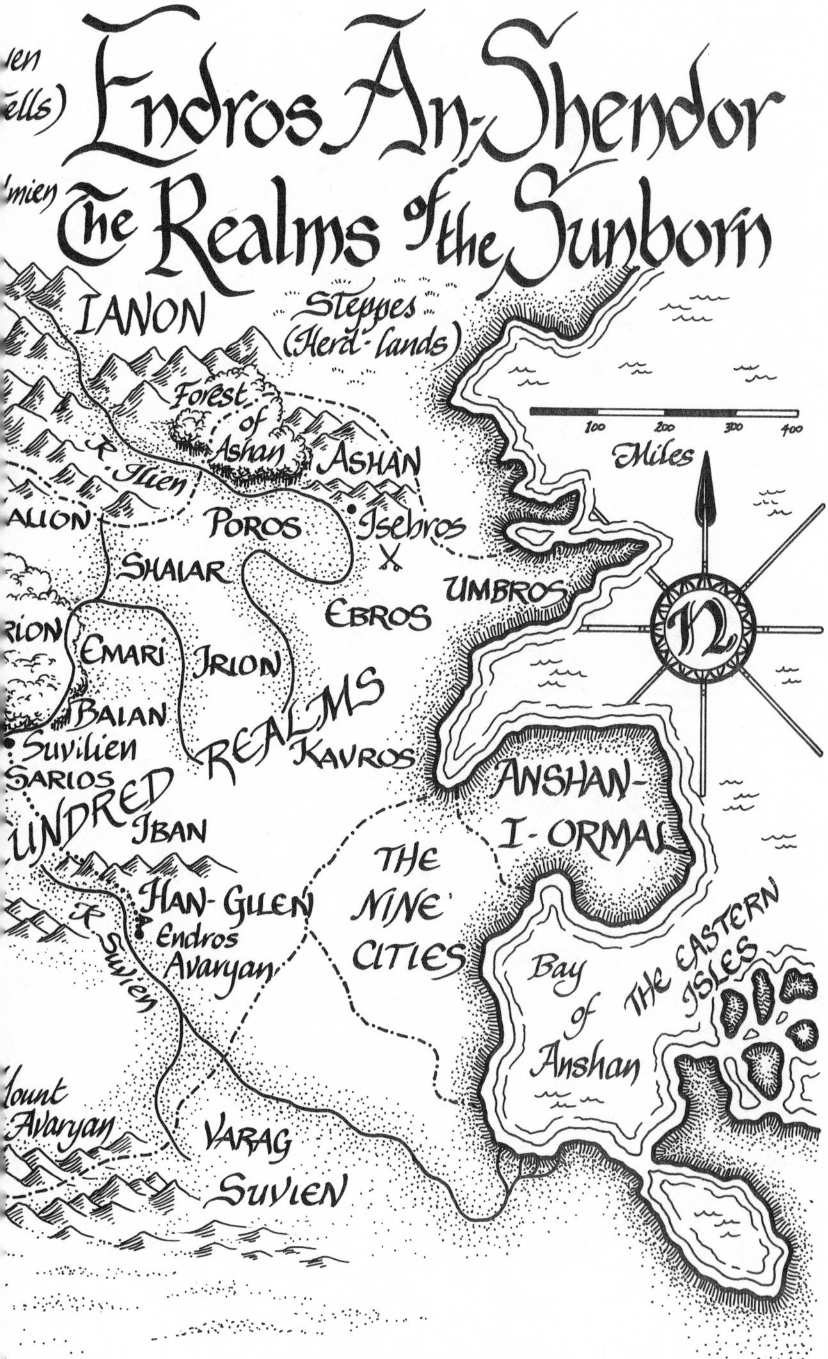

Endros An-Shendor
The Realms of the Sunborn

ien
ells)
mien
IANON
Steppes
(Herd-lands)
Forest of Ashan
ASHAN
R. Ilien
ALLION
POROS
Isebros
SHAIAR
UMBROS
EBROS
RION
EMARI
IRION
REALMS
BAIAN
Suvilien
KAVROS
SARIOS
UNDRED
IBAN
ANSHAN-I-ORMAL
THE NINE CITIES
HAN-GILEN
Endros Avaryan
R. Suvien
Bay of Anshan
THE EASTERN ISLES
Mount Avaryan
VARAG
SUVIEN
100 200 300 400
Miles
N

ARROWS
OF THE
SUN

Endros Avaryan

"His majesty is in a rare mood this morning."

His majesty, having flung back the shutters to let in the newborn sunlight, turned in the flood of it and laughed. "His majesty is his majesty this morning. What's rarer than that?"

Vanyi stretched in her tangle of pillows and coverlets. She was warm all through, and not with sunlight.

He was bathing in it, pouring it over him like water. Sun's child, that one, morning-born, bearing the Sun in his hand. It flamed there, gold born in the living flesh, mark and price of his lineage: *Ilu'Kasar*, brand of the god.

She, who would have welcomed more sleep, still found it in her to smile at the god's youngest child. "Oh, there are rarities, my lord, and there are rarities. But not every day sees a ten years' regency ended, or a throne taken that's sat empty so long."

He came out of the light, but it was on him still, limning with gold the arch of a cheekbone, the angle of a shoulder. "I should be terrified, I think," he said.

"Probably," said Vanyi. She sat up, drawing knees to chest and clasping them. She shivered. It was not the warmest of mornings, bare spring that it was, and the sun though bright was cool.

Warmth wound about her: coverlet, and Estarion's arms about that, and his white smile. "I had all my panic terrors yesterday. Today I'll be pure arrogance."

"Joy," said Vanyi. "Leave a little room for that."

He left more than a little: enough for both of them several times over.

She noticed before he did that they had a watcher. Green eyes blinked at them. Ivory fangs bared in a yawn.

"And a fair morning to you," said Vanyi, "milady ul-cat."

The great cat-body poured itself across their feet, rumbling with purr. Vanyi worked her toes into fur the color of shifting shadows, sleek and almost stiff without, soft as sleep within. Estarion ran a teasing finger down her ribs. She yelped and attacked him until he cried for mercy.

The next visitor announced herself more properly than the cat had. The page was young enough to look everywhere but where his master was. There was no telling if he blushed: he was a northerner, and dark as Lady Night. "My lord," he said. "Sire. The Empress Regent—The Lady—Your mother—She—"

"Let her come in," said Estarion before Vanyi could speak. She could have hit him. She scrambled at blankets, cursed the hair that knotted and tangled and got in the way, and added a choice word for young idiots of all-but-emperors who did not care who saw them naked in the morning.

He kissed her into fuming silence. Knowing—damn him—what his mother would see: her son making free of his favors with his lady of the moment.

"Not that," he said, drawing back, smoothing her hair. Reading her through all her shields and her magery, and hardly aware that he did it. "Never that, my love."

Vanyi let her gaze fall. Even when she was angry, his touch could make her body sing.

The empress found them almost decorous: Vanyi with the coverlet drawn to her chin, Estarion stretched across her feet with the cat. He raised himself on his elbow and smiled his sweetest smile. "Mother! I hadn't thought to see you here so early."

"Hardly early," said the empress. "The sun has been up for a long hour." But she smiled, and kissed him on forehead and cheeks with ceremony that was all love.

One could see, thought Vanyi, where Estarion had his darkness and his slimness, and much of his height. He did not have his mother's beauty. His face was pure Varyani: high-cheeked, hawk-nosed, neither ugly nor handsome but simply itself. He looked like his firstfather, people said, Mirain, who had called himself the son of the god: gone these fourscore years, and four emperors since, and Estarion the fifth of them, sixth in the line that sprang from the Sun. From Ganiman his father he had the thick curling hair of the western blood, and the family profile; and, through some alchemy of breeding, his eyes.

He was born to be stared at, but he hated to be stared at for that. When he was younger he had cultivated a concealment of flamboyance, made a fashion of hats and hoods, or worn garments so outrageously cut or colored that lookers-on forgot his single, and singular, oddity. He had grown out of that. But he still would not linger in front of a mirror, or happily remind himself that he was at least in part a westerner.

It might have been simpler if the rest of him had not seemed pure northern tribesman. But his eyes were Asanian, and worse than that: royal Asanian. Eyes of the Lion, they called them in the west. Pure and burning gold, seeming whiteless unless he opened them very wide; astonishing in that dusk-dark face.

He was not thinking of them now, regarding his mother with every evidence of content. But he said, "Do you mind terribly? That I'm taking your titles away?"

"I mind," she said, "that I am laying all the burdens on you, and you so young still."

He sat up sharply. The cat growled, startled. He soothed her with an absent hand. "I'm hardly a child any longer."

"You are a man," his mother agreed willingly, "and most well grown. And yet . . ."

"It's time," he said. His voice was steady.

"Time and past time," said the empress regent. "No; that office I lay down in all gladness. But I am still a mother, and to a mother her child is always and ever that, though he wear a beard of august silver, and hold empires under his sway."

Estarion's hand went to his chin. There was no silver in the stubble there, nor would be for a while yet, Vanyi reckoned.

The empress smiled and held out her hand. "Come, Starion. Your servants have been waiting this past hour and more."

He was up almost before she finished speaking, kissing her hand, casting himself upon the mercies of his bath-servants. The empress did not move to follow him. Vanyi, who had known better than to think herself forgotten, restrained herself from pulling the blanket over her head. She met the dark stare steadily. "Lady," she said.

"Priestess," said the empress. Her tone was cool.

"Are you sorry," Vanyi asked, "that virginity is no longer a requirement of priesthood?"

"Hardly," said the empress. "My son would object strenuously if you were sentenced to the sun-death."

"Ah," said Vanyi, "but would you?"

Her heart was beating hard. She had been Estarion's lover these past three seasons, and yet she had never exchanged more than brief courtesy with Estarion's mother. Vanyi knew what the court thought of her who had walked straight from the road of her priestess-Journey into the emperor's bed. What the empress thought, no one knew. Vanyi was mageborn and priestess of the Sun. The Lady Merian was a wisewoman of the north, priestess of the goddess who was the dark behind the sun, mistress of mages. Her soul was a blinding brilliance, her thoughts a shape of silence.

She said, "My son is very fond of you."

"I rather think he loves me," Vanyi said. There was a snap in it.

"He has a warm heart," said the empress. "And you were his first woman."

Vanyi's cheeks were burning. No doubt they blazed scarlet. It was all the color they ever had. Corpse-woman, people called her here, because she was as white as new milk, and they were all black or brown or ruddy bronze. Even the Asanians were, at worst, old ivory.

But Estarion loved her pallor; loved to cup his dark hand over her white breast, and marvel at the play of blue veins under the skin.

"Yes, he fancies that he loves you," the empress went on, gentle and cruel. "He knows he cannot marry you. You are a commoner, and an Islander at that."

"You tell me nothing I haven't long known," Vanyi said. "Why didn't you stop me when I first set eyes on him? I might have gone away then. I was appalled at myself: that I had such thoughts, and he so high."

"I trusted in your good sense," the empress said. Vanyi stared. The empress smiled. "You know what you are, and what you are not. You will not be empress: you are too thoroughly unsuitable. But you give yourself no airs; you claim no advantage, though he would give you the moons if you asked for them. You bear him no child, nor shall, while the bonds of the Journey seal your womb. And," she said, "you are very good for him."

Vanyi had nothing to say. The words had drained out of her.

"Remember," the empress said, "how his father died. How he had taken his son with him into Asanion after too long a sojourn in the east, for the heir to the throne must know all of the empire he would rule; and how, when he came to the city of kings, to Kundri'j Asan, his death was waiting for him. No clean death in battle, but poison in a cup, and malice wound about it, and sorcery sealed within it."

Vanyi knew. Estarion never spoke of it, but others did, round about; and she was a mage of the temple in his city. His father had died as he watched. He had known the poison for what it was. He found the mage who had wrought the poison, and mustered all his power of heart and soul and mind, and made of it a weapon, and killed the man who had killed his father. He lost his power for that, and nearly his mind. He was twelve years old. A child, but never a child after.

His power had come back, but slowly, and never in the measure that it had had. Of memory he had nothing, save that sometimes he dreamed, and woke screaming. And he would not go to Asanion, or speak of it save as he must, or grant more than cold courtesy to its people who came to pay him homage.

"Before you came," his mother said, "we had begun to fear for him. He had seemed to be recovered from the black days, in mind if not in magery; and then once more, as he became a man, the darkness closed in. Never a night passed but that he dreamed, and dreamed ill. He strove to hide it, to wall it with such power as was left to him. But we knew. We were in great dread for his sanity."

"He is perfectly sane," said Vanyi, more stiffly than she liked.

"He is," said the empress, unruffled. "We owe you a debt for that."

"But not enough to give us leave to marry."

"His empress must be bred to it," said the daughter of a mountain chieftain.

"And I was bred to the nets and the boats and the fish." Vanyi considered rage, but found it insufficient. "What, when he takes his proper bride, and I take my leave? What if the dreams come back? What will you do then?"

"We shall settle that when we come to it," the empress said. "No law forbids him a concubine, or a lover of choice apart from the woman who shares his throne."

"His empress might have something to say of that," said Vanyi.

"She may," the empress said. "She may not." She bent her head. It was almost a bow. "For this day and for the days until he takes his bride, you have my blessing. Prosper well, priestess of the Sun, Guardian of the Gates. Cherish my son."

"Always," said Vanyi. That much at least she could promise.

* * *

Time was in the north when the king came naked to his throne, and proved to his people that he was male and whole and fit to rule. Estarion might have liked that: he had no shame of his body, and he loved to be outrageous. But the south was a staider place.

Estarion had not wanted excessive ceremony, and he would not suffer the tenfold robe of the western emperors. In the end he consented to be a southerner in trousers and embroidered coat, with his hair in the single plait of a priest, and no ornament but the heavy golden torque of his priesthood. The high soft boots and the trousers were white unblemished, and the coat was cloth of gold. Against it he was all the darker, his eyes all the more brilliantly gold. He did not, for once, try to hide them.

Vanyi, anonymous among the priests and the lesser nobles, watched as he passed in procession. He was aware of her: a ghost-hand lay brief against her cheek, a ghost-smile warmed her from within. Most of him was centered on the rite. For a moment she walked within him down the long aisle between the white pillars, from sun to shade and back to sun again, and before him, looming larger as he came closer to it, the simple chair set on its dais. The wall behind it burst and bloomed in gold, the rayed sun of his fathers, image and remembrance of the god. But he saw nothing of the gold, no more than he saw of the people who thronged the hall and filled the courts without. The throne was waiting.

He had never sat in it. He was too young and it too strong, his regents had thought, for the fragility of his mind. It was a simple thing, a chair carved of pale stone, neither silver nor grey but somewhere between. But there was mighty magic in it. It was carved of dawnstone, the stone that woke to the coming of the sun, and imbued with the power of his line.

It was glimmering, Vanyi thought. Faintly; difficult to see from so far, with so many bodies between. But it was more silver than grey.

He was closed to her now. For a moment she was empty, bereft; then she shook herself, bolstering the wards about her thoughts. Far behind them, deep and safe, she allowed herself to smile. A year yet, and four days: that long she had to wait until her Journey was done. Then the oath was ended. The bonds of her womb were loosed. And she would give him the gift she most longed to give: an heir of her body. Let another be empress if it would please his princes and his lady mother. Vanyi would bear his son.

The throne gleamed clearly now, a pure light that though pale was never cold, like the sky at the coming of the sun. She could not see Estarion's face. She knew that it was rapt, like the rest of him. Drawn toward it; bound to it.

He paused at the foot of the dais, with the high ones about him. The empress in royal white, tall and cold and beautiful. The chancellor of his empire, elegant southern prince with his startling bright hair. Priests of Sun and Shadow, god and goddess, torqued in gold and in black iron. The lords of his council in their manifold splendor, from bearded, kilted, glittering northerner to clean-shaven trousered southerner to robed and turbaned syndic of the Nine Cities. And one lone westerner in the fivefold robe of a prince, wearing an ambassador's fluted hat.

They surrounded their emperor, overwhelming him. Then he mounted above them. His mother followed, and his chancellor, a step behind, at right hand and left. On the last step he paused. They passed him and turned. They were of a height, northerner and southerner, dark woman and bronze-skinned man with his hair the color of new copper. They bowed to one another and held out each a hand.

Estarion laid his hands in theirs and let them draw him upward. He was taller than either, and for a moment he seemed very slight, almost frail.

He straightened. Vanyi saw his head come up, his shoulders go back. They were broad, those shoulders, for all the narrowness of the rest of him. He inclined his head to each of his regents. They bowed in return.

He turned. His face was a shadow against the sudden blaze of thronelight. His eyes were full of it.

Without great ceremony, but without haste, he sat. The thronelight blazed like the full sunrise. Vanyi staggered with the power and the glory of it—the great singing surge of exultation. Terrible, magical, awful thing: it knew its lord and servant. It took him to itself.

2

Drums beat, pulse-beat. Slow, slow, then swifter, rising up and up to a rattle of panic-terror.

The boy ran.

Sometimes as he ran he was himself: wind in his face, breath in his lungs, fire in his blood. Pain, sudden and sharp, as a branch caught his hair and tore it at the roots; or a stone turned underfoot and pierced the unprotected skin; or a thorn sank claw in his side.

Sometimes he was wholly outside of himself. A bird, maybe, in the dark of the trees, looking down at the pale naked thing running from it knew not what, leaving its panic-trail of flesh and blood and acrid human scent.

The law said, Run. The drums said, Run. Therefore he ran.

The mind paused. Saw wood, twilight dimness, sweat-streaming bloody self running from nothing at all, and said, *Why?*

It mastered the feet, slowed them, willed them to a standstill. The heart was harder, and the breath in starved lungs; those, it left to heal themselves. It brought its scattered selves together and bound them with its name.

"Korusan!"

No.

"Koru-Asan!"

Better.

He opened his eyes. The wood was gone, had never been, except in his mind, and in the rattle of the drums. They were silent now. He stood on stone, in walls of stone. Rough tunic rasped on skin as whole as skin could be, no mark that was not long since won, no scar that had not healed.

Cold metal touched his nape. He did not flinch, even inwardly.

"Strong," said the voice behind him, that had known his name. "And self-willed."

"Blood of the Lion," said the man who stood in front of him. The man had no face. None of them did, of all who stood about him: clad in black from crown to toe, not even a glitter of eyes through the swathing of veils. Korusan, whose face was bare for any to see, made of it a mask and schooled his eyes to stillness. They would always betray him, those eyes, unless he mastered them. He was named for them: Koru-Asan, Goldeneyes. Yellow eyes. Eyes of the Lion.

"Proud," said the one behind, the one who held the knife. "Haughty, if truth be told. And why? His blood is none of ours."

"It has its own distinction." Dry, that, from one who stood in the circle.

"And its own destruction." Cold and soft. Korusan stiffened at it. Infinitesimally; but here of all places, now of all times, there could be no concealment. "He will be dead before he is a man; and if he lives to get a son, what will that son be, as weakened as the blood has grown? Dead in infancy, or witless, or mad—if any are born at all of seed so sore enfeebled. Such is the Brood of the Lion."

"He will live long enough," said the dry voice. "He will do what he is born to do."

"Will he live so long?" the cold one inquired.

Run, said the law. And Korusan had run. Keep silent, it said. And he had kept silent. Running had won him nothing but pain. He said, "I will live as long as I must."

"You will be dead at twenty," said the cold one, the cruel one. "You fancy yourself strong enough now; and with magic and physic and training, so you are. But those have their limits. I see the darkness in you. Already it sinks claws in your bones."

"All men die," said Korusan steadily. "It is a gift, maybe, that I know what I shall die of, and when."

"Is it a gift, too, to hate those who willed this doom on you?"

He laughed. They started, those grim men in their circle, and that lightened his mood immeasurably. No one ever laughed in this rite, under this questioning. "They are dead who condemned my house to its death—man without woman and woman without man, lifelong, and never a child of any union but one; and that was their weakness, that they permitted her to live. Or maybe their cruelty. They would know that the sickness was in her, the blood-beast, the thing that goes down from father to son, from mother to daughter, and weakens and twists and kills. But—hate them? No," he said. "No. It was never their choice that she wed daughter to son and son to daughter, and they likewise, to preserve the line pure. If I hate anyone, it is that one. She was a fool, my ancestor. Far better had she done as her brother did, and wedded with barbarians."

"Then the Blood of the Lion would truly be lost," the dry voice said. Not so dry now; there was a whisper of passion in it.

"It is lost in any event," said Korusan. "My sisters are dead or idiots. I may die before I can sire sons. But before I die, I will have our blood-price. The blood of the Sun is more robust than mine, but it too resides in one man, and one man alone. And he has no son."

"That we know of," said the cold one.

"There is none." A new voice, that. It spoke with surety, from an unveiled face. Korusan regarded the man in grey who emerged from the circle. He was not afraid, though he saw the man's shadow, a woman in black, as barefaced as he, and as deadly keen of eye. Lightmage, darkmage.

He raised a brow. The lightmage met his stare blandly and said, "He has no son. No daughter, either."

"I hope," said Korusan, "that he refrains from women, then, until I hold his life in my hands." He smiled at the mages. "You will see to that."

They were affronted. He watched them remember who he was.

The knife shifted on his nape. He spun. The world ran slow, slow. Still, almost it failed to slow enough. He lost a lock of his hair, a drop of blood. He won the knife.

The one who had held it now held a length of uncut gold. Korusan grinned at him and finished what he had begun: set blade to the uncut mane of his youth and cut it away, lock by heavy lock, and stood up a man. The air was cold on his unprotected neck. His head was light. He ran fingers through cropped curls, tugging lightly at them, but never letting down his guard or his weapon.

"No," he said, "I am not of your blood. No bred warrior, I. I was bred to be your master. Bow then, Olenyas. Bow to your lord."

He did not think that he had appalled them. They knew what they had raised. But knowing in the head and knowing in the belly—there, he thought, was a distinction they had not made. There were no eyes to read, to uncover resentment or regret, or even fear, until the one whose knife he had won lowered the outer veil. And then—and this he had not looked for—the inner.

It was a younger face than he had suspected, and more like his own than he could have imagined, even knowing the women and the barefaced children. The Master of the Olenyai regarded him with eyes well-nigh as pure a gold as his, but white-bordered in simple human fashion, and no fear in them, nor overmuch regret. Then they lowered, and he went down, down to the floor, in the full prostration. "You are my lord," he said, "and my emperor."

"I am not the emperor," said Korusan.

"Then there is none," the Master said. He rose. His eyes came up. That was permitted of Olenyai, to look in the face of royalty.

"I do not wish to be emperor," said Korusan. "I would be Olenyas."

"May you not be both?" the Master said.

Korusan was silent. He had spoken enough foolishness, and far beyond the limits of the rite. He reversed the knife in his hand and bowed as initiate to Master, and returned the knife to its owner. The Master accepted it. Korusan drew a slow breath. If it had been refused, then so likewise would he; and he would be emperor without a throne and Olenyas without the veil, rejected and found unworthy.

The fine steel flashed toward him. He stood his ground even as it neared his eyes. Even as it licked down, once, twice, and the pain came stinging. He kept his eyes steady on the Master's face. Ninefold, the scars on that cheek: from cheekbone to jaw, thinly parallel like the marks of claws. One for each rank of his ascent.

Korusan said, "I will not take second rank for my blood alone."

"Nor do you," said the Master. He wiped the knife clean of Korusan's blood and sheathed it. "You could be swifter in defense."

"I was swifter than you."

The Master's hand was a blur, but Korusan caught it. The Master smiled. "Better," he said, then snapped free and slapped Korusan lightly on the unwounded cheek. "That for your insolence. And this," he said, "for your wit." He set hands on Korusan's shoulders and leaned forward, and set a kiss where his hand had stung. "Now you are Olenyas. Be proud, but never too proud. Be strong, but never so strong that you betray yourself. Be swift, but never as swift as your death. And take the oath as your kinsmen have taught you."

Korusan knelt and laid his hands in the Master's, looking up into that face which now he was entitled to see. He was aware of other faces, strange and yet familiar, and eyes that he had known when all the rest was wrapped in darkness. But for the moment he saw only the one, and the two that came up behind it, lightmage, darkmage, filling the Master's shadow. He shuddered a little inside himself. Magic he knew, because he must know it. Magic he had, because it was bred in him, like his eyes, like the death that would take him while lesser men were still no more than boys. But he had no love for it.

"It is our custom," the Master said, "to give the oath and the protection, and to seal them in bronze, and bind them about your neck."

"But for you," said the lightmage, "bronze is too little a thing, and a binding of chain too feeble. You, we seal and bind with the Word, and with the Power that is behind the Word."

Korusan felt it in his bones like the fire that had filled him in the wood. He fought instinct that would have risen and swelled and thrust the magic away. He let it crawl through him, though he shuddered at its touch. He hoped devoutly that his stomach would keep its proper place. It was never his most obedient servant; and he had not fed it since this rite began.

Preoccupied with keeping his belly quiet, he barely noticed the wrench and twist as the magic pulled free. He did see the lightmage sway, and the darkmage steady him. He heard the woman mutter, "Goddess! He is strong." And the man: "Hush! He hears us."

Then he knew that they had not spoken aloud, but as mages spoke, in the silence behind the words.

The lightmage met his gaze directly. "You are strong," he said, "but unschooled. Beware of arrogance. It will destroy you."

Korusan's lips stretched. It was not a smile. He spoke the words then as the Master bade him, words that meant everything and nothing after the touch of magic. The magic had sealed him to this rite; the magic, and the blood that ran down his scored cheek. The words were for his brothers, his Olenyai. To serve where he must serve, to command where he must command; to do battle for lord and land and kin; to show his face never but to his brothers, and to protect the secrets of his caste— *His* caste, he thought, half wry and half in pain. Only while it served him, and until his vengeance was won.

To protect, then, while he lived, and to defend to the death.

He was warrior born, warrior bred if not to the blood. Their enemies were his enemies. He was all of their kin, as they were all of his. He took the robes and the veil, the knife and the swords. He sealed them with his blood.

Robed, veiled, armed, he danced. The circle opened itself for him and to him. He danced to the drums, and their beat now was swift, but that swiftness was joy. He drew his swords. They were steel, and they gleamed in lamplight and firelight. He spun. He leaped. He sang. *"Ohé! Ohé Olenyai!"*

Others sprang into the dance. Steel rang on steel. It was like a battle, it was like a willing woman. He whirled in its center. He was all of them, and all of himself. Korusan. Olenyas. Lion's cub. Warrior born, warrior raised, born to die young. Lord and weapon of his people. Arrow shot from the bow: an arrow in the Sun.

Kingship. Majesty.

It was stronger than wine. Stronger than dreamsmoke. More dizzying even than the scent of Vanyi's hair, wonderful sea-sweet masses of it, and she wound in it, gleaming in moonlight and starlight and the nightlamp's flicker.

Estarion reined himself in. That was the throne, making him its own. The fire he carried in his right hand was shrunk to a sunlit warmth: painlessness after pain so long and so relentless that it shaped the world about it.

He turned his hand palm up in his lap. Without the price of pain the *Kasar* was a beautiful thing, beautiful and improbable and all perfectly the god's creation.

He closed his fingers carefully over the bright burning brand and looked up. His people waited for him. Eyes fixed on him, faces a blur of black, brown, bronze, gold, and one beloved white-bone glimmer. She was afraid for him. He gave her warmth and a promise.

His mother shifted all but invisibly, reminding; admonishing. He smiled at her. Grinned, she might have said, though he did try to damp it down. One grew accustomed to it, she had told him. But it was splendid, this first heady draught of empire.

He raised his branded hand. The silence, that had been absolute, shattered in one glorious wave of sound.

They paid him homage one by one, from the highest to the lowest. They wore the bright edge from his joy, but nothing could rob him of it.

Vanyi was not in the endless train of his people. When she came to the throne, it would be to sit beside him in it, empress to his emperor, mother of his heir. She was gone now about her duties: mage, priestess, guardian of the Gates between the worlds. Those would not wait for any man, even a man who was lord of the world.

They came without pause or diminution, to bow at his feet, to kiss his hands, to murmur the words that made them his people, and to hear him seal them with a word and a smile. His throat was raw. His face ached with smiling, his neck with bending to acknowledge bows or tribute. His backside, he decided, would do much better with a thicker cushion; and that almost betrayed him into laughter. The stout merchant in front of him received a smile that made him blink, dazzled, and the freewoman behind looked mildly smitten.

The one behind them, well out of proper order and walled in retinue, neither smiled nor appeared enraptured with Majesty incarnate. Estarion went cold.

There had been others of that ilk among the lords and princes. One could hardly avoid them. They were half of his empire, as his advisors never tired of reminding him. But he could not abide them. Oily yellow people with flat snake-eyes, bowing and groveling and thinking scorn at eastern barbarians. When he could read their thoughts at all. They thought slantwise, round corners; they made his head ache.

The Asanian lord bowed low. He wore the five robes of a prince, one atop the other, slender ivory feet bare as befit one who need walk only in palaces, straw-gold hair uncut and bound behind him with plaited gold. He bowed to the floor, prostrating himself, and his entourage went down with him, concerted as a dance.

Their minds were a babble of nonsense. They were warded, with magery in it. Not that the mage could be a priest of Avaryan, or Estarion would know it; nor could it be a mage of the old and broken Guild. No: it was but one half-hidden servant, grey man in a grey gown, with eyes as flat as coins.

Estarion set his teeth against the pain of that protection. Some small remnant of his power had come back since he lost it in the time he could not remember, when he had wielded it like a weapon, and killed the mage who killed his father; but it had come back flawed. Nothing could test his shields without his knowing it; and that knowledge was a stabbing pain.

He meant to say the words that set the prince free to rise. Pain locked his jaw upon them. Pain, and anger. How dare any mage, or any man, try his defenses here, where he was emperor? It smacked of contempt, if not of treason.

The moment stretched. The prince and his entourage lay on their faces, unmoving. The court began to shift uneasily.

"Estarion!" his mother hissed in his ear.

He recoiled from the sound of it, and from the rebuke that came as much from within as from without. "Get up," he said. Snapped. In High Court Asanian; but the inflections were all awry. He had addressed the prince of five robes as a minor eunuch of the Middle Court.

His lordship rose with grace they all learned in childhood. The others were less polished, or less composed. Their anger grated raw against his aching brain.

A prince could not declare death-insult against an emperor, but Estarion had made no friend in this one. The Asanian spoke the words of homage in precise, icy syllables, each inflection meticulously and lethally correct. His entourage did not echo him. That was insult less than mortal but more than minor.

The prince bowed again to the floor. This time he rose without Estarion's bidding, and bent his head a careful degree. Giving the emperor pardon. Forgiving a barbarian his ignorance.

As he began to back away down the long silent aisle, Estarion stopped him with a word. He stood stiff and still, and he did a terrible thing, a thing that no Asanian did to the emperor enthroned. He looked up into Estarion's face.

Estarion met the yellow eyes. They fit that face: old ivory, old gold, carved smooth and sleeked with scented oil. Their stare was bold beyond belief, as Asanians thought of it, and profoundly, wonderfully shocked.

Estarion smiled. "Am I what you expected?" he asked sweetly, in High Asanian that had remembered itself and given the man his proper rank.

The Asanian's gaze dropped, as did he, full on his face, all grace and dignity forgotten, and in him only fear. He had meant defiance, that was in every line of him, and contempt for the emperor who would not walk in the west and yet called himself lord of Asanion. He had forgotten, or chosen to forget, that there was Asanian blood in the barbarian, blood of the Lion, blood imperial.

He fled, there was no other word for it. Estarion sat back in his throne and set himself to be markedly gracious to the Islander who came forward shakily, almost creeping in the Asanian's wake.

Estarion stood in the middle of the robing-room and stretched. No servants beset him. He had locked them out, and bought a few moments' quiet.

There was wine on the table. He filled a cup, drank a heady draught. He ached, inside and out. Some of that was hunger. But he could not go to the feast until the servants, tyrants that they were, gave him leave. He must make an entrance, and so must enter last.

He circled the room, skirting the chests and the clothing-presses. His mood was odd, unsettled. The Asanian had taken the splendor out of it. The man had been testing him; and he had not done well. He had let himself be caught off guard. He had betrayed his weakness.

"I may be young," he said to the air, "but I am not stupid. Nor completely ignorant of my failings."

"Goddess forbid that you should be."

He whipped about. A locked door was small barrier to a mage, and his mother was one of rare power. Likewise the one who bulked behind her. Great tall northern barbarian in beard and braids and baubles—strangers never suspected the cultured delicacy of that mind, nor knew him for the great mage and scholar and priest that he was.

They were together more often than not, priestess of the dark and priest of the light. It was a jest in some quarters that they were like the old Guildmages, matched in their magic, darkmage and light. They had shared Estarion's regency, and shared his raising once his father was dead; they were not always of a mind, but they never failed to come to an accommodation, one way and another.

The Lady Merian settled herself in the room's one chair. She never looked less than queenly, but her eyes were tired. Estarion set a cup in her hand. She wrapped long fingers about it, gratefully maybe, but she did not drink the wine that was in it.

Avaryan's high priest in Endros betrayed no such hesitation. He drained his cup and set it down, and sighed.

Estarion looked at them both. Anger pricked. He was emperor, and these two not only invaded his solitude, they reduced him to a child.

"I cry your pardon," his mother said, reading him with maddening ease. "There is too much to say, and too little time to say it."

"Is it nothing that can wait until the morning?" Estarion demanded.

"I think not," said Lord Iburan. He was unwontedly quiet, almost grim, though his eyes on Estarion were gentle enough. Not angry, then. When Iburan was angry, mountains trembled.

Iburan laughed. "Do they? Come now, youngling, tuck in your thoughts. They're flapping like flags at a feast-day."

"Maybe I want them to." But Estarion shored up all his walls and slammed shut the gates and locked himself in the keep. Iburan winced. Estarion was briefly, nastily glad.

"Estarion," his mother said. Her tone was a warning.

He bit his tongue, then said it in spite of her. "Was it all a sham, then? Shall I be your puppet still, and you the empress regnant?"

Her eyes narrowed: the only sign she gave that he had struck the mark. "You will learn to rule yourself. Or so one may hope. You are young yet, and I have raised you ill, maybe; protected you too well, and shielded you from good as from harm."

"What, the good that's in Asanion?" Estarion met her stare. "It comes to that, doesn't it? I'm emperor of Asanion, too."

"So," she said. "You do remember it."

"I never forget."

"You never fail to regret it, either." She set down the untouched cup and pressed fingers to her brows. "Ah, child, I did ill and worse than ill to keep you here in Keruvarion. You should have gone long since to Asanion, and conquered your fear of it."

Estarion reared up. "I'm not afraid of the west!"

"No," she said too gently. "Only of the people in it, and the memories it may hold."

Estarion opened his mouth. No words came out. He shut it with great care.

"You cannot continue to shun Asanion," his mother said, "or to offend its lords and princes. We have spoken for you through the years of your youth. That now is over. You must speak in your own name, for your own honor."

"You must rule all of your empire," said Iburan, "not only the east or the north. The west should know you, and know you fair. And not as one who loathes all that it is."

"I do loathe it," said Estarion, breaking in on their antiphon. "I've seen it. I know it. I despise it."

"You remember nothing of it." Merian's voice was as calm as her eyes. "One fool passed all our guards and protections and destroyed your father. It could have been a northerner, or a man of the Hundred Realms. It could have been anyone at all."

Estarion's heart set hard and cold. "You never loved him, did you? He gave you a throne and an empire. He, himself, man and lover, was nothing to you."

Her hand was so swift, the blow so sharp, that he never saw it, or even felt it, till it was done. His own hand flew up. But he could not strike her, no matter the heat of his temper. So well at least she had reared him.

"Never," she said, soft and still. "Never say such a thing again."

Iburan's voice was deep and almost harsh, but there was calmness in it, and peace. "There now. Be still. You're on the raw edge, both of you."

"So we are," said Merian. Her voice for once had forsaken its sweetness, and its grace that set an empire in awe of her. "So we must continue to be. That one who faced you, Starion, came out of Asanion to defy us all, and not you alone. Keruvarion is yours by right and by choice. Asanion is a conquered kingdom. Thus it reckons itself. It chafes at the rule of barbarians and mongrels. My dear lord did ill when he took me to wife and refused the woman his council had chosen for him."

"An Asanian woman." Estarion shivered through the dregs of his temper. "Then I would never have been; or been far other than I am."

"Surely," said Merian, "and I could never have endured a rival. But Asanion took its revenge, takes it still, and forgets nothing. And never, never forgives."

"Then what's left to us?" Estarion said. "Civil war? Asanion chafes, it always has, but in the end it gives in. You saw how yonder princeling was, once I made him see what else I am."

"What you would rather not be." Iburan sounded tired. "He saw that, too. Be sure of it."

"What if he did? They're slaves born, all of them, even the princes. Once he knew that I have blood-right to his homage, he gave it. He'd have slit his own throat if I'd ordered him to."

"There," said Iburan more wearily than ever. "There you have it. Half of your empire is Asanian. Half of *you* is Asanian. And you know no more of the truth of yourself or your empire than a blindfish knows of the sun."

Estarion's head throbbed. "It is *not* half of me! It's a trickle in the tide that I am. No Asanian has tainted my blood since Hirel himself."

" 'Tainted,' " said Merian. "Dear goddess help me. And you believe it."

"Is it false?" Estarion asked her.

She did not answer.

He swept his hand down his body. "Look at me. What do you see? Northerner, as pure as makes no matter. Except for this." His fingers clawed as if to rake his eyes; but he knotted them into fists. "If my father erred, then so did Varuyan before him, and Ganiman before that. None after Sarevadin endured an Asanian marriage. And she was married to Hirel Uverias, who was like no Asanian who ever was, or ever would be."

"No," said Iburan. "He was nothing remarkable, except that he loved a foreigner. And that, he always said, was a doom of his line."

"So it is," Estarion said slowly. He caught himself before he said something he would regret. He would not bring Vanyi into this, or soil her with its touch.

"Estarion," said Merian, "listen to me. The time is ill, but it will never be better; and you must know, and accept. When your father wedded me, he promised his council that his son would not repeat his error."

"It was an error to marry for love?"

"For him," said the empress mother, "and for his empire, it was. It killed him. You must not err as he erred. You must do what he failed to do. You must take a bride in the west."

"No," said Estarion flatly.

He could not say that he had not expected it. He had ears, and wits. He knew that his council did not approve of Vanyi. She was a commoner. Her father fished off the coast of Seiun isle. She brought him no wealth or power, nor any dowry but herself.

But an Asanian. A yellow woman. Serpent-breed, to breed serpent-children.

His gorge rose. He would not do it. He could not.

"You will consider it," his mother said. "That much at least you will do."

"I have considered it," he said. "I refuse it."

"Have you ever even seen an Asanian woman?"

Estarion rounded on Iburan. "Why in nine hells—"

"How can you judge anything unseen and untested? Before your priestess came, you shuddered at Islanders and called them corpse-folk and fish-people, and reckoned them less than human."

"Islanders never killed my father," said Estarion.

"That's Asanian, you know. That obstinacy. That unwillingness ever to forgive."

Estarion laughed. It hurt. "You can't have both sides of it, foster-father. Either Asanians are sorely misunderstood, or all my vices are theirs, and none of my virtues."

"How can you know until you know them? You can't avoid them forever, no matter whom you choose for your empress. Asanion has had no emperor in its palace since your father died there. Soon or late, you'll have to face it and them."

"Are you telling me that I should ride west in the morning?"

"Hardly that," said Iburan, impervious to the weight of Estarion's irony. "You'll need a cycle or two at least to settle this half of the empire. But then, yes, I think you should begin a progress into the west. People are expecting it. They need to see you, to know what you are."

"As yonder princeling did?"

"Even so," said Iburan. "If you have nothing better to give them."

"God," said Estarion. "Goddess. That would be war."

"So shall it be, if you let him go back unchallenged to his people, and tell them what you did to him."

Estarion shut his aching eyes. It was no quieter in the dark. "I don't suppose one could apologize." The word caught in his throat.

"One could," said Iburan. "But he's only one man. What

he did . . . he acted for a whole realm. That realm must see you. It must know that you belong to it as to the rest."

"My father took such counsel," Estarion said. "He died for it."

"He died because no one would believe that an emperor, a mage born, needed protection from magery in his own palace. He died because we were fools, Estarion."

"Yes," Estarion said. His throat was sour with bile. "You were fools. All of you. He too. I. Everyone." He swallowed hard. "I'll be a fool. I'll go. Damn you, foster-father. I'll go."

"Soon?"

Estarion's head was splitting. No one was trying to get into it—it was not that kind of pain. This came from within. It made his sight blur, and made him say, "When Brightmoon comes back to the full. Four days—no. Three. I'll go into the west. I'll face my demons. I'll make myself remember. But I won't—I *won't*—bed an Asanian woman."

"That is as the god wills it," said the god's priest. There was no triumph in his voice. He was never one to gloat over victories, was Iburan of Endros.

4

SILENCE RULED THE heart of Avaryan's temple in Endros, silence so deep it seemed to drink the light, to transform the hiss of breath to a roar and the murmur of blood into thunder. No foot fell, no voice spoke. Even the air was still, wrapped in the temple's veils and bound with magery.

Vanyi kept vigil in her due turn, now praying to the omnipresence of the god, now casting nets of power on the seas that were the mageworld. Most often there were two to watch and to pray, but on this day of Estarion's enthronement, all mages who could were set to guard the palace and the emperor. He was more valuable by far than the Magegate that shimmered where wall should be. That might fail or close, but mages could restore it, however high the cost. If Estarion died, there would be no heir of the god on earth; and that would be beyond repairing.

Strange to think of him so, and to know what he had been in the morning, tousled laughing boy-man covering terror with exhilaration. Her power twitched, yearning toward him, but the magewall barred it. And she was forgetting her duty. She traced the patterns of the dance, sang the song that sustained the Gate. Dance and song were part of her, had always been part of her. Even on the shores of Seiun, fingers raw from mending the nets, nostrils full of the stink of the fish, her feet had known the steps, her voice the notes. Mooncalf they had called her, and witch, and changeling, with her sea-eyes and her hair the color of moors in autumn. She knew the speech of the gulls, felt in her bones the sway of the tides.

That was far away now, long ago. She stood in this chamber as in a globe of glass, and even the pull of the moons was faint, overwhelmed in the roar and reach of the Gate. There was sea on the other side of it, tides that were no tide of this earth, waves heaving and falling on a shore that looked like dust of rubies, or like blood. As she watched, it blurred and shifted, and she looked into darkness full of stars; but stars that were eyes, great burning dragon-eyes staring into her own. Seeing her. Knowing her for what she was.

She gasped. A Word burst out of her, raw and barely shaped. The stars blinked, steadied. They were only stars.

A shudder racked her. The worlds changed: that was the way of Gates. Most were alien. Some were horrible, hells of ice or of fire, swarming with demons. None had ever left her as these stars had, crouched on her knees, heaving as if she had taken poison.

She scraped wits and power together. They were thin, threadbare, but they were enough to cast a net.

The seas were calm. Nothing swam there but what belonged in that place. Mages about their workings. Lesser folk dreaming, asleep or awake. Spirits of air and fire at their incalculable pursuits. No threat. Nothing to fathom that instant of horror.

She pulled in the net. Her heart had ceased its hammering. Her knees were steady again. The sweat dried on her body. She went down on her face before the Gate, and began the prayer of the sun's descent.

Estarion came to his chambers much earlier than Vanyi had expected. It would have been like him to leave the lords' feast and go down into the city and pass the night with his people, drinking their beer and singing their songs and showing them why they loved him. He never calculated that, or thought of it as politic. He liked them, that was all.

He had been in the city: the beer-scent came in before him. He was in plain city-walking clothes, his court robes long since laid away. She heard him calling goodnights to the battalion of his friends, and them chaffing him for turning lily maid while the night was young. "Maid!" someone cried. "And what's he got inside, then? Maybe he's got the right of it. Who's for a fine warm woman to while the night away?"

They roared at that. Estarion laughed and shut the door on them.

Vanyi looked up from the book she had been staring at for longer than she could reckon. Estarion was a shadow beyond the lamp's glimmer. She mustered a smile for him.

He moved into the light. There was no laughter in him, no sign that she could see of the face he had shown his friends. This was somber, almost grim.

"Troubles?" she asked him.

"No," he said. He gave himself the lie: snatched the rings from his ears, flung them at the wall. They clattered to the floor.

Carefully, precisely, she rolled the book shut and fastened the cords. "Disasters, then," she said.

He dropped his coat more gently than he had the rings. "When Brightmoon is full, I'm going to Asanion."

She stared at him.

"Surely someone told you?"

His tone was nasty. She ignored it. "I came direct from the temple. Everyone else was in the hall or elsewhere."

His long mouth twisted. She wanted to kiss it. He said, "I looked for you after your Gate-duty should have been over. I thought you would come to my banquet."

"I wanted to." She shivered. It was cold in the room, she told herself. She had dismissed the servants when they came to light the brazier, then forgotten it and them. "I was more tired than I thought. I slept a little." And waked to nightmares, and sought refuge in a book of which she remembered nothing, not even its name. "By the time I could have come, you were gone into the city."

He pulled his heavy plait over his shoulder and tugged at the bindings. They were stubborn. His brows knit.

She worked her fingers under his. They were stiff, quivering with tension. He let his hands fall, let her unwind the cords, loosen the braid. His hair was his great beauty, thick and curling yet soft and fine as silk, so black it gleamed blue. She filled her hands with it.

His body was taut. She kissed the point of his shoulder. He barely eased. "Why?" she asked. "Why exactly now?"

He told her all of it, words honed to a bitter edge. The Asanian, the test—he made little of it. Too little, maybe, but she was not ready to solve that riddle tonight. But his mother's command—

"I'll go west," he said through gritted teeth. "I'll face my demons. I'm no coward. But I won't—I *won't*—be stud bull to a herd of yellow women."

"It need only be one," Vanyi said. Her voice was steady. She was proud of that. "So. It's a long way to Kundri'j Asan. Long cycles of the moons. A year, maybe, at the pace of a royal progress."

"A year and three days?" His smile was thin. He kept count, too. "Not likely, my love. They'll have me over the border as fast as the court can travel, and into the Golden Land, marshaling parades of yellow women."

"Teaching Asanion that you are its emperor."

"It does need lessoning," he said. Breath gusted out of him. "God and goddess, Vanyi. I thought I was safe from this for years at least. There's empire enough here to keep any man occupied."

"Except that it's yours entirely, and always has been, and always will be. Keruvarion knows you, loves you. Asanion has never seen you."

"It saw plenty of me when I was younger. I do remember that much," he said, sharp, almost angry. "They marched me about like a prize calf. They dressed me in so many robes I could barely move, and perched me in a litter, and made me sit like an icon for people to gape at."

"You were a child then," Vanyi said. She did not know where the words were coming from. The earth, maybe. The cold thing that, a little while ago, had been her heart. Had the empress mother been trying to ease the blow this morning, telling her that she could never be empress? She worked the knots out of the emperor's shoulders and said to him, "They never knew you as a man. Now you'll show them. You'll teach them to love you as your easterners do, for the brightness that's in you."

"I'm as dull as an old stone," he said, with the soul burning so fierce in him that her mind's eyes were dazzled, and his eyes lambent gold, and gold burning in his hand. She felt the wash of it, the pain that would have sent any other man into whimpering retreat, but only sharpened his temper and made him rub his hand against his thigh.

She caught it, held it to her cheek. It was no more than humanly warm, stiff with the metal that was born in it, holy and impossible. All the heat burned within. "Oh, my lord," she said, and her eyes pricked with tears. "Oh, my dear lord. How can anyone keep from loving you?"

"You're besotted," he said. But a little of the tautness was gone. Not all, yet enough that he could lie down, and let her hold him, and be soothed into something resembling peace.

Dark. Stars. Eyes. Teeth that gleamed in the blackness. Maws opened wide, gaping to devour.

"Vanyi!"

She clutched at warm solidity. Estarion's voice thrummed out of it, deeper always than one expected, with a singer's purity. She clung as much to the voice as to the body, gulping air. He stroked the rigid line of her back. "Hush, love. Hush."

She pulled free. She was laughing, hiccoughing. "No! That's my part. You're the one with nightmares."

"Sometimes," he said, "one has to share." He was barely smiling. His eyes were as dark as lion-eyes could be, all pupil, and about it the thin rim of gold.

She burrowed into the warmth of him. The dream was fading in his brightness, the horror shrinking to insignificance. She had forgotten to eat after her vigil in the temple, that was all, and the oddity in the Gate had come back to haunt her empty stomach. No mage alive knew all the secrets of Gates. Maybe the Guild had, that in its prime had made them and used them and ruled them with fabled power.

The Guild was long since fallen. Vanyi was not supposed to regret that, or to wish that it had survived long enough to teach her what she yearned to know, of Gates, of magic, of the worlds beyond the world. But it was gone; only memory remained, embodied in the Gates.

Pride had laid it low. It had set empire against empire, Keruvarion against Asanion, striving to fell them both and set a puppet of its own making upon the doubled throne. But the puppet it had made had turned against it—and, wise cruelty, done nothing to destroy the Guild. Only let it be known what the Guild had done and intended, and offered a newer way to those who would be mages: the priesthood of god or goddess, and training in the temples of Sun or Dark. The Guild had withered, its twinned pairs of mages dead or lost. The robes that once had won such awe, lightmage grey and darkmage violet, were all faded, gone to the dim no-color of hedge-witches and hired sorcerers.

But the Gates endured. That one of them had gone briefly strange—it meant nothing. The priest who came to relieve Vanyi had said as much; and he was a mage and a master. She was initiate merely, priestess on Journey, mage in training. She was making nightmares of hunger and sleeplessness and a lover who might be taken from her.

Estarion did not know of this, nor would he. He had troubles enough. She attacked him suddenly with kisses. That made him laugh, reluctant at first, then more freely. Yes, she thought. Laughter drove away the dark. Laughter, and love; and that they had in plenty.

5

The City of the Sun lay in the arms of deep-running Suvien, where the river curved round a great prow of crag. To north and east the walls rose sheer. Southward they eased to a long level of windswept land and, half a day's journey down a smooth straight road, the white gates of its mother and its servant, Han-Gilen of the princes.

Westward was no wall but the river and the quays of ships and, black to its white beauty, that crag from which the city took its name, Endros Avaryan, Throne of the Sun. The sunrise bank teemed with men and beasts and boats. On the sunset side nothing walked, and no bird flew. The crag stood alone, dark against the sky, and on its crown a Tower. No window broke that wall, no gate marred its smoothness. Blind, eyeless, doorless, it clawed its way toward heaven.

Estarion stood atop the highest tower of his palace, on the northern promontory of his city, and glared across the river. He was nearly level with the summit of the black Tower, with the globe of crystal that, catching the sun, blazed blinding. But he was the Sun's heir: he could look unflinching on the face of his forefather. This, mere magewrought crystal, barely narrowed his eyes.

That whole Tower was a work of three mages conjoined, Sunborn king and Gileni empress and northern warrior, and they had wrought it in a night. "And why?" Estarion asked aloud. "Except to keep men off the crag, since any man who walked there must come down mad."

The cat Ulyai yawned vastly and stretched. She propped her forepaws on the parapet, leaning into Estarion. He wrapped an arm about her neck. "Have you ever seen a more useless braggart thing? Caves like lacework through that whole great rock, and tombs enough for a thousand years of kings, and he witches a Tower on top of it. And no way in or out, either, unless there's a Gate somewhere, or a key I haven't found."

Ulyai was not interested in the Tower across the river. There were ringdoves in the lower reaches of this lesser tower; she watched them with fierce intentness.

Estarion sighed. She would not care either that the Sunborn had left his bones there, and a story that he lacked the grace to die before he did it, but had himself ensorceled into sleep, because his empire was won, and there were no more battles to fight. He would rise again, the talespinners said, when the god called him back to his wars.

"It's only a story," Estarion said. "Or if it's true, it's so far away it doesn't matter. I'm all the Sun-blood there is, until I get myself an heir. I'm all the emperor this world will have." He shivered in the bright sunlight. "There's no Tower in Kundri'j Asan. He never came there, did the Sunborn. They stopped him before he marched so far. He was a madman, they say. I say he was saner than anyone else who came near him. He hated Asanion with all his heart."

"He was a fool," his mother said behind him.

He did not turn to face her. He had been aware of her coming, but he had chosen to take no notice. He had not spoken to her since the day of his enthronement, nor had she sought him out. A pleasant enough arrangement, he had been thinking.

"An emperor cannot hate the full half of his empire," she said. "Not and remain emperor."

"Is that what they hope for?" he asked, light, barely bitter. "That I'll hate them so much, I let them go of my own free will?"

"Maybe," she said.

His lips stretched back from his teeth. "Maybe I should do it, then. Give up Asanion. Leave it to rot in peace."

"It will hardly do that. More likely it will rise up and overwhelm the east, and rule us as it ruled us long ago, under an iron heel."

Estarion spun to face her. "Listen to yourself! Even you think of *us* and *them*. It's we in Keruvarion, they in Asanion. There's never been one empire. There never will be. Only irreconcilable opposites."

"If you think so," she said calmly, "you make it so. You have that power, Meruvan Estarion."

"I have too much power. Everyone has always said that. Too much power was never enough to save my father. Only to twist me and break me, and mend me awry." He laughed at her frown: laughter that tore his throat. "Yes, that's wallowing! I wallow extraordinarily well."

"You are too clever by half," his mother said. She was not smiling.

There was a silence. They had quarreled before—they could hardly help it: he had her temper, and that was as quick as her wits. But never for so long. Never for so much.

He would not be the one to end this. She asked of him what she had not had the strength to demand of herself. She could hardly fault him for seeing the flaw in it.

After a while she spoke, shaping the words carefully, as she did when she was holding anger at bay. "I am told that I am not to accompany you to Asanion. That I remain as regent in Keruvarion."

"There is a regent in Asanion," he said with equal care, but no more anger than she deserved.

"An Asanian," she said. "A great lord and prince, and loyal to the Blood of the Lion. But Asanian."

"Wasn't it you who said that I have to learn to face the rest of my empire?"

"The scars are deep. They will not heal in a day."

"Now you say it," he said.

"I have never failed to know it." She paused for breath,

perhaps to nerve herself, perhaps simply to let him simmer. "Will you take me with you?"

"Do I have a choice?"

"Yes."

He looked at her. He loved her, he could hardly deny that. But love and hate were womb-kin. Someone had said that once, long ago. One of his ancestors, very likely. It was something they would understand. "So," he said, pitching his voice light, easy, purposely exasperating. "You would come, then? And hold my hand? And pimp for me in the harems of the Golden Empire?"

She did not answer that. "The Red Prince is wise, and the people love him. He would do well as regent in your absence."

"Hal is barely older than I am."

"And you are emperor."

He accorded her a swordsman's salute. "Well struck! And suppose he forgives me for leaving him behind—what then, Mother? Do you think I'm not to be trusted, where I'm going?"

"I think that you will need me. Even," she said, "if you hate me for it."

She stood as straight as ever, her face as still, its beauty unmarred. But she was fighting back tears. He felt them burning in his own eyes.

Tricks. She was a master of woman-sleights as of the wiles of courts. And she had magery: she wielded it on him, and no matter the cost to his aching head.

He was softening. Fool that he was. He knew what she was doing; knew what she would do if she rode with him, if she had leisure to work on him through the long leagues to Asanion.

Maybe he needed the challenge. And it was true enough: he would need her wits, and her skill in bending men's wills. Especially in Asanion, where deception was a game of princes, and murder their pastime.

"Come, then," he said, "and do as you please. What I do, in the end, I'll do because I will it. And for no other reason."

"Have you ever done otherwise?" she asked.

She would not lock stares. She was too canny for that. She set a kiss on his brow and left him there. The scent of her lingered for a long while after she was gone.

It was nearer nine days than three before the court could be ready for the long road into Asanion. Even at that, the chamberlains were beside themselves with the haste of it all.

"Talk to the sergeants," Estarion said to the chief of them. "They can move an army of twenty thousand inside of a day, and you can't move a court of twenty score in a tenday?"

Nuryan fluttered and squawked. Estarion did not trouble to listen. "I'm going," he said. "In the morning. Anyone who can ride, will ride. Anyone who is late, is late."

"Sire!" his chamberlain shrieked. "The baggage—the wagons—your wardrobe—"

Estarion said a word both brief and vulgar. It shocked Nuryan into silence. "I'll wear what I can carry. There are cloth merchants in Asanion, no? And tailors. And, I trust, jewelers and hatters and cobblers—"

"An emperor wears no shoes in his palace." Nuryan truly was distraught: he had interrupted his emperor.

"He rides, surely? And walks elsewhere?"

"No," said Nuryan, "sire. He never leaves his palace."

So Nuryan might think. Estarion was of another mind; but that was another battle. "He has to *get* to his palace," he said. "And so he shall. I ride in the morning. The court may follow as it will."

The emperor rode out on a fine bright morning, with the sun a dazzle in a flawless sky, and a brisk wind to set his banners flying. The slow and the litter-borne and the baggage would follow when they chose. These were the swift and the mounted. The emperor's guard in its full ranks, blazing in scarlet and gold; the empress' guard in gold and green; a battalion of high ones, lords and ladies both, and guards and grooms and servants; and a little company of priests and priestesses, bearing no emblem, affecting no great estate, but each marked by the torque at the throat and the plait down the back. Vanyi was with them, a white face amid the black and brown and gold.

Estarion rode at their head. His senel was a black of the Mad One's line, blue-eyed, dagger-horned, with a star on his forehead; young enough to be a little silly with all the tumult, but wise enough to keep his temper in hand. Umizan snorted at Ulyai who paced beside him, but not in fear: he had been foaled among the royal cats. She snarled amiably at him and paced just out of reach of the sharp cloven hoofs, queenly oblivious to the crowds that lined the road. All of Endros seemed to have streamed outside the walls to watch their emperor ride away.

Their cheering rolled over him. It was heartfelt, but there was darkness in it. They were losing him to the west. Not forever, that he had vowed to them, swearing it by the Tower on its crag. But the last emperor who had gone to Asanion had sworn that same vow; and he had come back, but never living.

His bones lay under the Tower. Estarion could see it beyond the city's white walls: black crag, black horns, crown of crystal that caught the sun's light. He saluted it, flinging up his burning hand. The sun, escaping a wisp of cloud, struck the crystal and blazed.

Estarion laughed at the glare of it. "Until I return," he said, "watch well, old bones. Look after my city."

"You take that one too lightly," said Iburan.

Estarion slanted a glance at the priest, who had ridden up through the line and matched his mare's pace to black Umizan's. He was not smiling. "There is a power there," he said, "that would make a god tremble."

"Isn't that a heresy?" asked Estarion, bowing to the crowd, dazzling them with his white smile, giving Umizan leave to dance and flag his tasseled tail.

Iburan said nothing. But neither did he leave Estarion's side.

The people followed them far out of the city, mounted and

afoot, calling Estarion's name. At length even the most determined of them grew weary or felt the distance of their city and the sun's descent into the alien west. The last of them halted at the boundary-stone, the white pillar without adornment that marked the edge of Endros and the beginning of the Hundred Realms. It stood on a long hill cloven in two by the river, first outrider of the ridge-wall, and beyond it the land went up and up to a tree-clad height. It was nothing to the mountains of the north, but on that plain it stood high and haughty.

Estarion paused by the stone. "Go," he said to the rest. "I'll follow." Some hesitated, but he stared them down: even his mother. They rode on up the slope.

Umizan lowered his head to graze. Ulyai dropped down just beyond him and rolled in the sweet grass, singing a soft yowling song. Her mind was full of sunlight. No sadness there; no regret to be forsaking the city of her birth. All her kind remembered the free air and the wild places, even those born within Endros' walls: remembered it and yearned for it.

Estarion looked down upon his city. He could have cupped it in his two hands, as small as it seemed and as perfect, like a carving in ivory and gold.

He had left Endros often enough on journeys about his empire. But only in the east and the north. Never in the west. Never for so long or in such a mingling of anger and resentment, doubt and fear and piercing exhilaration.

Free. For however brief a time, for however unwelcome a purpose, he was free of those walls. It was terrifying, that freedom, and wonderful. That he went to a worse prison than he had escaped—it mattered, and yet after he was not sorry for it.

He touched heel to Umizan's side. The stallion snatched a last mouthful of grass and wheeled, turning away from the city and the plain. The Wall of Han-Gilen rose ahead of them, and the last of the escort riding slowly over the crest. Estarion wound fingers in the long mane. "Go," he said into the back-turned ear. "Brother, go!"

6

ESTARION'S RIDING FELL somewhere between an army's march and a royal progress: soldier-speed where land or weather allowed it, but long slow meanders through rough country, and pauses in this castle and that town and yonder temple. Once free of Endros he knew less urgency, or more patience. The pace was his to set, and he allowed his mood to set it, or Umizan's whim.

He rode in the swelling spring, up the long roll of Suvien with the Wall of Han-Gilen fading into mist behind him, through the hills and woods of Iban and Sarios, into the forest-ridings of Kurion. There the towns were fewer, the castles more frequent: crowning cliffs above the river, or warding islands in its center. Their lords were not always delighted to find the emperor at their gates of an evening, but he knew well enough how to talk them round. It was as simple as a word and a smile.

"The trouble with that," he said to Vanyi of a morning as they rode down yet another steep and twisting track, "is that once they have me, they don't want to let me go."

She had her hands full convincing her young idiot of a mare that she had come up this way; she could very well go down it. It was a while before Vanyi could answer. When she did, she was breathless and her face was flushed. Her words were calm enough for that. "Of course they want to keep you. You settle all their impossible cases, and physic their ailments with a touch, and bless their women and their cows."

"While my swarm of courtiers eats them straight into poverty."

"That's pride," she said. Her flush was fading; she pushed her hair out of her face, where it would fall no matter how she bound it, and smoothed the mane on her mare's sweating neck. Everyone else was waiting below, being patient and, in his mother's case, subtly disapproving. Vanyi took no more notice than he did. "They'll just expect the more from their vassals, or even from their equals, because they gave so much to you. Some will make a profit from it. You're a very useful guest, taking all in all."

He looked down at the mill and muddle of his escort, and the smaller party that belonged to the lord of the castle. That one looked ready to ride back up and discover what was keeping his majesty, but Iburan held him in what looked like easy conversation. Easy for Avaryan's high priest in Endros; excruciating, no doubt, for the lord of Inigal in Kurion.

Estarion rubbed his chin. One way and another he had been neglecting to keep it shaven. Laziness, his squire muttered. Good sense, he reckoned it. The stubble was ripening into a surprising luxuriance of beard. It itched now and then, but not enough to be a nuisance. Nuisance was cold water and cold razor on warm chin in the morning.

Vanyi liked to play with it. He grinned at her, touching the edge of her mind with a memory. She blushed gloriously and glared, but laughed through it. "I think," he said, "tonight, we'll make ourselves a camp. No towns a day's ride upriver of here, they tell me, and no castle past the meeting of the waters."

"But a great one there," she said, "and its lord waiting for you, like enough, if he's heard you're riding this way."

"So we'll summon him to be our guest under the moons. He'll reckon it a novelty."

"Not an insult?"

"Not with me to charm him out of it."

"Ah," she said, caressing him with the word. "You are incorrigible."

He kissed his burning palm and laid it on her cheek. "Bless you and all your lineage, my child."

She stiffened and went white, shocking him into stillness. "Don't," she said, strung tight. *"Don't* mock me so."

"Vanyi—" he began.

She shook herself so hard he heard the clack of her teeth. Her hair escaped the last of its plait and tumbled free, autumn-colored silk blowing in her eyes. She dug heels into her senel's sides. The mare grunted in surprise and shied, and nearly tumbled down the slope. Estarion gasped, snatched. Vanyi eluded him, scrambling mount and self together, half sliding, half running down the steep descent.

Once the road was level and the way clear in front of them, she found her voice again. It was tight, and it came close to trembling. "I'm not a cow," she said, "or a farmer's wife, for you to set a wishing on. I can't give you a child till my Journey is over. Don't make it hurt any more than it has to."

That was sharp, but just. Not that he would say so. He had his pride. He said instead, "Do you know, this is my Journey, too. I never had one before this."

"You have a dispensation," she said, with an edge still, but she was not refusing to speak to him. "And isn't it a life's Journey in itself, to be emperor?"

"Not without Asanion," he said.

Vanyi pondered that, gentling her senel as the mare objected to the slant of a shadow. Umizan snorted at her and lowered his horns. That was a mark of great disgust for a stallion to threaten a mare so, and she without horns to answer him. She laid her ears back at his presumption, but she settled somewhat.

"Yes," said Vanyi at length. "Yes, that's a Journey worthy of you, to go into the west and win it."

"If this were a proper Journey," Estarion said, "I'd be alone, or at most with one companion, and I'd go wherever the god led me."

"Isn't he leading you now?"

"No," said Estarion, but he paused. The road ran along the river through a colonnade of trees. Sun slanted through the branches, now dim, now dazzling. He gathered a handful of it as Umizan carried him through, holding it cupped in his palm.

It was warm; it tingled. No one else, even a mage, could capture light as he did. He tasted it. It was heady, like wine. It tasted of evening and of the west, though it poured from a rising sun.

"You see," said Vanyi, who could read him like letters on a parchment.

He opened his fingers to let the light drain away. Umizan sidled, restless. Estarion gave him his head. He stretched from trot to canter to gallop, running ahead of them all down the long smooth track.

They camped a league short of the meeting of Suvien and Ilien, still on the sunrise side of Suvien. There was a ferry below Suvilien's fortress, or so the guides said, and boats enough to bring them all across. Here the river was both deep and wide, its banks high but less steep than they had been or would be, and a level of grass and trees stretching round a long bend.

"Eddy there," the guide said. He was a dour man, a forester in the service of the lord of Kurion, and in no apparent awe of the imperial majesty. "Round that bend she wraps her arms round an island, Suvien does, and up past that is the castle and the rivers' mating. There's good fishing in the quiet place. People come down from Suvilien with nets and poles, and bring catches up for milord's dinner. He's partial to fish, is milord."

"His majesty will dine on fish tonight," said Estarion's squire. Godri took his duties to heart. He did not approve of commoners who spoke too easily to his emperor.

The forester raised a brow at him. "Who's fishing for it, puppy? You?"

Godri drew himself up. He was a chieftain's son from the deep desert south of Varag Suvien, and the swirling scars that ornamented his cheeks were marks of one who had killed a man in battle. He was neither the eldest nor the chief of Estarion's squires; he had won his place in combat, though he would have been mortified to know that Estarion knew.

He looked like a court elegant, with his delicate hands and

his slender grace. "We have servants," he said, "to do servants' work."

"Maybe I'll do it myself," said Estarion.

That silenced both of them. He laughed at their faces: matched astonishment and matched outrage. "My lord of Suvilien will be sharing our dinner tonight. See that he's received as his rank deserves."

"But—" said Godri.

"I am going fishing," said Estarion.

He escaped before they could marshal their resistance. There was camp to pitch, fire to build, mounts and baggage to see to. The lord of it all could slip away uncaught.

Vanyi's saddlebag yielded a hook and a coil of line, and a parcel wrapped in soft silk. She was with the priests, building wards about the camp. He touched the edge of her power, a bright singing thing like water in the sun. She was deep in the working, unaware of him save in her bones, where he was part of her. He set a smile where she could find it in the secret places of herself, and left the camp behind.

It was quiet round the bend of the river. Now and then the wind brought the sound of men's voices or the squeal of a senel. They comforted him, but they did not touch him. Escape was rare, solitude rarer yet. Even Ulyai was gone, hunting in the deep coverts. She would come back in the night, purring and replete, or she would appear in his shadow on the morning's ride, then ghost away again.

The air was colder here than in Endros. There summer would have begun after the long spring. Here it was spring still, the leaves young and green, and in hidden hollows a memory of snow. He paused to dip his hand in the river. It was snow-cold. He drank a little of it. Earth was in it, and snow, and something of the northern sky. That was the taste of Ilien that was born in the mountains of Ianon, first kingdom of the Sunborn, bastion of the world's edge.

He wandered along the bank. There was another bend

farther up, where the river curved round one of its many promontories. High and forbidding as that was, the one beyond it, they said, was greater. Suvilien sat on that. Kurion's lord would be coming down from it even now, riding a boat on the river.

Estarion could see none of that from here. This arm of the river curved round a steep wooded islet, running aground on a spit of sand before a trickle of it freed itself to run back into the greater stream. It was more pool than river, its current faint, its water deep but almost clear.

Fish would gather here. He knew that from Vanyi's teaching. She had not taught him as much as she knew, and at that he had kept distracting her, but he had a little knowledge of finned folk's ways. He eyed the stretch of water and the dance of winged darters on its surface, and, keenly, the swirl and flash of scaled body as it struck for the kill.

One of the treasures from Vanyi's silken parcel was like enough to the darters to please his eye. He mated the line with the delicate weaving of thread and down and hidden, deadly hook. Foolishness, the forester would have decreed. So had Estarion once, and been proved false a dozen times over.

He cast the line with its lure as Vanyi had taught him. The breeze was fitful but strong enough to lift the false darter and tangle it in branches, where it would catch nothing but curses. The brush of his magery lifted it from certain capture and sent it winging out over the water, to settle among its mortal kin.

The fish took their time in coming to the lure. Estarion let them. The sun was warm, the air was sweet. No one came to trouble him, no squire bent on duty, no tribe of lordlings questing for mischief. He cast his line, he drew it in, he cast again. Some of the shadows beneath the water had begun to draw nearer, circling, closing for the strike.

"There!"

Estarion jumped nigh out of his skin. The lure sprang out of the water. Living silver arced after it, fell short, vanished with a scornful flick of tail.

He whipped about. "You thrice-begotten son of a leprous—"

It was not Godri, nor any of the hellions who rode with him. It was not any face he knew.

"You jump," the stranger said, "like a plainsbuck in rut."

Estarion's mouth was open. He shut it. "That was my dinner," he said. Calmly. All things considered.

"This?" The stranger drew in Estarion's line with cool and perfect insolence, and inspected the damp and draggled thing on the end of it. "Little enough meat on these bones."

"Were you born a fool," Estarion asked, "or did you study to become one?"

"Clearly you were born rude." The stranger cast the line long and low and level, as a darter flew. It barely brushed the surface of the water. Silver flashed. Line snapped taut. "There," said the stranger, but softly, almost tenderly. "There now."

Estarion stared at the fish flopping and gasping at his feet. Blank bliss had transmuted into blank rage, and thence into plain blankness.

The stranger was a woman, he realized with a small but penetrating shock. It was not obvious. She was whipcord-thin, dressed in ancient hunting leathers, hair plaited as simply as a priest's, although she wore no torque. Her nose was as fierce an arch as his own, her skin as velvet-dark, but her eyes were northern eyes, black in white, under brows as white as the flash of her teeth when she grinned at him. She was old: and that too was not immediately obvious, for all the whiteness of her hair. Her skin was stretched taut over the haughty bones. She still had her teeth, and she carried herself like a young thing, with a light, arrogant grace that raised his hackles and set his pride to spitting.

She brought in another fish as quickly as the first, with ease that was like contempt. "You are a witch," he said.

"Oh, yes," said the stranger. "But here I'm a fisherman."

"Woman," Estarion said. His tone was nasty.

"You're jealous," she said. "Touchy, too. Here's enough for your dinner *and* mine. Where's your gratitude?"

"I'd have had my own dinner if you hadn't helped me out of it."

"And whose fault was that? This isn't milady's fishpond, where any idiot can drop a line in peace. There's a fair to middling army over yonder, and rakehells enough in it, and here are you, as if there was never a danger in the world."

"There isn't," he said.

"I walked right up to you. What if I'd been minded to stick a knife in you?"

"I'd have known if you were," he said. "Look here, whoever you are—if this is his lordship's personal pool, then tell him it's his dinner I'm fishing for, and would he mind not sending his servants to startle me out of nine years' growth?"

"You don't need that much," she said, measuring his length against her own. She was middling small for a woman in the north: he stood a head-height above her. She was anything but cowed. "And who says I'm anyone's servant?"

"You're from the castle, aren't you? You're not Lord Peridan, and you're not his mother either, from anything I've heard."

"Oh," she said, rich with irony, "I certainly am not that delicate flower of womanhood. I came here from Suvilien, but I was never a bondsman there, nor anywhere on this wide earth. I'm no one's servant but my own."

"And the emperor's," Estarion said. It was a devil in him, a stab of wickedness. She did not know who he was, that was clear to see. He was not about to enlighten her.

"Not even the emperor's," she said. "He doesn't own the whole world, or even the most of it."

"What is there beyond the twofold empire? Wastes of sand or wastes of ice—fine prizes for a lord who has everything."

"The Realms of the Sun are great enough, but they're no more than a single continent on a single face of this wide and turning world. There's land beyond the desert, youngling, on the world's bottom, and land beyond the seas, both west and east."

"And you've seen it?"

She paused to hook another fish. He was interested in spite of himself; he hardly cared that she took her time in answering. "Some of it," she said at last, having freed the hook of its bright burden and cast again. "The seas are wide, and some few of the ships upon them are brave enough to sail out of sight of land. Or storm carries them, and they fetch up on isles no man of our race has ever seen."

"Are there people there? Or dragons?"

"People enough, who speak strange tongues, and reckon us gods for that we sail on ships out of the sea. Dragons? Nothing so dull or so common. Dragonels as big as hawks, yes. And fish with wings. And insects like jewels, and furred beasts that sing like birds."

"Stories," said Estarion.

"Certainly," she said. "But true enough for that."

"But if they were true," he said, "then wouldn't the Sunborn have conquered them?"

A shadow crossed her face, too brief almost to see. "If he had known of them, he would have tried."

"Someone will, you know. Eventually."

"Or one of them will conquer us."

"Not while I live," said Estarion, forgetting his pretense. But she did not seem to hear him. She was drawing in another fish, the largest yet and by far the most determined to escape. He lent a hand with the line. Together, hand over hand, they brought the catch to shore.

"We'll feed an army with this," the stranger said.

"Not the one yonder," said Estarion. "That would take a whole boatload. But milord of Suvilien will have a dainty for his dinner."

"He is a glutton," she said.

It was hardly polite to say so, even if she had not been a commoner. Estarion forbore to rebuke her. She would not have listened in any case, and he had other matters to settle. "Do you have a name?" he asked her.

"Do you?"

"Estarion," he said before he thought; and scowled. "You?"

She half shrugged, half smiled. "Many. Call me Sidani if you like."

Wanderer, that meant. And maybe, a little, *Exile.* It fit her well enough. "Sidani," he said, marking her with it.

"Estarion," she said, still half-smiling. "I knew someone by that name once. His hair was as red as fire, and he had a temper to match. He married a priestess in Asanion. Fine scandal that was, too."

"That was the last Prince of Han-Gilen but three," Estarion said, "and he died young, and if you knew him, you must have known him in your cradle."

"Oh, I am terribly old," she said. "Are you named for him, maybe?"

"It's a common enough name in the south," he said. "You can't be as ancient as that."

"Why, youngling? Because you can't conceive of anything older than yourself?"

She wanted him to draw himself up haughtily and declare himself a man grown, he could well see, and then she could go on laughing at him. He said, "You'd have to be ninety at least, then, and you'd never be roving the roads. You'd have yourself a house somewhere, and a chair with cushions, and servants to run at your call."

"I had that," she said. "I wearied of it."

"But—"

She had stopped listening. She gutted the fish with a knife as lean and wickedly curved as a cat's claw, and strung them on a coil of the line, and presented them to him with a bow and a flourish. "Your dinner, my lord."

"And yours," he said. He did not know what demon possessed him, but he was not one to alter his word. "Come to camp with me. I can offer you a place by the fire, and all the dainties you can eat, and good company, too. Stories, even. Though maybe none as good as yours."

She frowned. She would refuse, he could taste it. He cast another lure. "You don't want Lord Peridan to eat all your hard-caught fish, do you?"

"That belly on legs." She spat just to leeward of Estarion's foot. "Very well then. I'll come. I hope you don't regret it."

So did Estarion. But if there had been evil in her, or any sorcery, he would have known; and his head was not aching even a little. Rather the opposite. He could not remember when he had felt as well as he did now. No pain, no ache of knotted muscles, no constant press and fret of rank and duty.

She cleaned her knife with a knot of grass and sheathed it at her belt. There was nothing feminine in the gesture, and everything female. He wondered how he could ever have failed to see that she was a woman.

"Well," she said in her deep sweet voice—nothing male in it, and nothing old either. "Are you going to dawdle the day away?"

"Yes," he said, to take her aback; then he laughed. "Come then, lady and stranger. Try your wits on the emperor's men."

ESTARION'S RETURN WAS somewhat less calamitous than he had feared. The camp was quiet; alarmingly so. Lord Peridan sat in the middle of it in a massive sulk. "The least," he was saying—growling—"the very least his majesty could do is to be present when his loyal vassal comes to attend him. Comes, it should be needless to say, at no little cost of time and inconvenience, not to mention the danger to his digestion, to dine at his rustic table, when the table in that lord's castle is renowned for its excellence, not to mention its comfort, and furthermore—"

Estarion swept a bow before him. It brought his peroration to a halt and began a new one. "And what, pray, are you? Who gave you leave—"

The man was a walking gullet, but he was a clever one. He heard the gasps. His eyes darted round the circle that had opened to admit Estarion. They settled on Estarion's face. The eyes, of course. Everyone always stopped at the eyes. "Sire," he said, as smooth as if the rest of it had been a litany of homage.

Estarion should not have spared a glance to see how the stranger was taking this revelation. She betrayed no flicker of surprise, and no repentance, either. The tilt of her brow almost pricked him to laughter.

He bit down hard on his tongue and schooled his face to blandness. "Lord Peridan," he said. "I trust your wait was pleasant. I bring a gift, as you see: a dainty for your dinner. Will you share it with me?"

Lord Peridan looked as if he had swallowed one of Estarion's fish, sidewise.

"Uncleaned," said Sidani's voice in Estarion's ear. He did not jump—in that much, training held. And how in the hells she knew what he was thinking—

No time now. He smiled at Suvilien's lord. "There, sir. Sit at your ease; Godri here will fetch you wine and whatever else you desire. And how is your lady? And your lady mother? Your sons are well, I trust? Your eldest son's son—a fine tall lad he must be, and ready soon to come out from among the women."

"In the autumn, sire," Lord Peridan said, warming perceptibly. Either he had forgotten his grievances, or he was choosing to play the game as Estarion led it. Estarion cared little which. This mountain of lard was his best defense against the storm that threatened in his mother's eyes, and perhaps worse, in Iburan's. He would keep it by him for as long as he could, and he would charm it into complacency, or he was no son of the Sun.

As he set himself to play the courtier, Sidani made herself a part of the camp. She did it with sublime simplicity: chose a fire, sat by it, began to tell one of her stories. He was aware of her, distant and yet close, as if she were a part of him; another thing to wonder at, but later, when there was time to spare for things that mattered. For now it was enough that she stayed.

"He has the gift," the stranger said. "No doubt of that."

Vanyi eyed her sidelong. The woman had come in with Estarion, walking in his shadow as if she had a right to be there. He never had got round to explaining her, nor had she seen fit to explain herself. She was simply there. People acted as if she belonged with them.

Idiots. Courtiers. If it walked with the emperor, it was his, and no one thought to question it.

Vanyi must have said it aloud. The stranger said, "What, like the royal cats? I like that, rather."

"What do you know of anything royal?"

"His thoughts exactly," the woman said. The fish had all gone to the great glutton of a lord, except one that came by Godri's hands, with his emperor's compliments couched in the elaborate phrases of the desert. She accepted it graciously, Vanyi granted her that, and she showed a mastery of phrase that left Godri blinking in awe. She did not, Vanyi noticed, include any of the many formulas of unworthiness. Nor did she try to decline the gift.

"And why should I?" she asked of Vanyi. "I caught it." She divided it neatly and laid half of it on Vanyi's plate. "Here, eat. It's as good as anything you'd catch at home."

"Fish of the sea is surpassingly fine," Vanyi said.

"But fish of the river is sweeter." The stranger disposed of hers with a cat's neatness and economy, and followed it with a noble quantity of lesser meats. In the middle of them she tilted her chin in the gesture that, where Vanyi was born, meant greeting, and said, "Sidani, they call me."

"Vanyi," said Vanyi. A mage guarded her name; but courtesy was older than magery, and deeper rooted.

This was not a mage. Vanyi was almost certain of that. Not a priestess, either. And yet she had an air of both. Maybe it was simply age, and arrogance that put Estarion's to shame. They were all like that in the north. They called southerners servile, and sneered at the grovelings of the west. Imperial majesty meant nothing to them except as they partook of it. They never forgot that the Sunborn was king of Ianon first, and Ianon was the heart of the north.

"I'm not Ianyn," Sidani said, "though my father was. I'm everything and nothing."

"You look Ianyn," Vanyi said. And stopped. "How do you do that?"

The dark eyes were as blankly innocent as a child's. "Do what, priestess?"

Read my mind, Vanyi said without words.

Nothing. No flicker of response. The mind before her was a clear pool, transparent to the bottom, and thoughts in it as quicksilver-elusive as fish. One, caught, was pleasure in the honeycake she ate. Another held nothing more or less terrible than Vanyi's own face, too white and sharp for beauty, but the stranger reckoned it splendid.

Vanyi did not like enigmas. Her body tensed to rise, to get

away. Her mind held fast. This was danger. Not for herself, she never feared that, but for Estarion.

She looked harmless enough, an old wanderer woman taking the emperor's charity. He was free with it, as Vanyi well knew. A priestess on Journey had come once to his city, with nothing to distinguish her from any of a hundred like her, except a gift of magery, and that was hardly uncommon in that city of mages and priests. But he had seen her, and he had singled her out. He had chosen her for his beloved.

No threat of that here. This woman was long past any such thing. And if she was not, she would not want a youth as callow as Estarion.

The glint of her eye belied that. But she could not know what Vanyi was thinking. There was no power in her. Vanyi had a gift for such things. She knew.

"Who is that woman? Where did you find her?"

Estarion was easy to entrap. Vanyi simply followed him into his tent when that interminable feast was over, evicted his squire with a well-placed glare, and set herself to do the squire's duties. Estarion made no effort to resist her, but neither did he answer her. He said, "I hope my mother doesn't take it into her head to try the same thing. Seeing Lord Peridan settled for the night won't keep her occupied long."

Vanyi shook his hair out of its plait and reached for the comb. He sighed under her hands. "So," she said, "before her majesty comes to take her own piece of your hide: Who is that woman?"

"A wanderer," he said. "She tells stories. She caught the fish I fed to his lordship. She says she was in Suvilien before she came down to the river and found me."

"His lordship didn't act as if he'd seen her before."

"His lordship doesn't see anything beyond his next meal. How did such a glutton ever get hold of a castle as vital as Suvilien?"

"Most likely he inherited it. Why not ask Iburan? He'll

know. And he'll be here on your mother's heels, you can be sure of it."

"Not if I can help it." He turned on the stool and clasped his arms about her. "Will you help me?"

She studied him. The new beard aged him, made him seem more a man, but from so close she could see the shape of the face beneath it, and that was still in great part a boy's.

"You trust too easily," she said. "What if the woman is an assassin? Remember the Exile who nearly destroyed the Sunborn in the womb, and came back when he was grown and tried to cast him down."

"There's no darkness in Sidani," said Estarion. "Maybe she is a little mad. Maybe more than a little. But she means me no harm."

Vanyi's arms locked about him, startling him into rigidity. "How do you know? How can you be certain? She's not what she seems, I know it. I feel it in my bones."

He eased slowly, though a remnant of tension lingered in the angle of his shoulders, the straightness of his back. "Maybe she isn't. She was a lord's bastard, I think. She has the air. What of it? She's neither mage nor sorceress. She interests me. I'd like to hear more of her stories."

"Child," said Vanyi tenderly. "Infant. Beloved idiot." His mouth tempted hers. She set a kiss in the corner of it. But she would not let him escape so easily. "I don't like her. Or," she said, "no. Not dislike, exactly. I don't think you were wise to bring her here."

"Maybe I wasn't," he said. "But when I did it, I felt that I'd done rightly—wise or unwise or whatever else it might have been. She won't hurt me. While I live, she'll never touch you but by your leave."

"She's no danger to me at all," Vanyi said. "That I'm sure of. Thank you, sweet child, for not suggesting that I'm jealous."

His eyes were wide with honest surprise. "Should you be?"

"She's beautiful in her way. And, as you say, interesting."

"She's *old.*" He sounded all of ten years old himself. He was not too badly offended when she laughed, although he said, "She is. She says she's ninety at least."

"A hale seventy," Vanyi judged. "Sixty, more likely. Or less—the road is hard on aging bones. See? She tells stories. Keep her for that. But don't trust her, or anything she tells you."

"Not even if it's true?"

She hit him, but the blow turned to a caress. He would have made it more. She pulled away. In time, just, to appear decorous when his mother stepped into the tent, and in her shadow as always, the high priest of Avaryan in Endros, lightmage to her dark as the old tales said. But they were not twinned mages. Not in any way the Guild would have understood, though it might have understood that they were lovers. It was obvious to anyone with eyes to see.

Vanyi was expected to leave. That was the coward's part, and the prudent servant's. She was neither. She busied herself about the tent, keeping to the dimmer places, for the little good it did, and cursing his squire for the perfect order he kept.

"Oh, come," said Iburan at last, half weary, half amused. "Sit with us, priestess. We'll not be flaying him alive quite yet."

She felt the flush rise to her cheeks, and knew they saw it. Her chin came up. If it was defiant, then so be it. She set a stool by Estarion's right hand, and sat on it, and waited.

For a long while no one spoke. Estarion seemed content to rest his eyes on the lamp, letting it fill them, and him, with its little light.

Again it was Iburan who spoke, who said what had to be said. "Suppose we consider the matter disputed: that you left the camp unseen. That you took a truant's liberty, and nigh caused a scandal by your absence. Suppose it argued, and the matter settled as well as it ever may be, at no great profit to any of us."

"And no great disadvantage," Estarion said. "Are you telling me that I'm to be forbidden any more such escapades?"

"We can hardly forbid you," said Iburan. "You are the emperor."

Estarion laughed, brief and bitter. "When has that stopped you? No, I wasn't wise in what I did. I didn't mean to be wise. Maybe the god led me. Have you thought of that?"

"Certainly," said the god's priest. "And which god, my lord? He of the east, who is light and truth, or he of the west, who is darkness and the Lie?"

"Aren't they both, in the end, the same?"

"Not in their consequences."

"You may argue theology until the stars fall," the empress said, clear and cold, "but it changes nothing that is. Estarion, mere error we can forgive. Idiocy, never. What if you had been killed?"

Vanyi kept her eyes scrupulously on her feet. One of her boots needed mending. Tomorrow, if there was time. If tomorrow came.

She felt the heat that burned in her lover's body. Heat of the sun, and heat of temper banked, flaring to sudden brilliance. Yet he kept his voice low. "If I cannot walk alone in my own empire, by my own river, under my own sky, then god and goddess forbid that I call myself emperor." He drew a breath so sharp it must have cut. "This is Keruvarion, Mother. In Asanion, yes, I'll walk low and I'll walk soft, and I'll never walk unguarded. Here at least, while I walk in my own country, let me walk free."

"Very pretty," she said. "Very foolish. Is a border a wall and a warded fastness, that no assassin should pass it?"

"Not here," he said, lower yet, and fiercer. "Not in Keruvarion. I'm not an utter fool. I have an art or two here and there. I can guard myself."

"So your father said," said Merian.

Estarion started, then went still. Those were cruel words, Vanyi thought, but—yes—necessary.

He looked rather more angry than convinced. But he did not argue further, nor say much at all, until his mother was gone. And then he only said, low, as if to himself, "He never died in Keruvarion."

"OH AYE," SAID Sidani, "I sailed the seas with Chubadai. He was never quite the pirate that they say, but he took what he wanted, when he wanted it, and if he wasn't too careful about how he paid for it, well then, as often as he stole it outright, he rendered its value in gold thrice over."

"Stolen gold," someone said.

Someone else jeered at him. "I'll wager he magicked it out of the sea-salt, to deck his lady with."

"He never magicked any for me," Sidani said. That made them all laugh. The nearest yelped: she had a hard hand. "Puppy! I was none so ill to look at when I was young. Though I grant you, I'd lost the best of it by the time Chubadai set eyes on me. I was a whip-lean mad thing with an ear for the sea-spells, and so he took me on, and sailed the world around."

Vanyi listened in spite of herself. There was always a crowd where the wanderer was, pressing her for one of her wild tales or coaxing her into a song. She could sing with a voice that time had barely blunted, and she could play the harp that one of the lordlings had given her. God and goddess knew, *he* could barely play it; and for a wonder he knew it. He was in love with her. He made no secret of it. They were all twitting him for his ancient lady fair.

But never where the woman could hear. And never with conviction enough to suit Vanyi. The damnable creature was looking younger by the hour. On the ferry across Suvien, though the swirl and rush of water made the mages ill, all but Vanyi who was seaborn, Sidani stood in the bow with the wind in her hair, and she laughed as the great ungainly thing rocked and pitched under the weight of its cargo.

Estarion was delighted with her. She had claimed one of the remounts for herself, a mean-tempered gelding who knew too well the use of his stunted horns, and she rode him as if she were born to his back. They rode for long hours knee to knee, trading tales; or sat by the fire of an evening, arguing the ways of men and gods; or sang together, dark voice and light, and sometimes, by a trick of the wind, Vanyi could not tell which was which.

The nights were another matter. He was all Vanyi's then, so wholly that often she wanted to weep. She kept a brave face for him, and braver, the nearer they came to Asanion. "I'll never leave you," he said, "nor send you away, unless you ask to go. I swear it, my love. No matter what comes of this—I'll never be aught but yours."

"Hush," she said, and stopped his mouth with her hand. His beard was well grown in, rich and full; she had trimmed it that morning, smoothing its ragged edges. She tangled her fingers in the curls of it. "Don't swear to anything. Just let us have what we have now, for as long as we may have it."

"Always," he said.

Her throat locked. She flung herself on him as if he were a feast and she were starving.

He fell asleep unwontedly soon. This traveling tired him, for all that he denied it. And the last few nights had been short of sleep: all of them in towns along the edge of the great wood, and all much beset with petitions for him to grant, dignitaries for him to entertain, affairs for him to settle.

In a day or two they would enter Asanion. Tonight they guested in another of the numberless towns; but Saluyan was less importunate than the rest. Its people had let him go not long after sunset. Its priestess was compassionate. "Poor my lord," she said where Vanyi could hear, "you need sleep more than we need your sleeplessness. Rest, sire, and be comforted. We'll not trouble you till you wish to be troubled."

He would have argued with that, of course, but the priestess was adamant. He would sleep, and her people would let him be. Wise woman. Stubborn too, to resist Estarion.

Not that one would expect any less from Iburan's kinswoman. In her the northern blood ran thin, though it gave her height and breadth enough to tower over people here. She was a brown-gold woman, brown-gold skin, gold-brown hair, brown-gold eyes: Asanian blood, Asanian face, but enough of north and east that Estarion barely bridled at the sight of her. He warmed to her swiftly, even when she opposed his will: and that was a rarity.

They were still awake, Iburan and the priestess, cousin and cousin. The empress was with them. Vanyi was hardly tempted to join their company. Nor was she minded quite yet to sleep. Restlessness twitched in her, and something deep, like an ache, or a cramping in her middle. It had been vexing her off and on for a day or two. Travel-weariness; anxiety for Estarion and for herself; too much riding and too little walking and not enough plain stillness.

She kissed Estarion's brow. He murmured in his sleep, but did not wake. She left him softly, pulling on such clothes as came to hand, and crept barefoot out of the room they shared.

This was the priestess' house, the largest in this town and for leagues about. Vanyi had counted ten rooms besides the room they dined in. Still it was hardly large enough for an emperor's train. Most of Estarion's escort camped outside the town; only his Guard and his closest companions shared his lodging.

Sidani should not have been one of them, and yet she was. Vanyi found her in the temple, or rather at the entrance of it, leaning against the doorpost. As Vanyi approached she moved aside, somewhat to Vanyi's surprise. She had looked as immovable as one of the pillars.

Vanyi wanted to pray at this altar, to beg the god's protection for her lover and emperor. The wanting was as keen as a blade, twisting in her center. And yet she paused. The wanderer's face was a shadow in shadow, her mind a singing silence.

"Do you want to come in?" Vanyi asked her.

"Do you give me leave?" Sidani asked. Vanyi could hear no mockery in her, and yet surely that was what it was.

"Do you need it?"

"Maybe," the wanderer said. "I cursed the bright god long ago, and his dark sister too. They took from me all that I loved. They left me in ashes."

"They do that," said Vanyi. "They give, and they take away. Else they'd not be gods."

"Maybe we need no gods."

Vanyi was not unduly shocked. One learned on Journey: not everyone yielded easily to the gods' will.

Sidani moved forward into the light of the vigil-lamp, almost as if she had forgotten that she entered a temple. Her face was still a shadow, but her eyes were bright, fixed on Vanyi's face. "For once I don't appall you. Do you agree with me, then?"

"You know I don't."

Sidani looked down at her feet on the fine colored pavement, and up past Vanyi to the altar with its undying light. Her hand rose to her throat. Something, some trick of the lamplight, caught the thickening of scars. Old galls.

Slave's collar? There were no slaves under the sway of the Sun.

Vanyi touched her torque. No slaves. But priests enough, and the torque a cruel weight, rubbing raw the necks of those who bore it.

"Yes," said the wanderer. "I was a priestess of the Sun. No one else has seen, do you know that? Least of all your great one, your holy one, your mage and priest and master. He's blind to aught but light."

"You ran away," Vanyi said.

Sidani laughed, harsh as a gorecrow's cry. "Ran, and was not driven? Can you be so sure of that?"

"You're not one to do anything but what you choose for yourself."

"That's a flaw in me," Sidani said. "Yes, I ran. I flung my torque on the altar, cursed the day I took it, and declared myself dead and damned. They wouldn't help me, you see. They wouldn't lend me their power when my beloved was dying."

Vanyi shivered. "They can be cold, the Sun's priests. They'll do nothing for one the god has touched."

"So they said of him. But they always hated him. He wouldn't believe in them, you see, or bow to the god. Not even in the end, when the Light was in his face." Her own was stark, racked with memory. "Oh, he was a cold, cruel, godless, heartless monster of a man, and I loved him with all that I was. He was the half of me. But for him, I would never have been."

"Chubadai?"

Sidani's lips stretched back from her teeth. "That fat pirate? He never laid a hand on me. He knew I'd take it off if he tried."

"He died, your lover. And so you turned apostate." The words were cold on Vanyi's tongue, with a tang of bitterness. "I . . . don't know that I could do as much."

"Why should you? He'll live long, your lissome lad, if an assassin doesn't get him first. My beauty was born to die young. He didn't age too terribly before he went—that much grace the god gave him. He just . . . went. One moment all there for me, and a good hot quarrel we had going, too. The next, empty, drowned in Light."

"You *fought* on his deathbed?"

Sidani smiled. "It was splendid. He insisting to his last breath that there were no gods, and all the proof in front of him, and I ready to strangle him if I didn't kiss him to death first. It took him just then, like lightning from the core of him: seized him and consumed him. No long slow withering into dotage for my lord. He went up like a torch." Her smile died. "That was glorious. But the priests who refused to give him life when he took sick—them, I never forgave. Nor ever shall."

"I should rebuke you," Vanyi said, "if I were a proper priestess."

"You're proper enough." Sidani strode to the altar with the air of one who dares her greatest fear, and turned her face upward to the lamp that hung above it. "There," she said. "There, god and father. See what I think of you. Will you strike me now? You dragged out my life for years past counting, half a mind that I was, half a spirit, half a soul. Take me, damn you. Put an end to this endlessness."

Her grief was like a wind in that holy place, bleak and cold. It was older than Vanyi, and stronger, with power in it beyond magery. It left her empty of thought or will.

Perilous. Some small part of her knew it, fought it. The rest fell before it.

Pain. Her cheek stung. She looked into a face she knew and did not know, black eagle-face, eyes—

"Your eyes are wrong," she said.

They blinked. Sidani drew back. Both of them were on the floor, Vanyi lying, she kneeling, sitting on her heels. Her eyes were perfectly ordinary northern eyes, if sharper than most. Why Vanyi had wanted them to be yellow, she could not think. Fuddlement, no more. They all looked alike, these northerners, with their faces like birds of prey.

For the first time in a long while, she yearned for a face that was like her own. Brown, maybe, with wind and weather, but white under it, and eyes sea-colored, and hair neither straight nor curling but something of both. Sharp-chinned, long-nosed, Island-bred, and no great waveless shield of land between herself and it.

Her fingers clutched at unyielding floor. Her stomach heaved. Laughter choked her. All these days, months, years, and now of all times she succumbed to the land-sickness.

No wonder people said they wanted to die. It racked her: knotted her stomach, cramped her belly, doubled her up gasping.

A thin strong hand stroked her hair back from her sweating face. Arms lifted her. A voice spoke, cursing softly and with great inventiveness.

"Not," said Vanyi. "Not your fault."

"Only about half of it." Sidani held her as she struggled, with ease that froze her into stillness. "Stop that. This place is too strong for you, with what I woke in it. I'm taking you where you'll be safer."

"Don't need—don't want—"

Little good that did. Vanyi was going to be properly and catastrophically sick, and soon. She hoped she would not do it all over Sidani's coat.

These new eyes above her were as they should be, bright gold with astonishment in the dark face, and the temper that flared in it was oddly comforting. Arms somewhat stronger and much more welcome closed about her. Anger trembled in them. "What's wrong with her? What did you do to her?"

"Nothing," Vanyi said before Sidani could begin. "The sea. It's too far. My blood—my tides—"

They were flowing out of her. Relentless, as if the moons had set hooks in her belly and torn it apart. As if—

"No!"

Her courses were strong. They always had been. But this was stronger than anything she had known. There was more in it than the tide of the moons, more in her womb than vows and emptiness.

The bindings had failed. They had made a child together, she and Estarion—neither of them suspecting, neither of them dreaming that it could be possible. And it died, this son, this daughter, it did not matter. The bindings, waking too late, closed in upon it. They killed it. Nothing that she did could stop it.

"What did you do to her?"

Estarion was much quieter this time. The anger was beaten out of him.

Neither of them had moved to fetch help. Sidani knew what to do: her hands were deft, catching the flood when it came, stanching it with cloths that she drew it seemed from air. One of them did not move as well as the other, he noticed with remote and bitter clarity. It was twisted somewhat, and its palm was scarred as if she had held it in a fire. Odd that he had not noticed before. Odd that he noticed now, or cared, when nothing should matter but Vanyi's life.

"I think," the woman said when Vanyi was quiet, more asleep than unconscious, "that you had somewhat more to do with this than I. Has she miscarried before?"

The word rang in his brain. "Mis—" He tossed his head. It would not come clear. "She can't! She's womb-bound. Spelled. She can't—"

"You forget what you are," Sidani said. "Did no one teach you to hold your seed until you were ready to beget your heir?"

He recoiled. "That's barbaric!"

Her laughter was weary beyond telling. Something in it struck him nearly to tears. "So. That much of Asanion is yours. Did your mother know what she was permitting? Or did she care?"

He could not think of that. Of what it would mean. That his mother knew, and had not prevented it.

"The goddess is a milder thing than she was when I was young," Sidani said, still in that tired voice, but without the terrible mirth. "But she's a cold one still, and heedless of life or light. I can't fault your mother, I suppose. She's but serving the power she's sworn to."

"My mother is not evil!"

"Of course not," said Sidani. "She's a good priestess and a strong empress. Your father chose her well." As if, thought Estarion, she had a right to judge. "But she did ill not to warn you that the Sun's seed is stronger than mages' bindings. That it could come to this."

He looked down at Vanyi. She seemed very small in the wide bed, very white and still. His heart twisted. "Oh, god and goddess. I could have killed her."

"Nonsense!" He jumped at the sharpness in Sidani's tone. "She's a good, strong wench—or she would be if your priests hadn't meddled with her cycles. Better for you both if she'd seen to it herself, and not trusted in someone else's bindings. Although," she added, musing, "even that might not have come to anything, you being what you are. *That* fire will burn in the void between the stars."

"What are you? How do you know so much?"

The bright black eyes slanted toward him and then away. There was nothing old in them at all, and nothing young. They were beyond age. "I tell stories. I live a few, maybe. Your grandfather got your father on a woman proven barren, proclaimed so by mages. He sowed his seed in the dry land, and it brought forth a bright fruit. She's no fallow field, this one, nor will be, now the gates are open."

Estarion's hands lowered of themselves to Vanyi's body, tracing the paths of life and magic. They ran clean and they ran straight, no knot of coiled spells beneath the heart. Blood had washed it away.

He began to shake. "Gods. Oh, gods. She'll be forsworn."

"Don't moan." Sidani gathered together bloodied sheets and cloths and made a bundle of them. "Someone will have to wash these."

"And explain them."

"Never explain," she said. "You are the emperor. That and no more is your explanation. But," she added, "if you insist, then your lady has had a particularly calamitous onset of her courses. They're never easy for her, are they?"

"No," said Estarion unwillingly. But, "Mages will know as soon as they see her."

"Let them. More fools they, for fancying that they could bridle Sun's blood."

He was not afraid of her, not exactly. But as he saw her standing there like a serving-woman with her armful of bloodied cloths, he knew suddenly and piercingly that she was more than he had imagined. Vanyi had seen it: blessed, damnable perception. She had not seen what was in her own body, not looking for it, not expecting it, and it had betrayed her.

"Go to sleep," said Sidani, dryly practical as any grandmother with a stubborn child. "She'll be sleeping for a while, and when she wakes she'll need you there, as strong as you can be. She wanted that baby too badly to be easy about losing it."

"But she didn't even know—"

The glance that raked him was burning cold. "Manchild," she said, "go to sleep."

And, like the infant that she reckoned him, he went. He sensed no sorcery in it. It simply was.

9

"A son! A son for the Olenyai!"

The cry rang from the tower of their stronghold, riding the notes of a horn. So it always was when a son was born alive, unblemished, and spoken for by the mages. Daughters were neither sung nor celebrated, although they suffered the same testing, the same speaking of mages, and the same hard fate if they failed: death, and casting out for the birds to feed on.

"That's another one for Shajiz," Marid said, down below in the court of swords, where he was alone but for his sword-brother. "What does that make now? Six? Seven?"

"Five," said Korusan. He was honing his right-hand sword; he had barely paused for the birthing-call.

Marid shrugged. "Then he's got two more coming. Remarkable. Do you remember when he was so behindhand in his duty that they were talking of forbidding him the women altogether?"

Korusan ran the stone down the bright blade and up again. "So they were," he said. His voice had no inflection.

Marid shot him a glance. Here where none could see them but Olenyai, he went unveiled. The single scar on his cheek was as redly new and no doubt as itchy in its mending as Korusan's: he rubbed it, fidgeting as he always did, for Marid was a restless man. "Some come late to it, that's all."

Korusan's hand stopped. He thought of clasping the sharpened steel, for the pleasure of the pain. "You have two sons," he said.

"So will you, when you get to it."

"I go to the women every night," said Korusan. "Every cycle of Brightmoon they name themselves and the men who have gone to them, and the seed that has sprouted in them. They often name me among the sowers. But never among the harvest."

"You're very young," said Marid, who to be sure was a whole year the elder.

"I was doing a man's duty while you were still a flute-voiced child."

"And who was it that I heard last cycle, singing descant with the girls?"

Korusan's sword sang into its sheath. There had been a moment while he raised it, when Marid's eyes had flickered, his hand twitched toward his own sheathed blade. But he would not begin battle, if battle must be. Not against his swordbrother.

Korusan would have liked to be as certain of himself. Olenyai were loyal to their lords and to one another. It was bred into them. But Korusan was not Olenyas—not in the blood, and not in the soul.

"I think," said Korusan. "I fear . . ."

He could not say it, even to Marid, who was as close to him as any living thing could be.

Nor would Marid set it in words for him. He was blind, was Marid, and deaf to what he did not wish to hear. "Shajiz was one-and-twenty when his first son was conceived; and he had been going to the women since he was twelve years old. Early manhood isn't early fatherhood, brother."

"Early is all I have," said Korusan. But not loudly. Not for Marid to hear. He thrust himself to his feet. "Maybe it will be tonight."

Marid grinned, transparent in his relief. "Maybe it will. Luck to your sowing, Olenyas."

"Luck to your reaping," said Korusan, "Olenyas."

The woman was willing. She was beautiful, also, as they often were, and she was skilled in the high arts. She could receive as well as give pleasure. Her murmur of thanks seemed honest, her smile unfeigned when he paid her the compliment of asking, "May I come to you again?"

She lowered her eyes as was proper, and said, "My lord, you may." And then she said: "Tomorrow, if it pleases my lord."

His heart should have been light. The women of the Olenyai were given to choose whom they would see a second time, as it was given the men to choose whom they would visit once. He had pleased her, then, and well.

But he was in a bleak mood as he left the place of the women and entered the place of the men. Harems in the world without, he was told, were scented, close-walled places. This was walled, to be sure, but its scents were simple ones: clean flesh, clean garments, the pungency of herbs or the sweetness of a flower in a woman's hair. Olenyai knew well the arts of simplicity. It made them strong; it taught them to focus on what mattered.

Men leaving the women's quarters walked a path well trodden through the years, up a stair worn deep in the middle, along a passage hung with tapestries so old as to have lost all color and figure and faded to the muted brown-grey of the stone behind them. Then they turned, either up to their own place—whether chamber or barracks—or down to the training grounds and the gates.

Although it was late, well past the midnight bell, Korusan turned toward one of the gates. It was unguarded. No one in Asanion would enter the fortress of the Olenyai, even if he had won his way so far. To pass those walls was forbidden any not of the Order, or of the House of the Lion. The lands that lay about it were not wide as princely domains went, but they sufficed to feed and furbish the castle; and they were guarded as the gates were not, by men in black robes with hidden faces.

He slid the bolt easily, for it was kept well oiled, and stepped into the cool of the dark before dawn. It had rained in the early night, but now all the clouds were blown away. The moons were glorious: blood-red Greatmoon at the full, silver Brightmoon some days short of it, filling the sky with fire, overwhelming all but the brightest of the stars.

There was someone sitting near the gate on a heap of stone left over from the building and grown now into the earth it lay on. In the bright moonlight the robe was silver, but it would be grey in the sun; the hair was frosted white, but would be youthful gold where eyes saw daylight-clear.

Korusan knew this lightmage by sight. It was a woman, and often about the castle. He had not seen her alone before, without her darkmage shadow. Here she had shadows in plenty, but none lived and breathed. They were all born of the moons.

Her eyes glittered as she turned them toward him. He knew better than to think that she had not been aware of him from the moment he opened the gate, and likely before that.

"It is odd," he said, "to see a lightmage here, under the moons."

"But they are as bright almost as day," she said.

"Almost," said Korusan. Perhaps he should feel his presumption. Olenyai did not speak thus easily with mages, as if mages were folk like any other. But he was not born an Olenyas.

"We all must understand our opposites," the lightmage said, "or they may consume us."

"Have you consumed your opposite?" Korusan inquired.

She laughed, a silver sound, so alien to her rank and to this place that he started. "Oh, my darkmage! He is a daytime creature; the sun sets, and he falls asleep, and sleeps the night through. But I can never sleep when the moons are high. Do you hear them singing?"

"I am not a mage," said Korusan.

She took no offense at the flatness of his tone. "Of course you are not. But you have the gift. I saw you when you ran the dreamwood."

"All your ilk saw me," Korusan said. "I could wish to return the favor."

"You pay the price of princes," said the lightmage. She clasped her knees, looking all of his own age, if that, and smiled at him.

He could strike her, and she would have no defense.

Not of the body. But that was not what held his hand: not knowing that she had magic. He had a use for her. "Tell me somewhat," he said.

She raised moon-silvered brows and waited.

He wondered if she had tried to enter his mind. Mages did that. He had felt nothing, no crawling of the spine that would have warned him. "Tell me this, mage. Will I beget a son?"

Her brows rose higher. "Do you take me for a village witch, to tell your fortune for you?"

"Will I?" he pressed her, stepping closer. She neither recoiled nor betrayed alarm. Her magic would protect her, no doubt, and she was sure of it.

"Truly," she said, "I am not a soothsayer. Find you a market, prince, and ask there."

He stood over her. She was complacent still, but she had to lean back a little lest he topple her. "Look inside me. Tell me what all your kind know. Will there be another after me? Or am I the last?"

"Are you not young to fret over that?"

He struck her, flat-handed, on the cheek. She looked perfectly astonished. No one ever laid hand on a mage. No one dared.

"You are older than I," he said, "but which of us is the greater fool?"

"I could blast you with fire," she said, no rancor in it, nor threat, but simple certainty.

He laughed in her face. "So you could; and kill your magic with it. Yes, I know that secret of your trade. Who does not, after the plot that succeeded so well for your kind? You disposed of an emperor; you maimed his son. But you betrayed yourselves to those with wits to see."

"We betrayed nothing that belonged to us," she said, and

now at last her voice had an edge of anger. "All who speak of that killing, speak of the fool who did it. No one knows who set him there, or who took his wits from him lest the priests discover the truth."

"No one," said Korusan, "but the Olenyai. And we are too valuable as we are. Tell me, mage. Tell the one whom you would make your emperor. Am I to be the last and only, and after me, nothing?"

"One will rule after you," she said.

"Indeed? And will that one be the Master of your Guild?"

She did not answer that.

"The blood has failed," he said. "Has it not? I remember, mage. When I was not quite yet a man, and one of my many fevers was fiercer than the rest, and you thought that I was unconscious, but I heard. You could save me, but you could not save my children who would be."

"Not I," she said. "That was not I."

"Are you not all one?" He stepped back, releasing her from his shadow. "It is true. I can beget no sons."

"You are young," she said, but faint, as if he had frightened her. "You cannot know . . ."

He wheeled. The moons spun. He flung himself through the gate. He did not care how he went, save that it was swift; or whom he trampled in going there.

When he stopped, it was not by choice of his own. He might have struck a wall, but there was only air, and a chamber lit with lamps—but none of them flickered as earthly fire would—and cold eyes regarding him from the cushions and coverlets of a bed.

The Master of Mages slept alone, or liked to have it seem that he did. He slept decently in underrobe and outer robe, and warmed his sparse-haired crown with a cap. He looked like a merchant from the provinces, but that was a deception.

"You are violent this morning, my lord," he said. "Did our youngest girlchild offend your highness? Does your highness wish her heart on a salver?"

"If I assented, would you give it to me?"

The Guildmaster smiled. These mages were all as complacent as cats. "I would, my lord, if it would content you."

"Anything for the prince," said Korusan with a bitter twist. "Anything at all. Except an heir."

"I am sorry for that," the Guildmaster said.

Perhaps it was honest regret. "So it is true," Korusan said.

"Even had the fever not made sure of it, we would have held out little hope," said the Guildmaster. "You are a miracle in yourself, with all the aid that we have given you, to keep you living, to raise you to manhood. We would not look for another such chance."

Korusan was prepared for it. He had looked for no gentler truth, but it was no easier to face for that.

"Olenyai gain rank," he said, "for the number of sons they sire."

"Not only for that," said the Guildmaster, "and not even for that among the highest. Any beast can beget young. It needs a man to rule men."

"And what is a man but a father of sons?"

"I have no sons," the Guildmaster said. "No mage of my rank does, or can. We make that sacrifice when we choose this path."

Korusan was not shocked. That too he had known, from what he had heard or suspected. "But you are not a prince, mage. You will not be emperor. And emperors must beget heirs."

"Not all of them do," the mage said, "or have."

"What, then?" Korusan demanded as he had of the lightmage. "What comes after me?"

"Do you care?"

Korusan drew up short.

"Do you truly care?" the Guildmaster asked him. "You live to take revenge against the Sun's brood. Once they are gone and you are dead, what does it matter who calls himself lord of the world?"

"It matters," Korusan said, "if that lord is the lord of your Guild."

"Why? Might not a mage rule as well as any man?"

Korusan stood up against the mage's wall and tasted the savors of rage, impotence, raw grief. And hate, always hate, like blood and iron. "So that is what you intend. Why trouble with me, then? Why breed me, raise me, keep me alive? Why not simply face the Sun-worshippers direct, and fight an open war? Surely it would be less trouble. Even," he said, "for cowardice as mighty as yours."

The Master of the Guild was not to be pricked by such words, however bitter they might be. "Perhaps we prefer the symmetry of this conflict, Sun against Lion. Perhaps the gods demand it, or fate, or the turning of the worlds; and if we defy it or seek to alter it, we destroy ourselves with our enemies."

"Perhaps you are afraid to face the Sun and its priests, because they are strong, and they may defeat you."

"We are stronger," said the mage, "and we are older in our magic. But secrecy is our armor, that is true enough. And we owe the Lion a debt. It took us in when we were driven from the Sunborn's empire; it protected us when his heir would have blotted us from the earth. We repay in you, in raising you to the throne that is yours."

"A barren throne," said Korusan. "An empty victory."

"Do you believe that, Lion's cub? It will be your throne, your victory."

"And I your puppet."

"You are no man's puppet," said the Guildmaster.

"What if," said Korusan, "when I had won the victory, when I had my throne—what if I ordered all of you destroyed? What would you do then?"

"We would fight," the Guildmaster said. "We wager high, prince, and we wager long. We gamble on your clemency, as we gambled on your being born at all, or living to stand here now, and show yourself in truth the Lion's heir."

"Flattery," said Korusan. But the anger had gone out of

him. He was cold within, and empty. Where another man had his little tribe of ancestors, he had a thousand years and more, an army of emperors. Where even the simplest man had hope of sons, he had nothing. Only emptiness and the line's ending.

"Perhaps it may console you," the Guildmaster said, "that your enemy has begotten a son, but the son is lost."

"And that too was your doing?"

"No," said the Guildmaster with all apparent calm. "His own priests did it for us, in womb-binding the woman who is his lover. Fools all. None bethought himself of what must come of working that spell on a Sunlord's leman."

Korusan's gorge rose. That his blood enemy should do what he could not do. That this fat merchant with his half-god's magic should gloat so over the death of a child.

He turned without speaking, without even the courtesy of a glance, and left as he had come, headlong. No wall barred him. Nothing stopped or slowed him but his own bones' weariness and the dawn breaking, and the rousing of the Olenyai to the morning's duties. His first duty was sword-practice. And though he ached within and without, he was glad of that grueling dance, glad of anything that bent his mind away from the dark.

VANYI HAD NO intention of feigning illness, or of suffering it. She could ride. She had before when her courses racked her, numbed with a potion the priestesses brewed for just such troubles as this.

Estarion could not move her, even when he lost his temper. She turned her back on the blast of it and set about readying to depart.

The drug numbed her body. There was pain somewhere on the edge of things, but it was no part of her, no more than the memory of what had caused it: what had broken, and what had mended, before Avaryan's altar.

She had lost nothing that she had known she had. She had gained a thing beyond hope. She could bear a child now. She could give Estarion his heir.

Through drug and distance and grim endurance, her entrails clamped tight. Only Estarion's presence kept her erect. She reached blindly for she knew not what; stared at what her hand fell on. For a long moment she could not guess what it was, could not name it or imagine a use for it.

Her fingers clenched. She had not even known.

"Who took off my torque?" she asked. Her throat was tight, had been since she got up, not knowing itself unbound, no more than her womb until it gave up its burden.

"Sidani," Estarion answered. "She feared you'd choke."

"Damn her," said Vanyi. "*Damn* her."

He reached for her. She slid away. Her hands trembled as she lifted the torque. It was deadly heavy, and cold. It locked like jaws about her neck.

She looked up into Estarion's face. "She was a priestess, you know. Sidani. Or whatever her name was then. She turned apostate."

"She told you that?"

"Would I lie?"

He stiffened as if she had struck him. She should kiss him, or say something to comfort him. Mind and heart were empty, void of comfort. It had bled out of her in the long grim night.

She shouldered her saddlepacks. The world spun briefly. Estarion spun in it, too bleak for anger. She walked away from him.

"You may go," he said behind her, "but I am staying here."

She stopped. She refused to turn.

"I promised the priestess that I would sing the tenth-day rite with her. That is tomorrow. I'll not leave till that is done."

"And when did you promise that?"

"Does it matter?"

The doorpost swung toward her. She caught at it.

He was there, hovering. She did not want him to touch her. "Let me," she said, thick enough to choke on. "Let me be."

"Vanyi—"

"Let me be!"

He retreated, too startled for hurt. That would come later. She did not want to see it.

He had mercy. He left her alone.

"That was well done," said Iburan.

Vanyi burrowed deeper into her nest of blankets. How long it had been, whether it was morning or evening, she neither knew nor cared. People had come in at intervals. Some had left food or drink. Some had tried to speak to her. She had shut them out.

Iburan was not to be deterred by anything as simple as blankets or a magewall. His voice followed her wherever she escaped. "Yes, you did well, to drive away the one who could best have healed you."

"The one who caused my pain."

He heard her. "So. You blame him."

She erupted from her lair. "I blame myself. I should have known. I should have prevented—"

"You should," he said. "Therefore you punish him for your own failing."

"No," she said. She shivered, though the air was warm. "No. I—" The rest would not come. She cried out through it. "Don't you touch him. Don't you dare! He knew even less than I."

"Why would I touch him?"

"Time was," she said, "when you would have taken us both and bound us to altars of iron, and turned the burning glass on us, and called down the Sun to sear away the source of our sin."

"Those were older days, older laws. The Sunborn came to free us from them."

"The Sunborn's descendant is too free altogether."

"You yourself said he didn't know."

She blinked. Her eyes were full of tears. Iburan was a blur beyond them, a shadow and a gleam. "It shouldn't matter. Every turning of Brightmoon this comes to me, to every woman. Why I do want to weep and howl at the moons?"

"Because this time it took more than the moon's blood. It took the child you made, you and he together."

"No," she said. "The moon didn't take that. *You* took it, priest of the Sun. You and the magic you wove."

Not he, not for her. That had been a priestess in the Isles, raising the great rite over the god's new-made bride. But he knew what she meant. "We had no way of knowing that this would happen. This time, when we weave the bonds anew—"

"You will weave no bonds," she said.

"You will bear him no child while your Journey endures."

His voice was soft, but there was iron in it. She met it with iron as strong. "Nor shall I ever bear him one, if you have your way. His heir will be a yellow woman's son."

"Will you defy your vows?"

She sat stiff. Her body ached, but worse was the ache in her heart. "Are you binding me?"

"You said that I should not."

It was too much, this war of wills. Her belly cramped. To yield to it—to crumple with a cry—that would be a clever diversion, and he would fall to it. She would not do it. "At this moment," she said, struggling to say it steadily, "when I think of him, I love him with all that I am. And when I think of him touching me, I shudder in my soul. Something is wrong with me, my lord. Something broke when the binding went away. Aren't you glad?"

"Child," he said. "Oh, child."

His compassion did not make her want to weep. It made her want to kill him. "Don't pity me!"

"That, I never have." He seemed at last to recall that he was looming over her. He sat in the chair beside the bed, sighing as he did it, as if with weariness. Sleights and calculation. She hardened her heart against them.

His beard was braided with gold this morning, evening, whatever it was. He stroked it as he sat there, eyes turned away from her, fixed on something only he could see. He looked nothing like Estarion, except that he was so dark, and yet she could not get that other face out of her mind. Callow, beak-nosed, yellow-eyed face. She loved it, she hated it. She wanted to enfold herself in the memory of it. She wanted to efface it utterly.

"You hurt," said Iburan, so low it was like a mountain shifting. "You strike out at anything that approaches you. Time will heal you. Time, and the nearness of those who love you."

"Not his," she said. "You'll see to that, I'm sure. It's best for everyone. He has to make an Asanian marriage. I'm an intrusion, an inconvenience. You never planned for me or wanted me, or anyone like me. You were keeping him for his royal bride."

"He kept himself. Sun-blood are always so. They do not—cannot—love lightly."

"And no wonder," she said. Bitter laughter burst out of her. "Seed, you men call it? Arrows, the Sun-blood have. Nothing is proof against them."

Iburan did not laugh with her. "What will you do, then? Take yourself away?"

"Wouldn't it be best?"

"It would give him great pain."

"Brief pain. Assuaged, I'm sure, by a procession of lovely ladies. Royal ladies. Ladies fit to be his queen."

"Do you hold him so light?" Iburan asked her, as if he honestly wished to know.

She looked him in the face. "Sometimes, my lord, I wonder. I wasn't raised to be a Sunlord's bride. When I told my father I was going to the temple, he beat me. Loving me, you understand, and determined to save me from myself. I was to be a wife in Seiun town, marry one of the boys who hung about making eyes at me, breed his babies and mend his nets and weave his sails. The temple was for other people, priest-people, people bred to it. The witcheries that haunted me would go away, my father said, when I had a baby at the breast. So they'd done for my mother, and she a sea-eyed changeling too. The sea took her, I told him. Should I let it take me? So I went away, walking straight in spite of my bruises, and when I took the torque, he wouldn't speak to me. What he would say if he knew what I'd gone away to, I dread to think."

Iburan said nothing. Eloquent, she thought. Subtle.

"You can't understand," she said. "You're all lords and princes. You don't know what it's like not to know for certain who your grandfather's father was, or where he came from. You can't imagine the clench of hunger in a lean winter, or the stink of fish in the summer's heat. You've never gone barefoot because you had no shoes, or worn the same filthy shirt the year round because there was no cloth to make another. And you've never—never—been spat on for a witch, not for anything you'd done, but for that you looked like a changeling."

"Estarion has."

She caught her breath. "Estarion is the highest of all high princes. He's as far above me as the sun itself. And he doesn't know. He doesn't think. He thinks he loves me."

"He does."

"He's a fool," she said. "There. I said it. I'll go away now. I'll set him free."

"If you leave now," said Iburan, "he'll go after you. He does love you, child. With all his great heart."

The tears were threatening to come back. She willed them away. "So I'm to make him stop loving me. Is that it? Is that what you want me to do?"

"I doubt you could."

"Oh, it's easy," she said. "It's as easy as a slap in his face. He's never been denied anything, never had to do anything he didn't want to do. Even this journey to Asanion is his choosing, though he imagines that his mother forced him into it. He's always known he'd have to do it. He let her work her will on him."

"And you? What will you do to yourself?"

"Do I matter? Do I, my lord, when you consider the empire, and the man who is emperor of it?"

There, at last, a question Avaryan's high priest could not answer. She regarded him in something like pity. "You won't bind me, my lord. I'll bind myself. I can read the god's will as well as you. I can see that I'm not meant for the emperor."

"I can see," he said, "that you need rest, and healing for the soul as well as the body. The servant will bring you wine. You'll drink it: I'll mix in an herb I know of. It brings nothing more deadly than sleep."

"Maybe I have a drug of my own."

"That is too strong in you. It makes you say things you never mean. Lie down now, and grieve if you must. It will help you mend."

Kundri'j Asan

ESTARION KNEW WHEN he crossed the border into Asanion. It was more than the softening of wild country into towns and tilled fields, forest tracks into roads, black or bronze faces into faces more truly gold and ivory. It was a thrumming in the blood, a quiver in the senses. Recognition—he did not want to call it that. Some part of him knew this earth, this air, this face of the world. It was not memory of his coming there half his life ago. It went deeper than that.

Half a day past the border, he stopped and dismounted and laid his hands on the earth. It was not so very different from the land he had left behind: rich black earth, fragrant with the rain that had fallen in the morning. It trembled under his touch. It knew him.

His companions were watching him as if they feared that he would break and run shrieking back to Keruvarion. He straightened. His right hand burned and throbbed. The earth that clung to it could not stain the gold in its palm.

He vaulted back into the saddle. "On," he said, snapping it off short.

The land knew him, welcomed him. But it lay crushed and flattened beneath the feet of the men who lived on it. There were no wild places. Even the woods were lords' possessions, their trees counted and reckoned for their worth, their beasts and birds preserved for the hunt or for their owners' pleasure. The rivers flowed in chains: locks and quays and bridges. The hills were tamed things, crowned with cities.

Worse still was the silence. People lined the ways to see him pass; came, it was evident, from many days' journey to look on their emperor. And when he was before them, they would not meet his eyes. They would not look at him at all, or cheer his passing, or speak when he spoke to them, but fell mute and bowed to the ground.

"All I see of them are their rumps," he said. "Their rumps, and the backs of their heads. How am I supposed to learn to know them?"

There would be no camps under the stars in the Golden Empire. On this, his first night in the west, he lodged with the lord of a town called Shon'ai. The man was endurable as Asanians went: old enough and secure enough not to be unduly touchy in his pride. Nor did he seem dismayed to be guesting the emperor himself.

"But he won't look me in the face," Estarion said. "What does he think I'll do to him if he does? Blast him with a glance?"

"It's their courtesy," Sidani said. What she was doing in the rooms he had been given, he did not know. She went where she would, did as she chose. Guards seemed to mean little to her, or princely privacy. She was adept at ignoring both.

Estarion was glad of her presence now: it gave him someone to storm at. Servants were no good for that. They cringed and fled. Godri was seeing that the seneldi were properly looked after. Vanyi was nowhere that Estarion could find, which was as well. She had been impossible since she lost the baby, would not open her mind to him, would not let him approach her, would accept nothing from him, no comfort, no anger, not even bleak endurance.

Sidani was the same as she always was. She sat in a chair like a throne, feet tucked up, hands folded in her lap, and watched him snarl and pace.

He came to a halt in front of her. He was breathing hard, somewhat to his surprise. The air was wrong here. Suffocating, even under the sky.

"You have a horror of closed spaces," she said. "You'll loathe Kundri'j Asan."

"What choice do I have?" he demanded.

She shrugged. "You could have been born a peasant's brat."

He dropped to the carpet at her feet. "No," he said. "I would have hated that, and wanted more. I wasn't made to be anything less than I am. Am I growing wise, do you think? Or simply arrogant?"

"You were born arrogant. Wisdom . . . you'll have it someday, if you live so long."

"Not now?"

"Now," she said, "you are a spoiled child. A dusty, dirty, sweaty one, who would profit from a bath."

She failed to make him angry, though she had made a noble effort. He bared his teeth at her. "I know why I keep you. To keep me humble."

"No man keeps me. I stay because I choose. To keep you humble."

He laughed. He did not get up at once, though a bath was a glorious temptation. "You keep me sane too, I think. Everyone else is so strange. Walking soft as cats, as if I'll go wild and tear them to pieces. Vanyi . . ." His throat tightened. "Vanyi shuns me. Because my body betrayed her."

"Not yours, youngling. She's not the mage she thought she was. She finds that hard to forgive in herself."

"Does she think I don't care? It was my baby, too."

"Did you want it as badly as she did?"

He could not answer that. He wanted an heir, yes. He had been bred and raised to want one. "It would be terribly impolitic, if my mother's to be believed. Then I wouldn't need an Asanian empress."

"That could be dealt with. There's the Sunborn's law, true, that the firstborn of the Sun's heir, whether son or daughter, is heir to the throne. But there's nothing in the law that the child's mother must be empress."

"It would be awkward if she weren't." He pulled himself to his feet. "They're waiting for me now. Hordes of them. Women of every size and shape, but only one color. I won't eat till I've passed them in review."

"It's not as bad as that," Sidani said.

"Do you want to wager on it?"

She said nothing. He took odd comfort in her disapproval. *She* did not want him to marry for cold politics. She cared nothing at all for such things.

"Only remember," she said. "They're people, not devils. Even if they do have yellow eyes."

He lowered his own. "I can't help it."

"Nonsense."

"They killed my father."

"A demented fool killed your father. Stop whining, child. He died, and that was an ill thing. You killed his murderer with magery, and that was a worse thing. It's none of it Asanion's fault."

"I don't need to listen to you," he said through gritted teeth. "I hear it from my mother, I hear it from Iburan, I hear it endlessly and forever, and it doesn't matter. Here, in my belly, I know what I know. Asanion will be the death of me."

"Poppycock," said Sidani. "You've stewed it in your innards till it's gone to bile, and not a drop of truth in it. You should have stayed here till you were whole again, or come back as soon as you could ride."

"How do you know what is truth and what is not?"

She smiled her terrible, sweet smile. "I've lived a little longer than you, child. There's nothing wrong with Asanion that a good scrubbing and a blast of fresh air won't mend."

"Maybe," he said, "I'll take the roof off the palace in Kundri'j. What will people say to that?"

"That you're stark mad. But they already know as much. You're Sun-blood."

She could drive him to the edge of rage, and back again to laughter. He bowed to her, all the way to the floor, and came up laughing, and went to his bath in better spirits than he could have imagined, his first night in Asanion.

* * *

The bath was none so ill. They wanted to shave him smooth, face and body, but he had been warned of that. The servants were men and boys, not women or eunuchs. Except one, maybe; he was beardless past the age one might expect. But he was the lightest-handed, and when the razors approached, he turned them aside before Estarion could do more than roll an eye at them. He even ventured a smile, which Estarion found himself returning.

When he was clean, bathed and oiled till he purred like Ulyai, they offered him garments. Not the ten robes of the imperial majesty, but a simple three, underrobe and inner robe and loose outer robe, all of them white, and the outermost embroidered with gold. It was not an insult, he judged, but a gesture toward his outland sensibilities. They fit him well, which was interesting. In the east he was middling tall; in the north a stripling. Here he rose to a towering height, even unshod as kings walked in their palaces.

Lord Miyaz's servants held up a mirror, a wonder of a thing, a shield of polished silver taller than Estarion by a full handspan. His face had grown no prettier since the last time he looked, though the beard lent it a degree of distinction. His eyes were a brighter gold than he remembered, bright as coins. Time was when he would have demanded a hat or a hood, to cast them in shadow.

Tonight he went bareheaded. The tallest servant bound his brows with a thin band of gold, confining his hair with no more than that, no plaits, no cords, no chains of gems.

He would never look Asanian, however they tried. Not with that face or that midnight skin. The robes made him seem even taller and narrower than he was. He was as exotic as a sunbird in a flock of finches.

He could hunch and creep and hope to pass unnoticed. Or he could stand straight, walk light and haughty, tilt his chin at its most rakish angle. Born arrogant, was he? Then let them see it, and think what thoughts they pleased.

The eunuch, who seemed to be the chief of servants, led him out of the baths and down a passage. He barely noticed its furnishings, if it had any. The air was full of mingled perfumes, amurmur with sweet voices.

He halted. "These are the women's quarters."

The eunuch regarded him without comprehension. He had spoken Gileni unthinking. He shifted to Asanian. "This is not the way to the place of feasting. Why are you leading me among the women?"

His guide bowed to the floor. "Majesty, forgive. The lady empress, she commanded—"

"So she would." Estarion lifted the boy—man—whatever he was—with hands that tried to be gentle. "Go on, then. Lead me where she bade you."

It was a hall of feasting after all, with tables laid, gleaming in the light of many lamps, and flowers banked about them, filling the air with their scents; but no food, no drink in the cups of gold and silver. And no sign of his mother. She was keeping herself out of it, then, or hiding behind an arras and a mage-wall, watching unseen. Wise lady. The feast stood arrayed before him, trembling or steady, white with terror or blushing scarlet with embarrassment, but every one gowned and jeweled till surely she could not move, and wrapped in veils to the eyes. Yellow eyes in plenty, but dark too, under brows of every color from dun to ivory.

No more than anyone else in this damnable country would they look into his face. But they darted glances. He caught a murmur: "How dark he is! And so tall. Can you imagine—"

The rest of it was drowned in a man's voice. "Sire," said the lord of Shon'ai, "for your majesty's pleasure, we have gathered a garden of flowers. Will you look on them? Will you taste their sweetness?"

Slow heat crawled up Estarion's face. He raised his chin a fraction. "I see a swathe of veils," he said, "and eyes too shy to look on me."

Lord Miyaz gestured sharply. The ladies glanced at one another. Slowly first one and then another raised a hand to her veil.

They were beautiful. He granted them that. Most were too smoothly plump for his taste, and some seemed barely out of childhood. Only one or two dared lift their eyes, and that only for a moment.

He walked down the line of them. They stood like troops on review, with the same air of mingled pride and panic. This was the battle they had been bred for, this war of beauty against beauty, lineage against lineage, and all triumph to the fairest.

He horrified them with his size, with his strangeness, with the rank he bore and the power he embodied. His head was aching. One of them at least was a mage. *Spy,* he thought. He could not muster the proper degree of wariness.

Even if he did not single out an empress, he was expected to choose one for his night's pleasure. That much of Asanian custom he knew.

His gorge rose. He came to the end of the line, turned. They watched him as birds would watch a cat: the same stunned fascination, the same willing acceptance of what must be. He was the predator and they were prey. So the world was made.

He mustered a smile. It was not, he hoped, too ghastly to look at. "My thanks," he said, "my lord and ladies. How can I choose any single lady from amid so much beauty? Will you dine with me, all of you, and enchant me with your company?"

The response was a little time in coming. He held his breath. If he had given insult, he would hear of it to infinity.

Then his lordship said, "The emperor is most kind, and most politic. Those men who wait without—"

"I'll go to them later," Estarion said quickly. "Bid them sit to their own dinner. When the wine comes round, I'll share it with them."

Thus providing himself with an escape. Lord Miyaz saw it, surely, but he bowed with every evidence of approval. "Wisely chosen, majesty." He smote his hands together. The eunuch bowed himself out. Miyaz remained, smiling, watchful, alert to the emperor's every need.

A prince's training had its uses. It taught a man to endure the excruciations of courtesy, to be charming when he would have preferred to turn and bolt. He spoke to every lady in that hall, however shy she was, however weary he grew of yellow faces, yellow eyes, yellow curls under silken veils. He put aside grimly his longing for a sweet dark face, or a sweet white one, sea-eyed, autumn-haired, and a body as supple as it was slender, and a voice that had never learned to giggle in chorus.

He left them smoothly enough, he hoped, to forget for a moment that he had chosen none of them for his bed or his bride. Their fathers and brothers and guardians were waiting for him, schooled to patience, and none quite bold enough to ask the question that burned in every mind. Frayed though he was about the edges, he had power left to charm them as he had their women.

Vanyi was not in the chamber when he came to it. He had dared to hope she would be, at least to quarrel with him. A quarrel would have lightened his spirit.

There were guards on the door: his own, he had been pleased to see when he came in, with eyes that would meet his, and minds that did not quail in fear of his presence. "Find Vanyi," he said to redheaded Alidan, "and tell her I'd welcome her company."

Alidan shifted his feet and looked uncomfortable. "My lord—"

"And when," Estarion wanted to know, "have I ever been 'my lord' to you, except when you were up to something?"

"My lord," Alidan said again. And when Estarion glared: "Starion, Vanyi said to tell you. She won't come to you at night any longer. If you want a woman, she said, you know where to find a sufficiency of them."

The world narrowed to a single, bitter point. Alidan, red

Gileni and no coward, flattened against the wall. His face was grey under the bronze.

Estarion spoke softly. "That's not Vanyi speaking. That's my lady mother."

"It is Vanyi," Alidan said. "Believe it, Starion. She told me herself."

"With my mother at her back, forcing her."

"No," said Alidan. "She was alone, and she wasn't under binding. Whoever put her up to it, she wanted it. She said so."

"Bring her to me."

"She won't come," said Alidan. "She said that, too. You'll sleep alone, or you'll sleep with a yellow woman."

Estarion took a step forward. Alidan flattened further. But Estarion had no mind to strike him, and none, upon reflection, to confront Vanyi. She would be guarded with iron and with magic, and if she said she would not see him, then nothing short of a mage-blast would win him through to her.

"Coward," he said to the wall she had raised about herself. It returned no answer.

12

THIS COLDNESS, THIS thing that was growing in herself, was nothing that Vanyi could stop. There had been warmth once, gladness, mind that met mind and knew no walls between them. Loss of the child had altered everything: broken, darkened, marred it perhaps beyond mending.

She loved Estarion still, down at the bottom of things. But it was very far down, and the heart that beat there was a tiny thing, globed as if in glass. When mind or tongue shaped his name, the light about it was warm. But when her eyes looked on him, the wall came up between them. He was other, stranger, emperor. His touch, she knew, would burn.

So he had seemed when she first came to Endros: alien, exotic, not quite human. The quick light wit that masked the knots of old scars, the sudden temper, the smaller things—the way he stretched all over when he woke, like a cat; or the turn of his head when he was startled; or his inexplicable and quite insatiable fondness for sour apples—were walled in with her love for him. She could not touch them.

It was best, she told herself. He had to marry in Asanion. He was too loyal in himself; he would never look at another woman while she was there to distract him. If she turned him away from her, even taught him to hate her, then he would look for comfort where it best served him, and surely find it.

She would happily strangle any woman whom he called beloved. But she could not—physically could not—make herself go to him. Even to face him; to lay her hand over his heart, just so, and know the power that slept in him, and know, know surely, that the child of this night would not die unshaped and scarce begun.

No one tried to talk to her. Estarion's lords and servants were too shy of the priestess-mage or too scornful of the commoner. The guards had no time. The priests had troubles of their own.

That, if she would let it, was cure and physic for her hurt. She had the land-sense—it was the first thing any mageborn child woke to knowledge of, and she had sea-sense on top of it, or water-sense at least. She knew how the earth welcomed Estarion: which was both pleasure and pain, because he had been so sure that it would recoil from him, and because that surety had become a part of her. But something had gone, or was going, awry.

"He's only partblood Asanian," she said to the priests and priestesses who had come from Endros, half a cycle's journey into the Golden Empire, when there was no one else to listen or to intrude. "And we all know what happened to him here. Is he twisting the worldlines, do you think? Or finding them twisted, and tangling them further?"

"If that were all it was," said Shaiyel, in whom the land-sense was so strong that he could wade in the earth as if in water, "then I could mend it with a word." He flushed under their stares. He was young, younger than Vanyi, and almost as pale as she. He kept well out of Estarion's way. He was half Asanian, and he favored his mother, though his eyes were narrower and his cheekbones higher and his hair straighter than any proper Asanian's. He never could understand why people thought him arrogant. He was like Estarion in that. He knew what he could do. Why should he pretend that he did not?

"It's not Estarion," Iburan said. He lounged on a bench against the wall, great black mountain of a man, dressed with uncommon plainness in the white robe that priests of the Sun wore in this part of the world. His beard was braided but ungauded, and his hair was in a single plait. In a little while they would all attend the sunset-rite in the temple of this city—town, rather, as Asanion reckoned it, smaller within its walls than Endros but thronged with double and treble the people.

"It's not the emperor," said Iburan again. "Except that, by living and breathing and walking in this country, he brings it about. I felt something like it when his father came here. Asanion never felt itself joined to Keruvarion in a marriage of equals. It would rule or it would have nothing, no matter the will of its emperors or their blood-right to its throne."

"But it accepts," said Shaiyel. "My mother accepted my father, though he was a slant-eyed plainsman. We are all one, she told me. We must be, or the sun will fall."

Iburan's smile concealed itself in his beard, but Vanyi felt it. "Not quite the sun that rides in the sky. But the Sun that rules out of Endros—yes, that could fall too easily if the half of the prop beneath it breaks asunder."

"One would think," said dour Oromin, "that nigh a hundred years of inescapable fact would impress itself on an empire's mind."

Vanyi faded into the shadows. They were saying nothing that she had not heard innumerable times already, and never to any purpose. On a field of battle half-begun, the heir of the Sun and the heir of the Lion, brought together out of all hope, had wedded their two empires. And spent the rest of their lives and the lives of their children struggling to keep that marriage intact. For a long while, maybe, they had been more successful than not. Then Ganiman died in Kundri'j Asan, and his son all but died taking vengeance.

Emperors in Asanion seldom died unaided. It was the way of their succession. But it was not the Sunlords' way.

Sunlords were too direct, she thought. They saw the world as a simple place, a pattern of light and dark under the sway of god and goddess. They did not understand Asanian complexities. Even that first heir of the two lands had had his mother's bright clarity of mind, and too little of his father's subtlety.

Estarion had no subtlety at all.

No matter what she thought of, she circled back to him. She

slipped out of that room full of priests and useless chatter, and sought the way to the gate.

This was a proper palace, as convoluted as an Asanian's mind. She lost herself more times than she cared to count, before she found a servant to direct her toward escape. The man was subtly, exquisitely contemptuous. *Barbarian,* he thought at her, not caring if she heard.

And so she was. She did not thank him: that would have set her below him. But she bestowed on him a coldly brilliant smile.

She was learning the shape and the taste of an Asanian city. Villages in the Isles huddled together above the sea, their faces turned inward toward the well and outward toward the boats and the nets. Towns in the Hundred Realms warded themselves in walls, but under the peace of the Sun they had allowed themselves to go to green, in gardens within, in fields and farms without.

In Asanion the walls were manifold. This town of Shirai had three, and gates so placed that one had to walk far round the circle from one to the next. The streets within the circles were an inextricable tangle of blank walls, twisting turns, sudden squares and crossroads often choked with market booths, or veiled women chattering at a cistern or worshippers thronging into a temple. Keruvarion had conceded mightily in suffering the worship of the goddess beside the god. Here the thousand gods had yet to diminish their number, for all the truth that was embodied in the emperor.

So many people crowded so close together could never be truly clean. The stench of them flooded Vanyi, all but drowning her. Their roar and seethe swept over her like a storm on the sea. She was seafolk, skyfolk. She was not made to live in such a place.

A thin thread of discipline kept her on her feet. She was tall here, and slight, borne along like a twig in a millrace. She did not try to fight the current. It fetched her up against a wall that had been the recipient of too many attentions; it reeked like a midden, or like a tavern in the morning after a long carouse.

But there was cleanliness within the wall, and quiet. She worked her way round to the gate. It was shut but not locked. It opened to the touch of her hand.

Which god was worshipped here, she did not know, nor did it matter. This was a holy place. Avaryan's temple would be full tonight, with the god's heir in the town, and the high priest from Endros come to sing the rite. Few people lingered here. A woman with a gift of fruit and flowers for the altar in the outer court. A circle of boys reciting lessons in front of their teacher. No priest that she could see, and no priestess.

The inner court would have been closed once to one of her sex. Maybe it was still. She did not care. The torque about her neck was passport to any temple in this world, even to the sanctuary, where the god's secrets were kept.

She did not need to go so far. This was a local god, perhaps, or goddess: it was hard to tell. The image above the altar was carved of wood black with age, clothed in robe upon robe of improbable, royal richness, and crowned and necklaced and garlanded with flowers. Its face was a mask of beaten gold, neither male nor female, blank, serene, unreachably beautiful. It had no eyes, only darkness. Its mouth smiled just perceptibly.

Here, she thought, was Asanion: a golden mask, an androgyne smile.

Strange how little it repelled her, or even frightened her. Maybe she had lost fear with the capacity to love, or in truth to feel anything at all.

She sat cross-legged on the floor. It was swept clean, she noticed, and sprinkled with scented water. Somewhere in the temple's depths, then, were priests with a care for their duty. She was aware of them now that she stretched her senses.

What she was looking for, she did not know. She had been led here as she had been led to Endros from the breast of the sea. The god's hand was light on her but firm. It did not ease the bleakness in her belly. Nothing could do that.

She let her body settle, her power open like a sail to catch the magewinds. They were treacherous here amid the crowding of so many minds, on land so long subdued that it hardly knew itself apart from the men who lived on it. And yet the winds were there, gusting and circling.

Voices. Mageborne, she thought; then shadows fell across the light. She was not visible, maybe: dark trousers, dark coat, dark cap, sitting motionless in shadow.

They spoke Asanian softly, barely above a whisper. "It is so?"

"It is so."

Men's voices both. The first was hesitant, the second eager—she would have said exultant. The eager one went on almost too fast to follow. "Oh, it is so! Out of the darkness he is come, the golden one, the Lion's child."

Estarion? Even in her half-trance, annoyance stabbed her. Could she never escape him?

"I don't believe you," the first voice said. "The yoke is heavier than it ever was. And now that one is come—the dark one. They say he has the eyes, but his face is a barbarian's face, like a black eagle. An army rides with him; the high ones bow down to him. How can any power free us from him?"

"Easily," said the second. "As easily as a knife in the dark."

"Not this time. They were innocents before. Now they know. They feel the hate we bear them."

"They are mages, too. And little good it does them. *He* is coming. He will strike them down."

"With what? Sorcery?"

Scorn, that, and a flash of fear. The second voice laughed. It was higher than the first, perhaps younger, and something in it spoke to Vanyi of more than simple courage: wine or dreamsmoke, or darker things. "He needs none of their sorcery. He *is*. He will throw down the false king and rule as the old emperors ruled, true blood and true spirit. No bearded barbarian mocking the throne of the Lion."

"You're dreaming. What did you get into this time?"

"Truth!" sang the younger man. "I saw him. Very well, if you insist—in my dream. But the prophecy is true. The time is come. The burning god will fall, and the Golden Empire win back its own again. Can't you feel it? Can't you hear it? It's coming—it's almost upon us."

"I hear the same old wishful wheezes I've always heard," the first voice said. "It's been, what? Fourscore years? Five? We're as strong under the yoke as we ever were. And now the black king is here. All the high ones fall in front of him. If there is a Prophet—and I admit it, I've heard people talking, too—what is he but a madman? We've had those before. They never came to anything but a head on a spike."

"This one is different," the young one said. "You'll see."

"I'll see him strung up for the crows," the older man said. He sounded ineffably tired, but behind the voice was a spark of hope: that Estarion would fall; that this prophet, whatever he was—dream, delusion, living lunatic—would set Asanion free.

Vanyi drew a careful breath. They still had not seen her. The young one went away singing to himself. The elder—and he was old, she saw as he moved into the light, an ancient yellowed creature in a priest's threadbare robe, with a broom in his hands—the old man kept silent but for the singing in his mind. The same song in both, wordless, wandering, but full of hatred for the invaders out of Keruvarion. It was worn so smooth, cherished so long, that it gleamed like a bloodstone in water.

She drew shadows about herself. Even so, she thought that the old man sensed her presence as the very old can, or the blind, by other senses than sight. He tensed, peering. She made herself nothing, no one, wind and shifting air.

It took all the courage she had to walk to that guarded door, to say to the men there, "I would speak with his majesty."

Men? They were boys, youths whom she knew, who smiled at her and asked after her. Was she well again? "We worried," said the slim brown boy from the Nine Cities. "He's going to be glad to see you. All those simpering yellow women are giving him the jaundice."

She burst out laughing, though she had thought there could be no lightness in her. "And of course no one can tell, he being what he is."

The other guard, a hulking lad from somewhere north of Ianon, grinned blindingly. "We won't tell him you said that. Go on, he's waiting for you."

Vanyi halted in the doorway of the inner chamber, stiff as a hound at gaze. At first she could not see him for the cloud of veils and perfumes and golden eyes. There must have been a dozen of them, and a fat personage beaming at them all and proclaiming in a voice much too sweet to be natural, "Oh, what joy! What delight!"

"Out." That voice at least was unmistakable. It had a growl in it. "Out, I said!"

"But," said the personage. "Majesty. They came all this way—all the way from Kundri'j, purely for your majesty's pleasure."

"Then let them go back to Kundri'j and give pleasure to men who want it." Estarion rose up out of the veils, his eyes hot gold with fury, and the raw edge of it in his voice. "And tell his gracious lordship—tell him to pay your full fee. Doubled."

"Trebled," fluted the personage, "with additions for our hardship. To come so far for so little—the roads, the inns, the brigands—"

"Out!"

"Well roared," said Vanyi dryly in the ringing silence.

Estarion stopped sucking in breath, stopped moving at all. He stared at her as if he had never seen her before. "Vanyi?"

"So I was the last time I looked."

"Vanyi!"

He was on her before she could stop him, arms about her, stronger than she remembered, whirling her in a dizzying dance. "Oh, love! Oh, lady! You don't know—"

Her mind set itself to go rigid, to fight free. But her body had other intentions. Her arms knew precisely where to go. Her lips knew what they wanted, which was to silence him. The taste of him was piercing sweet.

She pulled back so abruptly that he staggered. He looked as drunken as the youth in the temple. Her hands smoothed his hair back from his face, combed through the curls of his beard, clenched at her sides. "This isn't what I meant," she said.

He blinked. He was always the slower to come to himself. "Damn those boys to everlasting hells. Bless them for sainted idiots. Among the three of you, you saved me from a fate worse than death."

"What was so terrible about it? All those ladies need is a bath and a few days in the saddle, to make them halfway human."

"Not my saddle," he said with honest desperation. "Vanyi, beloved, whatever I said, whatever I did—"

"I didn't come here to forgive you," she said, so sharp that she brought him up short.

"But—"

"You can't be anything other than you are. I won't ask you to be. And you shouldn't ask me to do what I can't do. I can't be your empress, Starion. I've known that from the beginning."

"You have not." The giddiness was gone. Estarion was Estarion again, and ready for battle.

She forestalled him. "No, Starion. No fights. Not now. I came—" Her voice died. "I came as your priestess. As your servant. Will you listen?"

He did not want to: it was transparent in his face. But he had his training. "I will listen," he said, so tight that she could barely hear him.

She told him. The temple; the voices. The prophet they spoke of.

"Nonsense," he said as the old man had, in very nearly the same tone. "People are always talking. And the boy was drugged, you say. Demented. It's nothing but Asanion, being Asanion."

"No," said Vanyi. The power moved in her. She opened it to him, willing him to see as she saw, fear as she feared.

He would not. "Even if there is substance in it, what difference can it make? I'm guarded day and night. I'm watched over like an infant. I can't even visit the privy without someone peering over my shoulder."

"You still don't believe," she said. "No one does. Your guards let me in with cries of delight. What if I'd been got at by someone with a gift for sorcery? I could have sunk a knife in you while you whirled me round the room, or poisoned you with my kiss."

"Not you," he said, so sure of her and of himself that she wanted to shake him. "You do love me still. In spite of everything."

"I'll never *stop* loving you!"

She clamped her mouth shut. He had enough sense, for once, not to reach for her. Maybe he was too stunned by the force of her outcry.

"Estarion," she said after a long moment, in the steadiest voice she could manage. "Do this one thing for me. Trust what I see. Trust nothing else, not even yourself."

"I can do that without your bidding. Asanion does it to me."

"Then let it. You aren't loved here, Estarion. Maybe you can witch them into it—you've the gift, I won't deny it. But the hate runs deep, and it runs strong. They'll have their prophet if they have to make him themselves. They'll do all they can to destroy you."

"I knew that when I was in my cradle. You're forgetting, dear love. I've seen what they can do to me and mine."

She shut her eyes and pressed her fists against them. Tears burned, too hot to shed. "Damn you, Starion. Why can't you be as easy to hate as they think you are?"

"They don't know me."

Her fists dropped. She glared. "You arrogant—"

He seemed not to have heard her. "What can any of them

do to me that I haven't suffered already? Kill me? Then the god will take me."

"They can leave this empire without its emperor, destroy your kin and everything you love, roll over Keruvarion and crush it with bitter steel."

She heard the rasp of his breath, but his voice was light. "There is that," he granted her. "I'm guarded, Vanyi. I'm warned. What more can I do?"

"Show a little sense. Stop entertaining every whore in Asanion."

"Gladly!" His agreement was so heartfelt that she almost—perilously—smiled. "And?"

"And—" She stopped. He was seducing her. Keeping her there, tricking her with temper, leading to the inevitable, inescapable conclusion. Where was he safest? Under watchful guard. Who could guard him best?

"Not I." She hugged herself, trying not to shiver. "I'll speak to the guards," she said, "send one of them in to watch over you."

"I don't want to sleep with a guard."

"Then summon Ulyai, wherever she is. She's better for that than a dozen armed men."

"Ulyai hates cities in Asanion. She won't come inside the walls."

"She will if I tell her why."

"Vanyi—"

She would not hear him. She sent a messenger on the mageroads, a summons and a command. *The bright one has need. Come!* It touched the mind it sought, fierce cat-mind in the afterglow of a hunt, the rich taste of blood, the memory of the chase.

Some lord's park was less a deer. Vanyi felt her lips stretch in a grin as feral as Ulyai's own. This hunt was better, she told the cat. This was a mage-hunt, a man-hunt, ward and guard against the death that came out of the dark.

"She comes," Vanyi said. No matter that he knew. The words gave it substance.

Leaving him was as hard as anything she had ever done, and as purely necessary. He could not understand. She felt his anger swelling as she passed the door. She locked her mind against it.

13

Korusan did not remember how long he had been lying on this hard narrow bed that had been his since he rose to the second rank, in this cell with its tall thin window and its scrap of curtain for a door. But he remembered that he had been ill, memory that blurred into all the other illnesses. Most often it was fever, or a demon in lungs or heart or bones. This time it was lassitude that would not lift, and an ache without a source, that made his hands shake when he tried to curve them round a cup, and set him reeling when he would have sat up.

There were, as always, mages. They patched him together with threads of their magic, weaving over the other, older stitchings. He was as threadbare as an old cloak, and as like to fall apart.

He said so to the mage who tended him, when he gained strength enough to speak. It was the lightmage from the night by the gate, the last night he remembered clearly. She did not smile at his bit of wit. "You'll last as long as you need to."

"Am I your punishment?" he asked her.

She bent to the task of mixing a potion for him. It smelled less vile than usual.

"I am," he answered for her, since she would not. "Pity that you should suffer for telling me the truth."

"You knew it already," she said. Or he thought she said. The fall of her hair hid her face, and her voice was barely audible.

"Some things, one needs to be told."

"Some things were better left alone." She poured a measure of her physic and set the cup to his lips. He closed his hands over hers. She neither started nor pulled away. Her hands were cool. Her eyes met his. They did not pity him, which he was glad of, but neither did they warm for him.

So it would be with the women of the Olenyai, once they knew what this woman knew. "I would do very well among the wives of courtiers," he observed. "No fear of heirs who bear too faint a resemblance to their mothers' husbands."

"I suppose you are entitled to be bitter," said the mage. She wiped the cup with a cloth and laid it back among the jars of medicaments.

"You dislike me," said Korusan. Weakness made him blunt, and the potion made him bold. It was odd, to know both sides of that, and to know how little it mattered.

"No," said the mage.

"But I mean nothing to you, beyond the fact of my lineage."

"That's but a means to an end." She smoothed the coverlet over him. "Did you know that you are a legend to the people? They make a promise of you, and call you prophet."

He had not known. He was surprised that it could make him angry. "Whose idiocy is that? Your Master's?"

"You should be glad. The people are ripe for your coming. They have no love for the black kings."

"How can I be a prophet if no one sees my face or hears my voice?"

"Your face is a mystery, as every emperor's must be. Your voice is the voice of your servants."

"No servants of mine," said Korusan.

"We all serve you, my lord, from our hearts' center. You are the Son of the Lion."

He had taken joy in that name once, and swelled with pride when it was spoken. "I am the sum of my lineage," he said. "Which is nothing. How close did I come to death this time, when the old sickness took me?"

"Not close at all," she said, but she would not look at him while she said it. "You overtaxed yourself, no more. And it was a shock to discover . . . what you discovered."

Odd that she could not say it, when she could say so much else. "What greater shock will it be to mount the throne as emperor? Will I fall dead upon the dais?"

"Of course not," said the mage. "You are nowhere near as weak as you imagine."

"Oh, yes," said Korusan, "and I am so strong that I faint as easily as a girl, and rather more often."

"Maybe it suits some people to have you think so. Maybe they think it makes you more tractable."

He stared at her, speechless.

"You didn't ever think of that, did you? That maybe you aren't as feeble as that. An invalid could never be an Olenyas, or pass the tests of wood and steel, or live as a warrior lives, without ease or comfort. Keeping you slave to their mendings and magics—that keeps you slave to their will as well."

It could be true, he thought. And yet he knew his own blood, his own bones. He knew how brief his years must be.

Whether she read his thoughts, which mages said they could not do to a full Olenyas, or whether his eyes betrayed him, she said, "Oh, you won't live long. That's true enough. But you'll go all at once, not by these slow degrees."

"Why do you tell me this?"

She shrugged, a lift of a shoulder, a turn of a hand. "Maybe I don't dislike you. Maybe I feel sorry for you."

"Maybe you spy for the enemy."

She laughed. "Maybe I do! He loves our kind, does the emperor in Endros. He dotes so much on us of the Golden Empire that he won't suffer one of us in his presence."

"And yet he comes to Asanion. Or is that too a lie?"

"He comes," said the mage. "His mother drives him, they say, because she knows he'll lose us else. *He* loathes every step of the journey."

"Someone could kill him," Korusan murmured. "Then we would be rid of him."

The drug was taking effect. He wondered distantly if it was meant as the mage said, to weaken and not to strengthen him.

But he was too tired to care. He heard her say, "Someone may kill him yet. Or we'll leave it for you."

For me, he thought. Yes. That would be proper.

When he woke again, the lightmage was gone. He had another nurse, a silent Olenyai woman who would not tell him what had become of her. He did not see her again.

In darker moments he wondered if she had been set there to say what no one should say, still less a mage of the Guild that would have wielded him as its puppet. If she had died for it, or if they had stripped her of her power and cast or out. Or if, after all, she had the reward of a gentler posting, away from the terrors of this conspiracy.

The weakness passed—quickly, his nurses said; too slowly for his patience. He was back almost to full duties when he was called from one of them into the Master's presence.

The Guildmaster was with the Master of the Olenyai as Korusan had expected, and no one else but a lone veiled guard. He knew the eyes above the veil, the fret of fingers on swordhilt, Marid's presence a greater comfort than he might have looked for. Was that friendship, then, this fancy that one man at least was not hungry for his blood?

Before the Master of the Olenyai, Korusan lowered his veil and stood in silence until he should be spoken to. The Master's own veil was down, his face a little gaunter than Korusan remembered, a little more weary; but it was the weariness of a hard task well begun. When he spoke, he spoke not to Korusan but to the master of the mages. "He looks well. Will he continue so?"

"Now, I think, yes," said the Guildmaster.

"Good," said the Olenyas.

Korusan bit back words that would not have been wise. They could not dispose of him as they had a young lightmage, but they could master him with magic if they chose. Let them think him biddable, if reluctant; let them imagine that he was cowed.

"Prince," said the Olenyas, "we have somewhat that you should see. Will you come?"

Korusan bent his head, assenting.

He felt their eyes on him, and the cold brush of magic. He was still to them, empty of all but compliance. The eyes left him. The magic lingered, but after a time that too went away. Still, he kept up his guard and his veil, went where they led, said no word and offered no resistance.

"This, prince," said the Master of Mages, "is your empire."

Korusan regarded it as it lay on a table in a room somewhat less bare than others in this stronghold: it had hangings on the walls, new enough for the figures to be seen, and carpets on the floor, and a chair on a low round dais. That last had been brought in late and in haste, he thought; and likewise the table beside the chair, on which rested a single gleaming thing.

It was a mask of gold. It could not be the one that reposed in the palace treasury in Kundri'j Asan; that would be guarded incessantly.

By Olenyai. They were the trusted guards of emperors. They kept the treasuries, warded the inmost chambers, defended the Son of the Lion with their living bodies.

The mask was heavy as he lifted it. If it was not pure gold, then it was gold sheeted thick over lead. Its face he knew. It was his own. Its eyes were empty, blank.

"This is the mask of the emperor," the Guildmage said. "This you are born to wear."

They had had to remake it, he had heard, when the black kings came. Those were taller men than Asanians, leaner, longer-headed: too large by far to wear a thing made to Asanian measure. But this fit in his hands, seemed shaped for his face. "Then it is the mask of my ancestors," he said in wonder. "It is no makeshift nor forgery. But how—"

"It was given to us to be destroyed," said the Master of the Olenyai. "We chose not to obey the commands of kings who were not ours."

They would have called it treason, those bandit kings from the east of the world. "Yet the first of them was Lion's Cub himself."

"He broke faith," the Master said.

And that, Korusan reflected, was the greatest of all sins to the Olenyai.

He returned the mask to its place. The veil was a burden greater than gold; but that, he had earned. That, he would keep.

Nor did he sit in the chair that so clearly was meant for him. He took it from the dais and set it aside, and sat cross-legged where it had been. "I have as yet no throne," he said, "and no empire. Now what do you wish of me? To be persuaded to embrace your haste? Is there a purpose in it?"

He did not think that the Guildmaster was pleased. The Master of the Olenyai seemed to have expected this defiance. He raised his hand. A small company of veiled warriors came quietly from behind a tapestry, where must have been a door, and took station round the room. Guard-station, with Korusan in its center. It felt strange, awry, that he should be the guarded and not the guard; trapped in the center and not on the rim with Marid on his right and a second brother on his left and duty clear before him.

Korusan rested his hands on the hilts of his twin swords. They were solid, comforting. He was being tested, there could be no doubt of it. It was the Guildmaster's game, he suspected; Olenyai did not waste training-time in trifles. But perhaps the mage was not having all as he would have it. He was alone, no mages with him, surrounded by black-robed warriors.

The Master of the Olenyai took station at Korusan's right shoulder. "Prince and brother," he said, "be at ease. No harm will touch you. Only speak as your heart moves you to speak, and be silent as you will to be silent, and remember what we have taught you."

They had not taught him to sit as a prince in the hall of audience. But they had taught him to speak and to be silent, and to know what was sense and what was folly. He sat as straight as he might, composed his body as one should before battle, and waited.

There were but a handful of them, white-faced and staring, with the dazed look of men who had traveled far and long with their eyes blindfolded. Before that, maybe, they had traveled in curtained litters, taken here and there and round about until even the keenest-witted of them was hopelessly confused.

And here, where they had been brought at last, stood a circle of faceless men. Their eyes leaped to the one face bared among them all, that of the mage; but that was as blank as the mask upon the table. Then, as if reluctantly, they sought the center.

Korusan had leisure to study them. They were all Asanian, as indeed they must be. None bore the marks of rank. They looked like common tradesmen, priests of little temples, one or two in the garb of journeymen artisans, a smith from the look of one burly figure, the other perhaps a juggler or a player, with his long smooth hands and his mobile face.

When the Lion ruled in Kundri'j Asan, such creatures would never have been suffered in the presence of the emperor. But the High Court was all turned traitor, the Middle Court gone over to the enemy, the Low Courts fallen under the rule of the Sun-god's servants. Only the little people remembered what had been, who had ruled them before the black kings came.

Korusan's lip curled slightly behind his veil. The Sun-brood made much of its affinity for the common man. But in Asanion the common man despised his outland conquerors and yearned for the rule of his own kind.

Korusan looked at the pallid faces, the fear-rounded eyes, and knew only a weary contempt. He was bred to walk among princes. Not to beg charity from sweaty commoners.

Having ascertained at last that he, seated in the center, must be the one they came for, they flung themselves before him. None of them was clean. But none dared so vastly as to touch him, still less to stare at his hidden face.

Save one, who bowed down patently for prudence's sake, but kept his eyes on Korusan. "And how do we know," he demanded, "that this is the one we've looked for for so long?"

Korusan did not pause to think. If he had, he would have stopped himself before he went too far. In one hand he took the mask of the emperor. With the other he unfastened his veil. He held the mask beside his face. "Do you know me now?" he asked.

The bold one dropped down flat. But he was bold still, and wild with it. "You're younger than the one I dream of. And the mask, golden one: it too is older than you."

"Surely," said Korusan. "It is a death-mask."

"Ah! Poor god. He died young."

"Emperors often do." Korusan's arm was growing weary. He set down the mask again and said, "You have seen my face, and I am both Olenyas and Lion's heir. For that, then, you must die."

They started. Not one had failed to look up when their fellow spoke, to give way to curiosity that defied even fear.

"But I choose when you die, and how," said Korusan. "Now I let you live, so that you may serve me."

Their gratitude was as rank as their fear. When he was emperor—if he came so far—he would command that petitioners be bathed before they approached him.

"You are the Lion's son," said the one who dared to speak, the bold one, the player with his half-trained voice and his half-mad courage. "You are the chosen of the gods. You will rule when the black kings fall."

But, thought Korusan, there were no gods. "I will rule when my line is restored." And how briefly that would endure, with no heir to follow him.

They waited, trembling, on their faces. No one else moved, not the Olenyai, not the Guildmaster. He must speak, or the silence would stretch, and turn awkward, and then humiliating, and then dangerous.

There were words in him. Whether they were useful words he did not know, but they were all he had. "Swear to me now, men of the Lion. Swear that you will serve me. If you betray me, you die. If you lose this battle that is before us, you die. If you fail me in anything, for any cause . . ."

He paused for breath that came suddenly short. Their voices rose, finishing what he had begun. "If we fail you, majesty, we die."

This was power, to sit so, and to look down, and to know that these lives were his: his to keep, his to cast away.

"I am the emperor who should have been. I am the emperor who is to be. I am the heart of the Golden Empire. They who dream that they conquered me, they dreamed only, and they lied.

"And now he comes, my people: the barbarian, the savage, the bandit king. He jangles in outland gold. He speaks with the tongues of apes and birds. He goes naked, shameless as the animal he is; he wears the fell of a beast. And he dares to boast that he rules us. Will you deny him, my people? Will you refuse him? Will you turn your backs on him?"

"Aye!" they cried.

"We are but the least of the least," the bold one said. "Our allies are hundreds, thousands strong. Asanion is full of us. Wherever he goes, there he must find us, the false king. Whatever he does, he must run afoul of us. Shall we slay him for you, majesty? Shall we lay his flayed hide at your feet?"

Korusan stiffened. "The usurper is mine. But all that you may do to aid us, you will do. Go; remember me. Fight for me. Take back this empire in my name."

"He does have a talent for this," the Guildmage said.

Korusan caught himself before he spoke untimely. He rose from the dais, taking no open notice of the mage, and stepped down to the carpeted floor. He was dizzy; he had to struggle not to shake. He drew long breaths, calming himself, bringing his temper to hand.

"He is bred for it," said the Master of the Olenyai after a perceptible pause.

Korusan turned, still refusing to acknowledge the Guildmaster, and faced the Olenyas. "I trust that this mummery has been of use."

"Of much use," the Olenyas said. "Those were unprepossessing enough, but they have a great following. And now they know what they follow. They will serve you the more assiduously hereafter."

"There are no lords among them," said Korusan.

"Lords we have," the Guildmage said, "and many. They have no need for this spectacle."

"No? I should think that they would need it more." Korusan straightened his robes and raised his veil once more to conceal his face. "Am I done? May I go?"

"The emperor may go as he wills," the Guildmage said.

Ah, thought Korusan, but who was the emperor?

14

DARK. DARKNESS AND blood. Voices gibbering. Eyes—

Estarion flung himself headlong out of sleep.

The lamp flickered, burning low. Ulyai blinked at him. Her mind saw a cub under her gentling paw, and her tongue licking him until he settled, comforted.

He half-fell on her, wrapping arms about her neck, burying his face in warm musky fur. His breathing quieted. The sweat dried cold on his body. The shivering came and went. "I can't remember," he said to her. "I—can't—"

But he could. That was the terrible thing. He could remember too well. Deep down, where the darkness was, and the long fall into death and the soul's destruction.

Not his death, not his soul torn asunder and scattered to the winds of the mageworld. Oh, no. He had caused it. His power had done it, had killed the mage who killed his father, and in killing, slain itself. His power was maimed and perhaps would never be mended. The soul it had destroyed was lost beyond retrieving.

They thought they knew, those people who loved and guarded him. They gave him wisdom, gave him compassion, lashed him with impatience when they judged he needed it. But they did not know the truth of what he had done. To sunder a soul from a body: that was terrible. To shatter that soul—that was beyond any hope of forgiveness.

In the beginning, when the horror was new, he had let himself fall into the blessed dark. They had found him, dragged him back, shown him the way to the restoration of his power. He was weak. He had let them. He thought he could atone, if only by living and remembering, and suffering that remembrance.

Instead he had forgotten, or chosen not to remember. It was simpler. It won him Vanyi, who was water in a dry place, coolness in the terrible heat of his desert. And it had lost her. There was no escaping what he was. Even his body betrayed him.

He struggled to his feet. Ulyai growled and batted at him. She kept her claws sheathed. He evaded them, staggering away from the bed. His knees were as weak as a foal's.

Standing steadied him. He pulled on a robe and let his feet take him where they would.

Ulyai followed him, but she did not try to stop him. He was glad of her presence. She held him up when he stumbled.

It was a peculiarity of Sun-blood that it sought the heights. Mountains if there were any. Roofs else, and the stars that seemed dim and strange, and the night air. The roof of this house was made for standing on: it had a wall about the rim, and a garden of flowers sending their sweetness into the night. Estarion plucked one great moon-pale bloom and bore it with him to the parapet and leaned on the rail. It was not far down. Five man-heights, maybe. Six. Hardly enough to break one's neck. For that one needed a tower, or a crag.

"It doesn't work in any case," Sidani said from the shadows of the roof. "Mageblood saves itself. You'd find yourself flying, or landing as light as a bird on a treetop."

She came to stand beside him, leaning as he leaned. Brightmoon was down. Greatmoon's light limned her face in blood, dyed her hair as red as any Gileni prince's.

"You've tried it?" he asked her.

She held up her clenched fists and her lean corded arms. Old scars seamed them, tracing the lines of the great veins. "I thought that this would be surer. It only made work for a healer."

"But you're not a mage. No more," he said bitterly, "than I."

Her brow went up. The irony was pure Sidani. "And why,"

she asked, "does death seem so much more alluring than the life of an emperor?"

And why not tell her? He did not know her at all, no more than he could know a hawk in the sky or a fish in the sea. She could be his blood enemy. She could be the prophet Vanyi spoke of, though he doubted that Asanion would follow a woman, still less a woman who was a barbarian.

"Do you know," he asked her, "that it's possible, if one is a mage, to do more than kill the body of one's enemy? That one can kill his soul?"

"Nothing can kill a soul."

"I did."

She neither laughed nor recoiled. "What makes you think that?"

"The man who killed my father, hated us with a perfect hate," he said: "so perfect that I could only kill it by matching it. And in matching it, I destroyed it."

She pondered that. Either she chose to believe him, or she was better at feigning it than anyone he had ever seen. "Maybe it only fled too swiftly for you to follow."

"No," he said, though hope yammered at the corners of his mind. "I felt it shatter. It was indescribable. And where it had been, there was nothing. Not even the memory of a scream."

"They say you can't remember."

"I don't want to. Oh, there's darkness in plenty. I can't see my father fall. I don't know what I did when he died, or after his assassin . . . ended. But the ending: that I'll never forget. Not if I live a thousand lives."

"So. You're not as callow as you look."

He rounded on her. She smiled her sword-edged smile. "We were all young once," she said, "but it's fools who say it's either easy or simple. You looked the Dark in the face when you were twelve years old. You've been running from it ever since."

"Wouldn't you?"

"I've been running since before your grandfather was born."

Stories. But in this light, almost, he could believe them.

A rumbling drew his eyes downward. Ulyai leaned against Sidani, purring thunderously, while the strong old fingers rubbed the sensitive places behind her ears.

"You're not afraid of her," he said.

"Should I be?"

He bit his tongue. A beast as large as a small senel, fangs as long as daggers, claws that could bring down a bull at the charge: a fair lapcat, that. "She's not overfond of strangers," he said.

"I'm hardly that," said Sidani. "She's been my blanket, most nights, since we left Kurion."

"But—"

"Jealous, child?"

"No!"

Her teeth flashed white in the shadow that was her face. "Good. Then you won't mind that she found herself a he-cat in the forest of Kurion."

"There are no ul-cats in Kurion."

"Tell that to the forest king who, at Greatmoon's full, took a queen." Sidani regarded him in high amusement. "Surely you wondered what was keeping her so long."

"She goes her own way," he said stiffly. He looked down into the green gleam of eyes. They closed, opened again, in lazy contentment. "You are smug," he said to the cat.

"Well she might be. She'll bear her cubs in Kundri'j. They'll be purely delighted in the palace, to play host to a nest of ul-cats."

"Gods," said Estarion.

"So they will be. Asanians will worship anything, if it frightens them enough."

He shook her babblings out of his head. The last of the darkness went with it. She had meant that, maybe. She was more like Ulyai than anything human should be.

"Keep her with you," said Sidani, "until you come to Kundri'j."

A great weariness came over Estarion. "You too? Is everyone convinced that I'll fall over dead if I'm not guarded every living moment?"

"You won't fall. You'll jump. Or someone will push you."

"I'm not going to jump," he said.

"Not tonight." She turned her face to the great bloodied orb of the moon. For a moment he saw what she must have been when she was young. Haughty as a queen. Free-spoken as a man, or an empress. And beautiful: a beauty that smote the heart.

None of it surprised him. She was a northern woman. They were often so, in the kingdoms and among the tribes.

They were formidable when they were young. When they were old, they were terrible. This one drove him back to his bed with the edge of her tongue, and sat by him until he slept, and stood guard on his dreams. She and the ul-cat, one on each side of the gate, and nothing dark allowed to pass.

INDUVERRAN WAS THE gate to Asanion's heart, a city of gold and lead, flowers and dung, fierce summer heat and sudden stony chill. The cities that Estarion had seen and heard of in the Golden Empire were all old beyond reckoning. All but Induverran. There had been a city of that name in this place for years out of count, but the walls that framed it, the towers that rose within it, were none of them more than fourscore years old. Even Endros was older than that; but Endros was a white city, with a purity that time and men's habitation could not sully. Induverran struck Estarion with an air both grandiose and shabby, as if the land's weight had overwhelmed the new-raised stones, or memory bowed and stained them.

That memory was clear always beyond the walls. Induverran that was now stood apart from Induverran that had been, nearer a little river that had shifted since the first city was built. The old city stood in ruins like the charred bones of a demon's feast, grown over but thinly though the land was rich round about. No one walked there. Birds did not shun it, but neither did they linger, or build their nests amid the fallen pillars.

Induverran's lord sat his senel on the edge of the ruined city. He was a prince of five robes, of blood as pure as any in the empire, and Estarion should have detested him. But he had a hard clear eye in that yellow-curled head, and when Estarion readied to ride out of the new city and into the old, he was there waiting, mounted on one of the golden stallions for which his domain was famous.

The senel switched its silver-tasseled tail and stamped. Lord Dushai quelled it with a hand on its neck. "There they fought," he said in creditable Gileni. "There the mages hurled their blasts of power, and the beast of their mingled magics stalked and slew. And there," he said, tilting his chin toward the open plain, "the armies met."

"But not in battle," Estarion said. "My forebears stopped them: the Asanian and the Varyani, riding down upon them out of the living air, and raising walls of magic and of light."

"It was too late for the city," said Lord Dushai.

"They did what they could," Estarion said, struggling not to snap. That battle was nigh a century past. He was its consequence, with his lion-eyes and his northern face. They had faced one another across the broken city, the emperor of Asanion and the emperor of Keruvarion, son of the Lion and son of the Sun, and looked to end their rivalry in blood and fire. But their children had forged a peace. It had cost the high prince of Asanion his sole empire. It had cost the heir of Keruvarion far more.

Sarevadin. Estarion said the name to himself, like an incantation. Neither man's name nor woman's, given by a great mage and queen to the child of her body: manchild as he had been then, tall, redheaded, northern-skinned prince with a great gift of magery. Woman as she had ridden out of the Gate between the worlds, heavy with the heir of two empires, magewrought and magebound, but the Mages had had no power to sway her soul to their will. Only to rend her body asunder and make it anew, as they wished to do to the empire she was born to rule.

Estarion slid from Umizan's back. The stallion did not lower his head to crop the thin pallid grass, but followed as Estarion walked into the broken city. Others came slowly behind: Lord Dushai on his fretting, skittering mount, a line of guards, a thin scatter of hangers-on. No one else had been willing to leave the comforts of the new city for this bleak battlefield, not even Sidani who, Estarion had thought, would go anywhere.

The stench of blood and burning was long since washed

away. The taint of magery was faded almost to vanishing. And yet a power lingered in this place.

Here it began. Here the two empires met, fought, were joined into one. Here, where the grass began to grow green, the emperors faced their rebel children, and knew what they had done. Treason. Betrayal of all that their fathers had wrought, in the name of unlooked-for peace.

"They loved one another, the stories say," Estarion said. He did not care overmuch who heard, nor expect an answer.

Nonetheless he received one. It came, it seemed, out of a stone, but in Sidani's voice. "Only love would explain it," she said.

She was sitting on the ground, wrapped in a mantle that had lost its color to years and weather. For once she looked honestly old, a thin and ancient creature who shivered in the heavy heat of Asanian summer. Or maybe she was living in another time, in another season, when the wind blew chill over the plain, and death walked, and powers moved in the earth.

"Were you there?" Estarion asked her, half expecting a lie, half expecting it to be the truth.

She gave him neither. "Cold here," she said. "So cold."

When he touched her, her skin was chill. And the air already nigh to furnace-heat, even so early, with the sun barely lifted over the horizon.

"You're ill," he said.

She did not hear him. She was in delirium, or in a trance. He gathered her in his arms. She was as light as a bundle of sticks, and nearly as fragile, who had seemed as strong as a swordblade.

"Lord," someone said. Godri. Alidan stood behind him, and others of the guard, and a handful of Lord Dushai's men. Lord Dushai kept a little apart, saying nothing. What the emperor chose to do, his stance said, was the emperor's concern. Estarion almost loved him then, though he would never like so perfect an Asanian.

"Lord," said Godri, "we can carry her. Let us—"

Estarion ignored him. Umizan waited, unwontedly patient. He would carry the fire's child, for so he thought of her. Estarion saw briefly, dizzily, through the senel's eye: a shape of flame, red-gold at the heart, but burning dim now, sinking into darkness and cold.

"She won't die," Estarion said fiercely. "Stop thinking it!"

Umizan's ears were flat, but he did not shift or fret as Estarion set the shivering, burning body in the saddle. She was conscious enough to rouse as she felt the senel under her, to grip the beast's sides with her knees, to wind fingers in the long plaited mane. He walked softly, as smoothly as ever senel could, bearing her as if she were made of glass.

Once she was stripped of her worn clothes and wrapped in a soft robe and laid in the bed that had been meant for Estarion, Sidani slept peacefully enough. Her brow when he laid his hand on it toward evening was as warm as it should be, no sign of fever or of unnatural cold. She breathed well and easily. Her sleep was deep and quiet, without dreams.

He exchanged glances with Ulyai, who had come to fill a solid half of the bed. "Watch over her," he said.

The cat laid her head beside the woman's and sighed. She had been negligent. She had let both the bright one and the fire's child go out alone while she indulged herself in a fine fresh haunch of plowbeast. An ul-queen did not stoop to apology, but she could regret an indiscretion.

She would watch over Sidani. Estarion could wish himself as happily occupied.

Lord Dushai, perhaps mindful that a man could grow weary unto tears of banquets, had not laid on the usual feast or the usual parade of beauties. Both were to be had, but he had woven them into a new thing, as new as the hall into which he led his guest.

That was not the long narrow chamber Estarion was used to. It was as round as one of the moons, ringed in pillars and topped with a dome that seemed made of light. Nor was Estarion to sit at a high table, there to be stared at and remarked upon while he endured the fiery delights of the Asanian taste. There was a couch placed for him in the innermost of many rings of couches, a low table set between it and the couch beside, on which Dushai established himself, and in front of them the open center of the circle. Others reclined in the widening circles, some alone on their couches, some accompanied. His mother faced him across the open space, with Iburan seated upright at her feet. She raised a brow at him. He twitched a smile in return.

Servants brought food, drink. Estarion found that he was hungry. He was acquiring a taste for some of the Asanian sauces, though others were a sore test of his fortitude. The thin yellow Asanian wine went not ill with the more palatable of the dishes, and it was chilled with snow brought from mountains in the north and kept in deep cellars.

He had chosen to be cool, though it meant shocking his many-robed subjects. His kilt was of fine cream-pale silk broad-belted with gold and great plates of amber as yellow as his eyes. He was bare above it but for a pectoral of gold and amber and topaz, his hair plaited into the helmet-braids of the Ianyn kings. He had almost sacrificed his beard in the name of coolness, but contrariness forestalled him. Asanians never grew their beards, if in fact they had any. They reckoned it a barbarism. Therefore he kept his.

Barefoot, bareheaded, lightly kilted, he was as cool as human body could be, and almost content. The servant who had brought him wine set the flagon on the table and took up a fan, waking wind where there was none. He stretched out on the couch, propped up with cushions, nibbling a bit of spiced sweetness. People were staring in Asanian fashion, under lowered lids or out of the corners of their eyes. Poor creatures, wrapped in all those robes, compelled by custom to wear their hair unbound or knotted at their napes. The crop-headed, tunicked servants were happier by far than they.

His own people had had a little sense. Those who dared kilts, or who were entitled to them by blood and breeding, wore them with relief. His mother might have worn one herself, but she had greater care for Asanian sensibilities than he had. Her gown covered her from throat to ankle but left her arms bare. Its heavy raw silk revealed little of the body beneath, which was a pity. She had beautiful breasts, firm still and round though she had borne and suckled a son.

She bowed her head to the compliment, with a slight, wry brush of vision: himself as she saw him, a slender dark beauty with a noble breadth of shoulder.

Dark, yes, beyond a doubt. Slender—lean, for a fact, and not much hope of gaining flesh as he aged, if his mother's kin were any guide. They were all as ribby as spring wolves. Beauty . . . He laughed. Lord Dushai thought him amused by something someone had said. He let it pass.

His mother was pleased with him. And why not? As far as she knew, he had given up his corpse-faced commoner and accepted his lot, though not, yet, so far as to take to bed an Asanian woman. He did not even know where Vanyi was. Among the priests, most likely, or in the temple. She did not speak to him now; she did not touch his mind, nor respond when he sought hers.

No use to try. It only caused him pain. He drained his cup of snow-cold wine and held it out for the servant to fill. Lord Dushai addressed him, soft and clear under the muted murmur that was Asanian conviviality. "I have prepared an entertainment for you, majesty," he said, "which perhaps you have not seen before. We call it, if you will, a concourse of attractive lies."

Estarion's brows went up. This was new, and possibly interesting. He watched as black-clad servants brought lamps into the empty circle till it blazed as bright as noon. While they did that, others dimmed the lamps without, casting the hall into twilight.

He was aware of heightened alertness: his guards marking

the deepening of shadows. The beginning of an ache marked those who were mages, and the wall they raised about him. He made himself ease, endure, await what would come.

Once the servants had arranged the lamps to their satisfaction, they departed. There was a silence. It was a peculiarly Asanian thing: no stirring of restless bodies, no sighs of impatience, no muttered commentary. Even his Varyani were quenched into stillness.

Thunder rolled. Estarion jumped like a deer. Dushai's amusement brushed him, startling not for that it existed, but for that there was no scorn in it. He settled slowly, willed himself to smile as if at a jest.

Drums and flutes and horns, and instruments he had no names for. A consort of musicians marched into the light, arrayed themselves round the edges, settled to the floor, and never a pause or a soured note. The music they played was Asanian, rather like the yowl of mating cats, but, like their wine and their sauces, it grew on one.

He was ready, more or less, when the players came in. Their like haunted the roads of Keruvarion, wandering bands full of, as Lord Dushai had said, attractive lies. But these were no mountebanks. And they did not speak their parts. They sang.

Their tale was in his honor, of course, and apt in view of the morning. They played out the tale of Sarevadin and of Hirel Uverias, the dark prince and the golden. The one who was Hirel was Asanian, a beautiful boy with the fierce unhuman eyes of a lion. The one who was Sarevadin was a wonder: while he was a prince, one was certain beyond a doubt that he was male, but when she rose up out of the mages' circle she was a woman, and no hint about her of the man that she had been. No magery either, that Estarion could sense. It was all art.

He looked for a twist, for a stab of hostility in word or gesture. He found none. They were honest players, and their play an honest play. They did not touch on the tragedy of the Sunborn: the world he had sought to make, with the goddess bound in chains and the god triumphant over her, laid low by his heir's betrayal. He would have ruled alone, and set Asanion beneath his heel. His heir had set Asanion's emperor on the throne beside her, sacrificing all that she had been, because she saw no other hope.

This was all sweetness. Two princes loved one another across an abyss of enmity; two empires could never be reconciled but through the love of those who ruled them. An easy conclusion, for all the enormity of Sarevadin's sacrifice. A simple resolution. The old emperors were disposed of—Ziad-Ilarios of Asanion dead defending the life of Mirain's empress, that empress dead in spite of him, Mirain himself ensorceled in his Tower—and the Mageguild thwarted in its desire to rule the rulers they had made, and the lovers wedded on the field of battle. Soldier of the Sun embraced soldier of the Lion. Emperor clove to empress upon a golden throne. Joy ruled where had been only sorrow.

Estarion suppressed a snort. It was very pretty. Very convenient, too, for the talespinners. They never mentioned aftermaths. Emperor and empress growing old, emperor dying early as royal Asanians did, empress declining headlong to her own death, perhaps by her own hand, and Asanion chafing endlessly in the bonds of amity that they had forced upon it. Rebellions out of count, even a war or two, and their son dead in one such, and that one's grandson poisoned in the Golden Palace, and the last of their line presented with the consequences.

He would have liked it better if someone had come raging and foaming out of the shadows after the last aria and prophesied death, doom, destruction. Like Vanyi's prophet. That would have been nearer the truth.

The players finished their playing. The musicians concluded with a flourish. Asanians did not applaud; they rose and bowed. Estarion was pleased to follow their example. The players bowed in their turn, and it went back and forth, like a dance of odd birds.

Somewhat after he had had enough of it, he put an end to

it by stepping into the light. The players were startled, but they masked it well.

The Sarevadin, seen close, was less ambiguous as to gender than before. The northern skin at least was genuine; the red Gileni mane was not. Estarion bit his tongue before he asked what could compel a northerner to make himself a eunuch. The player had pride in himself. He met Estarion's eyes willingly, if warily.

The Hirel was older than he had seemed. His lion-eyes were clever shapes of glass with plain brown behind them, and a dun-drab lock escaping from the yellow wig. He was no more reluctant than his fellow to look an emperor in the face: a remnant maybe of the part he had played.

"You did well," Estarion said to them.

He never understood why a word from him could mean so much. It was the fact of his rank, he supposed, and the fiery thing in his hand. These players wanted to kiss it, as people did in Keruvarion but never in Asanion. Or maybe the commoners did; but he was not allowed to approach them, or to be approached by them. Emperors did not do such things here. They did not even speak to lords of the Lower Courts.

He had caused a scandal by addressing these players. He did not care. They were Asanian, mostly, but some of them had come from Keruvarion. This manner of singing the parts was a thing of the far west, where they had gone a season or two before, having an enterprising leader: the young eunuch, whose name was Toruan.

Relieved of his wig and his woman's dress, seated on the couch beside Estarion and partaking hungrily of meat and bread and fierce sauces, he was a pleasant, witty companion. He could deepen his voice almost to match Estarion's or lighten it to a woman's sweetness, but in itself it was soft and rather husky, not like a child's, but not like a man's or a woman's either. It was, Estarion thought, remarkable. He said so.

"Training," said Toruan. "That's why they do it: for the voice, to keep it from spoiling. Catch it soon enough, train it well enough, and it grows into this." He indicated himself with a hand as elongated as the rest of him; but his chest was vast, now that Estarion had his attention called to it. The gown had shaped it into a convincing semblance of a woman's breasts.

"You chose this?" Estarion asked.

The eunuch paused. For a moment his face went still. Then he smiled. The pain in it was almost imperceptible. "Of course not, sire. My clan was poor. A sickness ravaged it, took all the hunters and laid low our herds and left us starving. I was the best of what was left. They sold me for a wagonload of corn. The one who took me was kin to a master of singers in Induverran. He heard me singing at my work. He had his kinsman come to listen; his kinsman bought me, and made me a singer."

"The selling of slaves is banned in Keruvarion," said Estarion, soft and cold.

"They went over the border to do it," Toruan said. "They were hungry, sire. Their children were dying. My father and mother were dead, and I wanted to see more than our hunting runs, and be more than a wild clansman. It profited all of us."

"It fed them for a season at the most. It robbed you of all your sons."

"I didn't know it would come to that," said Toruan. "When they asked me if I wanted to be a singer, I was so glad, I sang. Then they gave me wine. When I woke from the drug that was in it, I found my price all paid, and no way to unpay it. I should have killed myself, I suppose. But I never quite worked myself up to it."

Estarion's tongue had a will of its own, and that could be cruel. "I . . . know about prices," he said.

Toruan stared at Estarion's hands—at the one that gleamed with gold and burned with unmerciful fire. "Maybe," he said, "you do." And maybe, thought Estarion, he did not. Not such prices as these.

Toruan consented to bring his players and his repertory of sung-plays to Kundri'j Asan, if not at once and not in the emperor's train. "That wouldn't be proper," he said. He was northerner enough to break bread and share speech with the imperial majesty, but when it came to traveling with it, he went all Asanian.

Lord Dushai was regretting, maybe, his novel entertainment. Estarion could read none of it in his face. There were still the women to endure, kept long past their time by the emperor's whim, and while they waited they had eaten and drunk perhaps to excess. Some of them were openly importunate. When clever soft hands slid beneath his kilt, he fled.

The chambers he had been given were quiet. No one stared or whispered. No one called him to account. He had offended a high lord, scandalized that lord's court, and insulted its women. And he was, it seemed, to be left to rest in peace. Maybe that was his punishment.

Ulyai was asleep on the bed, although she opened an eye at Estarion's approach. Sidani was awake. She had been lying so, it seemed, for a while. She looked much as she always had, neither young nor truly old, and the glance she turned on him was brightly ironic. "So, youngling. I take a fit and wake in your bed. Do I make the natural assumption?"

"It was the safest place I could think of," he said, "and the most comfortable."

She wriggled in it. "So it is. They've learned something since last I came here. This is a proper bed. They were always trying to drown me in billows of cushions."

"I had the servants get rid of those. Asanian beds aren't bad, once you get down to them."

"I never thought of that." She lay silent for a while. He hovered, wavered. The golden collar irked him suddenly; he extricated himself from it. Once it was gone, he found that he could breathe. He sat on the bed's edge. "Are you well?" he asked her.

"Was I ill?"

He shrugged a little.

"I was," she said. She sounded surprised. "I was cold, I remember that. I'd been thinking too much. Remembering."

"It put you in a fever," he said. "Iburan looked at you. He said it was nothing he could cure."

"No one can mend old age. Not even gods."

"You're not old."

"Infant," she said, "stop that. Of course I'm old. I'm ancient."

"You're not going to die quite yet."

"Alas for that." It was only half mockery. "Watching one's husband die is not pleasant. When one's son dies . . . that's harder. And when one's grandson is laid in his tomb, then, youngling, one begins to wonder if one isn't cursed. And such a curse! 'May you outlive all your descendants.' "

Estarion flung up his burning hand, casting the curse aside. The light of it made her blink. "Don't say such things," he said.

"What? Someone might be listening? Gods don't care. Men can't harm me."

"You are appalling," he said.

She grinned: a shadow of her wonted insouciance, but it was white and wicked enough. "Are you going to sleep, youngling, or do you have other sins in mind?"

His cheeks were burning. Still, he met her grin with one of his own. "You'll live," he said.

Godri had spread him a bed in one of the lesser rooms, with eloquent if wordless disapproval. Estarion went to it in something like gladness, once he had seen Sidani asleep again. Maybe he witched her into it. Maybe he did not need to.

16

THE NEW MORNING was if anything more heat-sodden than the one before. Estarion woke in a sweat, to sounds like muted battle. One of the voices was Godri's. The others he did not know, but he knew the cadence of Asanian speech. They had looked for the emperor in his bed, it seemed, and failed to find him.

He rolled to his feet, yawning hugely, stretching till his bones creaked. The battle was no longer quite so muted. He went out to face it.

Asanians were ridiculous about naked bodies. Bed-play to them was the high art, and they performed it, as far as he had ever been able to tell, in as many clothes as possible. They never bared more than faces and hands and feet, except in the bath; and then they pretended that they were robed to the eyes. They even wore clothes to sleep.

Absurd; lunatic in such heat as this. He entered the battlefield as he was born, with no covering but his skin. The silence was thunderous. Godri faced an army of Asanians, every one of them in a servant's tunic, and every one determined, it seemed, to pass or die.

On sight of Estarion, they dropped flat on their faces.

"Godri," he said. "Who are these people?"

Godri's eyes were battle-bright; his breath came hard. He steadied it enough to reply, "They say they belong to the Regent of Asanion. Who is, they say, on the road to Induverran this very moment. And who expects to see the emperor properly—as they say—bathed, clothed, and arrayed to receive him."

"And you object?" Estarion asked.

"They have," he said, "razors. And robes. And bottles of scent."

Estarion raised his brows.

"They informed me, my lord, that my services would no longer be needed. You are in Asanion now. Asanion will look after you."

When Godri was as precise as that, Godri was most dangerous. Estarion smiled slowly. "Will it, then? And I suppose I'm to wear the ten robes and the wig, and the mask too? And sit on a throne in the hall? And speak only through a Voice?"

"Yes," said Godri.

"Pity," said Estarion, "that I won't be doing any of that." He shifted from Gileni to Asanian. "Up, sirs. Listen to your emperor. The bath I'll take. But no razors, and no scent. My squire will see to my robing. If his grace the Regent is displeased, then I take it upon my head."

There was one use for Asanian servility. It kept them from arguing with royalty. The Regent's servants were not pleased in the least, but they could not protest. The emperor had spoken. They must do as he commanded.

They bathed him in blessedly cool water. They did not threaten him with razors or drench him with scent. They did object to the kilt which Godri proffered. "That will not do," the chief of them said—safe, maybe, because it was the squire he spoke to.

"It will do," Estarion said.

It was a royal kilt, scarlet edged with gold. The belt that went with it was rich, gold leaved over thickly carved leather, and he suffered the full weight of northern ornament: rings, armlets, necklaces, earrings of pure and heavy gold lightened with a gem or two; strings of gold and ruby woven in his hair, and threads of gold in the curls of his beard. He was blinding; dazzling; glorious. "Since," he said, "after all, I am receiving the Regent of Asanion."

"He's not going to approve," Godri observed.

"Alas for his grace," said Estarion.

* * *

The hall was as cool as anything could be in this climate. Its lofty dome held off the worst of the heat, and its many-colored stone kept to itself the coolness of the night. A pair of servants wielded gilded fans, cooling Estarion with their breezes.

The chair on which he sat was not too uncomfortable as thrones went. Asanians knew the virtue of cushions, too much so when it came to their beds, but thoroughly satisfactory under his rump. He rested his foot on the living stool that presented itself: Ulyai, who judged herself more truly needed where he was than with Sidani. She was not forthcoming as to the woman's whereabouts. *Safe,* she informed him in the image of an ul-queen laired with her cubs. He decided to trust her. In the circumstances he had little choice.

His own escort was present only in part. Most of the courtiers were still asleep or amusing themselves as courtiers could in a foreign city. His Guard was halved to those on day-duty. His mother was there, of course, and Iburan, and one or two priest-mages. Not Vanyi. Everyone else in that hall was Asanian.

A small shiver ran down Estarion's spine. So many yellow faces. So many minds turned on him, and not one level pair of eyes.

This too was his empire. These too were his people. They did not ask that he love them, only that he rule them.

He sat a little straighter. The walls about his mind were high and strong, but his head ached in spite of them. He knew the pounding of his mother's siege-engines. Disapproval was too mild a word for her response to the sight of him in the finery of her people. Even Iburan had taken his beard out of its braids and abandoned his kilt for the stifling confinement of a robe. He looked like a cave-bear in a coat, vast and ruffled and surly. But he was proper as Asanians thought of it. He was covered in accordance with his rank.

Maybe Asanians did not feel the heat as other people did. They did not sweat that he could see, or grow faint. They seemed content to stand for hours out of count, not moving, not speaking, not meeting his restless eyes.

His grace the Regent was in no haste to appear before his emperor. First he must come to the city; then he must be borne through it in his litter; at last he must enter the lord's palace and be received by the lord, and offered refreshment, and bathed and robed with honor and conducted to the hall. While Estarion sat fasting, sweltering, barely breathing lest he say something unfortunate. In Keruvarion at least he would have had a hallful of petitioners to keep him occupied. Here he was given nothing to do but sit.

It was designed to drive an emperor mad. But he was mage and priest before he was emperor. There were disciplines in which he had too little practice, and exercises of the mind that prospered well enough behind full shields. One of them was to draw all of his self inward save a sentinel behind the eyes, and focus it, and quicken time until movement without was a blur. In that shifted time he ran through the Prayers of Passing, first the invocation, then the doxology, then the petition, and at the last the praises. And as the last great singing line sank into the silence of his self, the blur before him slowed, and the world ran level again with his awareness. A wind ruffled the hall. An army marched in upon it.

The other face of time's quickening was time's slowing. Estarion took his leisure to examine the invasion. It was not as numerous as at first it seemed, or so headlong. It was simply determined.

He knew the livery of the Regent's guard, armor ornate to uselessness, lacquered and gilded till it rivaled his own finery, and all of it crimson and silver, the colors of his lordship's house. He knew their master, memory as sharp as a knife in the flesh, prince of seven robes, crimson on crimson on crimson, and the man within them aged cruelly in the years of Estarion's absence. But the ones who came behind, he did not remember, unless they were the shadows of his dream. Cold reason named their kind. Bred warriors. Olenyai.

Black robes, black hoods, black veils shrouding faces to the eyes. Twin swords, baldricked one on either side. Hands ivory-pale, eyes gold or amber, and none of them taller than any other, and that was small in any country but this; but even that smallness was deadly.

Asanion had bred its princes for a thousand years and more, for beauty, for subtle wit, for impeccably civilized viciousness. These were its warriors, bred as carefully as princes, reared and trained in secret, forbidden ever to reveal their faces. They were the dogs and slaves of the emperors, the soldiery of its warlords, bought and sold in captains and companies, bound to their lords by oaths and gold and, it was said, deep-woven sorcery.

Estarion had seen none of them since he came to Asanion. The armed men whom he had seen were men like any other, guards as he knew them in Keruvarion, free men taken into lordly service. There were no wars where he had gone, no emperor but the one, and that was himself. There had been no need of Olenyai.

He had all he could do to force his eyes away from them, to hold his face still while the Regent performed the nine prostrations of the Asanian homage. His following performed them with him, concerted as a dance. But not the Olenyai. The shadow warriors did not sacrifice vigilance even for the emperor's majesty.

The pain behind Estarion's eyes was near to blinding. He saw as in a broken glass, a thin glittering shard that held a remembered face. "My lord Firaz inShalion Echaryas," he said. "Well met again, and welcome."

"My lord Meruvan Estarion Kormerian Ganimanion iVaryan," said the Regent, stumbling not even once, "well met at last, and welcome."

Tidily put, thought Estarion. He did not remember that he had been fond of this man. One was not fond of Asanian high princes. One hated them, or one admired them, or both. This prince was as high as any but the highest, and he paid the price of his blood and breeding. He had been beautiful once as his kind could be. Now he was all gone grey, worn and ravaged with the years. And yet he was younger than the empress, whose hair had not begun to whiten, whose beauty was just coming into its prime.

They blossom young, said a voice in the deeps of his mind, *and they wither soon. They're all the more deadly for that.*

Memory; but when or where, or who spoke, he could not tell. Nor had he time to hunt it to its source. Lord Firaz was speaking: long elegant phrases of greeting, gladness, judicious flattery. But there was a barb in the tail.

"My emperor will know that he is now in my domain, under, of course, the imperial majesty. Those of the east who accompany him are freed to return to their places. Henceforth he will prosper in the hands of his western servants."

Estarion drew himself up slowly. He cut across a further spate of nonsense, but carefully, in High Asanian as perfect as he could make it. "Is my lord Regent implying that I should send back my escort?"

"Its task is done," said the Regent, "majesty. Your majesty's servants have been sent to your majesty's chambers. Your majesty's guard stands before your majesty. Your majesty's regent—"

"My servants? My guard?"

"As your majesty sees." The Regent's hand gestured slightly, gracefully. The Olenyai bent their shrouded heads. It was not humility. Not in the least.

"And if I wish to keep my own people?"

"These are your majesty's people."

Estarion closed his eyes, opened them again. His mother listened in unmarred serenity. He shot a bolt through the walls of his mind. *You knew!*

She inclined her head a fraction. *Wait,* the gesture said. *Be patient.*

He was in no mood for patience. "Suppose," he said, "that

we compromise. I keep my own Guard, and suffer your servants."

"These are your guard," said the Regent.

"We shall consider this," Estarion said, "later." He rose. "You are most welcome in our presence. But the sun approaches its zenith; the heat likewise comes to its height. Be free now till evening. Rest; seek what coolness there may be."

"That was peremptory," said the empress. There was no censure in her tone; simply observation.

"It was scandalous." Estarion prowled her antechamber. Her servant—as much a northerner as she, and blessedly silent—had rid him of his gauds and cooled him with a cloth dipped in water and herbs. The sharp green scent followed him as he paced. At the far wall he spun. "Mother, I'm not going to let him rule me."

"Are you clever enough to stop him?"

"You are."

She sighed. "Estarion," she said, "have you considered that it might be wise to yield? In body only. In spirit you remain yourself."

"I won't wear all those robes in this heat."

She frowned, but then, as if she could not help herself, she smiled. Here where only he and Zherin could see, she had yielded to simple sense and discarded her robes. Her beauty was garment enough in his reckoning, that and the pride that never forsook her, even when she slept. "I am not about to abandon you," she said, "if that's what you fear."

He would not admit that he had. "I don't want to lose my Guard. Or my squire."

"And your court?"

"They might be happier away from here." He began to pace again. "Mother, I can send them back. Most of them will be glad to go. But not Godri. And not my warriors."

"You do know," she said, "that under the compact of the empires' union, the heart of Asanion is Asanion's own. Firaz is doing no more than his duty—and granting you ample grace in demanding it no sooner than this. He could have met you at the border and not at the gate."

"He could have waited till I came to Kundri'j."

"He was wise to wait so long, but wiser to come so soon. Easier then for you to accept it, and come to the city in proper estate."

"If that's what he wants, then I'll ride in like a wild tribesman, and damn him and all his works."

Her gaze on him was level. He flushed under it. "Will you, Estarion?" she inquired.

"No, damn it." Her doubt stung him; her glance at his kilt and his braids. "Mother, I'm not a complete fool. I'll behave myself tonight: I'll even wear a robe. But he has to know that I'm not his puppet. I'll be as proper as I can be. I'll promise him no more than that."

"And me? Will you promise me to be more circumspect? Here they find it in themselves to endure your outland fancies. Kundri'j Asan endures nothing that is not Asanian."

"I'm not Asanian."

"You must learn to be."

His jaw set against her. "Maybe it's time they learned to see the world as it is and not as they would have it. The Golden Empire is gone. The Blood of the Lion is here, in me, black-faced bearded barbarian that I am. I am not ten robes and a wig and a mask. I am living, breathing, human power. And I rule them."

"Do you?"

Testing, always testing. He would hate her if he loved her less. He swooped down, set a kiss on her brow. "Can I do less than try?" he asked her.

She caught him before he could straighten, and held him with her hands on either side of his face. Her eyes were ages deep. The goddess dwelt in the depths of them. He was light and fire, Sun's child, bright noon to her deep night, man to her woman, son and emperor as she was mother and queen.

"My beautiful bright child," she said. The words were tender, but their edge was fierce. "I'll never call you wise. But neither will I stop you."

"Will you help me?"

"Only if there's wisdom in it."

"Then I'll try to be sensible."

"Sensible is even rarer than wise."

He grinned between her hands. "If I fall short of sense, then maybe I'll reach wisdom."

She cuffed him hard enough to bruise. "Puppy! Go, torment your servants, give me a moment's peace."

17

The battle royal between Godri and the Regent's servants was a ladies' walking-party to the war that Estarion found at the door of his chambers. The scarlet livery of his Guard held the way against the black regiment of the Olenyai. When Estarion came upon them, they were close to drawn swords.

His temper had, he thought, been holding up remarkably well. But this, after all the rest that he had had to endure, snapped the fragile cord of his patience. Just as a scarlet-liveried hothead went for a little snapping beast in black, Estarion let his temper go. *"Hold!"*

His battlefield bellow brought even wild Alidan up short, sword half-drawn.

Estarion drew a very careful breath. "Put away your swords," he said.

Alidan obeyed him. The Olenyas glanced at another of his like, his captain maybe. That one lowered lids over yellow eyes. The blade snicked into its sheath.

Estarion noticed, but he forbore to remark on it. "Now," he said. "What is this?"

The Olenyai went still. The Guard burst out in a babble of furious voices.

Estarion's hand slashed them into silence, and singled out the decurion of his Guard. "Kiyan. And you—Olenyas. Are you their captain?"

"I am captain of this watch," said the voice out of the veil. A quite ordinary Asanian voice, no power or terror in it. And no title for the emperor, either.

"Explain this," Estarion said.

The Olenyas did not answer at once. Kiyan the decurion

said, "Sire, they invaded your chambers, ordered your guards' dismissal, and informed me, when I came to settle it, that none but they will guard you. Is that so, my lord?"

"They have orders to that effect," Estarion said. And as Kiyan opened his mouth to speak: "But not from me. I have a matter or two to settle with the Regent. While you wait for that, let your two commanders come to an agreement. Both companies will guard me. Both, sirs; together and alike."

That was not at all to their liking. The Guard scowled; someone snarled. The Olenyai looked as supercilious as eyes could look in faceless masks.

A long look quelled the scowls. The Olenyai, who being Asanian would not meet his eyes, needed more. Estarion said, "My guards, my Olenyai. You are mine, no?"

"We are the emperor's," their captain said.

"Just so," said Estarion.

He stepped forward. They parted, Olenyai and Guardsmen alike. He escaped to the sanctuary of his chambers. Such as that was, with imperial servants infesting it and Godri brooding balefully in their midst.

Asanian custom permitted an emperor to receive a high lord in private, with no more than a servant or two in attendance. Estarion was careful. He put on the robes the servants chose for him, simple as such things went, inner and outer only, and thin enough almost to be endurable in the heat. He let them comb his hair out of its braids. He arranged himself as they—discreetly, politely, firmly—suggested, in a chair in one of the smaller rooms. It would have been a ghastly cupboard of a place, save that it opened on the garden. A fountain played just beyond, cooling the air and the ear.

Set up like an idol in a temple, watched over by a glowering pair of guards, bronze-dark narrow-eyed plainsman and black-robed Olenyas, Estarion received the Regent of Asanion. Lord Firaz came in unattended, which marked either very great insult or very great trust; his robes were no more elaborate than

Estarion's, and his manner was much less stiff than it had been in the hall. He insisted on a single prostration, but then he let Estarion raise him and set him in a chair a little lower than his own. He sipped the wine that the servant poured, great trust again, not to ask that it be tasted before he ventured it. He even abbreviated the dance of courtesies, restraining himself to a few dozen phrases in praise of the wine, the weather, and the appointments. The wine was drinkable, the weather wretched, the appointments no more and no less than they should be; but Estarion did not say so. It was his part to listen, smile inscrutably, murmur inanities.

After hardly more than a turn of the glass, Firaz approached the meat of the matter. "Your majesty—"

"Come now," said Estarion. "We're kin, or so I'm told. Let me be 'my lord' if you insist; or if you can bear it, let me be myself: Estarion."

"My lord," said Firaz. "I rejoice to see you so well reconciled to our ways."

"But," said Estarion, "I am not. I do turn and turn about as my fathers did before me: now of the north, now of the east, now of Asanion. None of them owns me. I belong to them all."

"You are in Asanion now," said its Regent.

"I had noticed," Estarion said mildly.

Firaz took the warning: his nostrils thinned. But he was not one to be daunted by imperial temper. "May I speak freely, my lord?"

"I would prefer it," said Estarion.

The Regent's eyes widened a fraction. Estarion tasted doubt, and a flicker of respect. "Very well, my lord. If I may say so without risk of grievous injury to your pride or to mine, your exhibition in the hall would not have been well received in Kundri'j Asan."

"No?"

Firaz went on doggedly. "I believe that you knew it, and that you did it for precisely that reason. Are you determined, my lord, to turn this half of your empire against you?"

"What if I were?"

"I would understand it," said Firaz. "I would not condone it."

"You don't think Asanion would be better served if it were rid of its pack of mongrels and upstarts, and an emperor of the pure blood set upon its throne?"

Firaz astonished Estarion. He laughed. "Should I say yes, and die for speaking treason? Or should I say no, and be hanged for imbecility? My lord, you are the Heir of the Lion. It is written in your face. If your servants are blind, or if they do not know you, then it were best you teach them to see. But not," he added, "quite so much as we saw in hall this morning."

"Why?" asked Estarion.

"Modesty is not to be explained. It is."

"I wasn't naked."

"You were." Firaz stopped himself. "My lord, I see clearly that you are no fool, nor do you do aught but as you choose. I would venture to ask that when you choose in Kundri'j, you choose the wise man's portion."

"And that is to do as you dictate?"

"I do not dictate," said Firaz.

"Your servants do. They ordered my squire, the chosen attendant of my journey, out of my presence. Your Olenyai had dismissed my Guard, at your command and in defiance of my will."

"It was your squire, my lord, who led me here. I see a Guardsman out of Endros and an Olenyas of Kundri'j at your right hand and your left."

"I discovered," said Estarion, "that my titles have a certain worth, even in Asanion."

"They are your servants, my lord, and your warriors. They but come to fulfill their duty."

"So they do. There will be, I hope, no further objections to my escort or to its disposition."

"Will your majesty see fit to indulge Asanian eccentricities in the matter of clothing and of conduct?"

"That depends upon the eccentricity."

"Will your majesty consent at least to observe the fundamental proprieties?"

"I will not ride in a litter. I will not wear the mask or the wig. I will, if I choose, walk outside of the palace."

Firaz paused, perhaps to gather patience. "My lord, will you learn to be an emperor in Asanion?"

Cruelly hard, that, to ask so direct a question. Estarion was almost minded to be merciful. "If you will teach me, I will learn as I may."

"It was for that, my lord, that I came."

"Then," said Estarion, "begin."

The art of wearing ten robes was like that of wearing armor. The seventeen inflections of the imperial salutation made a pretty, if wearing, game for a clever mind. The myriad minutiae of the courtier's dance needed a lifetime to study properly; Estarion had no patience for them.

Some of his courtiers went back to Keruvarion, bored with the long sweltering days in a city without useful diversions. Asanian court games wearied them rapidly: most required a command of high court Asanian, and few outside of the bedchamber demanded more of the body than a languid shift from one side of a chamber to another. Hunting did not amuse the exquisites of Asanian courts. That was a sport for winter, they sighed. Water games shocked them: one had to be naked for those. Mounted exercise and sword-practice were difficult where every open space was a garden or a concourse of people, and the plain was a furnace from dawn till sundown. Estarion's soldiers braved it, and those of his escort who were determined enough to cling to him. The rest took their seneldi and their guards and their servants and began the long journey back to, as they called it, civilization.

He would happily have gone with them. But he was the cause and the source of this exile in Induverran. If he left it, it must be to come to Kundri'j. And that would not be until Lord

Firaz, his tutor and his jailer, pronounced him fit for the High Court of his own empire.

Some things he would not do, here or anywhere, even in Kundri'j. One of them was to sit mewed in his chambers, speaking to no one save through guards and servants, walking nowhere save in walled gardens. That was the way of old Asanion, to keep its emperors as strongly prisoned as any miscreant, to cut them off from any stain of common earth.

That, he would not endure. "Either I am emperor or I am not," he said to his Regent. "And if I am, then I go where I will, within the bounds of safety or of reason. I may go guarded—I suffer that. I may go in robes, if you insist. But I will go."

There was nothing that Lord Firaz could say to that, except to request that his majesty permit an Olenyas to accompany him. A request from Lord Firaz was a thinly veiled command. Estarion saw no profit in disputing this one.

He did not like the Olenyai. They were protected by some magic that made his head ache with a constant dull throbbing; it kept him from reading them, or from learning anything about them at all, except what their eyes betrayed.

"And yet," he said to Godri, "I think they're loyal. Not to me, not that, but to the rank I hold."

Godri, these days, wore a permanent scowl. "And if they ever take it into their heads to suspect that you don't hold it any longer, they'll cut you down without a thought."

"The day I let go my kingship, you can be sure I'll be too dead to care what yonder blackrobes do to my carcass."

Godri's grin was feral. It vanished quickly. "Just have a care they don't speed the day. I see them sometimes, my lord. Staring at you. Measuring you for your shroud."

"Maybe they're only wondering how I'd look in a black robe."

But Godri had no stomach for levity. He muttered something dark.

"Godri," said Estarion. "Do you want me to send you home?"

For a moment Godri's face lit like a lamp. When it darkened, it was even blacker than before. "I swore oath, my lord. I'll stay with you till death or your hand set me free."

"I'll free you," Estarion said.

"No!" Godri seemed to shock himself with his own vehemence. He stopped, collected his wits and his expression. "My lord," he said at length, as calmly as Estarion had ever heard him, "you may send me away. You are the emperor. But what is to stop me from coming back?"

"You hate this place," Estarion said.

"But," said Godri, "my lord, I love you."

Estarion had no words to answer that. Godri spoke it as plain fact, with no great passion. It simply was. Like, Estarion thought, the sun's rising out of the eastern sea; or the dance of the moons; or the silences that shaped the notes of a song.

Thus Godri stayed. His scowl was a constant of Estarion's wakings, his caustic observations an antidote to the gagging sweetness of courtiers' speech. The servants learned to walk softly round him. The Olenyai accorded him a remarkable degree of respect.

"He has killed, and killed well," one of them explained. It was all he would say, and more by far than Estarion could get out of the others.

Of course a tribe of warriors would value a warrior's virtue. Estarion wondered if that was why they thought so little of him apart from the fact of his kingship. He had never killed anyone. Not with his hands.

Sidani was gone. Estarion had not seen her since he left her asleep in his bed, the second morning in Induverran. He heard of her here and there for a day or two: she was telling her wonted stories, walking her accustomed paths, recovered it seemed from the sickness that had beset her. Then he heard nothing. She was not dead—he would have known, he was sure of it. She had risen one morning, gathered her few belongings, and taken to the road.

He had not truly known her: she was too prickly for that, her shifts too odd. And yet he missed her presence, her biting wit, her gift for saying the unsayable.

Wanderers wandered. It was their nature. Talespinners had somehow to gather their tales. And maybe she loved Asanion no more than he did, who had shown the raw wounds of her soul on the battlefield of Induverran. Of course she had not fought there. She could not be so old. But she was odd when it came to her stories. She called them memories, and reckoned them her own. These, he thought, had grown too much to bear.

That she had left was no more than sense. But she had gone without farewell. That hurt. He had thought she valued him a little: enough at least to take her leave when she must go.

Her absence, Vanyi's continued and relentless coldness, his own gilded imprisonment, came together into a knot of misery. It was another burning morning, another searing day in this cycle of Brightmoon called Anvil of the Sun. He woke from a bleak and lightless dream, as he had been waking every morning since he learned to sleep alone. He went to the bath, which was ready as it always was, and the servants waiting, eyes that would not look into his, faces that would not warm for anything he said.

The water of the bath was cool on his fevered skin. The servants' hands were deft and light. One of those behind him, finding the knots across his back and shoulders, worked clever fingers into them: pain melting into pleasure. He was barely awake, or he would have resisted. He wanted those knots. He had earned them.

He did not know the servants' names; they would not tell him. This one, a dun-haired eunuch, stroked the tension out of him, saying nothing, offering neither love nor hate. There was a strange comfort in it. Perfect service, nameless, faceless, unobtrusive.

As his back eased, he felt the rest of him growing calmer.

All but one part of it. That, sensing his body's pleasure, rose to claim its share.

If he had been on his guard he would have quelled it before it began. But he was not entirely in his body. He drifted now in, now out of it, half asleep, half awake, haunted by the dimness of his dream. He watched the banner go up, distantly interested. Proper behavior would bid him do something discreet: sink down into the water in which he stood, exert the discipline he practiced too seldom, master the upstart.

He did none of those things. He stood slack, back arched into the hands that smoothed it with long slow strokes, and let his eyelids fall. There was a drugged serenity in it, a mingling of exhaustion and heat and hands that knew his most sensitive places.

How they came from his back to his front, he never knew. But what they did there, woke him abruptly and completely.

He could not bolt. The Asanian held him too firmly. In that appalled instant he saw the whole of the plot against him. Why take his life if they could take his hope of heirs instead?"

"No," he said. Tried to say.

The Asanian took no notice. The rest of them went about their business; he was aware of them, a prickling in his skin. He tasted no hostility, nor anything but calm preoccupation. This terror, this shame, was no more to them than duty. His majesty had need; this one of their number fulfilled it.

He was going to start laughing, and once he started, he would not be able to stop. It was pure high comedy to be trapped so, in such a predicament, and no escape that he could see. The nether half of him was delighted. It had been far too long since he took notice of it.

Very, very carefully he closed his fingers over those clever hands. They froze. "No," he said much more clearly this time, if no more steadily.

The Asanian actually raised his eyes. They darted everywhere before they fell, but for a moment they met Estarion's. "This is not what I wish," Estarion said.

"My lord needs," the Asanian whispered. He was young, little more than a child; he had the nervous look of too much breeding, like a fine stallion or a lordling of the High Court. They bred their slaves here as they bred their princes, and for much the same qualities.

"My lord needs discipline," Estarion said.

"I do not satisfy?" the boy asked. His face was white. He began to tremble.

"There now," said Estarion. "There. You satisfy me perfectly. Just not . . . in that. We don't reckon that a need, where I was raised."

The Asanian's eyes flashed up again in pure incredulity.

"Not *that* kind of need," Estarion said. He still had the child by the hands. He drew him to his feet.

The Asanian was pallid with shock, but he seemed to have mastered the worst of it. "Ah," he said. "My lord prefers the higher arts. Will it be a woman, then?"

Estarion opened his mouth, shut it again. "I don't need anything. Anyone."

He saw the crossing of glances, the silent speech that was not magery, but was as clear as any words. They had decided that he was a witling or worse.

"Not now," Estarion said. "Later. Maybe. If it suits me."

That mollified them a little. It did not convince them that he was a rational being.

Maybe they had the right of it. He stood in the shallows of the bathing-pool and knew that if he did not do something, he would run raving through the city.

"Kundri'j," he said. "Kundri'j Asan." They stared at him in Asanian fashion, sidelong and in glances. "I have had enough of this," he said to them, but in good part to the air and the memory of his Regent. "It is time I left here. I must go. I must come to Kundri'j."

KORUSAN HAD DWELT all his life in the castle of the Olenyai, in Kunzeran to the north of Kundri'j Asan. He had gone out in his training, ridden on the hunt, gone with the rest of the young Olenyai to the market in the town that was nearest. But he had never been farther than half a day's journey from the castle, and he had never walked in the city of the emperors.

To one place he went often, a place that he had made his own: the remnant of old forest that bordered the Olenyai's lands to north and east. He rode there of a morning in high summer, on the senel that he favored among those in the stable, and he rode alone as it best pleased him to do.

As he came under the trees he found one waiting for him. To the eye it was simply one of the brothers, an Olenyas like any other in robes and veils and twinned swords. But the carriage of the head and the glint of the eyes could belong to none but the Master.

Korusan knew the prick of temper, but he quelled it. He did not bare his face, nor did he speak.

The Master turned his mount beside Korusan's. They rode under the trees in silence. It was strangely companionable, for all of Korusan's displeasure at the loss of his solitude.

There was a place not far within, but off the wonted track, that Korusan had taken as a refuge. It was a clearing, not large, where a house or a small temple had been once. Part of a wall remained, and a bit of the floor, overgrown with creepers that flowered in the spring and fruited sweet in the autumn. Now, in summer, the flowers were gone, the fruit hard and green, but the shade was pleasant. There was water in a stream that ran beside the broken wall, grass for a senel to graze on, quiet to rest in away from the clamorings of duty.

Korusan had come here more than once with Marid, but he had not made it known to any other. The Master's presence surprised him in that it did not break the quiet.

Once he had loosened his senel's girth and unhooked the bit from the bridle and turned the beast loose to graze, the Master pulled off veil and headcloth. His hair was flax-fair, as tightly curled as a fleece; he dug fingers into it, smiling into the sun. "Ah," he said. "Here's a rare pleasure."

Korusan, moving more warily, freed his senel as the Master had, and bared his head. If he had been alone as he had hoped to be, he would have uncovered more than that; but modesty restrained him, even when the Master stripped to shirt and loose-cut trousers and waded barefoot in the stream.

The Master paused in dipping a handful of water, and slanted a glance at Korusan. "Do I shock you, young prince?"

"That depends on what you wish of me," said Korusan stiffly.

"You were always impeccable in your manners," the Master said: "more Olenyas than the Olenyai."

"Am I to consider myself rebuked?"

"Not at all," the Master said. "The young ones are always punctilious. It does them credit."

"I think," said Korusan after a moment, "that I am being made sport of."

"Is my prince offended?"

"No," said Korusan. He unbent sufficiently to put aside his outer robe, if not the inner, and to take off his boots. The water was shockingly cold. He did not stand in it longer than he must, to lave his face and drink a little. Safe on dry land again, he sat with knees drawn up, watching the Master out of the corners of his eyes.

The Master came out of the water and sat a little distance from Korusan, lay back on the grass and sighed. "There will be no such pleasures for me again, I fear. Tomorrow I ride to Kundri'j."

Korusan went still, body and mind.

"Before I am Master of Olenyai," the Master said, "I am captain of the guard of the Golden Palace. That duty has never beset me: I had but attained the fourth rank when Ganiman died. But now I must take it up."

"I had heard," Korusan said carefully, "that a company of our brothers had ridden from Kundri'j under the Regent's command."

"Yes," said the Master. "They rode to Induverran, where the emperor is, to await his departure for Kundri'j Asan."

Korusan's heart began to beat hard. "Then," he said, "it is time. He comes."

"He comes," the Master said. "And I must command his guard."

"You should have gone to Induverran," Korusan said.

"No," said the Master, but without rebuke. "I rank too high. It was only the Regent who commanded, you see."

Korusan did see. But he said, "The Regent summoned you to Kundri'j."

"I summon myself to Kundri'j, to prepare for the emperor's coming."

Korusan was shivering, but his body burned with fever. He did not trouble to curse it. It was only shock. "So soon," he said, "and yet it has been so long. . . ."

"Did I say that you would accompany me?"

Korusan met the Master's gaze. "I say that I will."

The Master's eyes narrowed. "Would you risk yourself so, in the very face of the enemy?"

"Where else can I be, if I am to destroy him?"

"Here," the Master answered. "In safety, under guard, while your servants serve you."

"No," said Korusan. "This, no one can do for me."

The Master frowned.

"I must see him," Korusan said. "I must know what he is." He raised his hand, although the Master had made no move to speak. "Yes, I have seen the portraits, heard the tales, had his every act and thought laid out before me with tedious precision.

I know that he favors sour apples, that he rides a blue-eyed stallion, that he has a training-scar on his right thigh above the knee. I know all that a spy can know. But I do not know him."

"Would you have him know you, and destroy you?"

"What can he know? I am an Olenyas, a blackrobe, a faceless warrior. And he is no mage, whatever he was in his childhood. He can work magics, if they are small enough, and he can read a soul if it is close and he is undistracted. More than that, he cannot do. So the mages say."

"Do you trust the mages, prince?" the Master asked.

Korusan paused for a breath's span. "I trust them well enough to believe that they have examined him and found him feeble. That they might have underestimated him, I grant you; but even they cannot read me."

"And that, prince, may be a fatal arrogance."

"Then I wager that it is not. I must see him, my lord. I must know my enemy."

The Master was silent for a long moment, eyes fixed on Korusan's face as if to limn it in his memory. "You were bred to hate him. Can you bear to stand guard over him, to dwell close to him, to be called his servant? Can you do that, prince? For if you cannot, then you have destroyed us all."

"I can do whatever I must," Korusan said, soft and level. "For if I cannot, then all your training has been in vain, and your hopes have failed."

"He is alien, prince. He is taller than any man you have seen. His skin is like black glass. He speaks Asanian with a barbarous accent, in a voice like mountains shifting. And for all of that, my prince, he has your eyes. Eyes of the Lion in the face of an outland beast."

"I have seen the portraits," Korusan said, still steadily, whatever his heart might be doing. "He has no beauty. He is merely strange. Strangeness I can endure, if I know that there is an end to it."

"I do not think," mused the Master, "that the mages would approve. They would call it folly to risk you so openly."

"And you, my lord?"

"I," said the Master, "do not approve. But I can understand. I too wish to see what kind of man he has become. He was an engaging child, for a foreigner."

"You knew him?" Korusan asked, startled.

"I guarded him. He coaxed my name out of me, but he never saw my face."

"And I have your face but not your name," said Korusan with careful mildness.

The Master raised his brows. "What, you do not know? My name is Asadi." He sighed. "Such nonsense, to conceal one's name. We never did so before the mages came among us."

"Before I came," said Korusan, "newborn of a mother who died before they took me from the womb, in a flock of mages. Would I know my own true name, my lord, if I had not insisted on it?"

The Master's lips twitched. "Perhaps not, my lord Ushayan inMuriaz. But your usename serves you well."

"It will serve me in the Golden Palace."

"And what of the truth that it embodies? All that any stranger may see of you is your eyes, and those alone suffice to betray your lineage."

"I will chance that," said Korusan. "Some of the Olenyai lines come close enough, and all of us walk faceless. Who will see aught but the veil and the swords, unless I wish him to see?"

The Master was wavering again toward resistance. Korusan steadied him with a last, strong thrust. "You are the captain of the emperor's guard. You have named me your emperor. I will enter Kundri'j; I will serve in the palace. Do you refuse me?"

He looked for anger, or for outraged pride. He received wry amusement: lifted hands, crooked smile. "You know that I cannot refuse my emperor."

Korusan looked hard at him, suspicious. "Is this a game you play?"

"Certainly," the Master said. "The greatest game of all: the game of kings." He rose and stretched, supple as a cat. "And it does please me to set a caltrop in the mages' path. They presume too much, my prince: of you, of all of us."

Korusan's heart eased its hammering. His fever was high still, dizzying him, but his mind was clear on top of it. He smiled slowly. "So they do, my lord. So indeed they do."

19

Kundri'j Asan.

Estarion said the name to himself in silence, like the silence that rode with him. Even the clatter of hoofs on paving stones was muted, the clink of armor among the guards, the snort of a senel as it shied at a dangling pennon. The sky was the color of hammered brass, the heat a living thing, breathing heavy on his neck, and he robed ninefold; not ten, not on his last march, for he was not yet come to the throne, and he would not wear the mask that made the emperor. He was mere high prince, then, with his bared face and his nine robes. He cared little for the count of the damnable things, only that he wore them. It was that or wear armor, and he would not come as a conqueror.

Estarion could not have felt less like an emperor. His body was dripping wet, shoulders and breast and thighs rubbed raw between the weight of robes and the unfamiliarity of the high Asanian saddle. He had not inflicted that torment on Umizan. The beast he rode was one of Lord Dushai's own, placid to torpidity but blessed with a coat the color of pure minted gold. Umizan's contempt for the creature was the only distinct thing in this blurred and sun-battered world. The stallion would have broken his halter when this ride began, and taught his rival a lesson, if Estarion had not forbidden and Godri mounted him. He could not shed that born rider short of flinging himself down and rolling; and that, even in his fit of temper, he was too sensible to do. He contented himself with flattened ears and horns lowered not quite enough for threat, keeping to the place reckoned proper for the squire who rode him, and stabbing Estarion with darts of acute displeasure.

I too, brother, Estarion said to him behind words.

Ulyai would not even pass the first gate. She tried. She clung as close as Estarion's idiot mount would allow, from Induverran across the plain to Kundri'j. But as the walls drew closer, her ears went flatter, her tail lashed more fiercely. Before the bridge that spanned the river of Asanion, broad brown Shahriz'uan, she halted. Her muzzle wrinkled, baring fangs. She could not bear the scent or the sound or the sense of this city of all the cities in the Golden Empire.

Her eyes were as close to pleading as an ul-queen's could ever be: pleading afire with rage. She could not cross the bridge. Not unless he laid his will on her.

And that, he would not do. *Go,* he willed her. *Be free.*

A yowl escaped her, a cry of protest. She wheeled. Seneldi shied. She broke through them, running swift as a shadow on the grass. The last horned idiot veered and skittered. Then she was free. The plain was open before her, her freedom calling. She sped to meet it.

Estarion's heart yearned after her. But he was bound by his word and his damnable duty.

He shifted in the saddle. His mount plodded on. The sun beat down. The city swallowed him.

Nine circles in the circle of the river, Shahriz'uan in its chains of locks and bridges. Nine levels as in the courts of this empire, from lowest to highest, from plain white marble to burning gold. It turned its splendor toward him, its high houses, its thousand temples, its broad plazas and straight ways, even its gardens and its cool places. The walls were hung with banners, the fountains flowing with wine and sweet perfumes, the way paved with flowers or carpeted with richness, priceless rarities to be trampled under hoof and foot.

He would happier have seen that wealth fed to the people who were not permitted to line the ways, the poor and the sick, the maimed, any who fell short of perfection. They were there: he felt them. There was hunger here, and sickness in this unrelenting heat. Squalor behind the splendor. A reek of dung beneath the heavy scent of flowers.

The imperial majesty was not to see such things, not to know of them, lest they sully him. His Asanian teachers had not said so in as many words. They knew it, as he knew that majesty must see everything, the dark and the bright, and know the face of death as he knew life. How else could he rule? How else speak for his people in the courts of the god?

He passed through the nine gates, white marble, black marble, lapis, carnelian, jasper, malachite, ice-blue agate, silver, and last of them all, the innermost, bright gold. It drank the sun's heat and poured it forth again, a blinding brightness, a fire as terrible as that which burned in his hand.

His mount halted unbidden. He raised burning hand to burning gate. It did not rock and fall.

It was only stone sheathed in gold. The sun was only sun, fierce with the breath of summer on Asanion's plain. His hand was flesh, his arm, his shoulder itching where he could not scratch.

Laughter welled in him. The Olenyai who rode ahead, the point of the spear, understood at last that he was not behind them. The court in back of him, the Guard, the servants in their multitudes, had begun to knot and tangle.

He was a great discomfiture to the heart of the Golden Empire. He kicked the senel back into its amble, and passed through the gate.

From Golden Gate to the Gate of the Lion was an avenue of lions, great stone beasts crouched on guard. The gate itself was a frieze of lions on the hunt and in the pride, rearing rampant to form the lintel and the posts. There was a joy in them that struck Estarion strangely in this joyless place, a delight in their play, even a welcome for this lost mongrel child riding under them, into the prison that was the Golden Palace.

Lord Firaz was waiting beyond the gate, on foot, attended by courtiers in the robes of princes. He greeted Estarion with the nine prostrations and the nine great salutations, less the tenth that was for the emperor enthroned. Then he took Estarion's bridle and led him inward, pacing slowly, as princes did in the Golden Empire.

The chain of courts opened and closed before them. In one they left the seneldi. In another, Estarion's courtiers found themselves politely but firmly directed toward another way than the one on which he was led. In the next, all but the core of his Guard fell back; but the bulk of the Olenyai were kept back as well, and that was a comfort. Lightly guarded, with the Regent ahead of him still, not quite touching him to guide him, he came to the heart of the palace.

The Sunborn had built the hall of the throne in Endros in the image of this: the Hall of the Thousand Years with its thousand pillars and its roof of gold, wide enough for armies to march in, and a floor of panels inlaid with jewels and gold, that could be lifted up from golden sand and dust of jewels, ruby, sapphire, topaz, emerald. The throne was moated so, behind a black wall of Olenyai.

In older days the throne had been a great bowl of gold lifted on the backs of golden lions. That did not please its last trueblood emperor. He had had it remade, suffering its lions to stand as they had stood for a thousand years, but setting on their backs a broad chair. Two could sit there on an abundance of cushions, taking their ease, and behind them a marvel of jewelwork: a lion rampant upon the face of a golden Sun.

Estarion faltered. He had come well-nigh to the wall of Olenyai, hardly marking the glittering ranks of the High Court, aware chiefly of the man who led him and the guards who paced behind, and the throne to which he came. It was not the great work of magery that was the throne in Endros, and yet it had its own power. Hirel Uverias had made it to share with his Varyani empress. Their son had sat in it, and their son's son. Their names rang in his memory. Hirel and Sarevadin, Ganiman, Varuyan, Ganiman. And now, if he did not falter, Meruvan Estarion.

He was dazzled, or ill with heat. He saw a shadow on the throne, a dark man, dark-eyed, with a sudden, brilliant smile. Not a young man, for he had married late, but still in the prime of his manhood, and gifted with the light bold spirit of his Gileni mother. He bore the weight of robes with easy grace, wore the mask when he must and smiled at it after, and was all the emperor that the Asanians could have wished for. And they killed him.

The throne was empty. Lord Firaz had just begun to perceive Estarion's hesitation. Before he could pause or turn, Estarion finished the stride he had begun. Briefly he wondered if the Olenyai would hold the way against him. But they parted smoothly, with no sign of reluctance.

Lord Firaz halted at the foot of the dais. Estarion must mount alone. One waited beside the throne, prince of seven robes with a face as like to the Regent's as a brother's or close cousin's, and in his hands, upheld with the barest hint of waver, the tenth robe, the emperor's mantle, woven of silk and gold.

It was as heavy as worlds. How the Asanian had borne it, Estarion could not imagine. He was a small man even for one of his kind, and yet he laid the mantle about Estarion's shoulders, hardly trembling with the effort, and secured it, and sank down in obeisance. It was not Estarion's part to raise him, still less to thank him. He backed down the steps and past the Olenyai, into the first rank of princes.

Estarion stood erect in front of the throne, though the mantle's weight strove to bow him down. The court lay flat to a man, all but the Olenyai, black motionless stones among the pillars of the hall.

Then at last Lord Firaz came up. He held the mask, the dreadful golden thing that Estarion had refused. It glittered in his hands. Blind eyeless face, Asanian to the last graven curl of its nostril, and beautiful in the way of these people: broad low brow, full cheeks, straight nose, lips that seemed as soft as a girl's. It was all smooth curves, no planes, no angles. It grew no beard. It never aged or scarred, or suffered the shame of a flaw.

Estarion reached, startling the Regent, capturing the mask. It was gold, and heavy, and despite the heat of the air it was cool. He lifted it. Its eyes were narrow windows on a world gone strange. Olenyai backs. The clean line of a pillar. A lord still prostrate, hair thinning on his skull, sadly exposed within the circle of his coronet.

Estarion lowered the mask before it touched his face. He kept it in his hands as he sat, giving in at last to the weight of his robes. Lord Firaz had recovered himself. Estarion could not tell whether he approved, or whether he chose to take the bargain he was given. He spoke in a clear, strong, trained voice, words as numerous as the grains of sand under the paneled floor; but all of them came simply to this: "Behold, lords of the Golden Courts. Behold your emperor!"

It was no more terrible than receiving homage from the throne of Endros. Estarion had not expected that. His back grew tired; his rump protested the long hours of sitting. Worse was hunger, but thirst was worst of all. This was a test of imperial hardihood, to bring him straight from the road into the hall, and set him down without food or drink or pause to rest, and compel him to accept the full homage of the High Court.

But he had done almost as much in Keruvarion, coming to audience from the hunt or the practice-field, forgetting to send for wine or water, and laboring till dark over matters of state. His mother was not here to call him away, nor did a servant creep up behind with a filled cup. That was not done in Kundri'j Asan. The emperor must not appear to be a human man, with a man's needs of the body. He did not even join in banquets, although his son and heir might do so.

Peculiar logic, Estarion thought, considering how many feasts he had suffered on his journey here. Then he had been the Varyani emperor, but not yet full lord of Asanion. Now that he would have welcomed a cup of water as a gift from heaven, he was forbidden anything but homage.

A weaker man would faint, or call a halt to the ordeal.

Estarion refused. He received the respects of every lord in that hall, singly and in companies, father or eldest brother with all his sons and brothers and cousins and hangers-on, each of whom must be named to the imperial majesty, and his place affirmed, his authority made certain by the emperor's decree.

There was none who came as that lord had come to the throne of Endros, defiant out of turn. Nor did his lordship appear among the princes of five robes. Estarion was cravenly glad. These Asanians were making the best of the emperor they had. They did not afflict him with hostility, nor did they try visibly to shame him.

The emperor did not speak at the giving of homage, which was a mercy. His Regent spoke for him, or his Voice if he had one. Firaz did duty for both. He said all that an emperor should say, in phrases as elegant as they were politic. No insults there, that Estarion could discern; no errors in the myriad shades of inflection.

He could grow accustomed to this. The knowledge chilled him. So many years, so many battles, so much hatred of Asanion and Asanians, and he sat here, surrounded with them, and he accepted it. Worse than that: he knew that he was born for it.

Maybe it was a poison. Or a mage's trick; though the ache in his head was for his empty stomach, and not for the touch of sorcery.

The last princeling came, made his obeisances, withdrew. Estarion sat unmoving, but no one else came forth. He was to rise, then. Stiff, struggling not to sway. The hall stretched endless in front of him. He must walk the length of it, mantled if not masked.

He could not do it. It was nearly sunset; he had not eaten or drunk since before dawn. He was drained dry.

He essayed a step. He did not fall. Another. It bred another. Like Asanians in their harems, spawning sons. That made him want to laugh, dizzily, weak with fasting. And was that a fast, then, this mere day's stretch? He had gone thirsty three days running in the cause of his priesthood, and fasted longer, until his body was a light and singing thing, and his soul stood all naked to the sun.

Pride, then. Stubbornness. He would not show himself weak to the court of his western empire. He hated them for testing him. He loved them as he loved anything that dared him to outmatch it.

He walked unaided from the hall down the passage that presented itself, into the room on which it opened. Servants waited there. The one who relieved him of the mantle won the most loving of all his smiles. The one who brought him water in a golden cup, gained a prayer of thanks unto the hundredth generation. It was not a eunuch, either, which was Estarion's good fortune. Ungelded servants were rarer, he had noticed, the closer one came to the throne. Were they afraid that the emperor would be seduced as women were, and bear a child out of turn?

He was too wise to ask them that. He drank the cool sweet water, and never mind that the boy who brought it had sipped it first lest it be poisoned. There were cakes too, and something with spices in it, and fruit, whole and sour-sweet. He was wise with a priest's wisdom. He did not gorge himself on either food or drink, but partook slowly, sparingly, letting each sip or bite settle well before he essayed another. The servants freed him from his robes while he ate, combed the tangles from his hair, indicated with Asanian subtlety that he could bathe when he was ready.

He wanted most to fall upon the couch that stood against the wall, and not wake till morning; but a bath was a potent enticement. He let himself be led into a chamber like a hall under the sea, all green and blue and sun-shot gold, with a play of tiled fishes, and a pool as wide as a lake, full of warm and ever-flowing water. He opened his mind without thinking, reached for the one who was not there, who had not been there in a bitter count of Brightmoon-cycles. *Vanyi, look. Here's a bit of your sea, all in the dry land.*

But she was gone, her mind closed away as if she had never been, or been part of him. He was alone.

Truly. None of his Guard had come so far, none of his court, his priests, not even his mother. She was in the queen's palace as was proper. If he would speak with her, he must summon her.

He opened his mouth to do it. Then he shut it, and likewise his mind. She had forced him to this. Let her know what she had done, and suffer its consequences.

VANYI WAS PROUD of herself. Having left Estarion to his own devices, she devoted the whole of her self to her duties and her priesthood. She was not even dreaming of him every night now, nor missing him for more than two heartbeats out of three. Sometimes, when they were still in Induverran, she had seen him from a distance. He looked well, if harried, and strikingly cool in the heat.

In Kundri'j Asan she did not see him. He was shut up in the palace behind the gates and walls of gold, where no woman walked and no commoner might go. She had her place in the temple of the Two Powers within the wall of lapis, in the third circle of the city. Its Worldgate was as potent as that in Endros, with holiness on it beyond its simple power, for it had been made by the Mageguild itself. This had been the guildhall, this house like any other in this circle of the city, neither the richest nor the poorest of those about it. Priests of god and goddess had kept it so after the Guild died out, altering it little save to set an altar in its central court. Common people did not know, maybe, what power dwelt here. Some came to worship, and the priests did turn and turn about in the rites, but most chose other temples.

It was a quiet place, for all its weight of memory. Vanyi could have been happy there, searching out its secrets, prowling its library that had been left when the images went away. Her old fascination with the Guild was whetted here, tantalized with glimpses into their lore and their magics.

Iburan refused the place of chief priest although he far outranked the mistress of the temple; he was content to serve where he was needed, to stand guard on the Gate in his turn, and to go rarely to the upper city and the high temple of Avaryan and Uveryen. He never said, nor indicated by glance or strayed thought, but Vanyi suspected that he was not fond of the high priestess. She was a proud cold creature of princely Asanian blood, such as raised steadier hackles than Estarion's; nor did she make a secret of her dislike for Iburan. Great northern bear, she called him, and other things less flattering.

Thus he did service like penance in the least of the temples in Kundri'j, and bowed his head and was humble, and made no move to put himself forward.

"She has no power," he said to Vanyi not long after they came to Kundri'j. She remembered it afterward as the day the lightning fell. In that hour it was simply another breathless, airless, hideously hot day, its only distinction that its sky was the color not of brass but of lead. She could feel the heat building, hammer on the anvil of the earth.

This temple had a garden of strange flowers—fruit of Magegates, Iburan said, and as secret as the rest of it. Vanyi plucked a blood-red bloom with a scent that both dizzied and steadied her, like her lover's kiss. She almost cast it away, thinking of him, but tucked it in her hair instead and sat on the rim of a fountain. The spray of water was cool on her hand.

Iburan plucked a fruit the color of a maiden's cheek in Asanion, and bit into it. "She's no mage, my lady Himazia," he said when he had chewed and swallowed. "She knows this temple only as a nuisance, a tendril of my jurisdiction in the heart of her domain."

"They don't have priest-mages here," Vanyi observed. "Not as they do in the east."

"They don't like to believe in magery." He spat out the fruit-pit, knelt, buried it carefully in a bit of open earth, watering it with handfuls from the fountain. "There now," he said to it. "Sleep well; grow strong, and bear fruit."

"It's not that there are no mages," Vanyi said after a pause, due respect to his invocation. "They have too many, maybe. Every lord has his sorcerer in grey. Do you wonder, sometimes, if the Guild didn't die out after all, or subsume itself into our priesthood? What if it survived in secret, in Asanion? A mage killed Ganiman the emperor. Maybe he wasn't alone when he did it."

"We never found an accomplice," Iburan said. He sat on the fountain's rim a little distance from her, and washed the fruit's sweetness from his beard. "The Guild died a natural death. Anyone will tell you so. After it failed to raise a puppet emperor on the throne of the two lands, and was subjugated to the will of Sarevadin and her consort, it withered into nothing. Mages had no desire to join a guild of traitors. Those who were willing or able to bear discipline accepted the torque. The rest took teaching from the priests and went their ways, sworn and bound to work no harm."

"All of which I know," said Vanyi sharply. "I heard it the first day I went to our priestess in Seiun and told her I wanted to learn. What if she was wrong? Consider what Hirel did to the army of his brothers, any one of whom could have supplanted him or his half-bred son. He shut them in the palace, gave them all that they could ask for—but no women. No children. If the palace galled them, they could leave freely, on one small condition. They must leave their manhood behind and go out as eunuchs. His sisters were free to do as they pleased, but they could never marry, never bear children to challenge his heir. It was a brilliant solution. Merciful, even. What if he did the same to the Guild?"

"He did, in his way," Iburan said.

"And if the Guild saw it, and saw through it? What then? Mightn't they have pretended to dwindle and vanish, but only gone into hiding?"

"It would be difficult," said Iburan, "to conceal such powers as they would need to raise, simply to train their young mages. We would know. We'd have sensed them long ago, and disposed of them."

"Not if they used Gates," Vanyi said.

Iburan sighed, but not with temper. "So. You've thought of

that, too? We've found nothing. You know that. You're a Guardian."

"I don't think," said Vanyi, "that we should grow lazy simply because we haven't found anything. They'd be expecting it, you know. The last Guildmage who would admit to it died when Varuyan was emperor. It's been a solid generation since. Time enough to dig in deep and build the walls high."

"Have you had a Seeing?" he asked her.

"No," she said. She was irritable: that surprised her. "You know that's not one of my talents. I'm just thinking. Maybe it's this place. It remembers. It doesn't like us much."

"That it doesn't." He was smiling. His beard hid the curve of his lips, but his eyes were warm, even wicked. "You are marvelously gifted with power; more, one might think, than you have any right to be."

That did not help Vanyi's temper at all. "I'm not too badly trained, and I have Gate-sense. I'm nothing more than that."

"But you are," said Avaryan's high priest in Endros. "It's time you admitted it."

"Why now?" she demanded. "Why here?"

"Because it pleases me," he said, "and because you've made a study of the Guild and its Gates, and your bones tell you to be uneasy. None of the rest of us is so troubled."

"Not even you?"

She had not meant her voice to sound as hard and mocking as it did. Iburan did not take umbrage at it. "Not even I. I'm jealous, I confess. If I were a shade less wise, I'd even be angry. Who are you, after all, but a priestess on Journey, and a commoner at that?"

Her own frequent words, spoken with exquisite irony. She blushed and glowered, and bit her tongue before she said something even more unfortunate than she had already said.

"Priestess," he said, wholly grave for once, "never let your lack of rank or lineage shield you from the truth. If your power tells you that you should be wary, listen to it. Heed it. Act as it bids you. And if you have need of me, wherever you or I may be, call on me, and I will come."

Vanyi shifted on the fountain's rim. Her body was as reluctant as her mind to accept what he was telling her. That she was not a priestess-mage like any other. That she was—could be—more than that. Maybe much more. More even than an empress.

Her body knew how to stop that thought before it ran wild. It had been long cycles since she had had a man, and would be longer yet, unless she let the priests restore the bindings. Her womb was open still, unspelled. It made a useful refuge from a harder truth.

Useful; and safe, which her body well knew. Even if she had not risked breaking her vows again, she would do no more than fidget under Iburan's splendid black eye. Everyone knew whose bed he went to when the temple did not keep him for itself. Everyone, that is, but Estarion. One way and another he had failed to notice, and people had failed to enlighten him. Wise of them. He would not be pleased to know how his mother found comfort in her widowhood. Sons could be odd that way. Every man's mother a saint, and every man's sister a maiden.

She stood up abruptly. "I have duties," she said; or something like it. She did not look to see if Iburan's smile turned mocking; or if he knew all of the reasons why she fled.

The Gate was at rest as Gates went, wandering with dreamslowness through its manifold worlds. This one could, if one but asked, come to the center and focus of the Gates' power, the Heart of the World. That stronghold stood amid bare and barren mountains under a moonless sky, on a world that had no name. Its center was a blaze like a hearthfire, but it was pure power. It had made the Gates in the beginning, and it had made an empress of a Varyani high prince, and in the end it had betrayed the mages who made it. Sarevadin was part of it, wrought in it. She mastered it and the Guild, and drew its claws; but not before it had killed her mother and her consort's father, and driven her own father mad. She never forgave the mages, never trusted them or granted them power in her empire. Therefore they dwindled and the priest-mages of Endros rose to take their place, but in subservience to the Sun's blood, and not in power over them.

The strength of the Gate here was such that three priests watched by night, two by day when the sun's power balanced that of the Gate. The other who watched now was a stranger, an Asanian girlchild, mute with shyness. Vanyi let her be. She would warm in time, as young animals did. Her magery was a bright and singing thing, as splendid as her outer seeming was dull.

They sang the rites together, the child's voice light, almost without substance, Vanyi's darker, smokier. The meeting of voice and power bred a silent amity.

They settled to prayer, content in one another's presence. Vanyi was aware in her body of the Gate at rest, the land under her, the air heavy with heat. The sky beyond the temple was like a roof, looming low, breeding thunder.

Well indeed, thought Vanyi. Please the god, the heat would break. She would be able to breathe again. People would stop snarling at one another; the city would retreat from its raw edge of violence. Nothing had erupted yet, perhaps for fear of the emperor's presence, but it was there, smoldering like fire under ash.

Almost without her willing it, her power divided itself. Part went on warding the Gate. Part ranged over the city, testing its mood.

She glanced at the Asanian priestess. That one seemed unperturbed. It was always so, her manner said. Kundri'j was an angry city. It smoldered; sometimes it burst into flame. Then people rioted, and the soldiers came, or if affairs were desperate, the Olenyai—this with a shiver of fear and sharp dislike. Now the emperor was here. People did not love his outland self, but his rank comforted them, and his presence in the palace.

Vanyi had no reason to be uneasy. She was not a seer. Old

tales were rankling in her, half-rotted fears, treason overheard in the temple in Induverran, strangeness in the Gate of Endros. This Gate was at peace. Its stars, when they shimmered past, were simple stars. Its worlds were worlds without fear.

And suppose, she thought, the Guild survived. It had made the Gates. Suppose that it could wield them, shape them to show only what the Guardians wished to see, while it drew in secret from their power.

There was an insect in the Isles. The male possessed a maddening incessant buzz, but did not bite. The female was silent; she drank blood, and left great itching welts where she had been. Silence was the warning, people said. When there was no sound, no evidence of the creature's passing, then one did well to be wary.

Fine way to drive oneself mad, thought Vanyi sourly. *I hear nothing, therefore I fear everything.* The Gate and the temple were at peace. The sky was readying to burst, but that was nothing to fear under this roof, in walls of stone and magecraft.

Guildcraft.

She got up abruptly, paced from end to end of the sanctuary. Her companion watched her wide-eyed. She tried to smile. It only drove the child back into her shyness.

This house was built by mages of the Guild. This Gate was their Gate. These stones were imbued with their power, however thickly overlaid with the power of the priests. If they truly had not vanished, if they chose to come through, they would be idiots to emerge here, into the Guardians' arms.

Such Guardians. One a year from full priesthood, the other little more than a novice.

"I'm losing my mind," Vanyi said aloud. The little priestess did not understand her broad Seiun dialect. She said in Asanian, "I wish this heat would break."

"Soon," the priestess managed to say, great boldness in one so shy.

"Now," said Vanyi. The word had no power in it, nothing but hope approaching desperation, but she could make it happen. She could shatter this heat, these clouds, this terrible, breathless waiting.

Magery was not for compelling the sky to do one woman's will. Such threatened the balance that sustained the world. If she broke the storm too soon, one domain's crops could wash away, another's wither in drought. She was no god, to make such choices.

She felt the power building above her. The Gate's shifting was quicker now, its edges sharper. Vanyi's power firmed itself, weaving more tightly with the Asanian's.

"This is a mother of storms," the child said. "Watch for the winds. They're treacherous. They like to spin and roar, and then they eat anything they find. But don't be afraid. If one comes near us, we can coax it away."

And if one would not be coaxed? If it were driven by living will, by the malice of an enemy?

It was only a storm. When it had passed, the heat would have broken, the air would be clean and cool and blessedly sweet. Vanyi would get her temper back again, and she would stop vexing herself with shadows.

Break, she willed it. *Damn you, break.*

The Gate was pulsing like a heart. Vanyi sent out a summons. Three would serve better here than two.

She did not wait to see who answered, but began to match her breaths to the pattern of the Gate. When they pulsed together, she shaped the notes of the breaking-chant. Beat, pause. Beat, beat, pause. Beat, pause, beat. Breaking that perilous rhythm which, sustained, could shatter the Gate.

It fought her. The storm was in it, lending it strength. The little priestess chimed a descant. The Gate wavered. Had it been a living thing, Vanyi would have reckoned it confused.

That too was dangerous. Confusion could shatter more easily even than that relentless beat-beat-beat.

A third voice entered the weaving, a third power like a pillar of light. It shored them up; it mastered the Gate. *Iburan.* The name was pure power.

All at once, with a roar like armies charging, the storm broke.

It was glorious. Freed of fear for the Gate, secure in the threefold weaving, Vanyi rode the lightnings. Winds raged; she laughed at them. Rain lashed the roofs of the city, scoured the dust from its streets, churned its lanes to mud. The river roared in its bed.

The heat was gone, shattered. The land heaved a mighty sigh. The lightnings ran away eastward, drawing the winds in their wake. The rain came down more gently.

Vanyi slipped back into her body. She was kneeling before the Gate, the little priestess on one side of her, Iburan on the other, all three clinging together. The Gate was restless still, but growing quiet as she watched.

All of itself, her voice soared up, chanting the god's praises. Iburan's wove into it, drum-deep; and the little priestess' like the call of a bird. They sang the storm away and brought back the sun, bright in the blue heaven.

But the Gate remained the Gate. And Vanyi's heart was not at ease, however much she willed it to be so.

21

"THAT ONE IS strong," a darkmage said.

The Guildmaster raised his eyes from the scrying-glass. They were red-rimmed; the lines of his face were slack with weariness. "Which? The black priest? We knew that long ago."

"No," said the darkmage. "The young one, the Island woman. I should fear her, I think."

"She is nothing," said the Guildmaster.

The darkmage looked as if he would have argued, but they had by then taken notice of the stranger at the door. Korusan suppressed an unbecoming stab of malice that even the great Master of mages had failed to mark his coming. They had been preoccupied—pressingly so, from the look of them.

He did not let his eyes wander to the scrying-glass, sorely though it might tempt them. He had yielded to one like it before, and been ill for days after. There was too much magic in him, he had been given to understand, and yet too little. Too much to be impervious to the lure of the visions in the glass, too little to defend him when they sucked at his soul.

"My prince," the Guildmaster said. "You are welcome in Kundri'j Asan."

No word of disapproval that Korusan should have come to this city. No suggestion of anger that he had dared it. "Is it not my city?" Korusan said. "Am I not to be lord of it?"

"In time," the Guildmaster said, "you shall."

Korusan circled the room and the gathering of mages, keeping his distance from the glass on its frame. "How marvelous," he said, "that you lair here, deep in the enemy's palace. And none of them suspects that you exist."

"One does," said the darkmage who had spoken before:

stubbornly, Korusan thought, and not at all prudently. "She pries into the library we so unwisely left intact. She questions what none of her kind should question."

"She is no danger to us," the Guildmaster said. "What can she know but that we were once strong?"

"She knows Gates," the darkmage persisted. "She could almost be one of us."

"Had she been one of us," said the lightmage who stood beside him, gently enough but with an edge of impatience, "she would have been known, found, brought among us before ever the Sun-cult had her."

"There are few of our order in the Isles, and those hard pressed by Sun-magic and sea-magic. She could easily have escaped them. As," the darkmage said, "she has escaped you even yet."

"Hush," the lightmage said, with a glance at Korusan. The darkmage looked stubborn but held his tongue. He would take up the battle again later, his expression promised.

Korusan wondered if this one would go the way of the lightmage who had been too honest in the face of his questioning. "Who is this woman you speak of? Is it anyone whom I should fear?"

"No, no one," the Guildmaster said, even as the darkmage said, "A priestess, a mage—she was the emperor's lover, they say she is that no longer, she—"

Mages closed in on him, silencing him, easing him out of the circle and the room. It was smoothly done. Korusan observed it with interest and a glimmer of pity. Outspokenness was never a virtue in an Asanian, whether he be mage or prince.

"My prince," said the Guildmaster when the importunate one was gone, "you are welcome here as always, but perhaps you would choose to rest from your journey in greater quiet than we can offer."

"I have rested," Korusan said. "My Master bids you attend him."

The master of the mages did not look pleased to be so summoned, even by the Lion's cub. Korusan was prepared for his resistance, and mildly disappointed when he acquiesced. "I will come," he said, "when I am done here."

Korusan inclined his head, all courtesy. "I wait upon your pleasure."

"You may go," the mage said, "my prince."

"I am bidden to accompany you," Korusan said.

"You accept a master's bidding?"

Korusan smiled in his veil. "I choose to accept it." He took the stance of the guard at rest, hands resting lightly on swordhilts, and set himself to wait. He was precisely in the path of any mage who wished to leave the room—fools, they, for trapping themselves where was but a single door. They must brush past him or walk round him if they would go about their duties.

They made no more workings while he watched, nor spoke unless it were from mind to mind. One of them covered the terrible beauty of the glass. Others cleared away the tools of their trade, odd small things that made Korusan's skin quiver. Their master watched and said nothing. When the last of it was done and its doer had departed past Korusan, the Guildmaster still did not move.

Korusan was in comfort, now that the glass was hidden. He could fight patience with patience.

The mage spoke abruptly. "Have you looked upon your enemy?"

"No," said Korusan. His voice was sharper than he liked.

"He is here. You know that, surely. They enthroned him these three days past."

Korusan had known. He was being tested again as always, his temper tried to see if it would break. "It is not the throne that makes the king," he said.

"There are many who would dispute you," said the mage. "The throne, the power, the backing of the courts and the armies—all those, he has."

"But I," said Korusan, "have you."

"Do you, prince? You like us little, you trust us less. If you could dispose of us, you would do so and be glad of it."

"But I cannot, and I will not, while your purposes serve mine. You have wagered all on this last cast of the bones—my bones, frail as they are. Only remember: you have called me your prince. As your prince I may command you. And I will look ill upon your disobedience."

"We will obey you," the Guildmaster said, "while you show yourself our ally."

That would do, thought Korusan. It must. He stepped aside, and bowed slightly. "Come. The Master of the Olenyai waits."

The two masters of their orders conspired at nothing that Korusan had not heard before. It had chiefly to do with Olenyai deployed here, mages deployed there, and rebellions fomented through the satrapies of Asanion. Of the emperor in this palace they said nothing.

And yet it was the emperor who mattered. Korusan left them, gaining a glance from the Olenyas and no apparent notice from the mage. Perhaps they thought that he went to the cell that had been given him. He thought of it, would have been glad of it, but his mind would not let him rest. It leaped and spun, driving him through this stronghold within a stronghold, this chief of the postings of the Olenyai.

Inevitably it drove him out into the palace. His robe and his veils granted him passage wherever he wished to go, except perhaps the harem; but that he did not approach. It was empty, he had been told, for the Sunlord had no woman but the priestess who knew Magegates, and she had left his bed. The queen's palace, which was occupied, tempted Korusan slightly, but the guards there were women, and some had magic. He veered away from them.

He was circling, he knew that. Round and round about, narrowing slowly to a certain center.

The emperor of Asanion had lived for time out of mind like a prisoner in his own palace. He had his chambers, and they were many; his courts, and they were broad; his wonted ways and his expected duties. But he did not pass the walls. He did not walk free in the world. That was the price and the sacrifice with which he bought his power.

The outland savage was shut up as tightly as any son of the Lion. Korusan half expected to hear him roaring somewhere deep within, but the halls were quiet, the chambers cool in the heat of the day. There were foreigners about, black men and brown men, even a few women; priests with their torques, guards in alien livery, a lordling or two eyeing the splendors of the palace as if he had a mind to buy. None of them ventured to question the lone Olenyas. They were afraid of him, he thought, catching their glances and watching them shrink aside. Wise fools. It was not his robe that they needed to fear, or even his swords. All his body was a weapon.

Of the Olenyai here, some were strangers. Many were not. One greeted him with Olenyai effusion: eyes that smiled, voice that called softly in battle-language for there was no one near to hear. "Brother! How did you come here?"

Korusan moved smoothly into position on the other side of the door that Marid guarded, and permitted a smile to creep into his voice. "I rode," he said. "And you?"

Marid slapped his right-hand swordhilt, half in mirth, half in exasperation. "You know what I meant. I thought the mud-robes would never let you loose."

"I let myself loose," said Korusan. "Whose door is this?"

"I think you know," said Marid.

"He is within?"

Korusan must have sounded more eager than he meant to: Marid raised a hand. "Down, lad! You can't have his blood yet. We're all under orders. We're to guard him as if he really were the emperor, and show ourselves loyal, and not a thought out of line."

"Have you seen him?" Korusan asked.

Marid's answer was cut off before it began. Footsteps approached them. They froze in the stillness of sentries, eyes schooled to blankness. The one who passed wore scarlet and gold, and his face—Korusan labored not to stare.

"What in the worlds—" he began when the creature had gone within.

"That is the emperor's bodyservant," Marid said. "Lovely, isn't he? He's a savage from the desert. He's killed a dozen men, they say, and he maimed a thirteenth to win his place by the emperor's side."

Korusan widened his eyes at that. "Truly? And was he born with such a face?"

"Oh, no. Those are his manhood-marks and his killing-marks, and some of them are for a prince. He'll talk to us sometimes. He's almost human under the devil-mask."

How strange, thought Korusan. How utterly foreign. His stomach was tight, but for once it did not want to empty itself. Perhaps it understood that he was here, at last, where he needed most to be.

He set hand to the door's latch. Marid frowned at him. "You aren't going to. Are you?"

Korusan answered by opening the door. Marid did not stop him. Duty bound the other to keep his post, but Korusan had no orders yet, and no ban upon him.

He knew these chambers within as if he had dwelt there all his life. They were the heart of his teaching, the place to which he had been born, in which he hoped to die. He walked in them like a shadow, faceless, unregarded: simply another of the Olenyai.

They were trusting in Keruvarion. That too Korusan had been taught, with some degree of incredulity; but his teachers averred that it was true. Now he saw the reality of it. All these open chambers, unquestioning guards, servants walking in and out; no locks, no bars in any place but one.

That one room had been the emperor's bedchamber. The

bar was new, the lock still bright from the forging. It did not yield to Korusan's touch.

"You! What do you there?"

He turned carefully, and not too quickly. The voice was sweet for all the barbarousness of its accent, speaking a rough but comprehensible Asanian patois. The speaker was half-expected, the tattooed savage in Varyani livery. He looked alarming, but his challenge held little hostility.

Korusan answered him in the same patois that he had spoken. "Do you hold his majesty prisoner?"

The emperor's servant looked narrowly at him, then shrugged. "What, are you new here? Of course we don't. That's where his father died. He won't go in, or let anyone else go in, either."

Such innocence. Korusan almost admired him for it. "The last emperor died these ten years past. Surely he does not bear the grief still."

"He can't forget. It almost killed him, too. He still has the black dreams."

"He is as weak as that?"

The savage's eyes glittered. "Only look at him, and you'll know that for the lie it is." He calmed himself visibly. "There now. You people don't know him; and mages are different, and Sunlords most different of all."

"It is clear to see," said Korusan, "that his servant loves him."

"So do all who know him." Someone called from down a passage. The savage snapped alert. "There! He's looking for me. Do your duty, blackrobe, but don't try to do it in there. He'll have your hide for a kilt."

Korusan followed the emperor's servant quietly, with steps that slowed, the deeper he went into the maze of chambers. Still he was not challenged. There were more of his own kind here, but they would reckon that he came under orders. And so he did if he was truly their prince, with authority to command himself.

The black king was in a chamber that had been meant for guests, but that he seemed to have claimed for his own. He must have come from High Court: his servant was divesting him of the robes.

Korusan had seen northerners since he came to Kundri'j. There had been enough of those in the palace, and others in the city and on the road. He had grown inured to black faces, arched noses, blue-black hair; he was prepared for towering height.

This was not a giant as his kind went. He was only a head taller than Korusan, and narrow, almost slight. He was long-legged like a colt, with some of a colt's awkwardness, as if he had not quite come to his growth; and maybe he would grow into the shoulders that seemed so wide against the rest of him.

No beauty, no. Ugly indeed, with that sooty skin, that blade of a nose, that long mobile mouth half-hidden in curling beard. His eyes were as keen a shock as Korusan had been warned to expect. They were all of the Lion, clear deep gold, no rim of white to lessen them, until he widened them at something that his servant said.

Korusan was braced for them, and for the coal of anger that burned his belly at the sight of them. He was prepared for strangeness, even for revulsion. But he had not expected to be captivated.

There was grace in that long body, something like beauty in the way the head turned, looking over his shoulder at the servant, who was struggling with the heavy masses of his hair. He smiled, white in that dark face, and said something in a tongue that Korusan did not know, that made the servant laugh. And Korusan was angry; no, Korusan was jealous, because neither of them had seen him, or cared that he watched.

He should have taken himself away, but he could not will his feet to move. This was the enemy of all that he was. This, taking its ease in these chambers that should have been Korusan's, casting off with patent contempt the robes to which

Korusan was born. Holding Korusan rooted with the purity of a line, long straight back, long plait down the center of it, long hand outstretched to touch the servant's shoulder, to rest lightly on it. "There, don't fret, I'll be well," the Sunlord said in Gileni. Korusan understood: he had been taught that tongue, the better to know his enemy.

Likewise in Gileni the servant said, "How can I not fret, my lord? You keep to yourself too much these days; and you left court so suddenly, as if you were ill, or worse. Won't you come out to the training ground? Won't you do a round with the swords?"

"Later," the Sunlord said, as if he humored a child. His voice was deep, like a lion's purr, but it had an odd clarity. The servant seemed troubled, opening his mouth as if to speak, seeming to think better of it. He withdrew slowly, giving his master ample time to call him back.

His master did not take it. Korusan, unmarked and undismissed, watched the outlander decide that he was alone. He stretched first, languidly, as a cat stretches, and yawned. His teeth were whiter than an Asanian's, sharper, the eyeteeth long and narrow and perceptibly curved.

He dropped the robe that still covered him. He was lean, skin stretched over smooth muscle, long bone. There was no softness to him. He was all planes and angles.

So strange. Hardly like a human creature at all. Korusan saw the glare of gold as the right hand came up, the impossible thing, the brand the priest-mages made when one of Sun-blood was born, swearing solemnly that it was bred there. But no living thing grew gold in its flesh.

The Varyani emperor wandered toward a curtained wall, caught at an edge, hurled back the hangings with vehemence that made Korusan start. Sun flooded the room. Through the dazzle of it Korusan realized that this was a bank of windows, and they looked down on the gardens. One by one the outlander flung them open, letting in heat as well as light. He leaned on a windowframe, seeming to care not at all if anyone below should see his nakedness, and said to the hot golden air, "Sometimes I think that my dreams are real, and the Golden Palace all the world, and Keruvarion the delusion of a fevered brain. Sometimes I imagine that I've never breathed any air but this, never walked on ground not smoothed before me, never worn less than the nine robes of a high prince. Was I bred for this after all, do you think, and not for that other world?"

He was speaking Asanian, not perfectly but well enough. "Hound," he said, still to the air. "Patient, silent guardhound. What do you think of me?"

Korusan went very still. It was foolish: his presence was known. But instinct had its own logic.

The Sunlord was dripping light. It ran down him in streams like water, pooling on the floor. Impossible. Sorcerous. Magic wrought to overawe the credulous, to frighten the yellow-faced spy.

But there was no denying the sight of it. Korusan slid toward it, essayed it with a fingertip. It burned and stung. He drew back carefully, keeping the corner of his eye on the barbarian. Emperor he would not call him, not naked and shameless, head fallen back, eyes closed, wallowing in his puddle of sun.

When the creature turned, Korusan was taken by surprise. He was cat-quick, and not above malice. "There, my hound. Run at my heel. See what I do, faithful slave that I am, and obedient emperor."

Pure insolence. Korusan would teach him manners. He smiled behind his veils, and followed the black king, not for obedience, but to see what he would do.

22

Estarion had won a few small skirmishes. Lord Firaz was winning the war.

He had had a bellyful of High Court this morning, walked out of it before he did something more unfortunate; and now he went back, dragging robes. He could not even say why he did it. Sun's heat, maybe, addling his brain while it made his body stronger. Or a pair of yellow eyes in a swathing of veils, and a subtle shimmer of contempt as they looked at him. It had not gone away when he commanded the Olenyas to play body-servant, which the bred-warrior did, and did well, with mute obedience. It was still there as Estarion made his second entrance of the morning, breaking in upon a court that was doing very well without him, throwing it into an exquisitely restrained flurry. He lost sight of the guardsman thereafter among all the rest, but he fancied that he could feel those eyes upon him still, judging him and finding him wanting.

High Court was excruciating as always. The emperor did not speak; his Regent spoke for him—as coolly now as ever, no shadow of rebuke, and chiefly in platitudes, greeting this lord who had come from the far western provinces, well-wishing that princeling for his taking of a new wife. His seventh, Lord Firaz murmured under cover of the man's prostrations, and a great heiress; which was well, for his properties were insufficient to support the tribe of his sons.

Estarion bit his tongue. Lord Firaz was revealing a surprising store of wit, much of it wry. His aplomb, Estarion knew too well, was unshakable, even for an emperor who fled and then came back, breaking every dictate of propriety.

The next petitioner to be presented wore five robes to the

princeling's three. It was, Estarion realized, a child. He had thought it was a very small man: the infant carried himself so haughtily, refusing to bow beneath the weight of his robes, wearing an expression so rigid that surely it would shatter.

His name was almost longer than himself, with three princely houses in it, and one royal connection. "He is come," said Lord Firaz, "to beg your majesty's indulgence, and your forgetfulness of his father's sins."

Estarion raised a brow.

The child spoke for himself, which was just within the bounds of protocol. "My father," he said in a clear steady voice, "is dead. He regretted deeply his dishonor. He took his life as the canons prescribe. He died bravely, and courteously."

"How can death be courteous?"

Estarion had never spoken aloud in that place before. He fancied that his voice echoed, deeper than Asanian voices were wont to be, and barbarously accented. The child was too young or too scared to be shocked. He answered, "He wished your majesty to know that he atoned for his disgrace."

"What was that?"

"Majesty," said Lord Firaz, soft and smooth. "His father was that one who, so we are told, dared defy you in your court in Endros Avaryan."

For a moment Estarion's mind was blank. Then memory filled it. An Asanian lord paying homage out of turn. Estarion's great error, and the Asanian's greater one as his kind would reckon it, looking direct on the face of his emperor.

This son had his father's face, now that Estarion had eyes to see it, though soft yet and unformed. But he had not, it seemed, inherited his father's recklessness. Estarion regarded him in disbelief, and in swelling horror. "He killed himself? Simply because he tested me?"

"One does not test the emperor." The child sounded like no child then.

No, thought Estarion. Let him have his name. He was Nizad of the house of Ushavaar. Nizad said, "We will pay penalty as your majesty decrees. He is dead, his ashes scattered on the midden, and the honor is taken from his name. What more your majesty will have, we will pay."

"No," said Estarion. His heart was swelling, struggling in the walls of his chest. "No. I'll have them trying to kill me if that's their pleasure. I won't have them die for me."

"He defied you," said Nizad. "He deserved his death."

"He did not." Estarion pushed himself to his feet. "There is no dishonor. Do you understand? He only did as he thought best. The shame is mine. I spoke ill to him. I never thought that he would take his life for it."

Nizad raised wide astonished eyes. But never, quite, into Estarion's face. Estarion came down, dragging the world-weight of robes, and took the small cold hand. The Court was appalled. Again. He did not care. "I give you back your father's honor," he said. "All else that was his, I return to you. He was a brave man. I grieve that he took his life for so little a cause."

"You are everything," Nizad said. "You are the emperor."

Estarion sucked in a breath. There was no reasoning with them, any of them. "Go," he said: the first thing that came into his head. "Prosper. Prove that I'm no fool for shocking the Court speechless."

A normal child would have laughed, or smiled at least. Nizad dropped down on his face. Even his babble was flawless, not an inflection out of place. Estarion could pause to wonder at it, amid all the rest.

"They are not like us," Estarion said to Godri. "They are not like me. How can I rule them? I can't begin to understand them."

His squire looked a little strange himself, drawn and silent. "I don't think they understand themselves, my lord."

Estarion wanted to pull off the damnable robes and kick them as far as they would go. But he had done that already, too often. He had done everything that a rebel could do, or a captive, or a spoiled child.

"And for what?" he said aloud. "They still surround me. They still torment me. They still overcome me, no matter what I do."

Godri had nothing to say. Poor Godri. Estarion defeated him as Asanion defeated Estarion. But Godri loved his master, and Estarion hated his.

Hating it accomplished nothing. Estarion stopped, struck with the thought. It had occurred to him before; it had been beaten into his head. And yet. Suppose . . .

He began to smile. Godri's eye rolled like a startled senel's, which made Estarion smile wider. "Suppose," he said, "I gave them what they wanted. What then, do you think? Would they let me be, and take the chains from me?"

"I don't know, my lord," Godri said in a tone that indicated that he knew, and that Estarion would not like to hear the truth.

"You don't think they will," Estarion said. "But I have to try it, do you see? I'm trapped whatever I do. If there's one small chance that I can be free, will you fault me if I take it?"

"You'll do what you'll do, my lord, whatever I say to you."

Estarion drew him into a quick, hard embrace. "Oh, my poor friend! Such a trial I am, and you never say more than a word. I do love you for it."

"Maybe you should hate me," Godri muttered. But he smiled as if he could not help it, and when Estarion told him what he meant to do, the smile burst into laughter. Most of it was incredulity, but some at least was mirth. "It may only be another skirmish, my lord. But such a skirmish!"

Fortified by Godri's approval, Estarion prepared his battlefield with care. The servants surprised him by clothing him in the robes he asked for, and astonished him by bearing his message to the one for whom it was meant.

Lord Firaz came in good time, unruffled as always. Estarion wasted no time in nonsense. Having seen the Regent served with wine and cakes—both approved by the dun mouse of a taster—he said, "I've sent out a summons to the High Court. I'm to marry in Asanion, they say. Well and good. Let each lord and prince present his marriageable daughters. I shall choose as I best may, and get it over."

The Regent did not so much as widen his eyes. "Shall we say, then, that the ladies of the Court are to gather in, perhaps, a hand of days?"

"No," said Estarion. "Today. At the next turning of the glass."

"Sire," said his lordship with extreme delicacy. "These are ladies of the High Court, not—"

"Surely," Estarion said, "they've been prepared for this since I crossed the border into Asanion. They'll come to me in the sixth hour. Or will you tell me that every marriageable woman in the High Court is not now in the city, waiting on just this summons?"

"Your majesty is perceptive," said Lord Firaz. His tone was dry. It did not quite imply that his majesty was also precipitous. "Perhaps rather the seventh hour, when the day's warmth is diminished somewhat, and the hour of rest is past?"

"I have rested," said Estarion. He smiled. "Will you stand with me, so that I may choose wisely?"

The Regent bowed to the floor, not without irony. "As my lord wills," he said.

The hall of queens lay in the inner palace, behind gates guarded by women of the Queen's Guard and eunuchs of the Golden Palace, in walls as much of silence as of stone. Here the pillars were carved in intricate fashion with twinings of vines and flowers, and the walls behind them were thick with figured tapestries. The sun that came in, came in through narrow lattices; light here was lamplight, great banks and clusters of them, burning oil scented with flowers.

Estarion paused in the passage behind the throne. He had not been permitted to come so far before. A company of guards had gone ahead, eunuchs of the Golden Palace, and more of them surrounded him, and still more warded his back. What they feared, he could not understand. His father had been murdered in the emperor's chambers, in that room which Estarion had commanded to be locked and barred, and to which he did not go. If an assassin came, it would be a bold one indeed who ventured the protections of the women's palace. One who penetrated the outer palace had to fear only death: One who came as far as this, would die long and slow, and he would die a eunuch.

From where Estarion stood, the hall was clear to see behind a shimmer of curtain, and filling with veiled women. They came with little evidence of haste and no more flutter than one might expect. Their fathers and their brothers were not permitted here, but must wait in mounting anxiety in the outer palace. Eunuchs guarded them, and mothers and aunts and cousins, some old enough, or bold enough, to drop their veils.

A tall figure moved among them, robed as an Asanian lady, but those slender dark hands were not Asanian, nor that unveiled face. Estarion had not known till he saw her how sorely he had missed his mother's presence.

He could not tell if she disapproved of his haste. It was too like him, she had been known to observe. He was like a cat, asleep or idling daylong, then leaping to the hunt, and never a pause between. Estarion admitted it. But he was not about to change his mind, even for his mother's sake.

The hall was almost full. Estarion's nursemaids, having ascertained that there were no rats behind the arras, consented to allow him past the door. He could see clearly through the veil, but no one would be able to see him. It was remarkably like being a child and spying on one's elders through the curtains.

He was to mount the throne, there to sit while each lady was brought to him and presented with due ceremony. But his mood was purely contrary. He dropped all but the innermost and outermost of his robes, which should be enough to satisfy even Asanian modesty, and left the bulk of his guards staring at the heap of them, and walked calmly round the veil.

They were, most of them, watching the throne and not the

curtain behind it. He was well past the dais before anyone moved. A ripple ran through the hall, a whisper that in Asanion was appalling rudeness. And better than that, to his mind, mutters of doubt, objections, even resistance. How could that be the emperor? It was a lanky barbarian in a mere two robes, like a commoner with pretensions.

His mother turned at his approach. The light in her eyes made him want to weep. He had meant to kiss her hand with cool courtesy, but he found himself embracing her instead, clinging hard if not long. "Mother," he said in the language of her tribe. "Oh, Mother. They wouldn't let me go."

"You've grown thin," she said in the same tongue. "You're naught but a rack of bones. What have they done to you?"

"I've done it to myself." He mustered a smile. "It's not as bad as it looks. I've been out of the sun too long, that's all."

"I should never have forced you to this," she said.

A small prick of malice moved him to agree with her, but he mastered it. "Hush now," he said. He bent to set a kiss in each of her palms. "We're being rude, you know. Shall we bring out our best Asanian, and set about finding me a wife?"

"Maybe," she said, still in the speech of her youth, "maybe, after all—"

He could not let hope grow, that she would relent, that he could go home, win Vanyi back, be as he was before: innocent, and happy. "Come now," he said. "Here is Lord Firaz, and he promised he'd tell me who is rich and who is beautifully bred. Will you show me who is sensible, too, and maybe not excessively horrified to contemplate a barbarian in her bed?"

"Most of them are fascinated," Merian said, this time in Asanian. She took his hand: the left, that was like any man's. "Lord Firaz, what pleasure to see you here. Your ladies: are they well?"

They circled the hall slowly. Lord Firaz, having exchanged courtesies with the empress, proceeded to present each lady, her lineage and her connections and her prospects as a mother of sons, as if she were a mare in his stable and Estarion a stallion at stud. Merian was charming, setting the nervous at ease, coaxing smiles out of the shy or the sullen. Estarion did not say anything. He was noticing who darted glances at his face, and who managed to evade him in his course. He had never felt quite so much like a necessary evil before.

He met a pair of coin-gold eyes in a blue veil. They did not drop at once, or shrink from the sight of him. They belonged to someone whose path never quite crossed his. There was someone else next to her, one of the shy ones, no more than a bowed pink-veiled head and a strayed yellow curl. A very small, bent person in black had them in charge, herding them with skill, determination, and a talent for keeping them out of his majesty's way.

His majesty said something to the woman whom Firaz presented, words he never afterward remembered. The blue veil was losing itself in the crowd, and the pink beside it.

There was one great use and pleasure in the office of emperor. People did not get in his way. Estarion left his mother being pleasant to a woman whose name he had already forgotten, and went in pursuit of the lady who would look him in the face.

Her duenna was almost too clever for him. The fierce old thing led him a merry chase, making good use of a gaggle of plump startled maidens and a knot of guards, and a convenient pillar. Estarion stretched his stride round that, and almost laughed.

Trapped, and thoroughly: cornered for a fact. He knew how to fill an exit simply by standing straight and gangling less, and letting his shoulders be a wall. He tried not to grin. Asanians, like cats, did not show their teeth except to display their armament.

He bowed as an emperor might, for courtesy: an inclination of the head, a slight tilt of the body. "Ladies," he said. "Am I so fearful a monster, that you should run from me?"

The shy one hid her veiled face in her sister's shoulder. The bold one looked straight at him, and she was laughing, surely, the more her duenna glowered. "You are not handsome," she said, "as the canons would have it. But you are very interesting."

She had a clear light voice, a little sharp maybe, but pleasantly so. Estarion raised a brow, which made her eyes dance the more, and said, "I would rather be ugly and interesting than handsome and insipid."

"You are not ugly," she said. "At all. Just . . . different. Does it come off?"

He looked down at his bare sufficiency of robes. "I should hope so," he said.

She did laugh then, clear and free. "Not those, my lord! That." She managed somehow, without moving or touching him, to make it clear that she was pointing at his hands, and not at their shape, or even at the Sun's gold.

He turned them. They were perfectly ordinary hands, burning brand aside: long and narrow like the rest of him, callused from rein and shieldstrap and sword. She set her small round hand beside them, all ivory as it was, with long gilded nails. "You aren't born that way, my nurse told me. They rub you with soot when you are born, and every day after, till the color takes, and you're all black, which is what they call beautiful. What color are you really? Nurse said white, like a bone. I think brown. If you were white, the soot would only turn you grey."

Estarion had never heard such nonsense in his life. "I'm all as nature made me," he managed to say. "Here. Touch."

He thought that she would not. But she stretched out a hand that shook only a little, and brushed the arm he bared for her. Timidly at first, as if she feared the stain; then more boldly, stroking light but firm, as one should stroke a cat.

"You have fur," she said, "like an animal."

"Like a man," he said. He should have been offended. He was merely amused. There was an innocence in her, coupled with a brazen boldness, that one seldom saw even in children, and never in maidens of breeding in the High Court of Asanion.

And yet slaves and servants did not dress in sky-blue silk sewn with silver, or betray glints of gold at ears and throat and wrists and ankles. The one who must have been her sister was all that she was not, modest and shy and ladylike in every particular, and her duenna was a smolder of resentment.

"Do you have fur," she asked, "all over?"

He had a rush of heat all over, in places he would rather not have thought of. "Not quite," he said. "Don't Asanians have any?"

"Not that they'll admit to." She looked him up and down. "I suppose I'll have my eyes put out, or my tongue, for being so impudent. If I have a choice, may I keep my eyes? I talk too much, everyone says so; my tongue would be no loss. But I do like to look at you. The others are so dull. All the same color, and soft, like bread before it bakes."

He laughed. The shy maid surprised him: she did not cringe, but lifted her head and looked at him. Her eyes were softer than her sister's, more amber than gold, and full of astonishing mirth. "What are your names?" he asked them both.

"I am Haliya," said the bold one. "And this is Ziana, and our dragon is Gazi, who thinks that I should marry someone proper, and not an outland conqueror. Ziana and I were born on the same day, to the same father, and our mothers were sisters, which makes us sisters too, twice over. We're not rich, or not very, though we're noble enough. Our house is Vinicharyas. It used to be very great in Markad, but now it settles for being middling ordinary in Kundri'j."

"You are not ordinary at all," said Estarion. He liked to talk; too much, some people thought. But she was like a river in flood.

"We know who you are," said Haliya. "Are you going to have me punished? Nurse said that people are shockingly free with their emperors in Keruvarion, but she did like to tell stories, and not all of them were as true as one might wish."

"Emperors in Keruvarion are people like anyone else," he said. And at the widening of her eyes: "Well. Maybe not like anyone. But anyone can come up to me and talk to me. Look at me, even. Touch me. Make me feel like something other than a poppet on a stick."

"You do hate that, don't you?" Her sympathy tasted real, if not over-warm. "So do I. I tried to run away to Keruvarion once. My father whipped me himself, with his own hands. He was stiff for days after."

"And you weren't?"

"He didn't beat me very hard," she said. "It runs in the blood, you see: running away. Especially the womenchildren. I could hardly help it. I'm older now, of course. I know what's proper."

"I ran away once," said Estarion. "I wanted to be a tribesman by the Lakes of the Moon, and hunt the spotted deer."

"Did your father whip you when they brought you back?"

The chill that touched him was less than he had expected. He could answer her calmly, even lightly. "My father was dead. My mother decided that I had too little to do. She gave me a princedom to rule for myself, and no one to help or hinder, unless I acted abominably."

"And did you?"

"I sulked for days. But the princedom couldn't run itself. Its steward was old and growing feeble, and its lords and barons were trying the bonds of their fealty, and the merchants were padding their profits, and the people, the poor people, didn't deserve any of it. So I had to behave myself, you see, and do what I could. Without insulting the steward, starting a war among the barons, or driving the merchants out, because we needed them to buy the wool and meat and cloth that were our wealth, and to sell the things we needed: wood for the looms, iron for the needles, herbs and earths for the dyes."

She was listening with every evidence of interest, but he

stopped himself. "There now," he said. "I was prince in Umbros till I'd learned my lesson, and then we found a princess for it, and I went back to the life I'd run away from. It wasn't so ill, once I'd thought about it."

"A princess?" Ziana asked, so unexpectedly that he looked at her sister. But the voice was not the same, not at all. This was soft and low, trembling with the effort of being so bold. "A princess to rule a princedom?"

Estarion found himself speaking more gently, trying not to frighten her. "She was heir to it, as close as made no matter. She would have taken her place long before, but she'd gone traveling to the Nine Cities to learn new ways of weaving and dyeing, and she had affairs that wouldn't settle all at once."

"She ruled," Ziana said as if to herself. "Do you hear that, Haliya? I told you that wasn't one of Nurse's stories."

"Of course she had a husband," Haliya said, "or a brother who could tell her what to do."

"She'd married in the Nine Cities," said Estarion, "that's true enough, but her husband wasn't minded to live in a shepherd's cot on the edge of the world, as he put it. She wasn't bitter about it, much. She had a daughter from him, to be her heir, and let him have the son, which they all reckoned fair, as such things go."

"I wish I lived in Umbros," Ziana said.

"It's not very elegant," said Estarion. "It's mostly moors and woolbeasts and shepherds. The palace is a manor house that grew. It's raw and cold in the winter, and what summer there is, is more rain than sun. We had fires in the hearths at High Summer, and winter rains by Autumn Firstday. No one had much use for silk, or for pretty things. They weren't sensible."

"Silk makes a great deal of sense," said Ziana. "It weaves strong and it weaves light, and it's warm when you want it, and cool when you want it. And it takes color like nothing else."

She was, in her way, quite as surprising as her sister. Estarion was enchanted.

"Ah," said Lord Firaz, sliding in beside him. "Sire, we had lost you. I see you have found Prince Alishandas' daughters. They are the jewels of Markad, born of mothers who were kin to the royal house. There have been mages in their line, and priestesses of the Sun—Orozia of Magrin, mage and priestess and friend to Sarevadin, was their father's grandfather's father's sister; and she was but the first of several."

"That is a noble lineage," said Estarion. Stupidly, maybe, but he was caught in amber eyes, and again in golden. Such wit and such willfulness; and here, where he had never looked for any such thing. He slanted an eye at his Regent. "I'm in a quandary, my lord. Here are two. How do I choose?"

"Why, sire, you take both," said Lord Firaz in some surprise. "You have no harem; that is hardly a disgrace, as new come as you are, but strict honor would dictate that you choose many ladies from the cream of the realm, to honor their families and to bear you strong sons."

"Many?" Estarion felt the slow flush rising. Bless his ancestry, it did not show. "How many?"

"Had you been high prince in Asanion," said Firaz, "you would have been expected to take a lady for each day of the year. Then on your accession to the throne you would double that number; and when your first son was born, treble it."

Estarion must have looked a perfect fool. He picked up his fallen jaw. "How on earth can any man please that many?"

Lord Firaz was amused: there was a glint in his eye. "He does his best, my lord."

"And Hirel had fifty brothers." Estarion shuddered. "I'm not Asanian. I'm Varyani. We take our women one at a time."

"In Keruvarion that is honorable, my lord. Here, it gives insult to all those fathers whose daughters might rise in the emperor's favor and enrich their families, and give them kin in the royal house—perhaps even on the throne itself."

Estarion had heard it before. Of course he had. But hearing and listening—those were not the same at all. "God and goddess," he said.

"Here we have a thousand gods," said Firaz.

"I won't—" Estarion stopped, drew a long breath. "Would honor be satisfied," he asked, "if I eased myself in gently? If I remembered the ways of the Ianyn kings, and choose nine ladies of beauty and lineage? Would that content the Court?"

"For a beginning," said Firaz, "it would, sire."

"Very well," Estarion said. "Choose me seven who you think will suit me, and who will find me, if not suitable, then at least endurable."

"Will my lord not choose his own?"

"I have," said Estarion.

The Regent's brows went up. "My lord honors me with his trust."

"I do," said Estarion. He stepped back, opening the way to the hall. The ladies did not seize it, he noticed. Their dragon, as they called her, seemed to have accepted the inevitable. Her scowl was no less fierce, but she had stopped flexing her claws.

THEY STOOD IN front of him. Nine of them. Nine veils, nine pairs of eyes, from warm amber to bright gold. Nine bodies so wrapped and swathed and swaddled that he could only guess at their shapes, though he had no doubt of their gender.

They had been parted from their protectors. Those would be deep in colloquy, one by one, with Lord Firaz and the empress, settling matters as honor required. The guards here were eunuchs of the palace, aged and discreet.

The room was small, smothered in curtains. Estarion followed his nose to one and swept it back. Light trickled in through a lattice. There was no catch, no opening. He snorted disgust and wheeled. They were all staring, women and eunuchs alike.

A chair stood against the wall. He sat in it, not to be at ease, but to keep from prowling.

This was not beginning well. He tried a smile, not too wide. None of them warmed, except Haliya, who was laughing at him. She raised a hand to her veil.

Women bared their bodies in Keruvarion with less ceremony, and less trepidation, than women in Asanion showed their faces. Estarion had no sympathy with it; or had had none, until he met those bright eyes. This was great bravery, and a great gift. She was giving him herself.

He did not know if she was beautiful. She was less plump than some, which Asanians would reckon a defect. There was a scattering like gold dust across her nose: remarkable. The color came and went beneath it. She was not quite brave enough to smile at him without her veil to hide behind.

The others, so exampled, unveiled themselves likewise. He

was careful to notice each face, to say something to each maiden, whether she blushed or paled, stared hard at her feet or raised her eyes daringly to the vicinity of his chin. Ziana was the beauty that her sister was not: an amber loveliness that paled the rest to milk and water. When she blushed, she blushed rose-gold. He could not help what he did, which was to rise and take her hand, and kiss it as if she had been the empress and he but a prince of her court.

He let her go not entirely of his own will, to face her sister again. Of them all, he had failed to speak only to her. She felt it: he saw it in the angle of her chin, in the hard brightness of her eye. He brushed her gold-dusted cheek with his finger. "Does it come off?" he asked her.

She did not laugh as he had hoped, or delight him with her wit. She drew herself up, straight and stiff and cold. "If I do not please your eyes, my lord, I shall leave you. But do keep Ziana. *She* has no blemish."

"Nor do you," he said.

"I am not beautiful. I am too thin. My face is blotched with the sun. One of my teeth is imperfect: it broke when I fell climbing the wall in our garden. I have a scar on my chin from riding my brother's pony over a fence too high for him, and—"

He felt his brow climbing. It stopped her. Asanians could not do that, maybe: he had never seen it in them. "I should want you to be perfect?"

"You are the emperor," she said.

"I do hate it when people say that," he said.

"Then I won't say it," she said. "Your majesty."

She was small as Asanians were, barely shoulder-high. And yet he did not frighten her. She kept her chin up as if she wanted it there, and glared down her nose at him. "Are you going to send me back?" she demanded of him.

"Do you want me to?"

"My wanting has nothing to do with it."

"I will if you ask," he said, and now he was as stiff as she.

She widened her eyes, which truly were beautiful, and

curled her lip. "But why should you? You own this empire and everything in it."

"I don't own you."

"You do." She looked straight into his eyes. "You can send me away. I don't mind. Maybe they'll let me go this time, and see how a woman can be a princess in Keruvarion."

"You do want that," he said. He did not know what he felt. Regret, maybe. Admiration for her outspokenness, so precious rare among her people.

"I wanted it once," said Haliya. "Then I thought I wanted to be a proper woman, and be a man's wife, and bear his sons. I'll not do that now."

"Why not, if I set you free?"

Her laughter was gentle, which startled him. "You really don't know, do you? You've seen our faces now. No one else will want us."

Estarion stood still. His heart had gone cold. "Then—all those ladies in all those cities—"

"Oh," she said, "they're safe enough, unless a man is remarkably silly about his honor. You didn't single anyone out, you see. You didn't say anything to them beyond the politest necessity. Whereas we've been your property since we walked through yonder door."

"That is ridiculous," Estarion said.

"It's custom. If you hadn't been the emperor, if you'd been a lord or even a prince, someone higher might be willing to take your leavings as concubines, or as servants to one of his concubines. We have no honor left, you see, that belongs to our kin. We only have what you will give. If that is nothing, then nothing is our portion. I don't mind," she said, "much. I know the way to Keruvarion."

She did mind. Even his little magecraft felt it. It was her honor she cherished, he knew that, and not his presence.

"I should set you free," he said.

"You can't do that."

"The emperor can do anything."

"Anything the emperor can do, he can do. He can't make a woman a man."

"Why in the hells should I want to—"

"She means," said a gentle voice, "that women live like this. Men go out, and ride, and run away to Keruvarion." Ziana blushed under his eyes. "Here, my lord, it's different."

Estarion threw up his hands. "You're going to drive me clean out of my wits. Then what will you do?"

"Madmen are like dead men," said Haliya calmly, but with a glint in it. "We'll be your widows. We can do whatever we like."

"Even go out, and ride, and run away?"

She lowered those bold eyes, but not before he saw how they danced. "I forget myself. Again. My lord."

"Oh, stop it," he said. "Could you bear to go to Keruvarion if you went with me?"

"In a carriage? With curtains? And guards?"

"On a senel. In trousers. With," he admitted, "guards. There's no escaping them."

"Will you promise that?"

He hesitated. She would not droop. She was too proud. But the light went out of her. He had her hands in his before he knew it, not tempted to kiss them, but not tempted to let them go, either. "I promise," he said.

Once Estarion had escaped as far as the queen's palace, he discovered that his jailers had lengthened his chain. He could go to his mother now if he wished, or speak to the women who were, in law if not in fact, his concubines. He was careful not to slight any of them. But he had begun with the sisters, and to the sisters he always returned.

It was perfectly decorous. There was a eunuch there always, and they sat demurely, hands folded in their laps, and watched Estarion pace. He amused them, he thought. The Asanian word for panther was the word for northerner too, and Ziana called him by it, blushing at first as if she had let it slip out, then when he smiled, making it her name for him. Haliya did not call him anything but "my lord."

He came to her in the morning, not long after that first meeting, so early that she was just out of bed and not yet dressed. He could hardly burst in on a lady in her bower, even a lady who belonged to him. He fretted and paced, while the eunuchs watched and eyed his companion with mighty mistrust.

Godri would never have come so far if Estarion had not invoked the full force of imperial ire. But there was no one else whom Estarion wished to trust with this.

Just as he was ready to give it up, Haliya emerged, wrapped in veils. Her glance at Godri was astonished. She would have been warned that there was a second man in her antechamber. But she could never have seen a desert tribesman before, nor such a richness of warrior-patterns on his face.

He had too much delicacy to stare at her. He relinquished what he carried, and stepped back.

"Go," said Estarion, filling her arms with Godri's burden. "Put these on."

She clutched the bundle to her breast, but stood her ground. "What—"

"Just go," he said. "Or we'll dress you ourselves."

She wheeled at that and ran.

"She has a fair turn of speed, for a lapcat," Godri observed.

Estarion almost hit him. "That is a lady of Asanion."

"Didn't I say that?"

Estarion prayed for patience. He needed it. She was so long in coming that he began to suspect she would not come at all.

At last she appeared. The trousers fit her: he had hoped for that. The coat was loose to spare her modesty, but it showed a great deal more of her than her wrappings ever had. The veil was an expedient of his mother's for the road into the Golden Empire, much like the headdress of Godri's people, or of the Olenyai.

He took her hand before she could stop him. "Now," he said, "come with us."

She had to trot to keep pace, but she went willingly, eyes bright with curiosity. Her hand was hot in his, clinging tighter the longer he held it. Eunuchs trailed after, expostulating.

The wall of guards stopped them all. Haliya regarded them in astonishment. "These are women!"

"So they are," Estarion said, amused.

"But they're guards."

"Guards can be women," he said.

"Then—you—"

"Oh," he said before she fainted with shock, "these are my mother's. I borrow them when I come here. My own Guard is safely male; but I can hardly bring them to this place, can I?"

"But," said Haliya. "They have swords. And that's armor. Is this a play? Am I to be the fool in it?"

"This is a gift," he said, and held his breath. She could refuse. She could slap him for his presumption, and run back to her gowns and her veils.

Or she could let him lead her through the gate that had opened in the armored wall. It closed behind them, shutting out the eunuchs. Estarion let his smile break through at last, and stretched his stride.

There was a courtyard that, Estarion had discovered, abutted one of the stables and yet was safely within the confines of the queen's palace. It took a little doing, but a senel could be brought in, with a eunuch groom to be properly honorable.

Estarion regarded the mare with some surprise. Godri had chosen her, there was no mistaking it. She was one of his own: desert-bred, sand-colored as they all were, less ugly-headed than most, with the beginnings of horns on her brow, rare in a mare and much prized.

"Godri," said Estarion. "This is—"

Haliya pulled her hand free of his and ran to the mare, and

flung her arms about the beast's neck. "No! Don't send her away. She's perfect. I don't *want* anything prettier."

Estarion blinked, taken aback. She had mistaken his intent too completely for words.

Godri laughed. "My lord, I think your lady has sense after all."

"She is an idiot," said Estarion. "To think that I would afflict her with a mount that was"—gods, the word tasted vile—"pretty. Pretty! That plowbeast I rode into Kundri'j is pretty. I'd have him for breakfast if I thought my stomach could stand it."

Haliya turned, still clinging to the mare. The beast preserved her aplomb admirably, even condescended to lip a strand of hair that had escaped the veil. Haliya glared. "Then why did you start to say—"

"I started to say," said Estarion, "that this is the best of Godri's herd, which is the cream of Varag Suvien. This is his queen, his beloved. He has given you a gift worthy of kings."

Her gaze dropped; her cheeks went scarlet. But she had spirit to spare. "Everyone else has tried to mount me on—on plowbeasts. With gilded feet. And ribbons."

Her disgust was profound. The mare snorted and caught her veil in long teeth, and plucked it off.

Godri had the wits to turn away. Estarion did not see the need to do the same. Haliya, bareheaded and vivid with defiance, mounted in creditable order. She did not ride badly, either, for a lapcat.

"How did you learn?" Estarion asked her afterward. She was damp from the bath, demurely gowned and veiled again, with her sister in attendance. "Did you steal your brother's pony and teach yourself to stay on?"

"I watched," she said. "From windows. Walls, sometimes. Even the roof, until Nurse caught me. I knew how to do it before I tried it."

"Did the pony think so too?"

She bristled at him. "I'm dreadful. Aren't I? You didn't say anything, but I saw you laughing with that painted savage."

"That painted savage is a lord and warrior of Varag. He is also," said Estarion, "the only one in Kundri'j whom I can honestly call friend."

That quenched her a little, but she was not one to let go a fight. "You were laughing at me."

"We were marveling. Godri says you'll make a rider."

"I'm not one now?"

"Do you think you are?"

She lowered her eyes. Her fingers knotted and unknotted in her lap. "My lord," she said after a while. "Did you mean that? About the gift?"

"I don't say things I don't mean."

Not that an Asanian could believe it; but Haliya was kind enough not to say so. "I may ride every day?"

"All day if you want to. I've given orders. They will," said Estarion, "be obeyed."

The eunuch on guard did not speak, but Estarion knew he heard.

Haliya took her time in responding. That was Asanian, that restraint. He had stopped thinking that it was coldness.

She stood all at once, with an air of resolution, and stepped forward. She folded her arms very carefully about Estarion's neck. He sat still, not daring to breathe. She was warm; she smelled of spices. Her lips were cool on his.

He drew back as gently as he could. "Do I take it that that is payment?"

She did not slap him. That would have been predictable. She caught his face in her hands. They were not cool at all now; not in the least.

He was gasping when she let him go. So, to his surprise, was she. He wondered if he looked as wild as she did.

Her hands were trembling. She let them fall to his shoulders. "You burn," she said. "Like fire."

"They say I'm the Sun's child."

Her fingers tightened. She looked ready to fall over; he steadied her about the middle. She was a pleasant handful, small but not as a child is, and sweetly curved. He did not even care that she was a yellow woman. Gold, rather, and ivory, and that sheen of dust from the sun: brighter since she came to the riding court, and touched with rose.

"We burn," she said, "when the sun touches us. Some of us change, and learn to bear it. Some of us are flayed alive."

"You go golden," he said.

"Oh, I burn, if I stay in it long enough."

"Do I frighten you?"

"Yes," she said.

She did not sound afraid, nor did he sense it in her. And yet it was the truth.

He had forgotten everything but the light in her eyes. She swayed toward him. Her hair was the color of wheat in the sun. The scent of her was dizzying.

They were alone in the room. He did not know at first how he knew that. Here in the circle of her arms, the world was clearer than it had been since he was a child. And yet when he looked past her, he saw no more than a blur.

If he asked now, she would give him anything he asked for. Anything he wanted. And cycles since he held a woman in his arms, since he knew that sweetness above all others.

She did not love him. He was a mage here; even shielded, he sensed what was to be sensed. He interested her greatly. She liked him: that was clear to see. It warmed him. She would give him her body as she had given him her face, willingly, even proudly, without regret that it was he and not another who must be her master.

Very gently he freed himself from her embrace. It was cold without, and grey, and the clarity of his seeing was gone. He set a kiss on her brow, chaste as if she had been his sister, and said, "Child, you are honey-sweet. But I'm no woman's master, nor are you my slave."

Her eyes narrowed. "It's that woman, isn't it? The commoner. You want her to bear your firstborn."

Estarion's heart clenched. "How did you know—"

She laughed, bright and hard. "We may live in chains, but we have ears. Everyone knows about the Island woman. She didn't want to share you, did she? She's selfish."

"Everyone doesn't learn to be as generous as an Asanian woman," Estarion said, trying to be light.

"She's not beautiful," said Haliya. "You don't like beautiful women. Except your mother. You like them to be interesting instead."

"I don't see faces," Estarion said. "Or I didn't, before I came here, where faces are so hard to see. What is in this place that trammels mages?"

"I don't know," she said. "I'm not a mage."

"Aren't you?" He shook himself. "No. You have it in your blood, clear enough. You wouldn't know what you have, without another power to strike sparks from you."

"Oh, I know that," she said. "That's not magery. It's only being Vinicharyas." One of the gifts of which line was to strengthen a mage's power with the touch of her body on his. Even if he had but a trickle of power left.

The quality of his silence alarmed her. "Is it something I should be afraid of? Have I hurt you?"

"No," he said quickly. "Oh, no. I never meant to scare you. I was only marveling at you. Will you forgive me?"

She took her time about it, but in the end she did. "You're so interesting, you see," she explained. "And really, once one grows used to you, rather beautiful."

24

" 'RATHER BEAUTIFUL,' " ESTARION said. "She called me that. It can't be for my face."

"The warrior-patterns wouldn't show on you," said Godri.

Estarion laughed. It was rusty: he was forgetting how. "Your father thinks they would. White paint, he told me, and gold. He thought gold would suit me very well."

"They'd cost you the beard," Godri said—with, Estarion noted, no little pleasure. Godri, good desert tribesman that he was, could not approve of the northern fashion.

"They might be worth it," Estarion said. "They'd shock Asanion to its foundations." He sighed and stretched. He had found a room with a window that faced westward, and disposed of the lattice with three very satisfying blows of a throwing axe. The axe was ancient and long resigned to exile upon a wall, but it had been pleased to do its duty again, albeit without due sacrifice of the enemy's blood. Nothing but dust and dead wood in that damnable lattice.

He folded his arms on the window-ledge and leaned out. The sun slanted long over the roofs and spires of the palace, and beyond them the descending circles of the city, and beyond those the river and the plain. The wind was almost clean up here, and almost cool. Summer, that had seemed so endless, was ending at last. Three days, and the sun would cycle round to Autumn First-day.

His father had died on the night of that feast. Ten years ago, less three days. He flexed his burning hand. "Who'd have thought I'd stand here again," he said.

"You remember?" Godri asked. "From before?"

Estarion shrugged, almost a shiver. "Sometimes I don't

know what I remember. What's dream, what's real, what's delusion. None of us is entirely sane, you know. We can't be. Not and be what we are."

"Mages?"

"Kings." He met the sun's glare. It was life, but it was death too, as all fire was. The Sunborn did not understand that. He tried to cast down the dark, naming it death and enemy. And so it was; but it was sleep also, and rest, and ease for the weary.

Nothing was absolute. Asanion was his prison, and yet he ruled it. He hated it; but he was learning in spite of himself to admire it. Even, in some part, to love it.

He turned abruptly. The room was dark after the brilliance of the sun. Godri was a shadow in it. "There's something," Estarion said, "I have to do."

Godri followed in silence. Estarion had made these rooms his own, but one suite of them was locked, its door barred. He laid his branded hand flat on the carved panel. Wood and gilding, carved caravans bearing tribute, memory that darted close and then away.

He did not have the key. That was in the keeping of the chamberlain. But he did not need it. He bore in his hand the key to every door. It was a power that tales did not tell of, and songs only hinted at.

The pain of the Sun's fire mounted almost beyond endurance, then suddenly subsided. The lock fell in shards. Estarion drew a shaking breath. "That was hardly necessary," he said to the air, or perhaps to the god.

The door opened to his touch. The hinges were oiled, the air within clean, touched but faintly with the taint of disuse. Death's stains were long since disposed of, Ganiman's body embalmed with spices and borne away into the east, to lie in the tomb of kings under Avaryan's Tower. The floor where he had fallen was clean, the bed mounded in cushions, no mark of his dying throes.

He had not died easily or quickly. Estarion had been there. Others remembered: they had told him. How he stood, how he would not speak, nor move, nor suffer any to touch him, but fixed his eyes on Ganiman's face. He had no memory of that. His mind had been far away, hunting a mage who was a murderer. He had not seen what the poison and the sorcery did to his strong beautiful father, withered and shriveled him, robbed him of voice and strength and wits, made of him a mindless mewling thing.

There was mercy, maybe, in that bar to his memory. When he saw his father, he saw him as he had been: tall robust handsome man, stern enough before his people, but light-hearted as a boy, and apt for mischief.

"The night before he died," Estarion said, "he led a whole regiment of his Guard on a raid against the queen's palace, abducted my mother and carried her away to this room, and held it against all comers. The uproar went on till dawn. People thought the palace was invaded; the eunuchs shrieked and wailed, and all the guards came out in arms. It was splendid."

Godri inspected an image that stood in a niche. "That's himself?"

Estarion did not need to look at it. "That's the Sunborn. Father was handsomer than that. Pretty, he said. He cultivated a beard and a severe expression. They only made him the more beautiful."

"You look like this one," said Godri. "Interesting face. He wasn't a tamed thing, was he?"

"And I am?" Estarion asked coldly.

Godri glanced over his shoulder. "Did I say that? You'll see reason now and then, when you've had your nose rubbed in it. Look at the eyes on him. Nothing reasonable about him at all."

"That was the god in him, I was always told." Estarion stood by the bed. He did not feel anything. It was not numbness, not exactly. More as if he had felt all that there was to feel, and there was nothing left.

Godri wandered on past the carving of Varuyan on senel-back, thrusting a spear into a direwolf's vitals. When he paused again, it was in front of a painted portrait. "Hirel and Sarevadin," he said. It was not a question. "Was his majesty really that young?"

"He'd not turned sixteen when his son was born," Estarion said.

"Well," said Godri after a pause. "The yellowheads don't live long. I suppose they have to get in their breeding while they can."

Estarion stood very still.

Godri did not seem to notice. "The lady was beautiful, wasn't she? That Ianyn face, and that hair, like new copper. They say your father looked like her as she was before she was a she."

Estarion had no difficulty in untangling that. He eased by degrees. "That's the Gileni blood. Not like the royal Ianyn. All beak and bones, those."

"You'd be less of both if you fed yourself better." Godri came round to Estarion's side and looked up him, black eyes bright in the swirling patterns of his face. "Is it bad?" he asked.

"No," Estarion said, too quickly maybe. But when he thought about it: "No. He was on the throne when I came to it. He's round about the palace, sometimes. But not here. This is only where he left his body behind."

Godri shivered but held his ground. "You're healing."

"If you want to call it that," Estarion said.

"It was well you came here, even if it makes you ill. Some fevers are necessary. They burn away old scars."

"Maybe," said Estarion.

The fever that was in him would not let him rest. He went to his mother for a while. She tried to comfort him, but she had her own burden of memories, and her own troubles.

The harem was waiting on his pleasure. One was very fine upon the lute; another had a wonderful voice. None was importunate, or tried to lure him to the inner chamber.

Haliya was not there. She was tired, her sister said, and had gone to bed. "But if my lord wishes . . ."

"No," he said. He listened to the singer and the lute-player. He said polite things to the others. When enough time had passed, he sent them away.

Ziana was last and slowest to go. He almost called her back. It did not matter that she had no love for him. Her beauty pleased him, and her calmness soothed his temper.

And if she conceived his son, what then? Did he want her for his empress?

He returned to his chambers in a mood as black as the sky. No stars tonight, no moons. Clouds had come up while he tarried; there was rain in the wind.

Guards hovered. Varyani, no Olenyai. Those were hidden in shadows. "Go," he said to the ones he could see, those who had been his friends, while he could have friends, before he was emperor in Asanion. "Go, rest, carouse in a tavern, do something that isn't fretting over me."

"But," said Alidan, "it's our duty to fret over you."

"I command you," Estarion said. And when they would not move: "I'm strangling with all the hovering and the watching, and knowing how you hate it. Some of you at least, be free for me."

"And if anything happens?" Alidan persisted.

"What can happen?"

Alidan refused to answer that, and rightly. But Estarion was in no mood to be reasonable. He drove them out, even Alidan, who needed main force.

His chambers were full of shadows. Some of them had eyes. He rid himself of them by dropping his robes and baring his teeth. Whether for fear of his armament or horror of his shamelessness, they vanished with gratifying speed.

There was always wine on the table by the bed. Godri insisted on tasting it. "Dreadful," he said, "but nothing deadly in it, that I can tell."

Estarion knew that already. That was another magery he kept, to know what was in the wine he drank. Or maybe it was only a keen nose. He downed a cup, and then another. Godri combed his hair out of its tangles.

"Do you notice," Estarion asked him, "what the Asanians do? They don't comb it, except on top. They let it set into a mat."

"So could you," said Godri, "if you didn't want to wear the king-braids again."

"Sometimes I wonder if I ever will." Estarion poured a third cup. The wine was strong, but it barely blunted the edge of his mood. Godri was no lady's maid: sometimes he tugged too hard. The pain was welcome. Less so the brush of his fingers as he plaited Estarion's mane into a single braid, bound and tamed it for the night. Estarion's skin was as twitchy as his temper. He almost wheeled, almost seized those tormenting hands. But they went away. Godri smoothed back the coverlet of the great bed and bent to trim the lamp.

Estarion let his body fall into the bed. Godri drew up the coverlet gravely, but with the flicker of a smile. "Good night, my lord," he said.

Estarion's growl made the smile brighten before it vanished. Godri went lightly enough to his own bed in the outer room. Fortunate creature. His moods passed as quickly as they came. He was even reconciled to Kundri'j; or close enough to make no difference.

Estarion lay on his face. The wine soured in his stomach. The coverlets were heavy, galling. He kicked them off. Cool air stroked his back. He rolled onto it, then onto his side. Canopy and curtains closed in on him. He covered his eyes with his hands. The dark was no more blessed than the nightlamp's glow. He ran his hands down his face, neck, breast. His fingers clawed. He clenched them into fists, pressed them together in his middle, knotted himself about them. He was not weeping. That much fortitude at least he had.

The dreams would be bad tonight. He had no power to turn them aside. The wine worked in him, dragging him down into the whispering dark.

* * *

Fear. Terror. Panic.

Estarion clawed toward the light. His breath shuddered and rasped. His nose twitched with the sharpness of sweat. His body could not move. He willed his eyes to open. Slowly the lids yielded. They were like stone. A thin line of light pierced the darkness.

He was not alone. His head would not turn, his hands were dead things. But he knew. There was someone else in the room. Breathing. Watching.

Magery?

A drug? And how, if not in the wine?

His power was as numbed as the rest of him. It could not lift itself, could not batter down the walls that it had raised. He was locked within. Trapped.

Laughter shivered through him. Oh, he was a fine image of an emperor, trapped and spelled and stinking of fear. Rats faced death with more grace.

That it was death, he had no doubt. It stalked him through the dimness of the chamber, breathing faster as it drew closer, though it tried to be silent. It could not know what senses he had, when he troubled to use them.

He gathered all of himself that there was. He did not try to open his eyes further, or to flex his fingers. When the blow came, he must be ready. He must move. Must. Move.

Under the world-weight of lids, through the veil of lashes, he saw the shadow that crept across him. Veils, draperies. A woman?

No. That scent was male: strong with fear-musk, and something else, cloyingly sweet. Dreamsmoke and honey. Something gleamed. Steel. Wealthy assassin, that one, and a fool, to carry bright metal and not black iron or greened bronze.

Move, Estarion willed his body. Must move. *Must.*

Nothing.

The knife poised over him. No face behind it, nor eyes, hidden in veils.

Fear was gone. There was only the will. To move. To *move.*

Steel flashed down.

Estarion lurched, floundered, dragged lifeless limbs, but he moved. Away from that glittering death, and up, into the shadow that bore it.

Two shadows. He crumpled bonelessly to the floor. The shadow with the knife locked in battle with a second shadow. That one had eyes and a face, and warrior-patterns thick on it.

Estarion's body struggled against the spell that bound it. Life crawled back, marking its way in pain. He could move hands, feet.

The shadow-battle swayed toward him. The knife was gone, lost, but its wielder had the strength of desperation. And wanted, still wanted, the life that flopped and gasped on the floor. The assassin lunged. Hands clawed for Estarion's eyes.

Godri struck them back. They yielded; one dropped. Estarion saw the glint of metal, black now, assassin's iron, curved like a cat's claw. Something—something he must know—

Godri caught the wrist that bore no weapon. The black knife arced, slashed past the patterns of his cheek, but drew no blood there. It darted at his hand. He seized it. By the blade, the idiot, the brave, mad, damnable fool. Gods, what it did to his fingers—blood welling, his face blank, unwounded hand twisting, clasping the assassin's wrist. Bone snapped. A shriek tore out of the veils, but the assassin would not yield, would not let go of that deadly blade.

Shadow reared up behind the shadow of the assassin. The veiled one stiffened. If he had had eyes, they would, perhaps, have gone wide. He dropped like a felled tree.

Godri swayed. He had the knife still, fist clenched upon its blade. Blood dripped. He did not seem to notice. He dropped gracelessly to his knees, who had always been as graceful as a dancer. "My lord," he said. Were those tears upon his cheeks? "Oh, my lord!"

With all the strength that he had, Estarion shaped words. "Godri. Godri, let go. The knife. Let go!"

Godri stared blankly at his bleeding hand, at the thing that he clutched in it. "It's nothing," he said. "I'll get a bandage—wrap it—"

"It is poisoned," said a clear cold voice. An Olenyas kicked the assassin's body out of the way and stood over them both. His eyes were all gold. "You are a dead man, tribesman. Whatever possessed you to take an assassin's knife by the blade?"

Godri drew himself up on his knees. "You're talking nonsense, yelloweyes." His breath caught. He swayed again, steadied, spoke through gritted teeth. "Don't listen to him, my lord. Did that vermin strike you? Are you hurt?"

"He never touched me," Estarion said. It was easier now, or would be, if he had not seen how grey Godri was, how his body shivered, his unwounded hand clenched and unclenched.

"Gods be thanked," Godri said. His voice was thin; he needed three breaths for the three words. "Oh, my lord, I thought you were killed."

"Spelled," said Estarion. He struggled to sit up. The numbness was fading. He was clumsy yet, as if half of him was turned to stone, but he could wrap arms about Godri, and know how he shivered and spasmed.

Just as Estarion's father had. But there was no mage to hunt, no assassin to kill. The Olenyas had done that.

"Fetch a physician," Estarion said. "Quickly."

"What use?" asked the Olenyas. "He is dead. Nothing can mend him."

"A mage can," said Estarion. He was growing—not angry. No. There was no word for it. It was too perfect, too blackly brilliant. "You are not going to die," he said to Godri.

Godri did not answer. The poison was strong in him. Estarion could smell it, could taste it in the air. It was vile, cloying-sweet.

He called his power to him. It was slow, it dragged, it trickled where it should have been a thin but steady stream. It was not enough even to fill the cup of his skull. With sunlight, maybe, it might have been more. There was no moonlight tonight, and no stars. Rain fell like tears.

Estarion gathered up the limp body. It was still breathing. He was sure that it was. It could not have stopped so soon.

"Well for him," the Olenyas said, "that it was quick poison and not a slow. He had no pain."

No doubt, for an Olenyas, that was compassion. Estarion found himself on his feet, hands fisted in Olenyai robes, shaking the man within as if he had been a child's doll. The Olenyas made no move to resist. "Don't," Estarion said. "Don't—ever—"

"I am not to tell the truth?"

"My friend is dead!"

It was a howl. The Olenyas heard it calmly, dangling in Estarion's grasp. "That is truth," he said.

Estarion dropped him. He landed lightly, hardly ruffled, no malice in the steady golden stare.

"My friend is dead," Estarion said more softly, "and I could not make him live. My friend . . . died . . . for me."

"He died for idiocy. And," said the Olenyas, "for you."

"I could kill you," said Estarion. He was quite calm. "You could have come before. You came too late."

"I came with the speed I had."

"You were supposed to guard me."

"You sent us all away."

Estarion gasped for breath. He should weep. He could not remember how. "You shouldn't—have— I'll kill you. You'll let me. You'll all die for me."

"I will not."

That stopped Estarion. "You exist to serve me."

"I exist to serve the throne. That one," said the Olenyas, tilting his shrouded head toward Godri's body, "lived and died for you."

Estarion had him by the robe again. He was not as small as some, Estarion noticed. Maybe he was young. His voice was so dispassionate that it seemed ageless, but it was light, as if it had not long been broken from child's into man's. The skin round the eyes was smooth, unlined, and white as ivory. The brows under the veil were dark gold. Maybe Estarion could see something of the face: straight long line of nose, smooth curve of cheek and chin.

Asanian. Estarion's belly knotted with disgust. He thrust the creature away, stumbled past Godri, half-fell where the assassin lay. The man's bowels had let go in death; he stank. Estarion swallowed bile, and stripped the veils from the face. Round unremarkable Asanian face, nothing to distinguish it from a hundred others.

"He was not of us," said the Olenyas.

It seemed to matter to him. Estarion stripped the body grimly, quelling the hot surge of hate. Calm, he must be calm. Later he could break. Later he could weep.

The dead man was plump and hairless—so that was true, they grew none save under the arms and between the legs, and shaved or plucked that. Full male; half unexpected, to find him no eunuch. No brands or marks or sigils but the knife that was in Godri's hand still. Nothing to name him or place him or bind him to anyone but himself.

"How do you know he's not Olenyai?" Estarion demanded of the one behind.

"No scars," the Olenyas said.

Estarion did not see how that could matter. He had scars himself. Anyone did, who trained at all for war. "Then what is he?"

"A fool," said the Olenyas.

"He was clever enough to come into my bedchamber, ensorcel me, and kill—" Estarion's voice caught. He must be calm. He must. Or he would be no use at all. "And kill my squire. That's not a fool. That's a mage, or a man who knows mages."

"Still," said the Olenyas, "a fool. He feigned to be of us. He is not. Those who sent him will be dealt with. You can be sure of that."

"You know—"

"We will."

Estarion rose. He was shaking again. "You will please," he said, "dispose of that carrion. And send for—send for Iburan. The priest, from Endros. You know him?"

"We know him," said the Olenyas.

"I'd rather my mother didn't know. And the ladies. Until tomorrow. Unless . . ." Horror smote him. "If there are more—if they've struck at her—"

"I shall see to it," said the Olenyas.

He was comforting in a strange fashion: so cold and so evidently unmoved, whatever Estarion said or did to him. When he had gone upon his errands, the room was suddenly very dark, full of the stench of death.

Estarion went back to Godri. He was growing cold, his body shrunken, all the quick grace gone out of him. He did not look as if he slept. He looked dead. Cold; empty. Lifeless.

Estarion smoothed the many plaits of his hair and straightened his limbs, as if he could care how he lay. The assassin's knife was locked in his hand. Estarion left it. Godri would have won the battle, if there had not been poison. He would have taken the small wound, bound it up, gone on unheeding as a warrior should.

"Asanion," Estarion said. "Asanion killed you. Asanion with its sleights and its poisons. Oh, how I hate this place!"

There were only the dead to hear. No guards. No servants. He had sent the guards away. The servants—and were they dead as well? Or spelled?

He sat on his heels beside Godri. "They should not have been able to do this to me," he said. "I should have known. My walls should have defended me."

Maybe they had. Maybe the dreams had been his walls breaking, his power resisting.

And what mage could do it? What mage would dare?

It was a drug, it must have been. A subtle thing, and slow, mixed in his wine or wafted in the air. Then it was a matter for the guards to discover, intrigue of the court perhaps, or a lord with a grudge. Asanion was full of grudges, and not the least of them that Estarion was lord of it and not an emperor of the pure blood.

Estarion's mind whirled and spun. It was better than weeping. Better than facing himself, and knowing that a man had died for him. A man who was his friend; whom he had loved.

The Olenyas came back alone. Estarion half-rose, braced for battle, and barely eased to recognize the eyes in the veil. "Where is Iburan?" he demanded.

"Coming," said the Olenyas. "As are the rest. I bade them hold back until I had given you warning."

"Send them in," said Estarion. But as the Olenyas turned: "No. Wait. Do you have a name?"

The Olenyas paused. "Does it matter?"

"Yes."

The Olenyas turned back to face him. The golden eyes were level. Lion-eyes. So, Estarion thought: the Olenyai bred them, too. Was he a prince of them, maybe? Or simply an accident of nature?

"They call me Koru-Asan," the Olenyas said. "Korusan."

Estarion laughed, sharp and short. "Yelloweyes?"

"Golden," said Korusan. "If you please."

"They call me that too, you know," Estarion said. "I've heard them talking."

"Your ears are keen," Korusan said.

"And my eyes," said Estarion with bleak lightness, "are as yellow as butter."

"As gold," said Korusan. He bent his head, which was Olenyai obeisance, or subtle mockery, and opened the door to the deluge.

25

IBURAN'S PRESENCE, MASSIVE and quiet, wrought order out of chaos. Estarion could happily have fallen into his arms and howled. But that was not given to a man and an emperor. He sat wrapped in a robe while guards and servants and a scattering of lordlings fussed and fretted. He watched them bear the assassin away to be hung from the wall with spikes, and Godri to be laid out with honor in the Hall of Glories.

It all went on without him. That was a wisdom he had come to long since. The emperor was necessary. He was the empire in his own person, his strength its strength, his progeny its hope of continuance. But for the workings of its days he was not needed at all, except to set his name to the greater ones, and to suffer the rest to go on as it would.

Iburan loomed over him. "Starion?" the deep voice said.

Estarion stiffened. He had wanted just this; now that he had it, he wanted to wound it, tear it, cast it away. "Godri is dead," he said.

"I grieve for that," said Iburan.

"Do you?"

Iburan sat at Estarion's feet. Easily, lightly, he laid his arm across Estarion's knees. Estarion could not escape him without oversetting him. There were shocked expressions among the servants; the lords whispered to one another. An emperor in Asanion was touched by no one but his bodyservants and his women, and by them only as he gave them leave.

Iburan, who knew that very well, looked long into Estarion's face. "No," he said at last. "You're not well at all."

"Should I be?" Estarion inquired. "Consider where I am."

"Where we forced you to go." Iburan sighed. "It would have been worse if you had never come here."

"Not for Godri."

"Is one young man, however beloved, worth the breaking of an empire?"

"Tonight," said Estarion very quietly, very carefully, "I can't answer that as you wish me to. I can only see that he is dead."

"You are not," said Iburan.

"That too I can't answer as you would like. I'm changing here, Iburan. I don't like what I'm changing into."

"What you were in Keruvarion, that was half of you. This is the rest of it."

"Then the half of me is a cold, hard, cruel thing, and it would gladly see whole ranks of men rent with hooks, if but one of them knew what was to pass this night."

Iburan did not flinch. "The half of you weeps for the one you loved, and longs to avenge his death. That's no shame, Starion."

"You have been a father to me," Estarion said. "Can you give me no more now than empty words?"

"I give what you will take. What have you done to your magery, child?"

"Asanion has done it," Estarion said.

"No," said Iburan. "You do it to yourself. You've shut it all away. If you had had your defenses laid properly, this murderer would not have come. And if he had come, and eluded you, you would have known who he was, and who sent him. Now he is dead. His soul is fled. There is nothing for a mage to discover, except that he hated, not you yourself, but what he thought you were."

"His emperor," said Estarion, tight and bitter.

"His conqueror. Still they call the Sun-blood that, after a lifetime of years."

"So I am," said Estarion with a curl of the lip, "if conquest it must be, to inflict myself upon an empire that does not love me."

"They don't hate you," said Iburan, "who know you. And

that's most of the High Court, these days, and much of the Middle Court."

"But not the people, who dream of prophets and of conquests undone, and conspire to be rid of me."

"Self-pity ill becomes you, Starion."

Estarion could not strike him. Not this man. Not that he was Avaryan's high priest in Endros, or that he had been a regent in Keruvarion, or even that he had been, in all but name, foster-father. It was simpler than that. "I know full well," Estarion said, "that you can break me across your knee. But I will not hear that you find me wanting. I have enough of that in myself."

"Then what will you hear? Your mind is locked shut."

"It always has been." Estarion leaned forward, nose to strong arched nose. "You left me here, Iburan. Why? You could have stayed; you could have been my bulwark. Instead, you left me alone."

"And how would it look," asked Iburan, "for the High Court to see me ever at your back, great black bear of a northerner, whispering in your ear? What then would they call you?"

"Conqueror," said Estarion. "Emperor."

"I came when you called me," Iburan said.

"Of course you did. There's no heir in the offing yet."

Iburan rose. The beard hid his expression, but his eyes were hard. "I shall always come when you ask, sire. Now will you ask me to go?"

"Gladly," said Estarion, all but spitting it.

Oh, well done, Estarion lauded himself. He had slain his friend with his folly, and lost his lover, and now he had driven away his foster-father. The faces about him now were all Asanian faces. All strangers.

And one that was no face, but a veil and a pair of golden eyes. They watched him steadily, a little fixedly, as if fascinated.

When he drove the others out, that one stayed. "One must guard you," said the Olenyas.

"They won't try again tonight," said Estarion. But he did not order the Olenyas to leave him.

Dawn was coming. He felt it in his bones, both ache and pleasure. He wandered the rooms with his golden-eyed shadow. No danger hid there, no threat but memory. Here was Godri's armor on its stand, there his box of belongings, pitifully little to matter so much.

Estarion had no tears for him. He turned away from the memory and the grief and walked swiftly, he cared not where. To the garden in the end, because it had no roof, no barrier to the sky. Rain fell soft, hardly more than mist.

Korusan was still behind him, cat-quiet. "You'll get wet," Estarion said.

"I'll not melt," said Korusan.

Estarion turned, startled. Wit, in an Olenyas? There was no way to tell. It was black dark, the Olenyas a shadow on shadow. "Why do you hide your face?" Estarion demanded of him.

"Custom," he answered with no reluctance that Estarion could discern. "Modesty, once. And if one cannot see one's enemy's face . . ."

"One can't tell what he'll do next," Estarion finished for him. "That's not so. It's the eyes that give it away. And yours," he added, "more than most. Are you a prince of Olenyai?"

"Olenyai are warriors," the cool voice said, "not princes." Then: "When we hunt an enemy to the death, we veil our eyes."

"Shiu'oth Olenyai," said Estarion. "Yes, I've heard of those. They're vowed, yes? And sworn to die unless their enemy dies first."

"Sworn to die with him," said Korusan, "when they take the great vow. Life is not worth living, you see, once the enemy is dead."

"I could understand that," Estarion said.

Korusan laughed. It was an uncanny sound in the dark and

the rain: young, hardly more than a child's, but old as mountains. "You understand nothing, my lord and emperor. What have you ever lost but what you could easily lose?"

"My father," said Estarion, sharp with the pain of it.

"Fathers die," Korusan said. "That is the way of the world."

"I gather you never had one," Estarion said.

"What, you think us born of the earth, or of a mage's conjuring? We are human enough, Sunlord, under the veils and the swords."

"How old are you, child?"

The Olenyas was not to be startled into anger. "I have fifteen years," he said calmly. "And you?"

"I thought everyone knew my age to the hour," said Estarion.

"Twenty-two years, twice six cycles of Brightmoon less two days and," said Korusan, "five turns of the glass, and one half-turn." He paused. Estarion held his tongue. "They say you will live a hundred years, if no one kills you first."

"You're here to avert that," said Estarion.

"Oh, yes," said Korusan. "No one will kill you while I stand beside you. I keep that privilege for myself."

Estarion laughed. It was the first true laughter he had known in Kundri'j. It swept the dark away; it brought back, however dimly, the light that once had been all he was. "None but you shall take my life," he said. "Here's my hand on it."

Korusan clasped it. His grip was warm and strong, strong enough to grind the bones together, had not Estarion braced against him. Estarion grinned into the night. This was terrible; it was wonderful. It suited his mood to perfection.

Korusan had been appalled when he followed the path of a suspicion and found a figure in Olenyai black, wielding a blade against the Sun's get. That was none of his plotting.

He was angry, first, while his body moved to do what was necessary. If this was one of the mages' puppets, he would take the price in their blood. Then he grieved, for he had conceived a liking for the Sunlord's servant. Neither anger nor grief got in the way of his lesser belt-knife. Swords were too great an honor for an assassin who dared robe and veil himself like an Olenyas.

After grief came stillness, and certainty. This life belonged to him. This prey was his; he would relinquish it to no other, no, not to death itself.

And, having claimed it, he was not about to let it escape him. He made himself the black king's shadow. He found himself admiring a creature who could stand in the rain until dawn, talking of everything and nothing. Of course he did not understand what Korusan meant by the oath he had sworn. He was too arrogant for that, and too much a child.

Korusan would be dead before he came to this man's years. His bones ached in the damp; old scars throbbed. But if a man could live as long as this one hoped to, then twenty-two was infant's years, and lifetimes in front of him still, and worlds to learn the ways of.

Most bitter of enemies he might be, but he was an engaging creature. Attractive, even, if one were fond of panthers. The grey morning showed him wet to the skin, hair a draggled tail, rain dripping from his beard, and eyes bright gold.

Korusan sneezed.

The lion-eyes went wide. "There now. See what I've done. I've caught you your death."

"I know where my death is," said Korusan, "and that is not in this place."

The Sunlord would not listen. He herded Korusan into warmth and dryness, got him out of dripping robes but not the veil, played servant as if he had been born to it. And if he knew what he served, what then would he have done?

He knew Asanian modesty. He observed it well enough, not even a glance aside, no touch that was not required. The robe in which he wrapped Korusan was black, and went round Korusan exactly twice, and trailed elegantly behind. The wine he poured was a vintage reserved for emperors. Korusan was startled that it stayed in his stomach.

"You're a delicate little thing, aren't you?" observed his lord and master.

Well for Korusan that his enemy recalled him to due and proper hate. He had been deadly close to conceiving a liking for the creature. "I could snap your neck before you moved to stop me," he said.

Estarion smiled down from that northern height. "I'll wager you could, if a sneeze didn't catch you. Your toes are blue. Why didn't you say something?"

And then, damn his arrogance, he went down on his knees and rubbed life and warmth into Korusan's feet. With his own hands he did it. Grinning, with all his white teeth gleaming. Thinking it a great lark, no doubt, to play the servant to his servant.

He was not even shivering, naked as he was but for a scrap of kilt. He was like a hearthfire, hot as fever, but Korusan knew that he was always so. Beast-warm. Beast-strong. His beard dried in ringlets. He was covered with curly fleece, breast and belly, legs and arms. But his back was smooth, and his sides, and his shoulders.

He was beautiful, as a panther is. Korusan shivered. Estarion leaped to his feet, all long-limbed grace, and fetched a blanket. Korusan flung it in his face. "Enough! This is unseemly."

"It will be more unseemly if you drop dead of a fever. I won't lose another guardsman, Yelloweyes."

"Golden," said Korusan.

A grin was all the answer he gained. Arrogant. Insolent. Thoroughly unrepentant.

Fool, thought Korusan, to make himself so easy to hate. So easy, and so unexpectedly difficult. One could despise his dreadful manners, and shudder at his alien face. But there was still that innocence of his, that transparent conviction that everyone must love him, simply because he was himself.

It would be a pleasure to kill him. But not now. Not too soon. Not until he could know why he died, and who had slain him.

III

Koru-Asan

Godri went to his last rest as best he might in this city of strangers. There was no sand to inter him for the season of the death-vigil, but fire they could give him, and a pyre in the Court of Glories outside the hall in which he had lain in state. Estarion sang the words of the rite, first those of Avaryan's temple in Endros, then those of the desert and the tribes. He sacrificed a fine mare upon the pyre, to bear the soul to its rest, and when it was time to kindle the flame, he called down the sun.

Estarion watched him burn. How long it was, or who lingered, he did not care. He had no tears. That troubled him. He should be able to weep.

He was walled in guards, surrounded by them, watched and warded till his nape crawled. And there were magewalls on him. Iburan's, no doubt, to defend him against a second assassin. He traced them in the ache behind his eyes.

His chambers were no refuge. No more was the harem. His mother was doubly and trebly guarded—they might, after all, strike at her, since they had failed with her son. In the hall of the throne, no one could approach him. Even the Regent stood outside the inner wall of watchers, speaking as Estarion no doubt would speak if he had the wits. Estarion wondered if Firaz counted this a victory in their long and almost amiable war, or a defeat. He could not come close enough to ask, even if the Regent would have answered.

Estarion's loss was not spoken of. Asanian courtesy. Grief was a private matter. One's servants spoke to the servants of the bereaved. Condolences came attached to gifts of minor value, a perfect blossom, a jewel, an image of the departed. Estarion was amazed to see how many small figures appeared in his chambers, the face of each painted with a reasonable likeness of Godri's warrior-patterns.

"They wish to be recorded," Korusan said of the givers, "as sharing your grief. So that you may suspect them less of wishing to slay him."

"No one wanted to kill Godri," Estarion said.

"That is understood," said the Olenyas.

"There are rites of thanksgiving in all the temples," said Estarion, "that I survived the attack. How many people will truly thank their gods, do you think? And how many will pray that the next attempt succeeds?"

"Do you honestly expect that everyone will love you?"

"I'd be content not to be hated."

Korusan shrugged. "Perhaps you should have asked to be born a commoner, or the lord of a little domain, where you could be adored and petted and never troubled with disagreement."

"Then I should better have been born a woolbeast. A blooded ram with nothing to do but grow fine wool and tup the ewes."

"You say it, not I."

Was he laughing? Estarion could not see his eyes, to tell. He was inspecting a tableful of death-gifts. His finger brushed a topaz on a chain. It was the exact clear gold of his eyes.

"Do you want that?" Estarion asked.

His hand jerked back. It was the first unguarded gesture Estarion had seen in him, the first that betrayed him as the boy he was.

"You may have it," Estarion said. "Everyone always gives me topazes. I have chestsful of them."

"Do you dislike them?"

"I like emeralds better. And opals of the Isles. Have you seen them? They're black or deep blue, and shot with fire."

"Like your hair with gold in it?"

"And red and green and blue." Estarion regarded him in some surprise. "You're a poet."

"I am a guard. What is there to do but study my charge?"

"I never thought of that," said Estarion. "Don't Olenyai do anything but guard? They sleep, surely, and eat. And practice weaponry."

"And unarmed combat, and the arts of the hunt."

"And the high arts?"

Korusan took up the jewel on its chain. His voice was as cool as ever. "I can read. I write, a little. I sang before my voice broke. Now I am like a raven with catarrh."

Estarion laughed. "That won't last. You'll sing deep, I think."

"Not as deep as you."

"That's northern blood. The priest, Iburan—he can sound like the earth shifting."

The topaz was gone, secreted somewhere in the swathing of robes. Estarion smiled inside himself. Strange how the world, like grief, could shift and change; how the hated shadow-watcher could become, if not a friend, then a human creature with mind and wits of its own.

"You didn't sleep last night," Estarion said, "and you've been my shadow all day. Don't you need to rest?"

"I slept while you were in Court," said Korusan.

"You've shadowed me since I came here, haven't you?" said Estarion. "It's hard to tell, if one isn't noticing. No faces."

"You see more than you admit to," Korusan said.

"Don't we all?"

The Olenyas moved away from the table. "It is a custom," he said, "for the imperial Olenyai to choose those who will stand in closest attendance upon his majesty. I asked to be chosen."

"Why?"

"I wished to see what you were."

"And what am I?"

"Interesting."

"Haliya says the same thing."

Korusan's eyes widened a fraction.

"A friend," said Estarion. "As Asanian as you, and as chary of showing her face."

"Your concubine," said Korusan. His tone dismissed her with the word. "And I am your servant."

"She talks like that, too. Or is that too insulting to contemplate?"

"You are not Asanian," Korusan said.

"Enough of me is," said Estarion, "to claim blood-right to this place. I hated that, did you know? I wanted to forget that I was ever anything but Varyani. I avoided mirrors, and cultivated hats and hoods, and let no one address me as Son of the Lion."

"You could have revoked your claim," said the Olenyas.

"Of course I couldn't," Estarion said. "It's mine."

"You are," said Korusan, "emperor."

"You hate me for it?"

"Should I love you?"

Estarion grinned and stretched, as if he could widen these walls with his hands and break through to open sky. "You are interesting," he said. "Fascinating. If you study me, may I study you?"

"The emperor may do as he wills."

"The emperor wills . . ." Estarion turned full about, dragging his damnable robes. His mood was as changeable as the sky, now sun, now clouds, now black night.

"Godri is dead," he said. "I should have died in his place. And the sun still shines. The clouds run over the vale of the river. The world cares nothing that I am lord of it, or that my people would cast me down."

"Or raise you up," said Korusan.

"I see," Estarion said in something very like delight. "The people would be death to me. You would be death to my self-pity."

"Does it give you pleasure to feel so sorry for yourself?"

"It gives me considerable gratification," said Estarion, "to think of throttling you in your sleep."

"Then we are alike," said Korusan.

Estarion flashed a grin at him. "Go away," he said. "Sleep. I promise I won't throttle you. This time."

The Olenyas went away. Estarion had not honestly expected him to. But he was tired: Estarion saw it in the droop of the shoulders in the black robe, in the slight drag of the step. A child, yes. A child who knew the use of the swords he wore, and who had slain an assassin with ease and dispatch and no slightest glimmer of remorse.

Other shadows came on guard. Estarion shut them out of mind and sight, and flung himself on the bed in the inner room.

The sun sank slowly into the west of the world. He felt it in his skin. That much was still his, the sun-sense, the land-sense. Asanion, and his father's death, had taken the rest of it away, locked him in himself. But the sun never left him.

He sat up, clasping his knees, resting his chin on them. He was smothering. Stifling. And tonight, if anyone came to kill him . . .

It was easier than he had thought. More fool he, for not thinking of it sooner. Dressed in his wonted armor of robes, he walked calmly and openly into the harem. His shadows halted perforce at the doors. He slipped into an empty chamber and bundled the robes into a chest there, and stood up in well-worn coat and trousers, with a hat in his hand. Still calmly, still openly, he walked through the maze of rooms and passages, empty of the thousand concubines that were the emperor's portion, bare and unguarded.

Haliya's riding court was deserted. She had been there earlier: the marks of hoofs were clear in the sand, a fall of droppings that the servants, careless or in haste, had missed. He circled it, keeping to the shadow of the colonnade. The door was barred but unlocked. The passage was empty. The gate opened to his touch.

He walked past the stalls and the drowsing seneldi, to pause in the shadow of the stable door. Grooms and servants walked past, some briskly, some idling in the long light of evening. He pulled the hat down over his eyes. What men did not expect to see, they failed to see. He squared his shoulders and put on the swagger of an emperor's guardsman at liberty, making his insouciant way to the stews and taverns of the city.

A shadow attached itself to him beyond the Golden Gate, well down the Way of Kings. He neither paused nor turned. But as the road narrowed and divided, he slid hunter-swift into an alleyway, doubled back, shot out a long arm to snare the shadow as it passed.

Olenyas. He had known that: the ringing in his skull was unmistakable. Nor did the eyes surprise him. All gold, and slightly more amused than angry.

"Yes," said Estarion. "You let me catch you. How did you know it was I?"

"Any fool would know," said Korusan. "No one else in this city walks like a hunting cat."

"Only half the northerners in my Guard," Estarion said.

"None of them needs a hat to conceal his eyes." Korusan shifted slightly. "If it does not trouble you overmuch, I would prefer to be throttled in my sleep, and not in a byway of the Upper City."

Estarion let him go. "You're not going to drag me back to prison."

"I would not dream of it," said Korusan.

"No?" said Estarion. "Back with you, then. I've no need of you."

"You have every need of me," said Korusan.

"Your emperor commands you."

"My emperor has sore need of guarding, if he will walk in his city, and his assassin's head barely cold upon its spike."

"They'll think I'm one of my own guardsmen."

"You reckon that an advantage? There is a fine art, my lord, to the disposal of a foreigner in Kundri'j Asan."

"In Endros we call it slugging and rolling. I've run the taverns all over Keruvarion. I can look after myself."

"I shall watch," said Korusan.

Estarion ground his teeth. "I order you to go back to the palace."

Korusan did not move. His eyes were level. Yellow eyes. Were Estarion's own so disconcerting?

He struck the boy's shoulder with his fist, rocking but not felling him. "Follow me, then. And keep your mouth shut."

Korusan's silence was eloquent. Estarion turned on his heel and stalked down the narrow street.

Kundri'j Asan after nightfall was a stranger place even than under the sun. The Upper City retreated into darkness and silence, broken only rarely by the passage of a lord in his litter, with his servants and his guards and his torchbearers. As Estarion descended, the streets grew narrower, the buildings meaner, the people more frequent with their noise and their smells and their crowding bodies. They jostled Estarion, pressed against him, groped toward the purse at his belt. He kept a grip on it and on the dagger beside it.

He should have been intolerably crowded. But it was freedom. No one knew him. No one fled from his path. Merchants importuned him, beggars plucked at him. Wanton women, all but naked save for the inevitable veils, leaned out of windows or beckoned from doorways.

He was not spat on, nor did a knife stab out of the dark. He smelled no conspiracy, heard no voices preaching riot. Of the prophet Vanyi had spoken of, he saw nothing, heard no word. But neither did he hear anyone speak of the emperor. His height and the color of his face brought silence where people stood together.

He had been where riot smoldered. Kundri'j was quieter than that. Happy, no, it was not that, no more than any city in Asanion. It seemed prosperous enough. The hungry were not starving. The beggars had the look of honest guildsmen. Priests and prostitutes shared street-space with no apparent hostility.

He should have been more easy as he walked, rather than less. He had been imprisoned too long. He had forgotten what it was like to walk where he would; and he had never been unknown as he was here. He could even, he suspected, have taken off his hat and met no recognition. The emperor was in his palace. He did not come down among his people, or sully his pure self with their presence.

There was something underneath. Thought, awareness, memory. Longing. Wanting something. Something that was gold, no shadow in it. Prophecy—prophet—

He halted, half-stumbling into a doorway. Something squalled and fled. He started, clutched at the doorpost. He was dizzy. His power felt raw, aching, like a limb too long unused.

A shoulder slid under his arm; an arm circled his middle. Korusan was a fierce warm presence, a familiarity so sharp it burned, as if it had always been, time out of mind. He let himself lean on the Olenyas, lightly, while his body mastered itself.

"You are ill," said Korusan.

"I'm well," Estarion said, "for the first time in far too long. It takes me like this. You shouldn't mind it."

"Mad," said Korusan as if to himself.

"Sane," said Estarion. "Here, stop fretting. I was tasting the city; it was stronger than I thought. It's been cycles since I could even begin to do it. There's something in the palace, I think, that throttles magery."

The boy's eyes were a little wild. "There is something in me—that—" He silenced himself so abruptly that Estarion heard the click of teeth. "My lord, you will come back to the palace. You have had enough of—tasting the city."

"I have not," said Estarion. "I'm not even halfway to where I'm going." He stood straight and pried the boy's arm loose. "I won't take a fit again. My honor on it."

Clearly the Olenyas did not believe in the honor of emperors, but he did not try to stop Estarion from going on. He clung as close as Estarion's own shadow, all but pressed against his side. Estarion sighed and suffered him. He was comfort of a sort, in his robes and veils, armed to the teeth.

The city cast them up at a gate in the third circle, on a quiet street lit at intervals by lamps. That was wealth, to pay men to set up the lamps and keep them filled, and light them at dusk and quench them at dawn. No taverns here, spilling their light and their custom into the street; no tawny-breasted women at the windows. Here all the walls were blank, the gates iron-barred.

The one Estarion sought was unlocked. It opened to his touch, admitting him to a soft-lit precinct, outer court of a temple as it seemed to be, unwatched and unguarded.

But there were watchers. His nape prickled; his head throbbed. He walked boldly into the light, trailing his shadow. "Greeting to the temple," he said, "and goodwill to its priests."

His words fell in silence. He passed from the outer court to the first sanctuary, deserted likewise, lamplit, redolent of incense and the evening rite. The altar was heaped with fruits and flowers. He bowed before it, aware of his shadow's stiff stillness, and laid a coin in the offering-bowl. Prayer he had none, except his presence.

The door behind the altar was open like all the rest. It led to a vestry, and beyond that to the inner house. The priests were all asleep, it seemed, or out upon errands. Estarion might have wondered that they kept so poor a guard, except that it was this temple, and this house, and these priests. They knew him. They admitted him without question: almost pain, to comprehend that.

Only the temple's heart was closed to him. He felt its throb in his bones, the pulse of the Gate under the care of its guardians. He could have forced the door. That power was in him. He did not choose to summon it.

Korusan was clinging to his side again, eyes darting, knuckles white on the hilts of his swords. Estarion touched him; he started. "Down, lad," Estarion said, making no effort to be quiet. "You're safe here. Nothing will eat you."

"And what will devour you?" the boy demanded.

"Nothing," said Estarion. "These are my people here. This is my magic that sets your hackles rising."

"I see no people. I smell no magic."

"It doesn't need your belief," said Estarion, "to be." He moved away from the warded door, following the tug of instinct.

She had a room to herself in an upper corner of the house. The way there was dim, deserted. Once a figure trotted past him. He made no effort to be invisible. The priestess took no notice of him at all. Anyone who came this far, it seemed, was judged to be harmless. He would have called it arrogance, had he known less of palaces.

Her door was latched but not warded. He opened it slowly.

She was asleep. His breath caught at the sight of her in lamplight, clothed only in her hair, with her coverlets fallen on the floor. The room was narrow, bare, no more than a cell. The only light in it was the single lamp, the only ornament the torque about her throat. There was not even a rug for the floor. And yet it was beautiful, because she was in it.

After so much ivory and gold she was blue-white, her hair ruddy-dark, her face sharply angled, her body thin but full enough in the breast, narrow-hipped, long-legged, free in her movements as a boy. She was not tall, but she seemed so, even asleep: she had that gift, to seem larger than she was.

He bent over her. She did not stir. Her scent was dizzying. And nothing in it but herself; no perfume, no sweet oils. He kissed her softly. She sighed. He pressed a little harder. Her lips parted; her arms came up, circled his neck as they always had, always would.

Her body went taut. Her eyes snapped open. She thrust him away. "What in the hells are you doing here?"

He sucked in a breath. "Good evening, Vanyi," he said.

She scrambled herself up, as far away from him as the wall allowed. "What do you think you're doing? Get out of here!"

He sat on the bed's edge. He was perilously tempted to laugh, or else to weep. Neither would have been wise. "I'm glad to see you, too," he said. "Have you been keeping well?"

"You've lost your wits," she said. "How ever did you escape? And what is that?"

He followed the line of her glare. Korusan stood rigid by the door, looking everywhere but at her. "That," Estarion said, "is my shadow. No one will kill me, he's promised. He reserves that pleasure for himself."

Her eyes narrowed. "You look dreadful," she said. "Don't they feed you?"

"You sound exactly like my mother."

"Damn it," she said. She rose, pushing past him. He did not try to catch her. She pulled a robe out of the clothing-chest and put it on, combed her hair with her fingers, knotted it at her nape. Estarion watched. Korusan endeavored bravely not to. She raked him with her glance. "You," she said. "Out."

He ignored her. Estarion bit back a grin. "Out, guardsman," he said.

The Olenyas took station just beyond the door. He could hear everything, surely, but there was no helping that. Estarion doubted that the boy spoke Island patois. He stretched out on the bed. "God and goddess," he said, "I've missed you."

"You should never have come here," she said.

"I'm safer here than I'll ever be in that gilded dungeon. Nobody recognized me in the city, Vanyi. Not one."

"Of course not. You're not in ten robes and a mask." She came to stand over him. "They must be combing the palace for you."

"Not at all. They think I'm in the harem."

He meant her to laugh at it, not to go bitterly cold. "So? And why aren't you?"

"None of them is you."

"I'm sure you've tested it," she said. "Repeatedly. To be sure. Is any of them pregnant yet?"

He sat up sharply. "No!"

"Pity," she said. "It must be tedious, keeping all those women happy. How many are there? A dozen? A hundred? Or do you lose count after a while?"

"Don't be ridiculous," he said. This was not going at all as he meant it to. She loved him, he knew it. He had felt it when he touched her, before she was awake to flay him with her tongue.

"And why shouldn't I be ridiculous? I'm your castoff, your commoner, the one who couldn't carry your baby. Now it's my turn, I suppose, and you're too polite to leave me out of your round."

He tried to be calm. She would think that. Of course. Everyone else did. "I haven't touched even one of them," he said.

"You don't have to lie to me," she said. "I'm jealous, yes, I admit it. I always did hate to let anything go, no matter how long it had been since I tired of it."

"Are you tired of me?" He rose. "Are you really, Vanyi? Or are you only bitter? Maybe you have a right to be. I should have escaped long ago, or brought you into the palace."

"In the harem," she asked, "with all the others? Well for you you didn't try."

"I wouldn't do that to you." He laid his hands on her shoulders. She did not try to elude him. That gave him hope, although her face was stony. "Vanyi, I swear by my father's tomb, I haven't touched any woman but you."

"Then you are a perfect fool." She wrenched out of his grasp. "I don't want you, Estarion. What will it take to convince you of that?"

"More than this," he said. "Your mouth tells me terrible things. Your body loves me still. Why won't you listen to it? I won't be in this place forever. We can go back to Keruvarion, be as we were. And when your Journey is over, you'll be my empress. Even Mother is almost reconciled to it."

"Listen to you," she said. "Your body tells me things, too. It tells me you don't believe yourself, not honestly. You want to believe it. You want me to fall into your arms, give you your night's pleasure, promise you what you can't take. You can't, Estarion. There's no going back, for any of us."

"There is," he said stubbornly. "Damn you, Vanyi. I love you."

"So you do," she said. "So much that you won't leave me alone when I ask, you creep up on me in my sleep, you all but rape me before I'm awake to know it."

"Rape?" The word caught in his throat. "That was rape? By the thousand false Asanian gods, I hope you never know anything worse."

She was white and set, hateful, hating him. He wanted to hit her. He wanted to weep in her arms for all that they had had, and that she would not let them win back. "Why?" he cried. "Why do you do this?"

"Because I must." Damn her calm. Damn her cruelty. "Take your shadow, my lord. Go back where you belong."

"No," he said. His hands clenched, unclenched. "Not without you."

"Then you will have to force me," she said, "because I will not go of my own will."

"Stubborn, obstinate, muleheaded—" He stopped for breath. "Vanyi! For the love of god and goddess—"

"For the love of your empire," she said, merciless, "no."

"When have you ever cared for my empire?"

"When have you cared for anything but what suited your whim?"

"God," he said, "and goddess. Godri is dead, Vanyi. I came to you—"

"You came crying to me, hoping I'd make it better. It's all I've ever been. A shoulder to cry on. A body to sate yourself with. You have a whole harem full of them now. Why do you trouble with me?"

"Because I love you!"

"If you loved me," she said, "you would go now. And not come back."

"Why?"

She turned her back on him.

He battered down the walls of his mind. He stretched a power gone soft and slack with disuse, and touched.

Walls. They were higher than his own, and stronger. When he pressed, they caught fire. They drove him stumbling back. They held him behind his own gates, warned him with lightnings when he ventured resistance.

A great anger swelled in him. Pain fed it, and grief, and the sheer bleak incomprehensibility of her hatred. For it was that. It could not be anything else.

"Very well," he said, soft and calm. "I shall not trouble you again. Madam." He inclined his head, though she could not have seen the courtesy. He left her standing there, cold hating obstinate woman, with her magic and her priesthood and her sacred solitude.

27

KORUSAN DID NOT say anything, which was a virtue Estarion could admire. Nor did he follow Estarion back into the harem. Estarion was somewhat surprised at that. He vanished into the shadows of the passage.

Estarion walked through the riding court in starlight, and into the harem proper. Its halls were as empty as ever, echoing faintly with his footsteps. He paused where he should turn to take the outer way.

Had Vanyi not given him full leave, all but commanded him?

He passed the first door, and the second, on which a eunuch stood guard. The servant bowed before him. He had half expected to be forbidden, late as it was. But this was his harem. His whim ruled it. Everyone said so.

Word traveled swiftly here. It was the lifeblood of the harem to know when its lord walked in it. They were awake, all nine of them, and waiting for him. They had been waiting, it was evident, for long and long. The youngest, the pretty child with the ivory curls, had fallen asleep in Ziana's lap.

They did not ask him where he had been, or why he looked so strange. He did not doubt that he did. His face felt stiff; his jaw ached.

Any, he thought, or all. Not little Shaia; she was barely come to her courses. Haughty Eluya, sweet-voiced Kania, Igalla and Maiana and Uzia and Ushannin, beautiful Ziana and her unwontedly silent sister. Any of them or all of them. They knew that this was a choosing. Their tension was palpable, although they strove to conceal it.

He circled the room as he had that first day, setting a kiss on each brow. Eluya was like marble, enduring him. Igalla's eyelids fluttered as if she would faint. Ziana offered him her lips, full, rose-gold, enchanting. Her perfume was honey and *ailith*-blossoms.

As before, he came last to Haliya. She seemed to expect it, to be resigned to it. Courtesy commanded that each lady be greeted properly; then the lord chose his favored one. She half slid away from him, easing his return to her sister. The others were all looking at Ziana as Asanians did, sidelong, measuring her.

He caught Haliya in his arms. She was too startled to do more than stare. When he lifted her, she was astonished. So much so that she did not open her mouth until they were in the inner room, and the door was shut and the bed was waiting and he had set her on her feet beside it. "You don't want me!"

"Would you rather I didn't?" he asked, sharply maybe. Maybe only aggrieved.

Her answer was as forthright as the rest of her. She reached as high as she could, clasped her hands behind his neck, pulled him down.

"Beautiful, beautiful, beautiful."

Her wonderment made him smile in spite of himself. Asanians did not, after all, practice the high arts in their robes. They made an art of getting rid of them. She made short work of his coat and trousers, shirt and trews. Marveling at him; reveling in him. Stroking him as if he had been a great purring cat, running fingers through his loosened hair, playing with his beard. She was nothing like Vanyi. She was both more innocent and more skilled. She knew what gave a man most pleasure, but it was all new to her, all wonderful.

The hard core of anger neither softened nor went away. But he had come to do grim duty. She was making it a pleasure.

He could more than once have put an end to it. Her boldness was half fear, her art half instinct. She was a maiden.

"We're very careful of that," she said, "when we have our training."

"You train? As if for war?"

She sat astride him. She was small, but her breasts were deep and full, her hips ample. He filled his hands with her. She filled herself with him, riding lightly, grinning down at him. "Am I not a brave warrior?"

"The bravest," he said, while he still could say anything.

Women in the east made more of their virginity than this western woman did. "For me," she said as they lay together, she in his arms, toying with the curly hair of his chest, "the hardest thing was to show my face. The rest of it was simple. I was so afraid you'd find me wanting. I'm not pretty, I know. I never was. I've been a great disappointment to my family."

"Even now?" he asked.

"Oh," she said. "Now they're all astonished. You were supposed to choose Ziana first. Is it that she's too beautiful? Are you trying the waters with me, to work yourself up to her?"

"She's interesting," he admitted, "to look at. But I like a woman who can talk to me."

"She's very witty. She saves it, that's all, for the inner room."

"Can she ride a senel? And shoot a bow?"

She struggled up. "How did you know about that?"

"Spies," he said. "Did you think the bow and the arrows just appeared on your mare's saddle?"

"I thought the grooms made a mistake and saddled her for one of the guards."

"A mistake they've made every day since," he said.

She hovered above him. Her hair streamed down, bright gold. It, like her eyes, like her breasts and her hips and her sweet rounded thighs, was beautiful. "I can be an idiot sometimes," she said. "Did you know that your eyes tilt up at the corners when you smile? And your tongue isn't pink, not really. It's a little bit blue."

"Isn't yours?"

She presented it for his inspection.

"Pink," he said, "all through. How odd."

"You are odd. You aren't all black, like a shadow. You're like glass. I can see underneath. What happens when you faint? Do you go blue?"

"My lips go grey," he said.

"We go green. And try to fall gracefully. It's an art."

He tangled his hands in her hair. "Is everything an art with you?"

"Everything." She swooped down to set a kiss on his cheek. "Oh, I do like you. Do you like me?"

"Very much," he said.

She did not say the next thing, the thing he dreaded. Maybe Asanians did not know about it. She wriggled down the length of him, doing things that he had not known a woman could do, with such delight in discovery that he could not help but laugh.

He had begun the night in grief and rage. He ended it in laughter. That was a gift. He had the wits to cherish it, and the one who gave it.

Estarion started awake. The bed under him felt strange, over-soft, scented with perfumes. He was alone in it.

He lay for a while, piecing together memory. Godri—Vanyi—Haliya—

He had dreamed that last. Surely he had. But this was not his bed, this billowing mound of cushions, and this was not his chamber, with its sweeps and swathes of curtains. He was naked in it, his body loosed, eased as only a woman could ease it.

The anger was still in him, the tight, hurting thing that thrust out guilt. Regret, he had none. They wanted him to choose. He had chosen. Haliya would do. She might even do well. As for the nonsense of love, that was forbidden him. Vanyi had made that very clear, clearest of all who undertook to teach him his duty.

He had been slow to learn it, but now he had it. He would

be the emperor they wished him to be. And since this was Asanion, he would be emperor as emperors were in the Golden Empire. Cold. Devious. Ruling as spiders ruled, from the heart of the web.

Servants appeared, knowing by some art of theirs that the emperor was awake. They bathed him, dressed him, brought him food and drink. He had little appetite, but the wine was welcome. When he had drunk the flagon dry, Haliya was brought in to him.

The laughing wanton lover of the night was gone. In her place stood an Asanian lady in a furlong of silk, painted and scented and jeweled and refusing adamantly to meet his glance. Even when he rose and went to her and tilted up her chin.

"Haliya," he said. "Whatever has come over you?"

Her face was tight, her voice stretched thin. "I am not a maiden now. I must be a woman."

"Who told you that?"

"It is custom," she said.

"Custom be damned." Her eyelids were gilded. His finger, brushing them, came away tipped with gold. "I liked you as you were before. Surely you won't be living your whole life now in all that silk? And paint—you can't ride a senel with your face covered with gilt."

"A woman never rides a senel."

"Even if her lord commands her to?"

Her eyes flashed up then, as bright as they ever were. "Does my lord command?"

"Your lord commands," he said.

She grinned, brief but brilliant. She smoothed a fold of her outer gown. "I do look ridiculous, don't I?"

"You look very splendid," he said, "and very uncomfortable. I much prefer you in trousers on your mare."

She blushed scarlet under the gilt, startled him by pulling his head down and kissing him soundly, and left him with a lightness in her step that looked fair to turn into a dance.

Her gladness warmed him. Too much, maybe. He sent for

another flagon of wine. It settled him, cooled his heart again, steeled him to be emperor.

Korusan stood guard on his proper chambers. Estarion did not know how to read the glance the Olenyas shot him, nor did he care. Much. It was not admiration, he did not think. Envy? Amusement? He was not about to ask. An emperor did not take notice of his servants, except to command them.

That resolution lasted exactly as long as it took him to endure his hour in the hall, and to hold audience with a company of princes, and—great wonder and rarity—to ride for a few brief moments in his garden. Umizan was more fractious even than usual. Estarion had to rebuke him, which was unheard of. "Brother," he said to the flattened ears. "Do you want me to set you free?"

The ears flattened to invisibility, and the stallion bucked, sharp and short.

"Yes," Estarion said, "and I don't want to lose you, either. But you're going mad here."

A blue eye rolled back.

"I can't escape it," said Estarion. "You can. Ulyai is long gone. I lay no blame on her: she only did what was wise. You can do the same."

Umizan half-reared, curvetted, lashed his tail as if he had been a cat. But when he had done that, he went still. His skin shuddered. He snorted.

Tears pricked in Estarion's eyes, the first in long seasons. "Yes, brother. It's wise. In the morning I'll send you away."

Umizan's head drooped. Estarion stroked his neck, trying to comfort him. "It won't be forever, brother. Only as long as I'm pent up in Kundri'j."

"He understands your speech?"

Estarion regarded Korusan in surprise. The Olenyas had been watching here as he did everywhere else. Estarion slid from the saddle, keeping his arm about Umizan's neck, smoothing the long mane. "He is my hoofed brother," he said, "and he comes of the Mad One's line."

Korusan walked round the senel. Umizan's ear followed him, but did not go flat. That interested Estarion. Umizan did not like strangers, and he detested Asanians. This one he suffered even to touch him, to run a hand down his neck and flank, to exchange senel-courtesies, nose to shrouded nose.

"He is very beautiful," said the Olenyas.

"You may ride him if you like," said Estarion, out of nowhere that he could think of.

"He will suffer me?"

"Ask him," Estarion said.

Korusan stroked the stallion's muzzle, taking his time about it. He did not speak. Umizan blew gently into his palm. He took reins, wound fingers in mane, vaulted lightly astride.

He rode well. Asanians often did. His hands were light, which was not common. He put Umizan through the dance of his paces. There was no telling behind the veils, but Estarion thought he might be smiling.

He brought the stallion to a halt in front of Estarion. His eyes were bright but his voice was cool. "Yes, you should send him away. He does not thrive in this confinement."

"So. He talks to you, too," Estarion said. He did not know that he was jealous. Interested, rather. Wary.

"He is not difficult to understand." Korusan swung down, stepped away, leaving the senel to his master. He did not do it easily: there was a drag in the movement, quick though it was.

Estarion had won in hard battle the right to tend his own senel. Korusan lent a hand, capable in that as in everything else he did. They were almost companionable, walking up from the stable, man and shadow, emperor and Olenyas.

VANYI STOOD UNMOVING for a long while after Estarion went away. The trembling began in her center and spread swiftly outward, till it buckled her knees and toppled her to the floor, gasping, fighting the tears that she would not, must not shed.

But she had fought them too long. She had no defenses left. She wept hard and she wept long, till her throat was raw and her ribs ached. And when she had no tears left, she lay where her fit had cast her, and she began to laugh. Weak laughter, laughter that, in its way, both sobered and steadied her.

She went down to the Gate. It was not yet her time to stand guard, but one of the priests there was pleased to gain an early escape, and the others did not vex her with questions. There had been nothing, no sign, no suspicion, either before or after the attempt on the emperor's life. It must be as rumor said: an assassin hired by rebels, with a warding on him, a common enough magic, within the powers even of a streetcorner mage. It had nothing to do with Gates or with the great magics.

There were no mages strong enough to oppose the priests of the temple. Those who served lords and princes in Asanion were trained often enough in Endros or in the Nine Cities, or trained one another under the eye of the temples. The wild ones, the herb-healers and wisewomen and purveyors of village curses, could do no harm beyond their narrow reach. What harm they did was punished swiftly by priests passing through on Journey, or by hunters sent out from the temples, or by lords' mages who did not suffer rivals.

That much good the Sunborn had done. Magic was a known thing now. Dark magic and death-magic were forbidden or carefully circumscribed. The mageborn need not suffer the sins of ignorance; the sorcerers, those who came to power through the word and the work and not through the gift of birth, had leave to learn their arts in peace.

Vanyi, mageborn and temple-trained, let her power bathe in the shimmer of the Gate. Its fire was cold and clean, its strength unwearied. She had been in the Heart of the World, that place like a fortress, where all guardians of Gates must go before they took up their charge. She had seen the flame in the hearth, walked in it and through it as part of her testing. She wondered now as she did then, that human creatures should have wrought such a thing, and made it everlasting. Not all or even most that was of the Guild was evil. It had striven to take power in the world, which was its downfall. In its day it had been a great and glorious thing, each mage a master of one of the faces of power, dark or light, and each paired with his opposite. That, the temples had lost. Some priest-mages served the god, some the goddess; they did not work together save in great need.

She was distracting herself from her folly, and from the lover she had driven away. And why not? This was hers, this duty and this calling.

As she stood her watch, a shadow paced through the door. It had been barred and warded; but the shadow took no notice of it. It wore a cat's shape, a cat's lambent eyes, its belly heavy with young.

Vanyi had been kneeling by the Gate. She rose slowly. The other Guardians were mute and motionless, as if enspelled. "Ulyai," she said, or willed to say.

Estarion's sister-in-fur heard: her ear cocked. She took no other notice. She approached the Gate as calmly as if it had been a door. It shifted, shimmered. She sat on her haunches to watch.

"Ulyai," said Vanyi. "How did you get in here?"

Ulyai set to work washing her paws. Where she had been, how she had hunted, there was no telling. She was no more magical than she ever had been, and no less.

The ul-cats of Endros' palace were a law unto themselves. They had their own courtyard and their own garden, lived and bred and hunted as they chose, came and went at will, and answered to none but the emperor or their chosen kin-without-fur. Ulyai had been Estarion's companion since he came back from his first sojourn in the west.

She had not followed him into Kundri'j. Wise cat. Yet now she was here, magical unmagical beast, watching the dance of the worlds.

Vanyi made no move to touch her. It was only prudence. She was as large as a child's pony, with fangs as long as knives.

She washed herself all over, meticulous as a lady's lapcat. Then she rose, stretched each separate muscle—was that where Estarion had learned it, or had she learned it from him?—and yawned enormously. The world-dance had slowed as it sometimes did. Ulyai's ears pricked. These were green worlds now, fields and plains and forests.

She crouched. Vanyi goggled like an idiot as the cat leaped long and high and light, into the Gate.

She caught herself the instant before she sprang in pursuit. The Gate pulsed and began to sing, a deep musical humming. Vanyi's magery uncoiled of its own accord, to slow the pulse, to damp the power.

Something.

Something watching.

Something flitting, shadow-quick, shadow-subtle.

Something in the Gate.

Not Ulyai. The cat was gone. Vanyi stalked the shadow through the flicker and shimmer of the Gate. Unwise, unwise, her training yattered at her, to do this alone, unwarded, unwatched—the priests with her worse than useless, rapt in a dream of Gatesong.

Nothing.

There had been something. Vanyi was sure of it. Something—someone—some power in the Gate, using it, passing through it.

All those worlds—might not they too have mages, guardians, wielders of Gates?

So they might. But this had a feel of this world, and not a beast, not a cat or a senel or a lesser creature stumbling into an ill-warded Gate. This shadow had moved with will and purpose, with intelligence, as a man would. A mage.

Priest-mages used Gates—rarely, with great caution, and never alone, for Gates were dangerous. But there had been none such since the emperor left Endros, no need and no occasion. If there had, she would have known; and likewise every other Guardian in the twofold empire.

She could not go to Iburan, even if he had been in the temple and not in the empress' bed. Not until she knew certainly what she had sensed. They had alarms enough, with the attempt on the emperor's life. They did not need this, which came to no more than a passage of shadows.

And maybe, she thought, she had dreamed it all. Her companions, who had seemed bewitched, were awake now and on watch; they remembered nothing, no ul-cat coming out of the night, no disturbance in the Gate. Both were her elders, and more skilled in magecraft than she; and she had had night-terrors of Gates before, eyes in the dark, presences on the edge of her senses. Nothing had ever come of them. She had too much magery, she always had. It made her see shadows where no shadows were.

Tonight in particular she was not the best of judges. She would wait and watch and see. If another shadow passed, another power betrayed itself, she would be ready. She would discover what it was that wielded Gates, and took no heed of wards or guards. And if it was not dream or delusion, was the Guild as she had feared for so long, feared and yes, hoped . . .

Then she would go to Iburan and the others. Then they would do what they must do.

29

Korusan sat in the shadow of a pillar, glowering at the door to the emperor's harem. He could pass it easily, if he were minded. Neither eunuch nor armored woman could stop him.

At the moment it did not suit his fancy to walk where, of men entire, only the emperor should walk. His majesty was within, doing what a man did in his own harem. He had taken an unconscionable while to work himself up to it, but since the night he went to the priestess in the Mages' temple, he had visited his concubines every evening and often nightlong.

Concubine. It was only the one, the Vinicharyas, and not the beauty of the pair either. A fair number of wagers had been won and lost over that. Korusan had a fine new sword and a string of firestones, for opining that a barbarian would more likely choose a woman who could ride and shoot than one whose only skill was to please her lord in the inner room.

They said that the barbarian was not unskilled in pleasing his lady and servant. For a barbarian. The lady was looking well satisfied.

Korusan had seen her. She rode her hammer-headed mare without a veil, thinking herself safe from scrutiny. Her hair was the true gold and her eyes were like the beaten metal, but her face was a little better than plain, and her mouth was too wide, and where the sun touched her, she freckled. He did not think, from what he saw of her in tunic and trousers, that she was very much more remarkable beneath them. A good depth of breast, yes, and ample hips, but no more than any woman should have if she was to breed strong sons.

His scowl deepened. If he had been a mage, he could have burned down the door with his glare. His majesty was going about it with a good will, to be sure. And it was no secret where Korusan walked and listened, that the emperor had succeeded already in breaking the mage-bonds laid on his priestess. They had been strong enough to lose her the child, but she should never have conceived at all.

There were no bonds on the lady in the harem. She was young, hale, of good fertile stock—her father had a dozen sons and daughters innumerable, and four of the sons were born of her mother. Wages now turned not on whether, but on when.

Korusan would get no sons. The pain of that was old now, the wound scarred over. It still ached when the soul's wind blew cold.

And that one, that upstart, that mongrel, could not fail even when he wished to. Such irony, thought Korusan. The Sun's whelp was getting sons behind that door, not even knowing that his shadow waited alone, nor troubling himself to care.

It would be a nuisance to dispose of the woman and the infant, if any of them lived so long. And suppose that there was no child. It was possible. Even Sun-bolts were not unerring to every target.

Suppose that the Varyani emperor went back to his priestess. She had driven him away ruthlessly—strong-willed as an Olenyas, and prickly proud. But suppose that she softened. She would not allow herself to bear a child until she was initiate; she wanted that, for a surety, and now that she had warning, she could guard herself against it.

She was besotted with the emperor. That was obvious even when she drove him out with curses. He was besotted with her. He talked about her endlessly, pacing and prowling, till Korusan knew every word she had ever spoken, every move she had ever made. He did not speak of his concubine at all, except to mutter that *she* was a sensible woman, *she* did not scream and strike at him for daring to breathe in her presence.

Korusan rose, working knots out of knees and back. The ache in his bones was fierce tonight. It was always there, gnawing on the edges, biding its time until it killed him. But he was its master still. He drove it out with a swift turn of the warrior's dance, leap and curvet, stamp and whirl and swift slashing stroke, down the length of the passage; and at the end a tumbler's leap and plummet and somersault. He came up breathing hard, laughing silent Olenyai laughter, striding out past astonished, staring eunuchs.

He had not expected to enter the temple as easily as the emperor had. Nor did he. There was a guard at the gate this night, a large and deceptively idle young clean-shaven northerner in a priest's robe and braid and torque. But there was no one watching the wall in the back, nor any magic to prevent a shadow from going over it.

The priestess was not in her chamber. Korusan tracked her by scent and sense and instinct to a room redolent with the scents of ink and parchment, bursting-full with books in their rolls and cases. A table stood in the middle of it, with a light like a star hanging in the air, magelight, clear and pure and blindingly bright. In that uncanny splendor her hair was the color of sweetwood, red and brown and gold intermingled, and her eyes the clear grey of flint. She had a pen in her hand and a roll of parchment before her, with words written on it, copied from the ancient and crumbling book at her elbow; but her head was up, her gaze fixed on the dark beyond the light. She did not look angry or sullen, or even sad.

As he watched, she lifted the hand that did not hold the pen, and traced an intricate pattern in the air. It shaped itself in red-gold fire, hovering after her hand retreated. She inspected it without astonishment, frowning a little, retracing one of its many woven curves. It flexed like a living thing, smoothed, flattened, sank down to the written page and spread itself there, as if it had been a bird and that its nest. Korusan fancied that it tucked its lacework beak beneath a latticed wing and went placidly to sleep.

A shiver ran down his spine. He had seen mages at their workings. They had worked on him more often than it comforted him to recall. But this was magic so calm, so matter-of-fact, performed with such ease and apparent pleasure, that it took him aback.

The priestess smiled at her handiwork and applied pen to parchment, writing smoothly and swiftly, as one who did it often. He recognized the characters of the Gileni script, but not the words.

He came to stand at her shoulder, moving as soft as a cat or an Olenyas. He watched her become aware of him. She was not alarmed. What Keruvarion must be like, that everyone he saw who came from it would let anyone walk up behind, and know no fear: he could not imagine it. Maybe it was that so many of them were mages. They thought themselves invulnerable.

Out of curiosity, and because she needed the lesson, he leaned forward, peering at the image she had made with magic. She started most satisfactorily. "Who—" He met her eyes. Her mouth snapped shut. What came then was tight and hard, as through gritted teeth. "Tell him no. I will not go to him, summoned or unsummoned."

Korusan should not have been surprised. "He has not summoned you," he said. "He is with his ladies."

That might have been a misjudgment: she had a temper, and it thrust her to her feet. She was smaller than he. Interesting. He had thought of her as tall. She was so, if she had been Asanian, but for an easterner she was a small woman. "Then why are you here?" she demanded.

Presence of mind, too. Korusan was beginning to like this odd fierce creature. He shrugged at her question. "I had thought," he said, "that you might wish to know to what you drove him."

"Why? What profit is in it for you?"

He gave her a part of the truth. "I would wish that a lady of good family not bear mongrel offspring."

She very nearly struck him. He could have eluded her, if he chose to. She knew that: she showed him her teeth, and her flattened hand. "Sometimes," she said, "you people are repellent."

"And you, madam, are without flaw?"

She returned to her seat. She was not wary of him, which was either courage or great folly. She took up the pen and turned it in her fingers, but her eyes lingered on him. "You're his shadow," she said. "They all call you that. Do you dog his steps because you love him, or because it pleases you to hold his life in your hand?"

"I am his guard and his servant," said Korusan. "But for me, when the assassin struck, he would have died. Do your people understand life-debt?"

"We understand that Asanians are anciently inscrutable, and Olenyai worst of all. Does life-debt mean that you are bound to him until you set him free?"

"And he to me." Korusan inclined his head. "You understand much."

"He wouldn't agree with you." The pen snapped between her fingers. She laid down the shards of it carefully, as if she feared to break them further. "What do you want with me?"

"To understand you," he said.

"Why?"

"Because," he said, "my master loves you."

Her fists struck the table. "Stop it! Will you stop it? Bad enough that he hounds me and haunts me and drives me to distraction. Must I have his every slave and servant doing the same?"

"Why?" asked Korusan. "Has anyone else come to you?"

"No!" She lowered her head into her hands. It was not defeat, nor was it weariness. It was violence grimly throttled. "Go away," she said.

He went. She had not expected him to. But he was not Estarion, to resist will as well as word. She raised her head from her hands. The shadow of him lingered in the room: a shape of veils and silent movement, soft voice and wide bright eyes. Feverish, she thought. As if he were ill, or touched with something of his master's fire.

She swept up the first thing that came to hand: an empty scroll-case, solid and heavy. With all her force, she hurled it at the wall.

The silence afterward was blessed. She stared at the dent the case had made in the plastered wall, and called to mind each line of that faceless shape. He had eyes like Estarion's, lion-eyes as they called them here. She had thought them plain Asanian until she came to this place and found that eyes in the Golden Empire were much as elsewhere, more often yellow than brown, but never whiteless like an animal's.

Shaiyel was not unduly disturbed to be roused in the middle of the night, although the priestess with him blushed and hid her face from the light. It was a sin in Asanion, Vanyi recalled out of nowhere in particular, for a grown man to lie in bed alone. Shaiyel smiled at her, welcoming her, offering what hospitality a priest could in his cell: a seat on the stool, a cup of water from the jar.

She declined them. "Shaiyel," she said. "Tell me about eyes of the Lion."

His own widened. They were amber-gold, large, round, and quite human. "They are the mark of the blood imperial," he said.

"Always?" Vanyi demanded.

He clutched a robe about him and rose, pouring a cup of water, sipping it before he spoke. "There have been lines of slaves," he said, "but they never prospered. Too many defectives. Too many incorrigibles. It's something in the blood. It goes with the eyes, maybe; I don't know. I'm neither physician nor healer."

"What of the Olenyai? Do they have a strain of it, too?"

"Very little is known of them," Shaiyel said. "I suppose it's possible. I've never seen one who, as far as I could tell, was anything but plain Asanian. Purer blood than most, maybe, and better breeding; but there are lordly houses that can claim as much."

"Have you noticed the emperor's shadow?" She spoke of Estarion without her voice breaking. She was proud of that.

"Ah," said Shaiyel. "That one. He has life-debt. I wonder if Starion knows what that means."

"I doubt it," said Vanyi. So: that much was true. "Do you think that any of the old royal line survived?"

"Certainly," said Shaiyel, drawing her into a knot until he said, "Starion is the last of it. He even has the eyes. His son will, too, if he goes on as he's begun."

"No," said Vanyi, thrusting pain aside. "I don't mean Estarion. Could there have been others who were full Asanian? Didn't Hirel let one of his sisters marry?"

"Jania," said Shaiyel. "Yes. But that was far away in the west, almost to the sea. And her line died out, I heard, as the slave-lines did, and for much the same cause."

"And," said Vanyi to herself, "there's no way they could have gone among the Olenyai. The blackrobes don't take in strangers. Do they?"

"So we're told," Shaiyel said. "Their lines are more sacred to them than our altars are to us. We can break an altar if we must. They won't break their bloodlines."

Vanyi shook herself. "This place . . . I'm starting at shadows. He came this evening, you see. The Olenyas. He seemed curious, as if he were inspecting me. I think he wants to breed me to his emperor."

It did not come out as lightly as she wanted it to. Shaiyel touched her hand in sympathy. "There's no understanding Olenyai. Maybe he wanted to see what you were, and he'll come back again when he judges it time, and ask you the question that's in his mind."

"Probably not," she said. "I told him to go away. If he wants his fortune told, there are mountebanks in the market who can do it better than I."

"But is any of them the emperor's beloved?"

"I don't *want* to be—" She broke off. "Shaiyel, I don't like it, that he came to me. He's not what he seems to be. I know, Olenyai can't be read, they have a magery on them. But there's something under it. And it frightens me."

Shaiyel had no comfort to offer. She left him as soon as she could, sooner maybe than was polite.

Dawn surprised her. She had been walking nightlong, back and forth through the temple, round about its gardens, up the street and back again. When she realized that she could see her hand in front of her without the aid of the lamps, she was standing at the crossing, poised to turn back toward the temple.

She drew a breath. The city was waking about her. Some of it had never gone to sleep.

A woman without a veil, walking the open street, was a scandal, but a priestess in robe and torque, hair plaited behind her, was not reckoned as other women were. Once or twice people spat just past her. More often they bowed or gave her room.

The palace admitted her without question. Some of the guards were Estarion's own from Endros. It half warmed, half pained her that they were still there. They greeted her with pleasure, even with fondness. They were all full of the emperor's nights in the harem: not meaning to be cruel, but it was clear, was it not, that she had set him free. And it would be a wonderful thing, or a dreadful one, if he sired a son in Asanion, of an Asanian woman.

She was almost glad to enter the perfumed confines of the queen's palace. The empress had done what she could to make it bearable: torn down hangings, discarded cushions and carpets, flung windows wide. It was still a stifling prison.

Vanyi had to wait to be admitted. She did not mind overmuch. Servants brought breakfast, which she nibbled at, and offered diversion. She accepted the book. She refused the lute-player.

She was beginning to think that she had acted too quickly. What could the empress do? Vanyi had nothing more than vague suspicions, an intrusion in a Gate, an Olenyas with the eyes of an emperor. Plain sense would bid her consider that she was a woman still unbalanced from the loss of a child, further shaken by the loss of a lover, and prey to wild fancies.

Just as she gathered to rise and escape, a eunuch entered and bowed. "The empress will see you now," he said.

The empress had been celebrating the rite of the goddess: she was still in her robes with her hair loose down her back, and a look on her as of one who has not quite returned from the gods' realm to mortal reality. Vanyi, who had forgotten the sunrise-rite in her distraction, knew a stab of guilt. It did nothing to sweeten her mood. She managed a punctilious obeisance, even a proper greeting.

Merian forestalled it before it went on too long. "Enough. This may be Asanion, but I prefer the usages of Keruvarion. Will you sit? Have you eaten?"

"Your servants saw to it, lady," Vanyi said.

"Then you will pardon me if I break my fast in front of you."

Vanyi inclined her head. Merian's servants brought a much lighter repast than they had offered Vanyi, bread only, and fruit, and water scented with the sour-sweetness of starfruit.

The empress seemed to take an endless time about her frugal meal, chewing each minute bite, swallowing, pausing as if in prayer before she took another. Vanyi was ready to scream by the time Merian put down the last bit of fruit half-tasted and waved the rest away, and said, "Tell me."

"I know about Estarion," Vanyi said, which was not how she had meant to begin at all.

"Everyone knows about Estarion," said his mother. "Do you want him back?"

"No," Vanyi said, "damn it. Everyone asks me that, too."

"Including Estarion?"

"I'm the one who drove him to it."

"So you both may like to think." Merian sat back in her tall chair, as much at ease as she ever allowed herself to be. "My son is quite excessively dutiful, and quite clever at casting blame on others for the pain it costs him."

"I had a great deal to do with it," Vanyi said. "Don't try to tell me I didn't. It's what you wanted, isn't it? I hear she's even a hoyden, as Asanians go. He gave her a senel, and she rides it every day."

"She is quite charming," said Merian, "and very forthright in her opinions."

"I'm sure that delights him."

"It is what he is accustomed to."

Vanyi wanted to laugh, but if she did, she would burst into tears. "He does like a woman who will give as good as she gets."

"Even now," said Merian. She sighed. "He is changing. Asanion has altered him."

"For the better?"

"For the worse." The empress rose and began to pace. Vanyi had never seen her restless before. She walked to the wall and spun. "No. Not for the worse. I cannot reckon it, or him. He comes to me, he speaks, he is courteous, he is everything a son should be. And yet he seems to me to be walking in a dream."

"A nightmare," said Vanyi.

"Yes." Merian closed her eyes for a moment. "And since his squire died, there is no touching him at all, mind or body. He has closed himself off altogether."

"He . . . came to me," Vanyi said through a narrowing throat. "He wanted . . ."

"Of course you refused," said Merian. Vanyi could not judge her tone, whether she meant to lend comfort or to prick with scorn. "If you had accepted, you would have broken your vows."

Comfort or scorn, it did not matter. "So he went to the Asanian woman," Vanyi said. "And now he belongs to her."

"You should not envision her as a snare or a temptress," Merian said. "She is a child who was born to breed princes."

"And so she will," said Vanyi. "But I didn't come to speak of her. Or even, directly, of him."

Merian waited, one brow lifted.

"You know his Olenyas," Vanyi said. "The one who never leaves him."

"The one who bears the life-debt." Merian sighed. "I know him."

"Have you noticed his eyes?"

"Should I?"

"Have you?"

Merian half-smiled. "You think that he is a lost heir to the Golden Throne?"

"Couldn't he be?"

"It is possible," Merian said. "And if it were, would he have slain the assassin who was striking at my son?"

"He might, if he had in mind more than simple assassination."

"Such as?"

"Revenge," said Vanyi. "Payment for all the years of Varyani rule in Asanion. That's why your husband died, isn't it? Because he dared to be emperor, and to be a foreigner. Estarion has an advantage his father lacked: the one thing, the sign that marks Asian royalty."

"There is somewhat more to him, and it, than that."

"Of course there is," said Vanyi. "And there's more to this blackrobe than life-debt or loyalty or any other Asian claim to virtue. He's shielded from magery—"

"They all are," said Merian, cutting her off. "They wear a talisman; they have done so for as long as anyone remembers."

"Yes, and who makes the talismans? Who raises the wards?"

"Mages," said Merian.

"Mages of the Guild?"

"The Guild is dead."

"What if it's not?"

Merian stood in front of her, eyes level upon her face. It was not a challenge. She was not, Vanyi thought, the enemy. "Do you have proof?"

"No," said Vanyi. "Not yet."

"Why do you think it, then? Might there not be mages in Asanion as elsewhere, who may be willing, for a price, to set a simple spell? Or they may be Olenyai themselves, those mages. Why not? It is a useful thing for a warrior and a guardsman to be protected against magic. We do the same for our own, when we think of it."

"I can't explain," Vanyi said, though she hated to show that weakness. "It has to do, a little, with Gates, and feelings in my bones. If I can gather proof—if I can prove that the Guild survives, and that it is using the Gates—will you stand by me?"

"What will you do if you find proof?"

"Confront them," said Vanyi. "Discover their purposes. If they mean the empire no harm, then well for them. If they're up to their old tricks . . ."

"You may of course be obsessed," the empress observed.

"I know that." Vanyi quelled her temper. "My lady, much of magery is in the bones and the instincts. We forget that, with our training and our tests, our rules and laws and vows."

"You would instruct me, priestess?"

The empress was not angry. Vanyi allowed herself the flicker of a smile. "I'm instructing myself. I have nothing more than a feeling and a fear. I tell myself that even if there is a threat, there's nothing at all that would suggest the Guild."

"Except that your uneasiness began in connection with Gates."

"Yes." Vanyi rubbed her aching eyes. "And the Guild made the Gates. I'm even hoping it's they, and not something else—something incalculable. There are a million worlds out there. Who knows what moves in them?"

"And the Olenyai?"

"Maybe there I am jumping at shadows. They're uncanny enough, and they know it. And that boy has lion-eyes."

"Everything in Asanion is shadow," said the empress. "And

I am priestess of the dark between the stars, and I—even I—would give heart's blood to be in my own land again."

Vanyi would give her sympathy, but she had little enough to spare for herself. "So would we all," she said. "Lady, if you judge it wise, would you go to your son? Warn him. Tell him not to trust his Olenyai, and least of all the one who clings closest."

Merian took her time in responding. When she did, it came slow. "I will speak to him."

THE MESSENGER CAUGHT Estarion as he dressed for the harem. "Majesty, if you please, your lady mother would speak with you."

He paused. It was late, and Haliya was waiting. He had a new tale to tell her, that he had heard in court, and a song that would make her laugh. He was eager for her already; he had had to call off the servant who would have eased him when he thought of her.

"Tell my mother," he said to the messenger, "that I'll see her in the morning. I'll break my fast with her, if she will."

The messenger bowed to the floor. "Majesty, she said that it was urgent."

"And I have urgent business," said Estarion with a flash of temper. "In the morning. Tell her."

The messenger was Asanian. He could not argue with his emperor.

When the eunuch was gone, Estarion drew a breath. He should go, he knew that. But he was feeling contrary tonight. He wanted, needed, what Haliya could give. He would only embarrass his mother, or lose his temper, or say something they would both regret.

He approached the harem with a clear enough conscience. Haliya was not ready for him: the room in which they met was empty. He settled there with the wine and sweets that waited, drinking the wine, toying with the sweets. He had arrayed a whole army of sugared nuts, with banners of dried starfruit and a honeycake general, before the door opened.

It was not Haliya. He half-rose. "Ziana. Is she—"

Ziana made obeisance with grace and composure. "My lord," she said.

"Is Haliya ill? Has something happened?"

"Oh, no," said Ziana. "She's quite well."

Annoyance made his voice sharp. "And she sent you to keep me busy while she sees to more important matters?"

Ziana raised her eyes to him. He would not call it hurt, what was in them, but he had not pleased her. "Nothing is more important than you, my lord."

"Then why—" He stopped. At long last his mind had caught up with the rest of him. She was wearing what a woman wore when she came to her lord in the evening. It covered her voluminously, but it was made to come off of a piece.

"My lord," said Ziana, "we talked about it, Haliya and I. We thought that you might not know. There are courtesies, you see. And prudences. Since the harem is as it is, and women are as they are, their lord cannot afford the luxury of a favorite. Oh," she said as if he had spoken, "he may have one, of course. But he can't see her and only her. It isn't fair to the others."

Estarion was speechless.

She went on bravely. "So, my lord, we decided that since you likely might not know, and since you have never had a harem before, that we would help you. It's not strictly proper, mind. You should have had us all in together, and chosen one of us again, but not the same one as before. A truly dutiful lord would do that every night; we don't expect that, or even want it. Once in every hand of days is more than ample."

And he had spent every night with Haliya for a Brightmoon-cycle and more. "You must think me a perfect boor," he said.

"Oh, no, my lord," said Ziana. "You don't know, you see. And you do mean well. Haliya is very, very pleased with you. She's told me everything that you like, and I've thought of more that may delight you." She moved closer, which was great boldness, and dared to touch his cheek.

Her hand was soft and cool. He shivered. "I don't—" he said thickly. "I don't think—I'm made for this."

"Of course you are, my lord." Her gaze was kind. "Haliya

said you could be shy. Who'd have thought it? So tall as you are, and so proud."

"I'm not tall inside," he said.

"But you are." She laid her hand over his heart. "We've decided, all of us, that you are beautiful. The canons deny it, of course. They call for ivory, not ebony; gold, not raven; smooth sleekness, not nerves and bone and angles. The lion in a cage, not the panther in his lair."

"You are beautiful," he said dizzily, "by any canon."

"I was bred to be," she said. "Haliya's colors are better than mine, but I have the bones. And amber is permitted, even preferred in some of the poets."

"I don't know that I want to choose," Estarion said.

"You don't need to. You have us both. And all the rest, too. Eluya looks like a tigress, but she has the softest touch in the world. And Ushannin learned the high arts from a great master in Ishraan, who named her her best pupil. And—"

He silenced the rest of her recital with a finger on her lips. "I'm not ready to think of more than one woman at a time," he said. "Even two are more than I know what to do with."

"You'll learn," said Ziana. "It's not so hard. And you're certainly man enough to master it."

She was not speaking in figures. Asanians were half appalled, half fascinated by northerners' size as by everything else about them. And while Estarion was not a large man as his mother's kin would reckon it, that was still rather more than an Asanian could lay claim to.

The swift heat rose to his cheeks, but never as swift as what rose below. He stood abruptly and turned his back on her. "I can't do this," he said.

"Of course you can, my lord," said Ziana. From the sound of it she was trying not to laugh. "You do want me. And I want you. Very much," she said.

The honesty of that, and the plea clothed in pride as in fine silk, made him turn to face her again. "Do you really? And why?"

"Because you are ours," she said. "You belong to us as we belong to you. And because you are beautiful. And because . . . I like the way you talk to me. Even when you are being rude."

"I'm rude?"

"Sometimes," she said. "It's refreshing. You always say what you think, you see. And we almost never do."

"Haliya does," said Estarion. "I think you do, too."

"It's our besetting flaw," Ziana said.

"Don't mend it," he said. "I forbid you."

"As my lord wills," she said demurely, but her eyes were laughing.

She was, in her way, as enchanting as her sister. He had known that before. He had not properly comprehended the wit that inhabited the amber beauty.

His body decided for him. It stepped forward; it found the fastening of her robes. He paused. She was trembling, but not with fear. She did want him. Goddess knew why, goddess knew how, but there could be no mistaking it.

He had taken Haliya, and she had been glad of it, and had accepted it. Ziana took him. She was honey and fire and swift intelligence. Such splendor as that was, to be lost in the body's pleasure, and to look into eyes that knew and cherished every moment of it, and every inch of him.

"I don't understand," Estarion said somewhere in the night, when his body rang like the bell after the peal, but his mind was wide awake. "I don't see how a man can love three women at once, and equally, and treasure them all."

"How does a father love his children?" Ziana asked. "He may have a dozen or a hundred. But there is enough of him for all of them."

"That's different," said Estarion.

"In its way," she said, "yes." His hand cupped her breast. She laid her own over it, lacing her slender ivory fingers with his long thin ebony ones. "I'm glad you say 'equally,' my lord. It's a great honor."

"It's you who honor me." He kissed the top of her head.

Her hair smelled of honey and of *ailith*-blossoms. "I don't think I know myself any more. I wasn't raised for this, or prepared for it."

"I think you were," she said. "Only you didn't know it."

"There's a spell on me. I know that." He felt it, wrapped about him, swathing his will and his power, smothering them. "It's in the stones, or in the air. I don't know which. But it's not meant to harm me. Simply . . . to bind me here."

"Isn't that what honor is, and duty? A binding?"

"Are they always sealed with magery?"

"I don't know, my lord," she said. "I know nothing of magic."

Nor did she. He clasped her to him and made himself laugh. "You have a magic all your own. See, I'm enchanted, enraptured, enspelled."

"Silly," she said, but she indulged him. And yet, in a pause: "You won't always stay here. You'll go back where you came from."

"I'm lord in Keruvarion too," he said. "I have to travel through my empire." But not now. Not soon. Not while he could foresee.

"When you go back," she said, "take me with you."

"Your sister made me promise the same thing," he said. "Did you conspire in it?"

She frowned, shaking off his levity. "I know you'll take Haliya. She rides, and she can shoot a bow. I can't do either. Will you still take me?"

"Would you be willing to learn?"

"No," she said, "my lord. I'm afraid of seneldi. I know that makes me a great coward. But I would like to see a place where a woman can rule."

"Then you shall," he said.

"Promise."

"On my right hand," he said, dizzy again, drunken with her. She kissed his burning palm, a cool touch, soothing the fire. But not the fire that was in the rest of him.

31

The emperor did not see the empress mother in the morning. First he was late in coming from the harem; then there was a matter of state too urgent to put off; and after that he was expected to sing one of the Sun-cult's rites in the great temple.

Korusan made certain that no more of her messengers reached him. It was simple enough. The slow wearing of time, the Regent's persuasions, Godri's death, Vanyi's rejection, seemed to have broken Estarion's resistance. He closed in upon himself. After his blue-eyed stallion was sent to run the fields and mount the mares in Induverran, he did not go to his riding-court. With autumn the rains had come; there was little pleasure in walking in his gardens. He went to the harem still, but, Korusan noticed, somewhat less often than before. As the days ran on, he took to sitting in his inner chamber with a book unrolled on his knees, but the pointer never stirred by more than a line. One day he did not even open the book; the next, he left it on the table and sat quiet, staring at nothing, saying nothing.

He was alert enough in court and when he went to the harem. He did not seem to be dying of a broken spirit. He was quiet, that was all. Still. Unmoved and unmoving, neither content nor discontented, neither happy nor sad, simply being.

Korusan hated it. The bright, restless, eternally unpredictable barbarian was gone. In his place sat a poor shadow of an Asanian emperor. He still would not wear the mask, and he still kept his barbarian beard, but that had the air of habit too long ingrained.

On a grey raw morning between the harem and the High Court, Korusan found him in his bath, eyeing the razors in their case. He was testing one of them on his arm.

Korusan had no memory of movement, but the razor was in his own hand, the case clapped shut and his free hand clamped on it. Estarion was quietly amazed—that too so unlike him that Korusan wanted to shake him. "I'm not about to kill myself," he said.

"No," said Korusan. "Merely to lose yourself."

Estarion's brow went up. He tugged at his beard. "There's more to me than this."

"Will you become all Asanian?"

"Is that so unbearable?"

Korusan returned the razor to its case and secreted it in his robes. "I prefer you as you are."

"Barbarian."

"Barbarian," Korusan agreed, "and honest in it."

That gave Estarion pause. And Korusan: Korusan understood, at last, too much.

The summons came as he changed guard at midday, while the emperor held court and the grey rain came down. Marid brought it, walking lightly, with a brightness in his eye that was more than simple love for his swordbrother. "The Masters," he said. "They bid me tell you. It's time."

Korusan stood still. Marid stared back at him, amber eyes, black veil, restless fingers on the hilts of his swords. "At last," said Marid, "you shall have what is yours."

Korusan drew a careful breath. "I shall speak with the Masters," he said. "Guard well, guardsman."

Marid's eyes laughed with the irony of it. "I keep his life for you, prince."

"Hush, brother," said Korusan. "I am but a guardsman here."

"Indeed," said Marid, unrepentant, "guardsman."

Korusan prepared himself carefully. He put on his best robes. He armed himself with all the weapons that a warrior might carry: the swords and the dagger that anyone might see, the others that were known only to the Olenyai and to the dead, who had known the bite of them. When he was the perfection of an Olenyas, he went to his Masters.

Korusan passed the guards and the watchers and the hidden ones who made his hackles rise. That he was protected from them was little comfort. They were shadows on the edge of vision, voices on the edge of hearing, movements not quite sensed. His instinct, inevitably, was to hunt them down.

It was quiet in this stronghold within a stronghold. No women or veilless children dwelt in this place. They were all men and warriors here, doing their turn in the emperor's service; and they were trained to silence.

He found the Masters together in the room behind the hall. There were attendants of the Guild among the Olenyai, robed in violet and grey amid the somber black. Korusan chose not to notice. He was awaited: he was not challenged at the door, or forbidden entry. He entered with beating heart, chiding himself for a fool. Was he not the son of the Lion? Did they not call him lord and rightful emperor?

He was still but an initiate of two ranks' standing, and please the nonexistent gods, no mage at all.

A warrior did not trouble with preliminaries unless they served his purpose. Korusan bowed to his own Master for true respect, and to the Master of the Guild for careful courtesy, and said what he had come to say. "It is not time."

Neither of them betrayed astonishment. The mage seemed about to smile as one smiles at a child who thinks itself a man. Master Asadi lowered his veil, which was a mark of great trust in this company, and said, "We believe that it is time."

"No," said Korusan. He did not bare his own face. That was noted, he knew, although no one spoke of it.

"Why?" asked Asadi.

"Because," said Korusan, "it is not."

"Are you a seer," the mage inquired, "or a thaumaturge, to know the art of times and places?"

"I am the emperor's shadow," said Korusan, "and I hold his life in debt. How fare the rebellions, my masters?"

"Well," said Asadi, "and prospering. But they need their prince and prophet. They need your conscious presence."

"Soon," said Korusan.

"It were best you do it now," the mage said. "The people are fickle, and the emperor's mages are not all fools. The more we do, the greater our workings, the closer we come to setting you on your throne, the greater the danger of discovery."

"I see," said Korusan, "that you are afraid for your secrecy. Wise, that. Prudent. But the time is not yet come. Your magics are succeeding—they are your magics, I trust?" He received no answer, but he had expected none, nor needed it. "The emperor is mewed in the palace. He stirs forth less with each day that passes. He is learning to be content with his harem and his court and his confinement. He has no knowledge of aught but what he sees and hears, and that is nothing. When he is perfectly closed in, venturing forth no longer even to preside in court, then we may move."

"Then will be too late," the mage said.

Korusan studied the man. His face was sleek, complacent, deceptively harmless. His eyes were as cold as ever, as quietly merciless. They did not fall before Korusan's stare.

Korusan smiled. "You are a worthy opponent," he said, "but I am the Lion's cub, and I hold the Sunlord's life in my hand. I judge that we must wait. Now is too soon."

"When will it be time?" the mage demanded. "Can you judge that? The Sunlord may have little magery that he can wield at his will, but he casts spells with his simple presence. The light of his eyes can bind worlds."

"And you dare oppose him?"

The mage did not bridle at Korusan's mockery. "I have not his native power, but neither have I maimed and squandered what is mine. You, my young lord, have no magery, no power but what guards your mind from intrusion. You are easy prey for the spell that he casts."

That could indeed be true. There was a remarkable fascination in the black king, more than his oddities might account for.

But Korusan was no fool or child, to be snared by outland magics. "When I am ready, I will kill him. I am sworn to it. His life is mine, mage. Remember that."

"I do not forget," the mage said. "Do you?"

Korusan laughed, cold and clear. "Never for a moment. Do you think that I sit idle? I have him in my power. He calls me friend, he tells me his secrets, he speaks to me as much as he speaks to anyone. I shall teach him to love me. And when he has learned it well, then, mage, I shall strike."

"Be swift, then," the mage said, "or we shall fail."

"We will not," said Korusan. "I shall slay him with my own hand."

"Soon," the mage said, like a chorus in a song.

It occurred to Korusan afterward to wonder that he had won so easy a victory. Perhaps after all the Guildmaster granted him the right of his lineage.

Or perhaps, he thought, the mages did not need his complaisance to do what they willed to do. Their spells were sapping Estarion's will with his strength. In time he might care too little to live. Then he would rob Korusan of the life that was Korusan's, take it with his own hand, and spare the mages the effort of disposing of him.

Not, Korusan swore to himself, while he had power to prevent it. Estarion must care that he died; must know who slew him. Else there was no purpose in aught that Korusan did, and he was but a puppet after all, to dance at the mages' whim.

32

Toruan the singer had come back.

Estarion learned of it by accident. As he was returning from court by another way than the usual, in part to avoid a gaggle of lords who sought to waylay him, in part to vary the monotony, he heard the singer's name just as he turned a corner, and paused. Two of his Varyani Guard idled in the passage, new come it seemed from the city, warm with wine. "He's doing a play for the High Court tonight," one of them said. "One of Lord Perizon's men owes me a fortune at dice. I'm going to make him pay me off by getting me into court. How do you think I'll look in yelloweyes livery?"

"Beautiful," said his companion.

The other cuffed him. "Go on, laugh. I was a pretty thing before that bastard broke my nose for me."

"Lovely," his companion agreed sweetly. "The whole fathom and a half of you."

They would have brawled happily in the corridor, if one, the plainsman with his sharp narrow eyes, had not caught sight of Estarion. He pulled the northerner about, wide-eyed both, bowing arm in arm like players on a stage.

Estarion looked them up and down. "I don't suppose the two of you could be troubled to escort me to court tonight."

"No, my lord!" the northerner said. "Yes, my lord. My lord—"

Estarion left him still babbling. He was weary suddenly, as he was too often of late, weary to exhaustion. But he would be glad to see Toruan again. He mustered the will to send a messenger and the wits to inform the servants before he rested, that he would attend court that evening; and there was Ziana to think of. Or Eluya. It was time to change the guard again in the harem.

All the more reason to avoid it tonight. He stood while his servants freed his body from its robes and his hair from its inevitable knots, and when they went away, lay on the couch that was closest. Korusan was nowhere to be seen. The Olenyas on guard was the nervous one, taller and narrower than the run of them, with fingers that could never be still. After a while his twitching grew unbearable. Estarion ordered him out. He went without protest, leaving Estarion in peace.

Estarion drowsed, neither truly asleep nor truly awake. Some part of him resisted; protested; begged him to wake, move, do something. But he was too tired.

It was not Estarion's custom to attend court in the evening. His servants informed him so, at length. He took no notice. They dressed him in robes so heavy that he could barely move, and crowned him with gold, and touched his eyelids with gilt. He had not allowed that before. Tonight he did not care. He would have let them shave him, even, if Korusan had not taken the razors. Odd child; presumptuous. He still had not appeared. Estarion hoped that he was resting well, or whetting his swords on slaves, or whatever Olenyai did when they were not on guard.

The court at night was a restless glittering thing, lit with lamps, flashing with jewels and gold, murmurous with voices and music and even laughter, soft as the canons prescribed, and deep. No women's voices. No ladies, and no women of lesser repute, though those, Estarion had heard, might come forth later, after the wine had gone round.

His presence gave them pause, but only briefly. Custom, which was always their salvation, bade them bow as one, grant him the accolade of silence, then return to their dance of precedence. He was neither expected nor permitted to join in it. His place was to sit before and above them, and watch, and be silent.

His two guards and he were the only men in the hall who were not Asanian. And, when they appeared, Toruan and certain of his troupe.

The court quieted at their coming, settling to chairs and stools that servants placed for them, making a circle before the throne. As they had in Induverran, the musicians came forward first, took their places, began to play. The singers followed.

This was not the masque of Sarevadin and her prince, nor was it any tale Estarion knew. It was Asanian, maybe, yet Toruan sang in it. He was the lord in his palace, or perhaps the god in his temple, to whom the people came for guidance or for healing or for surcease from their troubles. He wore a white robe, which was royal or divine, and he carried a mask, an Asanian face, which sometimes he held before him and sometimes he bore at his side.

He did not speak to the people who came to him. Another did that. And what that one heard, he rendered differently to his lord. A man would ask for aid against his enemy, and the speaker between would sing to the lord of praises sung and tribute promised. A woman—a eunuch in a veil, surely—would beg him to heal her child of a sickness, but he would hear that she asked for his blessing on her womb. A youth would bid him attend to a great injustice, and he would hear that he must work stern justice in the youth's demesne. The people cried their grief. He heard only praises.

The people, given false coin or none to heal their ills, grew angry with their lord. Or with their god; it still was not clear which he was. They came together. They resolved to beg him, all of them at once, to listen, to hear them, to give them what they needed. Bread for their bellies, for they starved. Wine for their throats, for they thirsted. Healing for their children, for they were dying.

And he heard only praise. He smiled, he blessed them, he sang sweetly of their joy and their prosperity. The louder they sang of grief, the sweeter he sang of contentment, until their patience shattered. They rose up. They tore him from his throne, rent his mask asunder, slew him in a roaring of drums and a rattle of sistra and the thin, high, sweet descant of his unshakable complacency.

"That," said Estarion, "was quite the rashest thing I have ever seen. Preaching sedition in the High Court of Asanion—it's a wonder they didn't rend you limb from limb."

Toruan was somewhat grey about the lips, but he laughed. "Oh, they wanted to. But not in front of you."

"You're not safe after this," Estarion said.

"I am if you say I am," said Toruan. He drank off the wine that Estarion's servant had poured for him, and held out the cup to be filled again. His hand was shaking.

"Why?" Estarion asked him.

Toruan closed both hands about the newly filled cup. His eyes searched Estarion's face. "You didn't understand, did you?"

"I understood," Estarion said, amiably enough, he thought, but Toruan's fingers tightened till the knuckles greyed. "Granted that they keep me like a prisoner of state, can you honestly say that matters are as bad as you showed them to be? Or that I am that perfect a fool?"

"I never thought you a fool, my lord," Toruan said. "But you are cut off here from anything that hints of reality."

"Who put you up to this? My mother? The temple? My court in Keruvarion?"

The proud eyes lowered; the eunuch hid his face behind his cup. "I did receive a messenger from the empress mother. But that was after we decided to do it, my lord. We've been in the towns; we've traveled the roads. We know what people are saying to one another, and what they're threatening to do."

"Rebellion against the barbarian on the throne?"

"That, my lord, and more."

"Surely not," said Estarion. "I'm here; I came as I was ordered to come; I've taken what's mine, and done what's expected. Those are old grievances and empty threats."

"They are not," said Toruan, "my lord."

"So," said Estarion. "You were put up to it. Who was it who wrote the songs for you? Iburan? He's a fine fast hand with a verse, and he doesn't get on well with the high priestess here. He'd want to wake me up to that, I'm sure. As if there were anything I could do. I've no authority inside the temple."

"My lord," said Toruan, "I spoke to the priest, I confess it. He was your mother's messenger. He said that you'd protect us even if you were angry; you're too honorable, he said, and too honest to do otherwise. But we had our play all written. We were going to take it to Keruvarion."

"What, and foment rebellion there?" Estarion was not angry, not yet, but his temper was slipping its chains. "Isn't it enough that you've incited the High Court almost to riot? Not that they'd ever show it, but they were running over lists of poisons, and hiring assassins."

"You needed to know," said Toruan, as stubborn as ever a northerner could be, and as perfect an idiot. "The priest thought so, and the empress mother. You won't listen to them. They thought you might at least give me a hearing."

"So I did," Estarion said. "So did the court; and I'll be hard pressed to get you out of here unpoisoned. What do you want me to do? Go back to Keruvarion?"

"Open your eyes to what's outside of this palace." Toruan flinched a little at Estarion's expression, but went on stubbornly. "It's bad, my lord, and getting worse. They use your presence here as a weapon. They call you conqueror. They swell your Guard into an army, and have it raping and pillaging Kundri'j."

"When I was in Keruvarion," said Estarion, "they called me conqueror. They had me scorning to set foot in their country, and despising all that they were. At least now they have me here to carp at."

"They killed a tax collector in Ansavaar."

"They have a deplorable propensity for killing tax collectors. That was seen to, surely?"

"They overran the troops sent to punish them, and fortified the town, and there they sit. They've declared themselves free of your sway."

"Have they?" Estarion half-rose, then sat again and sighed. "It will be settled. I'll attend to it."

"Then you'll attend to the rest, too? It's a plague, my lord. You know what sickness is, how it comes to a man, and he passes it to his wife, and she to her baby, and the baby to the cat, and round it goes. And maybe they all live, and maybe one or more of them dies. And that is the way of the world. But if it goes beyond the one house, if it runs through the town—then it's not so little any longer. It's pestilence. It wipes out whole cities, strips the land of its people, lays low the demesne. That's what this is, my lord. It's not a little thing, a rebellion that refuses to die of age and exhaustion. It's young in strength but old in rancor. It won't give way at a word, even if it's you who speak it."

"How odd," mused Estarion. "They spend all their strength to see me here, and now that they have me where they wanted me, they do their best to lure me out again. Aren't they ever satisfied?"

Toruan did not understand, or did not care to. He said, "My lord, I won't say you're badly advised, but you aren't hearing what goes on outside of the palace. It's worse than it was when you came here. Much worse. In some towns I'm afraid for my skin. They see it, you see, and start to growl."

"My guards have had no trouble in Kundri'j," Estarion said. "Nor did I, when I went out. I was barely noticed."

"This is Kundri'j," said Toruan. He looked about at the chamber in which they sat. "How do you stand it, my lord? You must be suffocating."

"One learns to endure it," Estarion said honestly enough, and somewhat to his own surprise. "Tell my mother that it was a valiant effort. She and her priest will see that you are protected. You may choose to take yourself and your people to Keruvarion, where your art is a new and wonderful thing.

But," he said, "you may not be wise to give them your tragedy of folly. They don't hire assassins. They see to it themselves, and promptly."

"Our play was for you," said Toruan. He set his cup aside untouched, and dropped to his knees in front of Estarion. "My lord, we are yours, all of us, but we're a vanishing few in the mobs of Asanion. They've been stirred up. Their old hates are new again, and their fears are stronger than ever. Maybe you can't go out among them as you could in Keruvarion, but if you knew, if you kept yourself aware of them, all of them—"

"I am as aware as emperor can be," Estarion said. He was weary again, aching with it. He had hoped for an evening's pleasure, for an hour's brief escape from his troubles, and this well-meaning idiot had only made them worse.

He was not to blame. The empress had got at him, and Iburan, who thought himself subtle. They would know how little Estarion was deceived by their cleverness.

He dismissed the eunuch as politely as he could, sending him under guard to the empress' palace and charging the guards to defend him with their lives. It would, he hoped, suffice.

He almost smiled, thinking of the court, how appalled the lords had been, how hard they had fought to conceal it, because the emperor professed himself pleased. No doubt they thought him a simpleton.

He wandered his rooms, more restless than he had been since he could remember. Servants kept creeping out of shadows, begging to serve him. He herded them out. The guards were more tenacious, but they could at least be banished to windows and corridors.

He tried to sleep, but sleep would not come. He read a few lines in his book. He drank more wine than he should, enough to make him light-headed, and walked for a while on the roof of his summer-room, under a sky as restless as he was, until the rain drove him in.

As he came down from the roof, a shadow met him. He

smiled with the first honest pleasure he had known since morning. "Yelloweyes," he said. "I've missed you."

Korusan did not say anything. That was like him. Estarion passed him, drawing him in his wake, chattering of he knew not what. It was a restlessness of the tongue, close kin to that of his feet.

Somewhere in the maze of rooms, between the room of silks and the armory with its golden panoplies, Korusan stopped. Estarion's shadow was cold without the Olenyas in it. He turned. Korusan stood as straight and stiff as the pillar beside him, with eyes that burned. Fever, thought Estarion. The boy was perfect Asanian: he hated to be touched. But Estarion was not to be thrust aside for this. "You're burning up," he said.

"It is nothing," said Korusan. But he shivered.

He was ill, there could be no doubt of it. Estarion considered the wisdom of knocking the child down and sitting on him and shouting for the physician. It would be a fair battle. Korusan was arming for it already, tensing under his hand. He lowered it from the brow to the shoulder, which was rigid. "You should have this seen to," he said.

Korusan's hand flew up. Estarion braced to be struck aside; froze as the boy's fingers closed about his wrist. "I am often ill," Korusan said. His voice was coolly bitter. "It is nothing to fret your majesty. It will pass as always, and leave me no worse than before."

"And while it's passing? How well will you guard me, when you can barely stand up?"

"I can stand!" he snapped, wavering as he said it, but not loosing his grip on Estarion's wrist.

Estarion tripped him, caught him as he fell, braced for a fight. Korusan offered none beyond a sulfurous glare. Estarion laughed at it and carried him inward.

The bathing-room was warm and quiet, its pool of ever-flowing water murmuring gently to itself. Estarion set Korusan on the rim and held him there. "Bathe," he said. "It will cool you down."

Korusan stared at the water as if he had never seen its like before.

"You do bathe, I suppose," Estarion said with tight-strained patience. "Or do you lick yourselves over like cats?"

Korusan hissed at him, so like a cat that he laughed. "We bathe. But not," the boy said, "in public."

"I'll turn my back," Estarion said.

Korusan lifted his shrouded head, as haughty as any emperor, and as short in his temper. Estarion met his glare, gold to gold. Something shifted. In Estarion, in Korusan; he did not know. Maybe the earth had shrugged in its sleep.

Gold, he thought. They were not the color of coins; that was Haliya, as close as made no matter. They were clearer, a color between amber and citrine, now as flat and hard as stones, now as soft as sleep. Thick long lashes, dark gold, and fine arched brows a shade lighter, and skin as clear and fair as ivory.

Korusan lowered the lids over those remarkable eyes, and raised them again, almost as if he were succumbing to sleep. Estarion caught him before he could tumble into the water. But he was steady on his feet. He was taut still, but not as rigid as before, easing slowly. He reached up past Estarion's arm, and with sudden force, sharp enough to make Estarion start, stripped off headcloth and veil.

Estarion's breath caught. Even after those eyes, he had not expected beauty such as this: an image carved in ivory. No line drawn awry, no mole or blemish, no flaw save two thin crimson scars that ran straight and deliberate from cheekbone to jaw. They only made him the more beautiful.

"If you had been a woman," Estarion said, "singers would be making songs of you."

"Not in Asanion," said Korusan. He ran fingers through cropped yellow curls, pulling out tangles with ruthlessness that made Estarion wince. "It is wanton to sing of a lady or an Olenyas."

"Or a prince of the court?"

"That," said the boy, "I am not." He said it strangely, but that was his fever: he was shaking again, cursing himself. With the same ferocity that had startled Estarion when he bared his face, he wrenched free and shed his robes and his weapons, all of them.

Beautiful, yes, and clad in scars and a single ornament, a topaz on a chain about his neck; and so young, caught between boy and man, slender but with breadth coming in his shoulders, taut-muscled as a swordsman must be, light on his feet as a dancer, even dizzy with fever. This time as he swayed, he caught at Estarion. His hands fisted in robe and tore.

Estarion had stopped trying to guess what the boy would do next. He was not afraid. Probably he should have been. A bred-warrior's body was as much a weapon as one of his swords, and if anything more deadly. But there was no death here, unless it were in Korusan's sickness.

The air was cool on his bared skin. He shivered lightly. Korusan touched him. A spark leaped, jolting them both. He laughed. Korusan recoiled; then sprang, lion-swift, lion-strong, bearing him down in a tangle of limbs and robes.

Estarion struck tiles hard enough to jar the breath from him, guarding his throat by instinct, seizing what presented itself: a shoulder, a wrist. Korusan twisted with boneless suppleness. His body was burning hot, fever-dry. Estarion let him hurl himself sidewise, guiding him, toppling them both into the water.

It closed over them. Korusan's legs locked about Estarion's middle. Estarion thrashed. Drown—he would drown—

He burst into blessed air, gulped, scrambled feet beneath him. Korusan clung with blind ferocity. Gasping. Weeping? Face buried in Estarion's shoulder, arms inextricable about his neck, chest heaving with sobs or with battling for breath. His weight was as light as it was strong.

Estarion's hand found itself stroking the boy's back. Its sleekness was all muscle, its bones just perceptible—thin as Asanians went, and smooth as they all were, like ivory. And cooler, maybe, than it had been.

He sank down carefully, braced against the pool's side, alert for mischief. But Korusan offered none. His breathing quieted. His clasp loosened, though it did not let go. It was trust, Estarion knew with sudden clarity. Estarion could thrust him under and hold him, and he would not fight.

His head moved on Estarion's shoulder, from side to side as an infant's will, seeking the breast. But no infant this. One hand crooked still about Estarion's neck. The other explored the long curve of neck and shoulder and arm, and up again, over belly and breast and throat. Pausing there, as if tempted; but tangling itself at last in beard. Estarion looked down past clenching fist into eyes gone wide, all pupil, in a face as white as bone, and the blood-red slash of scars.

Estarion traced the line of them with a fingertip. "Sword?" he asked.

"Knife," said Korusan. His voice was as cool as ever. It seemed to come from elsewhere than that stark face. "One for initiate. Two for honor. Because I showed myself worthy in the battle that made me Olenyas."

They fought to win the veils and the swords. Of course. Estarion should have known without asking.

"Are you all so beautiful?"

Korusan looked startled. That was rare. It made Estarion laugh, at which the boy scowled. "What does beauty matter?"

"Little," said Estarion, "if one wears veils to hide it. Is that why? To keep people from thinking you pretty idiots?"

"You who deny your own beauty: you think to be a judge of mine?"

"I'm not—"

Korusan tugged. Estarion swallowed a yelp. The boy's teeth bared. They were white and even, no flash of barbarian fang, but sharp enough as they sank into his shoulder. Estarion howled. "Hells *take* you!"

Korusan pulled his head the rest of the way down.

It began, Estarion observed with dreadful calm, somewhere in the vicinity of his tailbone. It felt most nearly like the spark of magery swelling into fire, searing up his spine, bursting through his skull. He would not have been surprised at all if this young lunatic had bitten off his tongue and spat it into the water; but he seemed content to settle for devouring Estarion alive. Lips first, cheeks, chin, throat—nip of teeth there, but not quite to draw blood—breast and still-throbbing shoulder, arms, hands, barely shying from the flame of gold. And breast again, and belly, and—

Estarion heaved them both up bodily, dripping by the pool. Korusan made no effort to steady himself on his feet, but sank down, arms about Estarion's knees. Estarion's banner was up and flying. He could not tell if Korusan was awed. He looked stunned, but that might only be fever.

Estarion pried him loose. He had to kneel to do it. It set Korusan eye to chin, which was better than what else he had been staring at. Estarion kept a grip on his wrists, though he made no move to break free. He was, Estarion noticed, a fair figure of a man himself, for one still half a boy.

There was nothing girlish about him, for all his beauty. If there had been, Estarion could not have done what he did. Taken vengeance. Kissed him hard and long. And when they were both reeling, drawn back. He held Korusan's wrists even yet. He let them go.

"You are velvet," said Korusan, "and steel."

"Steel," said Estarion, "and ivory."

"Your life belongs to me," Korusan said.

"And yours to me," said Estarion. It came from he knew not where, but when it was spoken, he knew it for truth.

Korusan rose. He neither swayed nor staggered. He drew Estarion up.

Estarion could stop it now. He knew that. He need only

resist: pull free of that hand, speak the words that waited on his tongue. This was nothing that he had ever looked for, or wanted. He had seen how some men were with beautiful boys. He had not understood them. He was a man for women, always, since he was old enough to know what a woman was for.

This went beyond man and woman or man and boy or—if he were honest—man and man. It was certainly unwise for an emperor to discover a passion for his guardsman. It could very likely kill them both. And it did not matter in the least.

Korusan's fever had changed. It was a whiter heat now, a fiercer burning, and it knew precisely how to cure itself. Estarion, Sunborn, panther's cub, had never thought to be a cool spring or a healing draught. He found it wonderfully strange.

It was not like loving a woman. Vanyi was as fierce, Ziana as serpent-supple, Haliya as quick to know where was his greatest pleasure. None of them was so close to his own strength.

They grappled like warriors. They made a glorious shambles of the bed, tumbling from it to the floor, ending in a knot of cushions and carpets, gasping. Estarion was dizzy. Korusan was breathing quickly, stretched the length of Estarion's body.

Suddenly the boy laughed. It was edged with hysteria, but it was true mirth. He ran sharp-clawed hands down Estarion's sides. Estarion spilled him over, set knee on his chest, grinned down at him. He grinned back. "Am I a match for you?"

"Almost," said Estarion. He bent to seize another kiss. It lingered, softened. No war this time. No contest for mastery. Long, slow, impossibly sweet. Bodies so different, and so much the same.

Not all the dampness on Korusan's cheeks was sweat. Estarion tasted the sharper salt of tears. Korusan would have raged, had he known that Estarion knew. Estarion kept silence, and held him long after he had fallen asleep. Even in dreams he kept a shadow of tension, a memory of the warrior that he was. But not in his face. That was a youth's, a boy's, more beautiful than any girl's.

Estarion eased himself out of Korusan's arms. Korusan

stirred, murmured, but did not wake. His brow was cool, his fever gone.

It had lodged itself in Estarion. He bathed quickly. His robe was rent, but there was another in the clothing-chest. He put it on. He bound his hair back in a thong, out of his face. He had not, yet, begun to shake.

His shoulder ached; his ribs stung. Vicious, that one, before he let himself be tamed.

What he did then . . .

Estarion was striding swiftly. His robe swirled in the wind of his speed. He nearly cast it off. A guard's eyes restrained him, and the gleam of lamplight on bronze.

The spear drew back before him. The guard—broad brown plainsman's face, name forgotten somewhere in Korusan's shadow—flashed a smile. Estarion had none to return.

There was no peace on the roof, no stars, and a thin cold wind blowing, cutting to the bone. The winter of Asanion was begun. Estarion barely felt it. His vitals were all fire.

The sun was coming. He should sing it into the sky. But he was empty of either prayer or song.

"Do I love him?" he asked the dark. "Do I even like him? Does it matter at all?"

The dark kept its counsel.

"I never meant this," Estarion said, "or anything like it. I'm bewitched, ensorcelled. And I don't care. Why can't I care? Is he doing it to me? Will he kill me when he has me in his power?"

Korusan had had Estarion in his power many times this night, and had done nothing but love him. It was love, love as cats knew it, with claws. Estarion was a pitiful excuse for a mage, but some things could not elude him. The boy's heart was his.

Fierce, prickly, deathly dangerous, marvelous thing. Clasping him was like clasping a naked blade. Estarion had never known anything like it, or conceived of it.

Now he had it. Now he could imagine it. And he would not give it up.

The empress' palace was quiet, its guards alert, but silent when he bade them be. If she was not awake, she would be soon: the goddess' servants made a rite of the last darkness as did the god's priests of the first light. He advanced softly through the rooms, from latticed light to latticed shadow, through curtains that strove to snare him in silk, past guards who bowed if they were Asanian, or bent their heads if they were Varyani. Women and eunuchs all. No men here. None but Estarion.

His body was bent on proving it. Again. And he had called Korusan insatiable. He was like a man waked from too long a sleep: waked to find himself wrapped in chains, but those chains were falling one by one.

He must rule in Asanion. There was no arguing it. But he could not rule in Kundri'j Asan. It was stifling him, throttling him, robbing him of wits and will and magery.

His mother knew. He had been shutting her out as he had done to them all, all who could teach him to be wise.

The last door was shut and, he would notice later, barred. It barely gave him pause. Locks had never mattered much between them, not when there was such need as this.

The lamps burned low. He had night-eyes; dimness mattered little. He saw the tumble of her hair on the pillows, black untouched with silver; the curve of her cheek like the arc of a moon, the swell of her breast, the hand that moved upon it, broad strong-fingered hand that was no woman's that Estarion had ever seen.

Estarion froze. Shadow distilled itself into shape. It would tower over Estarion's slenderness. What Korusan was to Estarion, Estarion was to this: slight smooth-skinned stripling. But Korusan was stronger than he looked. Estarion was weaker. Weak to spinelessness.

Iburan opened eyes unclouded by sleep, or by guilt, or

surprise. It was Estarion whose privates shriveled, whose cheeks burned.

"Fair morning to you," said the man who had been his foster-father. And, for what clearly was no single night, father in more than name. Even, maybe—

Estarion's hand flared to sudden pain. He gasped.

To have been such a fool. Such perfect, utter, unconscionable fool. To have seen it full before his face, how they were always together, always in accord, never separated for long or at great distance. To have seen, and to have failed so utterly to see.

He wheeled.

"Starion!"

His mother's voice. He shut his ears to it, to everything but the truth.

He had been asleep. Now he was awake. He had been blind. Now he could see. He raised hands to his eyes, his lion-eyes. One hand that was dark. One that was burning gold. The agony of it was exquisite. It made him laugh. It was that, or shriek aloud.

"Starion!"

His name pursued him, but it could not hold him. This truth had shown him what he must do. He was free, and freed.

KORUSAN WOKE ALONE. He knew at once where he was, and what defenses there could be if anyone struck to maim or to kill. There were more of those than anyone could imagine who was not Olenyas, to see a slender youth naked and forsaken in the emperor's bed.

Not even a servant hovered. He regretted that somewhat. The creature would have had to die for having looked on Korusan's face.

Estarion would die. But not yet. Korusan had been delirious with fever, but not so much as to have lost awareness of his purpose. To have gone so far, so soon . . . no, he had not intended that. Nor expected so easy a victory.

If victory it had been. His fingers flexed in the silk of the coverlets, remembering a very different silk, with panther-strength beneath, and the red heat of blood. No shrinking there, no priestly scruples, and if no art, then instinct enough to make in time a master.

Korusan had meant to take the outlander by surprise. And so he had. But the outlander had surprised him in turn. Not by being Asanian—gods forbid, if there were gods—but by being himself.

Love was nothing that Korusan had time to know. Obsession he had already, and no room in it for another. This, he had no name for.

"I have you now," he said to the air with its memory of Estarion's face. "You belong to me. No one else shall take you."

He smiled. No. No one else. Least of all a woman who could bear Estarion a son.

The Masters would be most displeased. He was to slay this

upstart and any offspring he might sire, and claim the throne to which his blood entitled him. To slay with love, to prevent the siring of offspring at all . . . they would not understand. They were not the Lion's brood.

Only Estarion, whose eyes were lion-eyes—only Estarion could comprehend it.

"I the darkness," said Korusan, half in a dream, "you the light. I the image of ivory, you of ebony. Uveryen-face, Avaryan-face, now the one, now the other, matched, opposed, lovers and warriors . . ." He laughed, although he wept. "You were to wake alone, I to escape before you could snare me in your magics. How dared you claim the part that was mine?"

"Did I?"

Korusan started, surging to his knees. Estarion leaned against the pillar of the bed, more like a panther than ever in his tautness that masked itself as ease. His expression was calm to coldness; and that, in fiery Estarion, was perilous.

"I thought you would be gone," Estarion said.

"So should I have been." Korusan composed himself with care, sitting on his heels, hands on thighs. "You should never have let me come to this."

"What?" Estarion's voice was sharp. "Guilt? Humiliation?"

"You."

"I'm sorry."

He was. Korusan bared teeth at him. "Do you regret me?"

Estarion looked down as if searching for a lie. Korusan watched his fist clench and unclench beside his cheek on the carved whorl of the pillar. It was the right, the branded fist. He had pain there: Korusan had seen it before, how he flexed it or, when he thought no one was watching, rubbed it along his side or his thigh, or simply held it beside him, knotted, trying not to tremble. It was a magic, the tales said, to keep Sun-blood from waxing too proud.

When Estarion spoke, he spoke slowly, eyes fixed on his feet. "I can't regret you or anything that I've done with you. I suppose I should. You're so young, and I—"

"Oh, you are ancient." The scorn in Korusan's voice brought the lion-eyes up, wide and improbably golden in that outland face. "You are ages old, ages wise, an elder, a sage, a patriarch." Korusan rose to face him. "You have seen but a fifth part of the life that your god has granted you. I have lived three parts of the four that have been given to me. I am *old,* Sunlord. I am a brief breath's span from the grave."

"That's not true."

"That is most true." And it was nothing that this of all men should know; but Korusan could not stop himself. "My blood, the blood that gives me this beauty you make so much of—it bears a price. We die young. Very young, Sunlord."

"Not that young," said Estarion. "You'll see forty. Fifty even, if you're fortunate."

"I shall not see twenty," Korusan said.

"Nonsense," said Estarion, flat and hurting-hard. "It's hard enough to tell with only eyes to go by, but the rest of your Olenyai aren't children. All the others are men grown."

"Not I," said Korusan. "Not my line. I am the last of it. After me there are no others."

"Then why—" Estarion stopped himself before he came too close to the truth. "Never mind. You're still sick, aren't you? You're seeing death in every shadow. You won't die. I'm not going to let you."

"No one has such power," Korusan said.

"I do."

Korusan laughed, because he always laughed at death and folly. He who had no magic, still had eyes within, half of training, half of his own nature. He saw the death that slept in him, blood and bone. It was waking. Years and training, medicine and magic, had lulled it, but even the Sun's power could not drive it out. It was sunk too deep.

Estarion's hands on him were burning cold, both pain and exquisite pleasure. "You'll live," said Estarion. "My word on it."

"Great lord," said Korusan. "Bright emperor." His mockery was bitter. "Will you swear not to outlive me?"

"That's in the god's hands," Estarion said a shade too quickly.

"Spoken like a priest," said Korusan, "and like a king." He smiled. He felt Estarion shiver. "If I am not clad and veiled very soon," he said, "every servant in the palace will know my face."

Estarion let him go. Korusan paused, considering wisdom and unwisdom, and prices, and velvet over steel. Abruptly he spun, seeking the refuge of his veils.

It had all come upon Estarion at once: Toruan's message, Korusan's fever, his mother and Iburan proving him a fool beyond fools, then Korusan again, with death lodged in his bones. He did not pause to think. He had paused too long, thought far too much, until there was no reflection left in him at all. It had taken what magic was left him. He found none, though he delved deep. He was empty, ringing hollow. There was not even pain to mark where it had been.

What stirred in him, he told himself, was relief. An emperor did not need to be a mage, still less the poor maimed thing that he had been for so long. He had wealth to hire the greatest of masters, power to compel obedience even from the likes of the Lord Iburan of Endros, who danced the dance of dark and light with the empress mother of Keruvarion.

His servants were there to bathe and robe him, as they were every morning. He allowed the bath. He forbade the robes. When he received the Regent of Asanion, it was in royal richness, but such as it was reckoned in the princedoms of the east: embroidered coat, silken trousers, boots heeled with bronze and inlaid with gold. His hair was tidily plaited, his beard cut short.

Firaz seemed undismayed to see his emperor gone back to outland habits. "I shall see to the Court this morning," he said, "and assure them that your majesty is well."

"No need," said Estarion. "I'll tell them myself. Some of

them will be needing to muster forces, armed and otherwise. It's time we dealt with this little matter of rebellion."

"Majesty," said Firaz, "there is no need to vex yourself. All that need be done, your servants shall do."

"I vex myself," said Estarion, "sitting in this silk-lined cage, hearing nothing but what my servants judge fit for me to hear."

"Ah," said Firaz. "That one shall be dealt with also, and swiftly."

Estarion's smile widened. "He already has, my lord. I saw to it last night. I trust there will be no additions to my undertaking."

The Regent inclined his head a fraction. Estarion watched him narrowly, but he did not look like a man startled in guilt.

Firaz had waged long war to make an Asanian emperor of an outland savage, but he was an honest man. God and goddess knew, if he was either traitor or enemy, it was much too late to escape.

Even in Asanion an emperor had to place his trust in something. Well indeed: Estarion would trust his loyal adversary. "When I came to Kundri'j," he said, "I rode at speed, and I kept the company of princes. In that, I think, I was mistaken. Tomorrow when I ride out, I ride as I was used to ride in Keruvarion, among my people, teaching them to know my face."

Firaz drew a sharp breath: a great betrayal, for an Asanian. "Majesty! That is deadly dangerous."

"So," said Estarion, "it is." He sat back, stroking his new-clipped beard. That was tension, but maybe the Regent would not know it. "I will go, Firaz. You will go with me or remain, as you will. But Kundri'j has held me long enough. It's time I saw the rest of Asanion again, and reminded it that it needs no dreams or prophets."

"In the teeth of winter, my lord? Will you not wait until the spring comes round again?"

"Will the siege in Ansavaar wait for a prettier season? I'm

going to break it, my lord. I'd like to find a living city when I go in, and not a hill of starveling corpses."

"My lord, you cannot do that."

Estarion almost laughed. "Am I the emperor, my lord Firaz?"

Firaz bowed to that, but his back was stiff. "You are the emperor, my lord Estarion. And the emperor does not ride to battle."

"Then that tale is a lie which tells of Ziad-Ilarios at the battle of Induverran, and he not only emperor but Son of the Lion, of the pure and ancient blood."

"His heir was gone," said Firaz. "His empire was overrun. He had no choice."

"He had other sons—half a hundred of them, or so they say. And he put on armor and rode to war."

"You have no son," Firaz said, "nor any hope of one, if you are killed in pursuit of this folly."

"If I die," said Estarion, "I'll die free and sane, and not mewling like a beast. Which I shall be, good my lord, if I am pent much longer in this palace."

Firaz opened his mouth as if to reply, but shut it again. He bowed low. Perhaps it was contempt that held his face so woodenly still; but Estarion thought that it was not. He was afraid for his emperor. His emperor was touched, but he was not going to yield for that. "Now," he said. "The Court."

The Court astonished him. It was barely shocked to be addressed direct, and it received his commands with aplomb. It seemed like Firaz to have been expecting something of the sort, though maybe not so soon. Estarion could not tell among the bland faces, who was pleased to see him abandon the safety of walls and guards. Some, maybe, wondered if he were being subtle, to lure out his assassins. Others would be certain that he courted his death.

So he did. If Asanion killed him, he wanted to die under the sky, not smothered in silks. And maybe he would live. Maybe the rumors were all lies, and the rebellion a falsehood, a distillation of discontent that had not come yet to open battle.

If Asanion had a war-council to match that in Keruvarion, no one would admit to it. The emperor spoke, he issued commands, they were obeyed. It was convenient, in its way. No one but Firaz dared to tell the emperor what he could not do.

"It will of course be done," Estarion said, smiling sweetly. "Yes, my lords?"

None of them protested. None even met his eyes.

"Will they do it, do you think?" Estarion wondered when he had gone back to his lair again. "Or will they conveniently forget?"

"They will not forget," said Korusan.

Estarion slanted an eye at the Olenyas. He was robed and veiled and armed as always, no difference in him that Estarion could detect, but his nearness was warm on Estarion's skin. And only yesterday he had been a stranger, a voice without a face, cool and remote.

"What," Estarion mocked him, but gently, "will you hunt the laggards down yourself, and make them obey or die?"

"Yes," said Korusan.

"Do you ever laugh?" Estarion asked him. "Or dance for the simple joy of being alive?"

There was a difference after all: Korusan would meet his eyes and not slide away. "I dance," he said, "with swords."

"Everything you do is about killing," Estarion said.

"I am Olenyas," said Korusan.

Estarion sighed. He knew every inch of that body, and every scar on it; and he had enough of his own to know what weapons had caused most of them. He did not know Korusan at all. Except that he was doomed to die young. And that he danced with swords.

He would ride with Estarion, he and a company of his fellows. The Olenyai had not questioned their emperor's command, or even rolled an eye at it. They did flaunt it a little in the faces of his Varyani Guard, which marked them human after all, and which made the Guardsmen snarl. If Estarion could persuade those warring warriors to mingle freely and in friendship, he would have no difficulty with the rest of his twofold empire.

The servants had left Estarion with his shadow and a tableful of delicacies, none of which Estarion was minded to taste. He would not rest before the sun went down, or sleep tonight. There was too much to do. But for an hour, because the emperor did not eat in company, he was granted a respite.

He held out his hand. "Come here," he said.

He knew a moment of exquisite uncertainty, mounting to terror. Korusan was Asanian, and Olenyas, and incalculable. He might have meant not love at all, in the night, but something like war, and conquest: Asanion conquering Keruvarion in the bed and body of its emperor. If that was so, then he would refuse to be commanded; he would spurn Estarion, laugh, call him a lovestruck fool. So he was; so he could not help but be. He was besotted with a pair of golden eyes, an ivory face, a heart as gentle as it was prickly-fierce.

Then the Olenyas came. He did not laugh; he did not cast Estarion's weakness in his face. He was less savage than he had been in the night, and yet more hungry, as if he had been starving and here was his feast. It was wonderful and terrible, like riding a stormwind, or dancing with swords.

He could dance. Naked first in Estarion's arms, clad in nothing but the stone that had been Estarion's gift; robed again after with swords in hand, whirling from shaft of sunlight to shaft of shadow. Estarion found swords of his own and the slight protection of trousers, and waited in the light. Korusan spun out of the dark, swirl of robes, flash of steel. Estarion laughed. Korusan was silent, but his eyes were burning gold. They danced the dance of steel and blood, swift, swifter, swiftest, and never a pause or a shrinking, though the blades were deadly keen and the dance in bright earnest.

They both knew it. One false move, one misstep, and blood

would flow. Now Estarion pressed harder; now Korusan. Korusan was a fraction the quicker. Estarion was a shade the stronger. He had the advantage in reach. Korusan could slide in beneath it if he let slip his guard, and slide away again.

Estarion was tiring. He had moldered in the palace too long; he had lost his edge. Sweat dripped into his eyes, blinding him. Korusan seemed as cool as ever, but Estarion heard his breath coming fast.

Without warning Estarion dropped both swords and sprang under and round the wall of steel, sweeping up the startled boy, whirling him about. He could have cloven Estarion asunder. Maybe he considered it, but then he let fall his own swords. Estarion set him down. The boy was furious—spitting with it. "Idiot! Lunatic! You could have been killed."

Estarion grinned, gulping air. "Oh, come. Don't sulk. It's no sin to be caught by surprise."

"I was not," said Korusan. From the sound of it, his teeth were clenched. "Had I been, you would have died."

"Not likely," said Estarion. He was gasping, running with sweat, beautifully content. "Gods! I've gone soft. We'll dance again, Yelloweyes. Every morning and every night, until I've got my wind back. Then we'll dance at noon, too, and whenever else there's time for it. And when we come to fight—"

Korusan was blushing. It could be nothing else. Head down, eyes down, and heat coming off him in waves. Estarion took pity on him. "Here, eat, while I wash the stink off. You're too thin by half."

"*You* are a rack of bones," said Korusan. But he did not try to hold Estarion back. When Estarion looked again, the feast was somewhat diminished, and Korusan had a cup in his hand, sipping something that smelled of thornfruit and spices.

VANYI WAS AT great pains not to betray her honest opinion, which was that the two in front of her looked like children caught in mischief. That one was Avaryan's high priest in Endros and the other the empress mother, only made it worse.

She made herself speak calmly. "You should have told him."

"Certainly we should have," said Iburan. He seemed torn between rage and laughter.

"One could argue that he should have been less blind," said the empress. She was pacing while the others watched, a restless panther-stride so like her son's that Vanyi's throat closed. "Whatever our failing, its result is interesting to say the least. I wondered if he would ever stir, once the palace had him in its net."

"More blindness?" Vanyi asked.

The empress spun on her heel. Her glance was sharp. "No, I did not know that it would do this to him. I hoped that it would heal his scars; that I had raised him man enough to rule as he was born to rule."

"Maybe," said Iburan, "it only needed time. He rides in the morning to settle the rebellion in the south."

That had the smoothness of long repetition; and the empress' reply, the harshness of long resistance. "He is not riding. He is running, as he always runs. Will he never learn that he cannot escape himself?"

"You do him an injustice, I think," Iburan said mildly.

"Then let him prove it to me!" cried Merian.

Both of the others let the echoes die. When Iburan seemed disinclined to break the newborn silence, Vanyi said, "There is something else, my lady. Isn't there?"

At first Merian did not answer. She looked young this evening, young and angry. Vanyi did not like her better for it, but it was easier to think of her as a woman and not as a figure of awe on a golden throne: a woman with a son whom she loved to distraction and sometimes despaired of, and a lover whom she could not marry. When she was empress regent she could not set any lesser man in her royal husband's place, not without forsaking her regency. Now that she had laid aside that office she was free to take a husband, but she needed the emperor's consent. And that, thought Vanyi, she was not likely to get.

That dilemma at least, Vanyi would never need to face. Everyone knew where Estarion spent his nights. If one of his women had not conceived a son, one would do it soon enough.

But not, she realized with a small shock, while he rode to the rebellion. Asanian ladies did not leave their guarded walls. They did not ride to war, even to wait in tents for their lords to return. And they were ladies, his concubines; not slaves or courtesans. They would remain behind.

Merian's voice startled her out of her reflection. She had to struggle to remember what she had asked, to understand the answer. "There is something else. He has done somewhat to his power. I would say that he had slain the last of it, but if he had, he would be dead."

Vanyi's heart clenched. Iburan spoke quietly, calmly. "He buries it deep, but it lives. Or, as you say, he would have died."

"When he came this morning," Merian said, "when he stood above us, I never even sensed him. It was as if he was not there. My body's senses knew him, but to my power he was invisible."

"Shields," said Vanyi.

"Shields leave a trace," said Merian.

"He's never been like anyone else," Vanyi said. "Why shouldn't he have found a new way to hide himself?"

"Completely?" Merian demanded of her. "So completely that he is not there at all?"

"Consider," said Vanyi. "When he was here before, he

nearly died, and his power was all but destroyed. He needed years to heal even as much as he did. Then all at once, before he was properly seated on his throne, he came back to this place where he lost his power. You know how he is inside of walls. These walls are higher and thicker than any he's ever known, and his faithful servants have taught him that he'll never leave them again. That's false, even he should know that, but how sensible can he be when he's locked in a cage? I doubt he even knew he had the key, until this morning."

"Did we give it to him, do you think?" asked Iburan wryly.

"You opened his eyes to something," Vanyi said. She sighed. "You'll pardon me for asking, but why did you call me here? I'm not his bedmate any longer. I can't bring him back to hand."

"Can't you?"

She rounded on Iburan. "What are you asking?"

"I think you know," he said.

"I won't," she said. "I will—not—take another woman's leavings."

"Jealousy," he said, "is a simple woman's luxury."

"I'm a fisherman's daughter from Seiun. As," Vanyi said with bitter precision, "you and your lady have never failed to remind me. I am not and never will be empress."

"What you are," said Merian, "is his beloved. He loves you still. Never doubt it. If he does as his duty commands, and does it with something resembling pleasure, who are you to fault him?"

"Maybe," said Vanyi, "I love him too much to let you use me, and him, as you are suggesting. You want me to lead him by the privates, straight out of this rebellion and back to his harem and his properly pedigreed ladies."

"No," said Merian without perceptible anger. "I wish you to keep him safe: to guard him with your power, since he seems to have lost the capacity to guard himself."

"And lead him back to his ladies." Vanyi pressed palms to her aching brow. "My father warned me, you know. Never get too close to the gentry, he said. Gentry aren't like us. They're cold as fish and treacherous as the sea, and when all's done and said, they'll look first to their damned honor and then to themselves, and never mind the blood they've shed or the hearts they've broken." She looked up into their faces. Iburan's was gentle, as if he could understand. Merian's was eagle-fierce. "Sometimes I wish I'd married that fat lout down by the harbor."

"You would be miserable," said the empress.

"My misery would be simple," Vanyi said. "It wouldn't be this hopeless tangle."

"You would have flung yourself into the sea."

Merian's lack of sympathy was bracing, in its way. Vanyi hated her with hate so perfect that it lacked even heat. "I'll force myself on him. I'll ride with him. Will that be enough for you?"

"Certainly," said Merian. "His heir must be of Asanian blood. I bid you remember that."

"I never forget it," Vanyi said. "Not for one moment."

Iburan followed her out of the empress' receiving room. She ignored him, difficult as that could be.

In the outer chamber a eunuch trotted past them. He wore white and gold: emperor's livery, with the shoulder-knot of a messenger. Vanyi paused. Everything in her wanted to be out of this place, back to her temple and her duties and her peace, but instinct held her where she was. She could stretch her ears, if she wished. She noticed that Iburan was doing the same.

There were no endless circling greetings and formalities. From anyone else in Kundri'j it would have been an insult, and the eunuch seemed to believe that it was. He did not know Estarion, or Estarion's mother.

Vanyi barely needed more than ears to hear him. His voice was high, and it carried. "The emperor bids you prepare to ride. He departs this city at sunrise."

The empress' response was calm. "Inform my son that I

have been ready since the sun touched its zenith. I shall await him at first dawn."

The eunuch seemed disconcerted: when he spoke again, his voice was less strident. "The emperor also bids you know that the priest of Avaryan in Endros will accompany him. He bade me tell you, 'I cannot forgive. But I can comprehend.' "

Vanyi's eyes darted to Iburan's face. It was perfectly blank.

In the room within, the empress said, still calmly, "Tell my son that I understand."

Iburan began to walk as if he had never paused. Vanyi found herself swept in his wake. She could not find words to say.

Outside of the palace, in the empty street, Iburan said them. "Clever, clever child. And oh, so cruel. Who taught him that, I wonder? Asanion? Or his mother?"

"What's cruel about it?" Vanyi asked. "He said he understood."

"He said it through a messenger," said Iburan, "and he said it within an imperial summons." And when she still did not understand: "He treated her like a vassal. And more than that. He let her know that he won't prevent us. He won't even keep us apart. Can you see what that will do to us every time we come together? We'll know that he knows. We'll shrivel with guilt."

"I doubt that," said Vanyi, with an eye not quite on the bulk of him beside her.

He laughed, sudden and deep, but it was brief. "No, it won't stop us. But it will slow us a little. Parents who disapprove, those are spice to a pair of lovers. Children in the same condition . . . they dampen the proceedings remarkably. They have such expectations; and they never, never forgive."

"If he knew how you laugh at him, he'd be furious."

"I'm not laughing," said Iburan. "He's dangerous, you know. I don't think he realizes that; and the rest of us tend to forget. When he was young, before his father died, he promised to be a great mage and king. He may never be the mage now, after all that's happened, but the king is there still. If he learns to stop running—if he accepts all that he is—"

"And if he doesn't do either, he'll be deadly, because he won't settle to anything, but will drag the empires after him wherever he goes."

"He'll break them," Iburan said. He tugged his beard. It looked naked without its plaits and its gauds. He seemed to miss them, raking fingers through it, scowling at the darkening sky.

Suddenly he straightened. "Come now. We've packing to do."

Vanyi hung back. "Shouldn't I tell him I'm going?"

"And have him say no? Don't be a fool. He's ordered me to go; I have to have attendants, it wouldn't be proper if I didn't. Unless you'd rather wait on the empress."

"Thank you, my lord," said Vanyi, "but no."

"She's hardly a monster, child."

"Of course she isn't." Vanyi did not mean to sound so angry. "It's only . . . we never seem to agree on anything. Except that we love that damnable, arrogant, impossibly infuriating son of hers."

"You are," he said, "quite dreadfully alike."

"I am *not*—" Vanyi bit her tongue. He was grinning at her. "Sometimes I wonder who's really his father."

"You should have known Ganiman," said Iburan. There was sadness in it, but above and about that, a wry amusement. "Starion comes by it honestly. If anything, his father was worse."

"That's not possible," said Vanyi. She strode forward down the broad street. After a handful of heartbeats she felt him behind her, broad as a wall and nigh as strong.

35

THERE WAS ONE duty that Estarion could not avoid, nor overmuch wish to. He performed it toward evening of that endless day, late enough to be polite, too early to linger. He would have left Korusan behind, but the Olenyas refused to leave him until he came to the inner door of the harem. Estarion half expected him to pass it. He halted and crouched in a shadow as he often had before, with no more evidence of disgruntlement than he had ever shown, if certainly no less.

Once past the door in the scented quiet, Estarion drew a shaking breath. There was a word in Keruvarion for what he was. Soldiers gave it to women who sold themselves in the street. In Asanion it was prettier. Here he was lord and emperor, and duty-bound to sire sons; and when duty did not bind him, he was permitted his body's pleasure.

His ladies were waiting. Tonight, he thought, he would choose Haliya, and damn the proprieties. When he came back—if he came back—he would return to the round of his duty.

They were all together in their usual silence, but the undercurrent was odd. Not rancor, he did not think, or jealousy. But tension certainly, and the salt bitterness of tears.

He kissed each one of them, taking his time about it. It was not, surprisingly, little Shaia who had been weeping, but Igalla with her elegant bearing and her queenly manners, and Eluya. Almost he chose one of them, but there was Haliya, dry-eyed and stiff-backed, and Ziana looking rarely unplacid.

He did not delude himself that he was loved. But they were fond of him, maybe, and they fancied that he owned them. He never had been able to talk them out of that. If he should be killed or if he should fail to come back, they could look for little mercy from an empire that had defeated him.

He had been steady, or so he thought, until he found himself leading both Haliya and Ziana to the inner room. He had not meant that at all. A choosing, yes, for courtesy, and a farewell as brief as he could decently make it, but nothing more than that. He ached even yet from Korusan's fierce embraces.

Or maybe he had been clever. He could hardly be expected to take them both at once, or to take one while the other watched. They seemed to think otherwise, it was true, and not to be discommoded by it. Maybe he should have chosen all nine at once, and escaped while they untangled themselves.

Neither of the sisters reminded him that he was being improper, or that he should have chosen Eluya or Igalla. Ziana fetched him wine spiced and warmed as he liked it. Haliya eased him out of coat and trousers, found his knots and aches, and set to work. Some were patently not practice-bruises. She did not remark on them.

He had not known how tired he was until those clever fingers stroked away his tautness. He had not slept since—when? He could not remember. His eyelids drooped in spite of themselves. Ziana had his head in her lap. He heard her voice as from far away. "You cut your beard. I like it so, like a fleece, curly and thick." She combed fingers through it, lightly, making him shiver.

Haliya stroked the lighter fleece of his body, breast and belly and loins. The rest of him was all but asleep, but his banner rose valiantly to greet her.

This was whoredom, harlotry, weakness of body and soul. A priest should master his passions. A Sunlord should rule them.

A Sunlord should sire sons. That was all he was meant for, when it came to it. If he died tomorrow, or if he never touched a woman again, there would be no heir to rule after him.

Necessity. That was the name of it. Very pleasant, lying here, with beauty beneath his head and brilliance at his middle.

Korusan would not be amused. He was jealous, that one. Asanians did not train their men as they did their women, to accept what must be accepted. Men owned. Women were owned.

Korusan would ride with his lord. These ladies would not. The voice of guilt was growing faint. Shame he had never had. He was blessed in his lovers.

He said so, later, when Ziana lay on one side and Haliya on the other, and he was renewed as if he had slept the night through. Ziana smiled from the hollow of his shoulder. Haliya said, "Will you say that when you've had a thousand lovers?"

"I'll never have so many," he said.

"You said you'd never have more than one. It's a longer step from one to three than from three to a thousand."

"Not likely," said Estarion. "I can be as Asanian as this, with you to show me the way. Even nine of you—that's within the realm of possibility. But no more."

"I would like it, of course," said Ziana, "if there were never more than nine. I'd see more of you then."

He kissed the smooth parting of her hair. "I should hate to see less of you than I do." She mercifully did not point out that he had not visited her in a hand of days. First there had been obligations. Then evening Court. Then Korusan.

He sat up abruptly, startling them both. "I have to go," he said.

Neither protested. That piqued him a little. Surely if they loved him they would beg him to stay.

Ziana brought him his coat, Haliya his trousers. They did not play with him, not much. Not enough to tempt him to linger.

But as Ziana fastened the last jeweled button, as Haliya set his foot in her lap for the boot, they both paused. Golden eyes and amber met, parted, fixed on him.

"Take us with you," said Haliya.

He did not think that he looked angry. He even laughed.

Ziana flinched. Haliya went stiff, and her hands on his foot tightened to the edge of pain.

"You know I can't," he said. He took care to be gentle.

"You gave your word," said Haliya.

"I promised that I would take you to Keruvarion. I'm not going there. I'm going south, and then maybe west, wherever need takes me."

"You will go to Keruvarion," Ziana said. "Once you're away from Kundri'j, nothing will stop you."

"Nothing but duty and necessity," said Estarion, "and a matter of rebellion in the provinces."

"I can ride," said Haliya, "and shoot. I won't encumber you. Your mother is going. She has women with her. Would one more be so great a burden?"

Ziana, who could neither ride nor shoot, was silent. Estarion spoke to her. "I promise you. When at last I go to Keruvarion, I'll take you, or send for you."

Her head bent. She did not weep. Tears were not a weapon she would use, if others served as well. He caught her hands that smoothed his coat, smoothed and stroked it. "You can't ride to war, my love. We'll all be on seneldi; the wagons will be only for baggage, and those we'll leave behind if we must."

"I ride," Haliya said at his feet. "I can fight. Take me with you."

Oh, he had trapped himself neatly, with Ziana to melt his heart and Haliya to bend his will. Ziana at least had sense to see the truth. "If you promise," she said, too low almost to hear. "If you send for me when you come to Keruvarion."

"On the Sun in my hand," he said, raising it to her cheek. She bore the touch of it, though her eyes went wide with terror. Maybe she feared that it would brand her. He kissed the cheek where it had rested, flushed over pallor, unmarked and unscarred.

Haliya was not so easily put off. "Take me," she said.

"Why?" he demanded with deliberate brutality. "What can

you do that a dozen others can't? I don't need you for my bed. I don't need you in my army."

He had struck, and struck deep, but she had her fair share of steel. Most of it was in her spine, and some in her voice. "Maybe you need me to remind you of what you're fighting for. Of what you have to come back to."

"I can't be trusted to remember it?"

"No."

His teeth clicked together. He could flatten her with a blow. Or he could laugh and pull her up, and keep his hands on her shoulders, and say to her, "You are impossible. And so is your whim. What will it do to your honor if I take you with me to war?"

"My honor is your honor," she said steadily. "I want to go, my lord. I won't make trouble for you."

"Your coming with me isn't trouble?" He lowered his brows. "If you come with me, it won't be as my bedmate. You'll ride in my mother's company, and you'll answer to her, and wait on her if she asks. If she bids you ride without a veil, you obey her. Do you understand?"

"Perfectly." She met his capitulation with admirable restraint. Her breath came quickly, but that might only have been discomfort. He unclamped his fingers from her shoulders. She kept her eyes level with his: one of her more interesting arts. "Is that the price, my lord? Not to see you at all?"

"You'll see me," he said. "I'm leading the march. But you ride with my mother."

She bent her head, but not her eyes. "And if you ask for me and she refuses, I am to obey her?"

"I could still leave you behind," he pointed out.

That quelled her, for the moment. She would whoop, maybe, when he was gone, and dance round the room. Or maybe not. There was Ziana still, watching and listening and saying nothing.

Haliya was the bolder, no question of it. Ziana, he suspected, was the braver. She accepted what she could not change. She had his promise, which he would keep. Her hand rose to her cheek, where he had sealed the vow.

That, when he left Kundri'j Asan, was what he would choose to remember: Ziana straight and still in the harem's heart, holding his heart in her hand.

Meruvan Estarion

It should have felt less like flight; and Estarion should have felt less like an earthbear dragged out of its burrow. He was persuaded to sleep, if briefly. As he woke to a raw cold dawn, a palace in tumult, and for all he knew, armies gathering to cut him down, he reflected that maybe he had moved too soon. It was winter, the feast of the Long Night well past and the sky closed in with clouds and cold. Armies would go if he sent them, to put down the rebellion. He had no need to go with them. On a bare day's notice, none but his own outland Guard and his Olenyai were ready: tenscore of each, and the hundred of his mother's guard, pitifully small for an army, barely enough to defend him if he was beset. If he waited a hand of days, he could have ten times that number; a full cycle of Brightmoon, and ten times that would follow him, out of the imperial levies.

There were armies where he went, under lords who were his vassals. And he was not going to fight if he could help it. They said that Sarevadin alone, without her consort, could ride from end to end of the empire with a company of guardsmen, and no one would touch her or offer her harm; and everywhere she went, her people learned to love her.

He was arrogant and more than arrogant, to dream that he could do the same. He was not Sarevadin but the last and least of her descendants. And when she rode, she had left a son under guard in Kundri'j, and a consort of impeccably Asanian lineage.

The consorts he had, eight of them, and the ninth ready, no doubt, and waiting for him to ride. The son he would get, god and goddess willing, when he came back. He was not going to his death. He was going to preserve his empire. And, he admitted, here alone in the dark, to save himself.

Asanion had lost its horror. Its people were people to him now, lovers, even—maybe—friends. He could not rule in this palace as the old emperors had ruled, as prisoners of their own power. But he could rule this half of his empire.

He had gained something, then, from his sojourn in the Golden Palace. Even his magery seemed a little less blunted by the walls about him, his mind a fraction less blind.

He lay in something resembling content, counting his aches and bruises. Korusan had not been there when he came out of the harem. He had been disappointed, enough almost to snap at the Olenyas who waited to fill his shadow, simply because it was not Korusan. But he had held his tongue. It was as well, he told himself as he calmed. He had much to do still, and then he should rest.

But if the boy had grown angry at the time Estarion spent with the women, if he had gone and would not come back . . .

Nonsense. Korusan had gone like a sensible man to prepare for the march and then to sleep. Estarion would find him in the ranks of the Olenyai, one pair of lion-eyes amid the simple human brown and amber and gold.

If his captain allowed it. If he was not commanded to remain in the palace.

He would come. He did as he pleased, that one. And he would please to ride with his emperor to war.

Korusan was not asleep, nor was he resting. He was facing the Master of the Olenyai yet again, for once without the mages or their master. Master Asadi had done an unwonted thing when Korusan entered his chamber, offered him food and drink to break his night's fast. He took them, aware of what they signified. From master to brother of the second rank it was high honor. From Olenyai commander to emperor in exile, it was the seal of an alliance.

Korusan was hungry, but he ate carefully, and drank sparingly of the well-watered wine. He was aware of Asadi's eyes on him. The Master was eating as lightly as he, and with as much sense of ceremony.

Custom forbade that they speak of anything but trifles until the bowls and cups were taken away, the wine replaced with a tisane of spices and sweet herbs, hot and pungent, to warm the blood for the cold journey ahead of them. Korusan sipped gingerly but with pleasure.

At length he set down the cup. He kept his hands wrapped round it, for warmth, and looked into Asadi's bared face.

"Do you approve of what the Sunlord does?" Asadi asked him.

He nearly laughed. "I disapprove of his existence. As for this, I think that he may be wise."

"To leave his guarded palace? To walk into the net?"

"Better to walk into a trap than wither in a cage."

"You love him."

Korusan kept his face expressionless. "You can judge that?"

"I can judge my Olenyas." Asadi sighed, gazing into his emptied cup. Korusan wondered if he had magery after all; if he could scry in the dregs of his tisane. Absurd. Insulting, to look on the Master of the Olenyai as a village soothsayer. "It will come to a crux, my prince. Then you will be forced to choose."

"What choice is there?" Korusan demanded with a flash of heat. "I am not a traitor. I do not forget what I am."

"But how will you prove it, my prince?" asked Asadi. His voice was gentle. "Our allies will force you to a conclusion. I hold them off as best I may, but my strength is hardly infinite. They wish this Sunlord dead. They will kill him, or break his mind, unless you move before them."

Korusan's stomach knotted and cramped. He should have known it would do that. But he was master of it, just. "All of you have plans and purposes, plottings that you labor to bring to fruition. So too do I. Are you as a great a fool as the mages are, to think me a brainless child, incapable of choosing my own times and places?"

"Hardly," said Asadi, "or we would never have yielded to you in this. And now the quarry leaves the lair. It will be more difficult for the spells to bind him while he rides under the sky."

"But also easier for death to take him," Korusan said, "where his defenses are dissipated, and any man may come at him. And he goes straight into the rebellion that the mages have fomented."

"So I argued," said Asadi, "and so I was permitted to conclude. But our allies are not well pleased."

"Let them be displeased," said Korusan, not without pleasure in the thought, "if only they grant me my will. Bid them loose their spells. We have no need of them."

"They will call it arrogance," said Asadi.

"And you?"

Asadi shrugged, one-sided. "I think that you may have more power over him than they believe, but less than you might hope. He goes where his whim moves him. Can you guide him?"

"I have no need," said Korusan. "He goes where I wish him to go."

"Into the fire, aye. And then, my prince?"

"And then," said Korusan, "we take him."

Asadi inclined his head. He did not quite believe it, Korusan could see. And if he was doubtful, the mages must be reckoning Korusan a traitor to all their cause.

Korusan lifted his chin and hardened his heart. So be it. Hate was older than love, blood stronger than the bond of flesh to flesh. He would do as he had always meant to do. Whatever it cost him.

The escort was waiting at sunrise. The emperor must be the last of them, for when he came, they would ride. Estarion did not find it difficult to drag his feet. Maybe he should wear the mail. Or the corselet. Or the full parade armor. Maybe his hair should be plaited, or knotted for the helmet, or—and at that his servants howled—cropped to the skull. Maybe he should go back to his bed and rise for morning Court, and forget that he had ever dreamed of escape.

In the end he wore mail, a glimmering gold-washed coat over supple leather, and he wore his hair in a priest's plait, with his torque for a gorget. He had a cloak for the people to wonder at if they ever looked up so high, white plainsbuck leather lined with golden fur—not lion, it was too clear a gold. Sandcat, the servant said: a lithe sharp-nosed creature the length and breadth of an Asanian's forearm, that lived in cities like a man. Estarion doubted that it went to war. Only men did that.

He pretended to break his fast. He drank the honeyed wine, picked at something that maybe had been roast plowbeast before they spiced and stewed it and wrapped it in thin unleavened bread. When it was well dismembered, he reached for the winejar to fill his cup again.

There was a hand on it before him, and eyes above that. Golden eyes.

The breath left him in a long sigh, even as Korusan said, "You grow too fond of the wine. If you will not eat, then drink this." He poured out warm thornfruit nectar, thinning it with water and a fistful of berries from a bowl.

Estarion eyed it with great mistrust, but he essayed a sip. "This is good!"

Korusan did not dignify that with an answer. He spread a napkin and began to fill it with the less fragile of the delicacies.

"What are you doing?"

"You must eat," said Korusan, "but you must ride, and the sun is rising. Will you keep your escort waiting?"

"My escort will wait as long as it must."

Korusan knotted the napkin and slipped it into his robes. Estarion wondered, brief and absurd, if the razors from the bath were still there somewhere, in a hidden fold.

The Olenyas tugged his robes into place, settled his swords in their sheaths, and said, "Your majesty is ready to ride."

His majesty was ready to upbraid him for an insolent child. He found himself, one way and another, striding through the maze of rooms. He gained followers as he went, guards, servants, people who not quite stared and not quite muttered and were, for Asanians, open in their curiosity. He hoped that he obliged them. He walked as tall as he knew how, and put on a swagger that was half despair.

Dank air struck his face. There was no sun. The sky was grey, with rain in its belly, or possibly sleet. He halted under it. If it rained—if there would be sun tomorrow—

The escort was drawn up in ranks, waiting for him. The black mass of the Olenyai, separate and haughty. The scarlet blaze of his Guard. His mother's strong women in their green livery, and she in front of them, warded in mail, armed with bow and knife and sword. Iburan was at her right hand in the plain robe he affected in Asanion, and his priests behind him. Some of them were women. One was Vanyi.

Estarion's jaw tightened. There was someone else in the empress' following, a small figure on a sand-colored mare. She had no escort that he could see. She had a mail-coat: where in the hells had she found that? The bow in its case he knew, and the arrows. He had given them to her. She had found a knife somewhere. No sword. He would have to find her one.

A groom held a mount for him. It was not Umizan: there had been no time to bring him from Induverran. Estarion paused to make this new beast's acquaintance. It was not one he knew, and not, he was pleased to observe, the golden plow-beast he had been forced to ride into Kundri'j. This was a tall striped dun with ell-long horns. Estarion smoothed the mane on the stallion's neck. It was striped like the rest of him, golden dun and glossy black. His eyes were amber, bright yet quiet. He breathed sweet breath into Estarion's palm.

Estarion mounted in a smooth long leap. The senel was steady under him. "Has he a name?" Estarion asked the groom.

The man dipped his head. "Chirai, majesty," he said.

"Chirai," said Estarion. The black-rimmed ears tilted back. Estarion gathered the reins. He could turn still, ride out of this court and into the stableyard, dismount, pull his walls about him.

Or he could urge the dun stallion toward the gate. His breath was coming in gasps. His hands were cold, even the one that burned and throbbed.

Idiocy. He was Estarion of Endros. He hated walls; he craved the open sky.

His senel settled it for him. As if he had given the command and not sat like a stone, Chirai moved softly forward. The rest fell in behind them.

The Regent of Asanion waited under the Golden Gate. There were men with him, lords of the High Court, and guards armed and armored. Estarion knew, looking at them, that they would stop him. They would offer battle; they would hold him captive until he died.

Chirai kept his steady pace. Firaz waited in silence. A spearlength from his mount's lowered horns, Estarion halted. "The emperor will pass," he said.

Firaz bowed his head. "Will the emperor reconsider?"

"The emperor must do as he will do."

Estarion barely breathed. Firaz looked full in his face, which was boldness beyond belief, had Estarion been Asanian. But he was not. He smiled a sword-edged smile.

"You are," said Firaz at last, "the emperor." It was a capitulation, and a challenge.

Estarion acknowledged them both. "Guard my palace," he said.

"Fight well," said Firaz, "and return well to that place which is yours."

"So I do intend," Estarion said. He touched heel to Chirai's side.

Firaz bent his own senel aside. As Estarion passed man and mount, he said, "Take comfort, lord Regent. If I'm killed, the next emperor can only be more proper than I am. And if I live—why then, maybe I'll have learned decent manners."

"One does not learn propriety in battle," said Firaz, "my lord." He bowed lower than he ever had, down to his stallion's neck. "May your riding prosper, my lord emperor. Believe that I speak truly; that I wish you well."

"I never doubted it," said Estarion. "Believe that too, my lord Regent."

Estarion emerged from Kundri'j Asan like a snake from its skin. Slow at first once he passed the Golden Gate and the lord who held it, with a tearing that was like pain. Then swifter, winding down the Way of Princes, rising from walk to trot to smooth rocking canter. Hoofs rang on paving stones. The silence of Asanian homage was profound and for once undaunting. The great fear was before him: the last gate; the bridge over the river, and the broad wall-less plain.

As he passed the gate and mounted the arch of the bridge, a thin rain began to fall. His cloak kept it out, but he was bareheaded, with nothing between him and the sky but a circlet of gold. He tipped his head back. He could fall, fall forever into the endless sea of cloud.

Rain kissed his face. His mount carried him with unruffled calm, down from the bridge and the river, stride by stride away from the ninefold walls. He fell out of the sky to the vastness of the plain, grey as clouds itself, and no walls, no walls as far as he could see.

His whole body shuddered. His mind shrank. It gathered all its force in its center; held, clenched in upon itself; and bloomed like a flower of fire.

He had power. He had magic—he, the maimed one, the blinded fool. He had never known truly how much he had, nor known how much of it was blunted within the walls of Kundri'j Asan. He laughed with the shock of it, half in incredulous joy, half in terror.

His escort spread behind him, Asanian, Varyani, divided as

enemies must always be. But there was a yellow woman in the empress' following and an Olenyas in his own shadow, black robe amid the scarlet of his Guard.

His senel bucked lightly, startling him. He gave the stallion his head. The stallion swung from canter into gallop, and from gallop into flight.

VANYI HAD NO need to ask who was the stranger in the empress' following. She was the only Asanian, and the only one mounted on a horn-browed mare out of Varag Suvien. The headdress was Suvieni too, the headcloth drawn up over the face and secured in a circlet. Vanyi knew who must have taught her that expedient.

So much, Vanyi thought, for Iburan's hope of wielding her in Estarion's defense. This chit of a child would see to that.

The first night out of Kundri'j, they stopped in Induverran. Estarion was reunited with his blue-eyed stallion: touching and unexpectedly amusing when Umizan met the senel whom Estarion had ridden from the city. The black charged upon the dun, ears flat, horns lowered, hoofs pounding. The dun stood with head up, alert but unalarmed. As Umizan surged for the kill, Chirai pirouetted neatly out of his path. When Umizan came back, raging, Chirai snorted as if in exasperation and eluded him again, and yet again. They danced the full circle of the field, until Umizan thundered to a halt, blowing and foaming, and stamped. Chirai flicked an ear, lowered his head, began coolly to graze.

Vanyi's sides ached with laughter. Even the Olenyai were amused. Estarion walked over to his sweating, seething, baffled blue-eyed brother, wrapped arms about his neck, and leaned against him till he quieted.

The rain had ended a little while since. Darts of sun broke free from the clouds, striking blue-black fire in Umizan's coat and Estarion's hair, turning Chirai's striped hide to bars of black and gold. Vanyi sneezed.

"Are you well?"

Vanyi glanced at the one who had spoken. Not so small, standing next to her: a palm's width the less, maybe, holding herself very straight in her desert tribesman's veil. She did not seem to know who Vanyi was. "Do you have a name?" Vanyi demanded of her.

She blinked at the sharpness, but she answered without hesitation. "Haliya. You?"

"Vanyi." It was not intended to be polite.

The Asanian's eyes widened. They were an improbable shade of gold, like coins. "Then you are—"

"Yes, I was his bedmate. I'd have thought you'd know."

Haliya blinked. Vanyi sensed no enmity in her, nothing but interest, and puzzlement that might be for Vanyi's rudeness. "Of course I knew," she said. "But he didn't say that you were beautiful. Your skin is like milk. Mine," she said with evident regret, "is more like well-aged cheese."

Fine ivory, Vanyi would have said, from what she could see of it. "He likes a pale-skinned woman."

"I don't think he cares," said Haliya, "as long as he finds her interesting."

There were people about, but none of them was listening. They were all watching Estarion. He mounted Umizan, bareback and bridleless, and rode him bucking and curvetting across the field.

Haliya sighed. "I broke my arm the last time I tried that."

"You didn't."

Haliya was difficult to offend. She laughed in her veil. "That's what he said, too, when I told him. But I did. I was a terrible child. Of course," she said, "when I went for that particular ride, it was my father's herd stallion, and no one ever rode him at all. I should have known what he'd do."

"I begin to see," Vanyi said slowly, and not without humor, "why he finds you interesting."

Haliya did a thing that left Vanyi speechless. She slipped her arm through Vanyi's and said, "I'm glad he brought you. I was afraid I'd be the only one."

Vanyi could not break free as easily as she might have expected. Haliya was strong, and although her eyes smiled, her grip was steely hard. "He didn't bring me," Vanyi snapped. "I came with the priests."

"I made him take me," said Haliya. "He didn't want to. He thought I should stay with the others."

"Why didn't you?"

"I wanted to ride," Haliya said. She sounded very young and very determined. "So he did mean it. He wasn't going to bring anyone for the nights. Is that a sickness, do you think? Or is it something they do in Keruvarion, to teach themselves about pain?"

Sometimes Vanyi wondered if Asanians were human at all. They did not think like anyone else she knew of, even syndics in the Nine Cities, who were surpassingly strange.

Haliya answered herself, since Vanyi was not going to. "He'll be choosing ladies in the cities, then. He didn't before, and he offended people. Now he understands what's proper."

"Don't you ever get jealous?" Vanyi demanded of her. "Can't you conceive of wanting him for yourself?"

"That's selfish," said Haliya.

"And you're a perfect saint?"

Haliya drew herself up, still holding Vanyi's arm, and said with dignity, "I do try to show a little honor."

"It's not honor where I come from," said Vanyi, "to let one's man go without a fight."

"Are you going to fight me? I'm no good with a sword, but I can shoot."

Alien. Vanyi pulled free and stood rubbing her arm. "The usual method," she said acidly, "is to exert oneself to gain the man's complete and total favor."

"So that's why he said he could only manage one at a time. He feared for his life."

Vanyi gaped at her.

Haliya patted her hand. "I suppose you can't help it.

You're foreigners. You don't understand the right ways of doing things."

"I see you've met the lady of the Vinicharyas."

Vanyi paused in folding the vestments from the sunset-rite. She would have liked to pretend that she did not know whom Iburan spoke of, but there could be no such simplicities among mages. "She's very . . . original."

"I would call her interesting."

"So would his majesty." Vanyi smoothed the last white robe and laid it in the traveling-chest, and turned to face him. "Were you expecting bloodshed?"

"Asanian women don't fight over men."

"So she told me."

Iburan closed and locked the box in which they kept the vessels of the rite. His fingers traced the inlay of its lid. "She brought no maid and no attendants. That's shockingly improper for one of her station."

"Surely the empress is chaperone enough."

"The empress can't be expected to wait on her."

Vanyi did not like where this was leading. "I may be a commoner, but I am not a servant."

"You serve the god," said Iburan.

"I do that." Vanyi kept her eyes level on his face. He was not allowing her to read it, or the mind behind it.

"I have been thinking," he said, "that she's very much alone. And Estarion isn't keeping her with him."

Vanyi should not have felt that stab of vindictive pleasure. "She told me that. She seemed to think that he'd be warming his bed with a selection of provincial ladies."

"Not likely," said Iburan. "Not on this riding, when he's a clear target for any assassin who happens by. As, I'm thinking, is she. She's Asanian; she rides like a man; she's clearly been corrupted. She would be a potent object lesson, and a valuable hostage."

"He hasn't thought to set guards on her?"

"He's set his mother on guard, and the whole company of her escort."

"But?" said Vanyi. "There is a 'but,' isn't there?"

"I think," Iburan said, and he said it very calmly, "that she needs more than that. She needs someone who can ride with her, keep her company, ward her with magecraft."

"There's Shaiyel," Vanyi said. And before he could object: "Yes, he's male, but he's Asanian. Isn't he kin to the Vinicharyas?"

"Distant kin," said Iburan, "and a man."

"His wards are as strong as mine. His land-sense is better."

"He's not a woman."

"I'm not the only priestess in this army!"

Iburan let the echoes die.

"Why are you asking me?" Vanyi demanded. "Am I being set a penance?"

"Maybe," he said. "Maybe you need lessoning in humility and forgiveness, and in the virtues of priestesses. And maybe," he said, "I think that you can protect her as no one else can."

"Because I want to kill her slowly for having what I can't have?"

"She doesn't have it now, either." He sighed. For the first time she saw that he was not a young man: saw the glint of silver in his beard, the lines of weariness about his eyes. "You could leave us all. You have your Journey still. The Gates won't break or fall for want of you."

"Wherever I am," she said, "the Gates are in me. It's like the land-sense, my lord. I have the Gate-sense. I always have."

She had not told him anything that he did not know. "Will you go?"

"Of course not." Vanyi was too tired all at once to be angry. "This is my Journey. I have no other."

"Will you guard the Lady Haliya?"

Vanyi laughed without mirth. "I haven't taken her hide yet. I don't suppose I will. Hide-taking is for men. They can afford the simple pleasures."

"Young men," said Iburan. "Old ones are as vexed as women."

"Would you know?" Vanyi took his hand, startling him a little, and kissed it. "I don't know why I don't hate you, my lord."

"Hate is a simple pleasure," said Iburan.

She stared at him. Then suddenly, and this time truly, she laughed.

38

VANYI WAITED TILL morning. It was not a failure of courage. It was sense. She would have one untroubled night's rest before she subjected herself to her penance.

And she did sleep. She prayed first, for humility and forgiveness, and the virtues of a priestess. The god gave her no answer, but she had not asked for one.

She was no humbler in the dawn's dimness, no more forgiving, but she had virtue enough to do as she had promised. As the escort arranged itself, Vanyi claimed her mare and led her to stand beside the Suvieni mare. Haliya was mounted already, shivering in the chill. Her eyes were bright with excitement. She greeted Vanyi as if she were glad to see her, but to Vanyi's surprise she did not vex the air with chatter. Maybe she had a sense of Vanyi's temper, or maybe she was too full of words to decide which she wanted to burst out with first.

Estarion came out last as always. The golden mail was put away; he was in his old familiar riding clothes, with mail showing under them, and a sword at his side. He looked as if he had slept well. He was smiling, saying something that made Lord Dushai laugh, pausing to greet people: lords, servants, hangers-on. His shadow was occupied as it always was now, by an Olenyas. The same one, Vanyi saw, the one with the lion-eyes. Her nape prickled. There was something different about him—about the two of them.

Of course there was a difference. Estarion was himself again, or close enough. The trapped look was all but gone from his eyes. He moved with his old grace, laughed with his old lightness. He even smiled at his mother, although he barely inclined his head to Iburan.

Vanyi he did not see at all. She made sure of that. There was no need for him to know what duty she had taken. He greeted Haliya with more than civility, standing full in front of Vanyi, so potent a presence that she almost forgot every vow she had sworn. Haliya was dignified. She did not fling herself on him or demand that he keep her with him. She said, "This is barely proper, my lord."

He smiled. "I won't shame you, then. Am I permitted to kiss your hand?"

She sucked in a breath, outraged. "My lord!"

"Ah then." His regret seemed genuine. "Fair riding to you, my lady. Send me word if there's anything you lack."

"I have everything I need," she said.

He went away to lead the march. Haliya did not watch him go, or sigh over him. She gathered the reins and said, "You must tell me how you do that."

"What?" asked Vanyi. And after a moment: "My lady."

"I'm not your lady," Haliya said. "Was it magic?"

"You aren't supposed to know about that."

"I'm Vinicharyas. We know too much about it." Haliya nudged her mare into the line of riders.

Vanyi kicked her gelding in behind. She had thinking to do. It was not supposed to concern Estarion, or the way he had spoken to Haliya. Light. Easy. Tender—yes, he was that. But not passionate. He was not in love with her. If there was a word for a man who was happily in friendship with a woman, then he was that.

It would have been better, Vanyi thought, if he had been madly in love with her. Passion died. Friendship had a way of persisting.

It rained more often than not as they rode southward out of Induverran. Estarion took no visible notice of it. The rest of them endured, most in silence. They were riding swiftly, but not at racing speed, and not precisely as an army to war.

There were armies mustering. Estarion made himself

known to them. They cheered him, albeit with bafflement, as if they could not quite understand that this was the emperor. The emperor was ten robes and a mask in the palace in Kundri'j. How could he be riding in the rain, bareheaded as often as not, and stopping to talk to commoners?

For he did that. It was something he had always done in Keruvarion, but in this half of his empire it was unheard of. His Varyani kept constant watch, but they did not try to prevent him. His Asanians looked sorely tried by it: hands twitching near weapons, eyes darting at every shadow. Vanyi heard the captain of Estarion's Guard say to the captain of the Olenyai, "Chin up, man. Do you think any of these mudgrubbers understands that that's the emperor in his own self?"

"They," said the Olenyas, "no. But others will know. And they can kill."

"Not while we're here to stop them," said the captain of the Guard.

Vanyi could admire his confidence. The land was quiet about them. Too quiet. As if it waited, or readied an ambush. Rumors told of violence, riots in the towns, people killed, a lord stripped of his escort and flogged like a slave and cast out naked upon the road. But that was west of their march, too far to ride in a day or even two. Estarion was dissuaded from turning aside. Matters were worse in the south, people said. He was needed more urgently there.

He did what he could, she granted him that. For those who rode with him, it meant sudden swift riding and then long pauses as he worked his way through a city or a town. He would have gone alone if his guards had let him. He even, more than once, climbed up on a fountain's rim or a market-table and spoke to as many as would listen. "You hear prophets giving speeches," he would say, "and prophets' disciples. Now hear what they're ranting against."

People thought him mad. Vanyi knew better than to think that he would care.

Vanyi, traveling unregarded in his train, found that she

could not hate Haliya, or even despise her. Haliya was a child, an innocent, an infant in the ways of the world. And yet she knew more of men and their follies than Vanyi had learned in half again her years. It was training, she said. That was what women did. They studied their men.

She was in awe of Vanyi. She said so the first day, when Vanyi informed her that she now had an attendant. "Of course I should have one," she said, "but I can't have you."

"Why not?" Vanyi asked. "Because I'm a foreigner? A commoner? A rival?"

"You are a mage," said Haliya, with a tremor in the word. "You are the gods' voice. How can they waste you on me?"

"They think I need a lesson," said Vanyi.

Haliya would not believe her. "I should be waiting on you. Is that what you're telling me? You don't have to be delicate. It's more than proper. Since you are mage and priestess and—"

"Maybe," Vanyi said, "we can wait on each other."

Haliya stopped short. She looked shocked, then she laughed. "That's outrageous."

"So is his majesty."

"There is that," said Haliya, as if it settled things.

She was not one to show awe in stumbling and in awkwardness. She did it gracefully. She let herself be looked after, but she did her share in turn. She kept quiet when she thought that Vanyi wanted it. Vanyi did want it, to pray or simply to think, but Haliya seemed to think that she was working magic. She never asked to see any. That would be improper, her manner said.

They had to share a bed most nights, when they were crowded into a lord's small house. If the house was large enough they shared a room: more of that endless Asanian propriety. Vanyi half expected to be offered more than a warm presence when the nights were cold. That was a way of the harems, or so she had heard. But either the tales were false or Haliya did not presume so far. She was a tidy sleeper, and quiet. At first she woke when Vanyi rose to sing the sunrise-rite, but after a day or two she merely stirred and muttered and went back to sleep, or feigned it.

She was always up and dressed when Vanyi came back from her hour among the priests. If she broke her fast she did it then, while Vanyi was away. Vanyi did not ask. She nursemaided the child the rest of the day, and the night too. Surely Haliya could be trusted to fend for herself in the morning. She was in exuberant health by all accounts, ate voraciously at the nooning and at evening, and slept as healthy children sleep, deeply and long.

What first made Vanyi suspicious, she did not know. A hint of greenness about Haliya's cheeks, one rain-sodden morning. A servant coming late to clear away the remains of her breakfast, of which she had touched nothing, not even the sweetberry pastries of which she was so fond. When Vanyi came in unexpectedly early—and maybe she did it by design, and maybe she did not—she was not at all surprised to find Haliya retching into a basin.

Haliya looked as guilty as a woman could look, and as defiant. She said, "I had too much wine last night. I should have known better."

Vanyi would dearly have loved to believe her. But there was no hiding the cause of her illness. Not from a mage.

Iburan must have known or guessed. Vanyi spared a moment to damn him, silently, to the deepest of the twenty-seven hells. Of all the guards he could have chosen for this duty, for all the reasons he could have chosen her, she was the least fit, and this the most unforgivable.

"You're pregnant," she said. "How long?"

Haliya raised her head. She looked dreadful; she was actually green. Vanyi had no pity to spare for her. She swallowed painfully, and grimaced. "I think six cycles," she said. "Maybe seven."

"You knew when you left Kundri'j."

Vanyi's voice was absolutely flat. Haliya shied at it, but nothing could stop her tongue from running on. "I wasn't sure.

I've missed courses before. They came on early, you see, but they never have been regular about it."

"You knew," said Vanyi. She was being unreasonable, she knew it. She did not care. "Does he?"

Haliya went even greener. "Oh, no! Don't tell him. Please. He'll send me back."

"And so he should." Vanyi throttled an urge to seize her and shake her. It was not mercy. She knew that if she did it, it would empty the rest of the little idiot's stomach. "I lost a baby on the ride to Kundri'j. Do you think he'll take even a moment's chance of losing this one?"

"They say that wasn't the riding. It was the magic on you. The priestess-thing. The bond."

True; and bitter beyond bearing. "What did you think you could do? Lie? Hide it till the baby was born?"

Haliya was recovering in spite of everything. She straightened; the color crept back into her cheeks. "I wasn't going to lie. I was going to tell him when we got back to Kundri'j, or when we came to Ansavaar."

"And I wouldn't have guessed?"

"You won't tell him, will you? It would be a dreadful nuisance to send me back now. You'd have to go, to keep me safe, and we'd have to be so careful. If anyone found out that I was his lady, and that I was bearing his son—"

"What makes you think it's a son?"

"It has to be," said Haliya. "You see why I have to stay, and why we can't tell him. He'd want me to go back, you see. And I'd be dead or taken before I got there."

And good riddance, Vanyi thought. But there was more of her awake now than shock and petty malice. It was not Haliya's fault that she had done what Vanyi failed to do. She had conceived, probably, the first night Estarion lay with her. The night Vanyi drove him away.

Vanyi had brought this on herself. She was learning, a little. She could see what her folly had won her.

Haliya could not even be smug, so that Vanyi could hate

her. "I know I should have stayed in the palace. But I couldn't bear to stay, and to know that he was gone, and maybe that he'd die. He could. They hate him out here. He travels like the sun, in a mantle of light, but that only makes it darker where his light doesn't fall."

Vanyi was not in a mood to listen to poetry, however prettily conceived. "You had better pray," she said, "that he doesn't take it into his head to keep you warm of nights. Men are only blind when we most want them to see. He'll know in an instant."

"That won't happen," said Haliya.

"You hope it won't. Hoping isn't happening."

"It won't," Haliya said. She peered into Vanyi's face. She was a little shortsighted, Vanyi suspected. It gave her an all too charming air of preoccupation. "You really don't know," she said. She sounded incredulous and yet resigned, as if to the foibles of foreigners.

"What should I know?" Vanyi demanded.

But Haliya was choosing to be maddeningly Asanian. "He was well taken care of, that night before we left. Too well, I thought. That's art to the high art, but there shouldn't be blood in it. He had hardly anything left for us."

"Who is she?" Vanyi asked. She was proud that she was calm, that she was thinking clearly, not screaming at the walls. "Someone else in the harem?"

"It's not a she."

Vanyi blinked. "Of course it's a she. He doesn't incline toward men. Even that lordling from Umbros, back in Keruvarion—beautiful as a girl, everyone was sighing over him, and he had nothing in his pretty head but wailing love-songs under Estarion's window—he got a smile and a word and a summons home, and that was that. Why would it be a man? How could he be . . ." She stopped. "Blood, you said? He drew *blood?*"

"Not much," said Haliya with that damnable Asanian aplomb. "More like a brawl in a pride of lions. It sounded like that, people said. Lots of scratches. Bruises in interesting places.

They thought it was murder, but it was only the two of them."

Vanyi had thought herself beyond shock. This she had never expected, never foreseen, never prepared for. "How could I not know?"

She was not aware that she spoke aloud until she had done it. Haliya was kind. "It was a surprise, wasn't it? I'd have sworn he wouldn't, either. But you can tell, the way they stand together."

"Who?"

"The blackrobe," said Haliya. "The Olenyas. Or didn't you notice him? I think he's young under the veils. And beautiful. Those eyes go with beauty more often than not. I expect he's fascinating, too."

Vanyi's knees gave away; she sat down. She had seen. She had refused to see. The shadow in the emperor's shadow. The bond that no mage could mistake, unless she willed it. They were lovers. Not two who kept one another warm of nights; not friends who happened to be lord and concubine. Lovers.

"There," Haliya said. "Don't faint. He won't take harm. Olenyai are sworn to defend their lord to the death. It was that one who saved his life, the night the assassin came, though it was too late for the squire from Keruvarion; so there's life-debt in it too. That's strong bonding, and strong protection."

"Pray," said Vanyi. "Pray to any gods you worship, that you speak the truth."

Haliya did not understand. She thought it jealousy, which was nothing an Asanian woman would admit to. And yes, Vanyi conceded, it was that; but only the shell of it. The core was cold fear.

She watched, now that she knew. She saw how it was. It was not the bright shining thing she had shared with Estarion and slain by her own fault, because she was both wise and a fool. This was a meeting like matched blades. They had been open with it, she and her emperor. The Olenyas had nothing open in him. He was all shadows and secrecy. But he was there, unfailing, fixed on Estarion as a cat fixes on its prey.

When she lost the child she had not known she was bearing, she had thought she knew what it was to be emptied. But Estarion still loved her; she was sure of it, and secure in it, even in casting it away. When he went to his harem, she had been jealous, bitterly so, but even then she knew that he would have preferred to go to her. Haliya bore his child, did the one thing that Vanyi wanted most to do, and now never would; but Haliya was not Vanyi, not his first woman and his first love.

The Olenyas was a new thing, a terrible thing. Vanyi was not afraid of any woman in Estarion's harem. She feared the Olenyas. She told herself that she was starting at shadows, dreading a harmless man because she could not see his face or touch his mind. What danger could he be? He was oathbound to protect Estarion. He could not bear a child or share the throne, or claim any part of the woman's portion. And while he preoccupied Estarion, no new woman could come to claim the emperor's heart. Vanyi should be glad of him.

Estarion did not look like a man enslaved by a devil. He was bone-thin, who had never had flesh to spare, but he was thriving. This riding suited him, this edge of uncertainty, even the wet and the deepening cold, till of a morning they woke to a world of glass, rain that had frozen into ice, and no riding anywhere until the sun had warmed the road. He passed the time in walking about the place in which they had passed the night, a town called Kitaz, ignoring his wall of guards, wandering into a wineshop and a leatherworker's and a jeweler's.

Vanyi wondered if he could sense the powerful discomfort of those he spoke to, unless they could convince themselves that he was not the emperor. Asanians did not want their royalty among them. It belonged in palaces, out of sight and, except for wars and taxes, the common mind. Royalty in their own muddy streets, haggling over a trinket, drinking their thin sour wine and thinner, sourer beer, was so far out of the way of the world as to be incomprehensible.

He had his shadow, always. They did not touch one another or exchange glances. They had no need.

She caught herself peering for marks of the lion-brawling Haliya had spoken of. Of course there would be none to see when he was in leather and mail, but he did not walk as if he were in pain. Servants, who knew everything, said nothing of uproars in the royal rooms. That his majesty did not sleep alone, they accepted as natural and proper. Like Haliya they approved of his choice of bedmate, although they wondered if the Olenyas kept his veils even then. None was quite bold enough to settle the wager. The tales were terrible of what befell a man who looked on a blackrobe's face.

She felt like a spy, or like a jealous wife. There was no one she could talk to. No man, certainly, even Iburan. This was not a man's trouble. Haliya did not understand. The empress . . .

Maybe. But not until Vanyi had more to tell of than vague fears and shameful jealousies.

On the morning of the ice, she walked in Kitaz herself. She had no intention of dogging Estarion's steps, but she found herself in his wake as often as not. It was a small town for Asanion, one broad street with a fountain in the middle, a tangle of lanes and alleys, a pair of temples and a market and the lord's house on the hill. His lordship was absent. Doing his duty in the Middle Court, his steward said. Hiding, Vanyi suspected, and hoping that the disturbance would go away.

When the royal progress came to the market, she worked her way ahead of it. The jeweler's shop attracted her with its glitter; she braved the jeweler's scowl to admire his work, which was very fine for the provinces. He could hardly order her out, priestess that she was, and she conceded a little to his modesty by wrapping her scarf about her face.

As she lingered and yearned over his treasures, contemplating her thin purse and her thinner excuse for needing anything so frivolous, the shop filled with light.

It was Estarion, that was all, bringing the sun in with him, and trapping her as neatly as if she had planned it. Which she most emphatically had not. He was not aware of her, not at first. He had turned to grin at someone outside, as at a victory. "See," he said. "No assassins."

His guards must have tried to enter in front of him. He always loved to thwart them. It was a game of his, that he had forgotten in Kundri'j but now remembered.

She did something to make him turn. Breathed. Twitched. Let fall the trinket in her hand. He came round like a cat, uncannily quick. The light that came to his face made her gasp. Not now, she thought in desperation. Not still.

Then his face went cold. And that, which she had wished for, was worse. Much worse. "Lady," he said.

"Majesty." She eyed the path to the door. He stood full in it. She never thought him uncommonly tall, not beside Iburan and his northern guardsmen, but he towered in this place, his head brushing the roofbeam. The door was barely wider than his shoulders. They had broadened since he rode out of Endros.

He was not as much the boy now as he had been. His face was leaner, its lines more distinct. He would never be pretty, nor would anyone call him handsome, but his beauty was coming clearer, the fierce beauty of the hawk or the panther.

She looked at him in something close to despair. She would never stop loving him. There was no use in trying.

At least she had not thrown herself into his arms. She wanted to, desperately. But it was the body's wanting. The mind knew that that was over.

Was it?

She spoke to silence the voice in her head, said the first thing that came to her. "Are you going to buy something for Haliya?"

"For her sister," he said. There was a slight but perceptible pause before he said it.

"I think," said Vanyi, "that this might do." She lifted what she had dropped. It was not the most elaborate trinket in the lot, but it was the most interesting. It was a pendant for the neck or the brow, plain bright silver like wings of flame, set with a jewel like silk turned to stone: bands of gold and amber and bronze that shimmered as the jewel turned.

Estarion moved closer. She almost fled, but there was nowhere to go. He did not touch her as he took the jewel from her fingers. "It's exactly the color of her hair," he said.

"I thought it might be."

He slanted his eyes at her. They were as bright as the jewel, but less changeable. "They tell me you're keeping Haliya company."

"Iburan ordered it," Vanyi said. If she sounded ungracious, then so be it.

He went a shade colder at the name, or maybe at Vanyi's words. "I'm glad she's well protected."

"You're not afraid I'll murder her in her sleep?"

"You wouldn't do that," he said, and he sounded like himself again. "I'll free you from her if you like. My lord high priest should have known better than to burden you so."

"It was to be a penance," said Vanyi. "It is still, most ways. But I don't want to be free of it."

"Even if I say you may?"

"You're not my high priest," she said.

He did not like that: his lips tightened as they always did when he reined in his temper. "But she is my . . . concubine." He choked on it. She was rather nastily glad. She would atone for that, but first she would enjoy it.

"Do you think I'll corrupt her?" Vanyi inquired.

"I think it must be agony for you to look at her."

"She's quite pleasant to look at. And you," Vanyi said, "have a high opinion of yourself."

She almost wished that he would hit her. He wanted to: she could see it. But he laughed. "I do, I confess it. I don't expect you to pardon me: I'm hopelessly unpardonable. But can you think of me, a little, with priestly charity?"

"How do you think of me?"

"You know," he said.

"No," said Vanyi. "I don't know anything. I thought I knew you once, when we were young together. But that was long ago. Maybe I never knew you at all."

"We're not fighting," he said as if to himself. "It's a beginning, I suppose."

"Or an ending."

"No," said Estarion, as if his royal will could make it true.

Vanyi looked up at him. He was so close that she had to tilt her head. She could have touched him, laid her hand over the beating heart, traced the line of his cheek. She could say the word and he would come to her hand. She had the power. It was as strong as magic, as certain as the laws that bound the worlds.

A shadow shifted behind him. Eyes fixed on her, lion-gold in faceless mask. They were not angry, nor did they hate. They laughed at her. They knew her as Estarion never would, nor ever could. All her sins and petty failings, her pride, her vanity, her penchant for stepping beyond her proper bounds.

Estarion shifted. He was not with her any longer, although he stood as close as ever. He was in the shadow's shadow.

The power was gone. The Olenyas held it, swallowed it.

Vanyi let him. Cowardice, wisdom, she did not care what anyone called it. A child who had never been born, a child who must be born, both bound her and held her helpless.

The Olenyas did not know that. She would have wagered gold on it. Nor was she about to tell him. He had his emperor. She had more. She had the emperor's heir, and the mother of the heir, safe in her charge. She had the empire that would be.

WHEN THE ICE had melted from the road and the sun shone down almost warm, Estarion led his escort southward again. He was numb still, mind and power, but the land-sense had little to do with the arts of mages. He felt the earth as if it were his body. Great aches and bruises, knots and tangles of dissension, a pain like sickness that spread outward from no common center. What he rode to was not the worst of it, but it made a beginning.

He was waking as if from sleep or from a long illness. The sun and the sudden warmth, in what should have been black winter, speeded a healing that had begun when he left the Golden Palace. He caught himself singing as he rode up a long slope. The scouts who ranged ahead were out of sight. His escort spread behind.

He glanced over his shoulder. Those whose faces he could see, flashed smiles. He smiled back. His Varyani were as glad as he to be out of Kundri'j.

"I'll have to do something about that," he said to Korusan, who rode at Umizan's flank. The Olenyas was mounted on Chirai. Umizan would not permit his lord another mount, and it had seemed a waste of good senelflesh to leave the dun behind. So Korusan had charge of him, and not unwillingly either, as far as Estarion could see.

Estarion hooked a knee over the pommel of his saddle, riding at his ease. "I can't live in horror of my own palace. What's to be done, do you think? Pull down the Golden Palace? Build a new capital?"

"First you need a solid empire for it to be capital of," said Korusan.

"Granted," said Estarion, "and a solid self to rule it. Sometimes I despair of that."

"A rather cheerful despair," Korusan observed.

Estarion unhooked his knee and swung down his leg and touched Umizan into a gallop, all in one swift reckless movement. Umizan reached the crest of the hill in three long strides, and plunged into a deep bowl of a valley.

No scouts, no token of alarm. Safe, then. Estarion let the stallion run as he would. The road was steep but smooth. A town huddled at the valley's end where it opened into sky, but the land between was cropland, fallow with winter. No one passed there. People kept to their walls and traveled as little as they might, between winter and the rumor of war.

He was well ahead of his escort. A glance back showed them on the crest, spreading out as if to scan the valley. Then they poured down into it.

Umizan slowed to a hand gallop, tossing his horns. Estarion laughed into the wind. It had a bite to it. Rain again by morning, his bones judged, or even snow.

What at first he had taken for a cairn or a shrine set up by the road, stirred as he approached it. Umizan shied and skittered sidewise. Estarion clutched mane, clamped knees to the stallion's sides. Umizan wheeled, snorting, horns lowered.

Estarion glared down the lance-length of them. Bright black eyes glared back. "That took you long enough," said a voice he had thought never to hear again.

"Sidani?" Estarion slid from the saddle, keeping a grip on Umizan's reins. The stallion stamped, still in a temper: and well he should be, fool that he had made of himself. "Sidani," Estarion said. He felt the grin break out. "Where in the hells have you been?"

"Ansavaar," she said. She nudged the stone at her feet. It shifted, yawned, opened eyes that gleamed green.

"Ulyai!" Her snarl and slash drove him back. He gasped, shocked. It was Ulyai—he could not mistake her. "Ulyai. Have you forgotten me?"

"Hardly," Sidani said. She pointed with her chin. Ulyai's back rippled. Three pairs of eyes appeared above it, two green-blue, one blue-gold. Three pairs of ears pricked. One by one the cubs tumbled over their mother's flank and rolled to the ground. Her foreleg caught and pinned two. The third, the one whose eyes would be gold when they were done changing, eluded its mother's grasp and leaped upon Estarion's foot, attacking it without mercy.

He swept the little beast up, wary of claws and infant fangs, and met snarl with snarl. The cub's jaws snapped shut. It stared wide-eyed.

It was darker than the others, almost black. "Yes, I look like you," Estarion said to it. Him. It was a he-cub. It let him ease it into the crook of his arm. In return he let it gnaw gently on his thumb. It began to purr.

"I expect you can explain this," Estarion said after a while.

"I expect I can." Sidani shouldered one of the two she-cubs and lifted the other onto its mother's back. She looked much the same as ever. Thinner, maybe, but then so was Estarion. He saw no sign of the sickness that had beset her in Induverran.

Estarion looked over his shoulder. His escort had come up at last. He called out to them. "Look! See who's been waiting for us."

His Varyani were far from displeased, but his Asanians did not know what to make of it. He laughed at them. "Here's a friend I've been missing. Guard her well, guardsmen. She's as kin to me."

Fine kin, Korusan thought, eyeing the wanderer woman as she chose one of the remounts—a cross-grained, slab-sided gelding that seemed to know her, for it lunged with teeth bared and then stopped, skidding, and all but fell over on its rump. She grasped it by the horns and shook it; it let its brow rest briefly against her breast. She swung abruptly into the saddle, taking no notice of the reins, and wheeled the beast about.

She had Estarion's reckless temper, that was certain, and

his fondness for monstrous cats. All through her juggler's tricks, the ul-cub kept its place about her shoulders. Estarion had another as dark and gold as he was, and the dam played mount to a third, pressing up against the black stallion's shoulder. The Varyani mounts snorted and sweated but endured; likewise the Lady Haliya's mare and Korusan's dun. The rest of the Olenyai were not so fortunate. Those who were not forcibly dismounted were run away with, or fought a pitched battle of man against maddened senel.

The woman surveyed the carnage with an ironic eye. It paused on Korusan, went briefly strange; then passed on. She sent her gelding forward with a touch of the heel, caught Estarion's glance, drew him after her. They divided in a long circle, seeming slow but in truth very swift, herding together the scattered seneldi.

Korusan followed slowly. Chirai was uneasy but willing, snorting and brandishing horns as he passed the ul-queen. She sat to watch the spectacle, and ignored him with queenly disdain. Korusan endeavored to return the courtesy. He had heard of the palace cats of Keruvarion; who had not? But their living presence was unnerving.

All his brothers' mounts were caught, and all of his brothers who had been borne away. It was bitter to be so humiliated before their rivals from Keruvarion. They bore it well, sitting straight and stiff on their shuddering seneldi. The emperor faced them. He seemed to be searching for words to salve their pride.

The wanderer rode her borrowed gelding down the line of them, with the cub draped purring over her shoulders. "There now," she said, her own voice like a purr, both rough and sweet. "It's only ul-cats. They won't eat you. Not while you serve your emperor."

Cleverly put. It gave the Olenyai time and grace to set themselves in order, but it warned them also, and showed them on which side they might find this stranger. They took the road again with the wanderer riding beside Estarion, talking a great deal of nothing, to the emperor's evident pleasure. The two of them had met, it seemed, over an escapade of his, and parted over one of hers. Where she had been since, or how she had come upon Estarion's own ul-cat and delivered the beast of cubs, she was not telling. She was very skilled at that. Almost, Korusan thought, as if she were Asanian.

The town at the valley's mouth would not let them in. It was no indication of disrespect, its lordling said. There had been sickness; it might be plague. He invited the emperor's escort to pitch camp in his fields and offered a penful of skinny woolbeasts for their dinner, but more than that he would not do.

He was lying. Estarion could not be such a fool that he failed to know it, but he refused to storm the walls. "They're not in open rebellion," he said, "and I'd rather camp under the sky than sleep under another roof."

It could have been worse thought of, Korusan admitted. Their camping place was broad, level, and easily defended. They had tents, there was wood and dung for their fires, and the woolbeasts were not too stringy once the cooks had done with them.

Estarion did not fulfill Korusan's greatest apprehension, that he would take his ul-cats to bed with him. The cub was too young to leave its mother for long, and she was content to idle by the fire with the wanderer for a companion. The emperor's tent was blessedly empty of animals.

The emperor's desire tonight was hot but brief; he fell almost at once into sleep. Korusan propped himself on an elbow, warm in the other's warmth, and considered the sleeping face. It had become a part of him. He knew no other way to think of it.

He laid his palm against Estarion's cheek. Estarion did not stir. He curved his fingers into claws, raked them softly through the curling silk of the beard, down the smooth line of neck and shoulder, round to the breast. Over the heart they closed into a fist.

"If the world were empty of you," Korusan said, "I should not wish to be in it." His mouth twisted. "I meant to snare you. I snared myself."

Oh, most certainly he had. He did not know when it had struck him. Perhaps that first morning, when he woke alone, and knew himself empty without Estarion's presence. Perhaps even before that—perhaps from the moment he saw this outland emperor, this upstart, this rival, this enemy he was sworn to destroy.

Estarion did not love him as he loved Estarion. Estarion's heart burned like the sun. Worlds basked in it, and it had warmth to spare for them all. Korusan's was a fiercer, frailer, narrower thing, a spark in the night. It had room for one love, and one great hate. Both of them the same. Both fixed here, in this heart under his hand, in this beloved enemy who slept oblivious, like a child or a blessed saint.

Korusan rose slowly. Estarion did not move. His branded hand lay half across him, glinting gold in the light of the lamp. Korusan turned his face away from it.

Robed, veiled, hidden in shadow, Korusan slipped from the tent. The fire had died down. The camp slept but for the sentries and, rising from beside the embers, the woman Sidani. Brightmoon was high amid swift-running clouds; Greatmoon hung low in the east, the color of blood. The twofold light struck frost and fire in her hair, now white as the bright moon, now red as copper. Her eyes gleamed on him. Her voice came soft, blurred as if with sleep. "Hirel?"

Korusan stopped. He had misheard. She had not given him that name.

She drew closer. They were nearly of a height. "Hirel? Hirel Uverias?"

"He is dead."

The words came flat and hard. She laughed. Moon-touched, he thought. "You promised me. If there was a way, you would come back. I never knew you'd come in the same body."

And how in the hells had she known whose face he bore? He felt stripped naked, he in his robes and his swords and his veils.

"Madam," he said with control that he had learned through hard lessoning, "you are mistaken. I am Olenyas; no more, if no less. The last of the Golden Emperors is dead."

"No Olenyas ever born could claim those eyes." She was close enough now that he felt the heat of her body, breathed the startling sweetness of her breath. She must have been beautiful in youth, a beauty to break the heart. It was in her still, here under the moons. She raised a hand. He shied, but she was too quick. The air was cold on his bared cheeks.

His hands leaped to his swords, but he did not draw them. Her eyes held him fast. Great eyes, dark eyes, eyes to drown in.

"I always forget," she said, "how beautiful you are."

"You must die," he said, gasping it. "You see my face."

She laughed. "I am dead, child. Years dead. Here," she said. "Look." She held up her hand.

Gold, gold turned to ash and grey scars; but there was no mistaking the shape of it. He had kissed its image just this evening, held its burning brightness to his cheek till he could bear it no longer: and Estarion smiling, not knowing that Korusan's trembling was pain—willing, joyful, fire-bright pain. They branded their emperors in Keruvarion, branded and ensorceled them; or the god did it, if one believed in gods.

"I tried to cut it out," said the madwoman, soft and deceptively calm. "I took the sharpest knife I had. I heated it in fire and began to cut. It was no worse than the burning I was born with. But the god was having none of it. The gold goes all the way to the bone, did you know? and wraps about it. And when I thought to cut off the hand, it was the knife that went instead, flared up and went molten and poured away. Thus the scars. The cuts healed clean, but molten steel is a match for any god. It took away the fire, and that I was glad of; but now it burns like ice."

"Gods," said Korusan. "You—are—"

"Sarevadin." She smiled. Yes: he saw it now. Estarion favored her, and in more than face. "You always were slow to know me."

"I am not Hirel!" Korusan snapped. "I am Koru-Asan of the Olenyai, and you are stark mad."

"Of course I am. All the dead are."

He gripped her shoulders. They were bone-thin, fire-warm, and very much alive. "You are no more dead than I."

"Exactly." She closed long fingers about his wrists, not to resist, simply as if it were her whim to know the swift pulse of blood beneath the skin. "Whose get are you? Jania's?"

His teeth clicked together.

"I never did approve of that expedient," she said. "Fifty brothers were a great inconvenience, but it was hardly kind to keep them locked in prison their lives long, and no sons to carry on after they were dead. Did any outlive me, do you know?"

"The last took his life before the fourth Sunlord died," said Korusan. He was falling into her madness, hearing her as if it were nothing to him but a tale.

"Ah," she said. "He lived long, for an Asanian. But Jania—I won the field there. We married her to a man in the far west of the empire. He was a good man, I made sure of that; he cherished her."

"She hated you," said Korusan.

"She did not," said Sarevadin. But then, slowly: "Maybe she did. She had hopes of me before I changed, and after, when I was as you see me, I let her brother send her away. She had the spirit that covets empires. Pity she wasn't born a man, and that she had so many brothers."

"Had she been a man, Asanion would never have fallen."

"Oh," said the old one, the empress who had been, who should have been dead, "it would have fallen, cubling, in blood and fire."

"So may it yet."

"In the end, yes. All things end. But not in this generation. He's a charming child, isn't he? He looks like my father."

"He looks like you."

"So he does, though I was prettier, even when I walked in man's shape. The god meant me for a woman, I think, but changed his mind. For a while." She brushed Korusan's cheek with her unbranded hand. The touch was like bone sheathed in raw silk. "Do you love him, youngling?"

Korusan wrenched away. The terror of it was not that she was dead and yet she lived. It was not even that she was the enemy, the one whom he had been born to hate—more even than Estarion. It was that he felt the power of her, the same power that was in her grandson's grandson. To dwell in his blood. To make herself a part of him.

Korusan was not her consort, not that great lord and traitor. Hirel Uverias was dead. Korusan might wear his face, and bitter penance that was, but he was no one but himself.

"You can't deny the blood," said Sarevadin.

He whirled away from her, back into the tent and the dimness and the blessed quiet. He shuddered with cold that pierced to the bone. So it was, fools and children said, when one spoke with the dead.

He lay again beside Estarion, pressed body to fire-warm body. Estarion half-woke, smiled, gathered him in. He struggled not to cling. Estarion was asleep again already, his arms a wall against the dark.

IT SNOWED BY morning, but lightly, drifting from a leaden sky. Estarion had them all up and riding by full light. A great restlessness was on him. It made Vanyi's skin twitch.

The heat of him made nothing of cold or snow. He was everywhere, it seemed, with and without his yellow-eyed shadow: now in the lead with Sidani, now riding back to speak with one or another of his escort, now bringing up the rear.

Haliya had been avoiding him with remarkable subtlety, managing always to be where he was not. Not that it was difficult. She needed but to stay close by Iburan, and make herself small when Estarion rode past.

But on this raw grey morning, Iburan's mare came up lame. He fell back to the rear and the remounts, calling to the others to go on, he would follow. Vanyi would have stayed to guard him—and in great relief to be freed from her other and more onerous duty. But he sent her away. He had Shaiyel and Oromin and a pair of the empress' warrior women, and he would tend his mare before he sought out another that would carry his bulk. He did not need Vanyi. Haliya, the leveling of his brows reminded her, did.

Haliya took what refuge she could among the empress' women. She was the only Asanian among them, and the smallest but for Vanyi. As Estarion roved rearward for the dozenth time, he checked Umizan's stride and swung in beside her.

Vanyi roused with a start to find her mare sidling toward Umizan with clear and present intent: ears flat, neck arched in the way mares had when they came into heat. Umizan would have been more than senel if he had been oblivious.

Estarion did not even see the mare or the woman who rode

her. His eyes were on Haliya. Haliya looked as serene as an Asanian woman could in her veils and her modesty, but Vanyi caught the trapped-beast dart of her glance.

Vanyi let slip a finger's width of rein. It was enough for the mare. She slashed at Umizan's shoulder. He veered, snorting and tossing his horns. Estarion cursed; and met Vanyi's eyes.

She would have wagered gold that, had he been as fair as she, he would have blushed scarlet. "Good morning, sire," she said.

Haliya's gratitude was an intense annoyance. He was blind to it. They were on either side of him now, hemming him in.

Vanyi was not going to make it easy for him, or for his lady either. She called her mare to order. It took time, and sufficient attention to keep her eyes from fixing on his face as they were sorely tempted to do.

She was aware even so that he looked from one of them to the other, and did battle with training against transparent cowardice. "My ladies," he said at length, stiffly. "Are you well?"

"Very well," said Haliya with perfect steadiness. "And you?"

It went on so, an exquisite dance of Asanian courtesies. Vanyi would not have believed Estarion capable of it.

Unless, she thought, he suspected something. He would not get it out of Vanyi, and Haliya was bred to keep secrets. In the end, and none too soon, he went back to the lead and the woman whose mysteries were nothing to do with him.

Haliya breathed a long sigh and let herself slump briefly against her senel's neck. "Oh, gods," she said, "I was so afraid he'd want me tonight."

"Not likely," said Vanyi. "Not with me here, watching him think about it."

Haliya did not understand, but she knew enough of Vanyi now to believe what she said of Estarion. Haliya's hand crept to her middle. It often did that of late. Vanyi was not finding it easier, the longer it went on. This should have been her child, her secret, her fear of being sent back to chains and safety.

Grimly she reined herself in. She had brought this pain on herself. She would bear it as she must, with a priestess' fortitude.

Simple to say. Unbearably difficult to do.

Korusan was wretchedly ill. It was the cold and the snow, and the fever that would not go down for any will he laid on it. He had managed to conceal his weakness from Estarion: rising before the emperor, pulling on his garments and his weapons, mastering himself enough to mount and ride. Estarion might have questioned him, but he took refuge in silence. When Estarion rode back to speak with his ladies, Korusan did not follow. Chirai's gaits were soft, his responses light. Folly to expect that a beast would understand a man's troubles, but the stallion seemed to be moving more carefully, smoothing his paces to spare Korusan's pain.

For there was pain. It was deep, in the bones, and it gripped with blood-red claws. He did not allow himself to be afraid. When the pain set deep, the mages had told him, there would be nothing that they could do. They had kept him alive his life long, nursed him through all his sicknesses, warded him with their magics and mounted guard on his bones. Now their protections were failing. He could feel them unraveling, fraying like silk in a cord.

He should have been dead in infancy like his brothers, or feeble of mind and body as his sisters had been. He was the last of his blood, the last child of the Lion. And he was dying.

But not now. Not, fate willing, too soon to do what he must do.

He was aware always of the madwoman's eyes on him. Sarevadin. He would have dismissed it as a folly of night and madness and newborn fever, but in the cold snowlight he knew that it was true. She even moved like Estarion, sat her mount as he did, with light long-limbed grace, held her head at that unmistakable, arrogant angle. How anyone could fail to see, he did not know. It was as clear as lightning in the dark.

She was dead, and he was close enough. It was said that the dead knew one another, even when they walked among the living. She tilted a smile at him, sweet and wild.

It widened for Estarion as he rode back from the excruciation of two ladies in one orbit. He returned it with ease that knew only innocence. Blind, blessed fool, not to know his own dead kin.

Estarion could not keep still. People noticed it, he saw how their eyes rolled on him, and how they looked at one another and sighed. He tried to keep down the pace, for the seneldi's sake if not for the riders', but Umizan was willing, and he was possessed of a bone-deep urgency.

The land pulled him southward, and stronger the farther he rode. The canker that was in Ansavaar was distinct and persistent, but there was another, closer, and it rankled deeper as the day went on.

When they halted to rest in a wood protected from wind and blowing snow, Estarion called in the chief of the scouts. The man was Olenyas, shadow-silent and shadow-quick. It vexed his Asanian propriety sorely to see his emperor go down on one knee in unmarked snow, but Estarion was in no mood to care for outland decencies. He smoothed the snow with his hand and took up a stick, and drew the shape of the land as his land-sense knew it. He marked the ache that was in Ansavaar, and the closer, stronger one that was on the road he followed, and looked up into the amber eyes. "What is this?" he asked, thrusting his stick into the latter marking.

The Olenyas would never show surprise, but he paused before he spoke. "You do not know, sire?"

Estarion bared his teeth. "If I did, would I ask?"

"That is a map, majesty," the Olenyas said. "Or so it seems."

"Indeed," said Estarion. "And this?"

"A city, sire. A day's ride from here, perhaps more in the snow. Pri'nai."

Estarion regarded the stick propped upright in the snow. "Yes," he said slowly. "Yes, that is what they call it. Pri'nai." He rose. "Can we get there by evening?"

The Olenyas seemed to have decided that all foreigners were mad, and Sunlords maddest of all. "We would be hard pressed to do it. And we would leave some behind. Your priest—his mount—"

Iburan could fend for himself. But Estarion was not entirely lost to sense. "No, we'd best not try to get there in the dark. And it will be dark early tonight. We'll camp as late as we can, and ride before sunup. We'll be in the city by midmorning."

"Unless the snow worsens," the Olenyas said. "Sire."

"It won't." Estarion swept his foot across the map, obliterating it. "It will clear by morning. We'll have the sun with us when we reach the gates. Then," he said, "we shall see what waits for us in Pri'nai."

41

THE SNOW ENDED in the middle night, the clouds scattered before a sudden wind. By dawn when Estarion was up and pacing, waiting for the rest to rouse, it was bitter cold, the stars like frost in the paling sky.

The sunrise was brilliant but empty of warmth. It found them on the road, hoofbeats muffled by the carpet of snow. Estarion was barely aware of them. He knew that Korusan was near him, that Sidani was beside him. He sensed the coming of another like a shiver on the skin: Iburan on a tall Ianyn stallion, towering over Umizan. Estarion would not glance at him. Even when he said, "There's trouble ahead."

"The whole west is trouble," said Sidani.

"Granted," Iburan said equably, "but there's worse here."

"We're riding under arms," Estarion said, "and in battle order."

"So I noticed." Iburan paused. "What drives you, Starion?"

"You need to ask, my lord of mages?"

"I need to ask," Iburan said.

That was meant to shame Estarion into sense. It pricked his temper, but it cleared his head a little. "Do you feel the land, Iburan?"

"I feel the trouble in it. Blood has flowed on it. Hate rankles in it."

"Yes," Estarion said.

"And you think that you can stop it?"

"If not I, then who?"

Iburan was silent.

"You don't think I'm arrogant?" Estarion asked.

"I think that you may be both more than anyone thought you, and less."

Estarion stiffened.

"Oh, he is that," said Sidani. "Who trained him? You? You didn't do badly, as far as you went. But you didn't make a Sunlord of him."

They rounded on her, both alike and both astonished. The irony of that did not escape Estarion.

She grinned at them. "Oh, he's emperor enough, priest—and more since he came to Asanion. He's still not all that he could be."

"He's young," Iburan said with a touch of sharpness. "He'll grow into it."

"Will you still be saying that when he's a greybeard? Because he'll be then as he is now."

"And how is that?"

Estarion wondered if she enjoyed the spectacle as much as he did. Iburan in a temper was a rare thing; Iburan struggling to keep from roaring was a wonderful one. She sat her evil-tempered gelding with grand insouciance and laughed. "Oh, such outrage! Look at him, priest. Isn't he a pretty thing? Fine wits, fine mind, and a light foot in the dance. He knows how to make people love him; and that without magery, because he assures himself that he has none. Why is that, Iburan of Endros? What makes this prince of mages so eager to deny the whole of himself?"

Estarion's laughter died soon after she began. She could not be saying what she said. She knew nothing of power, or of Sunlords, or of anything but wild stories. It was too much like hope; too much like all his prayers, before he had forgotten how to pray. "Woman, you are a fool. I have no power worth the name, nor ever shall again."

She waved him to silence. He had obeyed before he thought, for pure startlement.

Iburan answered her slowly, as if Estarion had never spoken: that too a goad to his temper. "He slew with power. He was slow to recover."

"So simple," she said. "So easy an escape. If you failed, or if you left his training half done—why then, it was never your fault, but his."

"We taught him all that we knew," Iburan said. Growling it. "And who are you, old woman, to cast reproach on me?"

"I am no one," said Sidani. "No one reproaches you. But one might wonder if you knew what you were doing. He was—he is—no common mageborn child. And yet you raised him as one."

"How else was I to raise him?"

"As his father's son."

"So," grated Iburan, "we did."

"Has he entered the Tower in Endros?"

Iburan looked ready to spit at her. "No one enters that Tower."

"Sun-blood do."

"I am not Sun-blood."

"So," Sidani said. She sighed. "One never allows for these things. If Ganiman had not died—if he had had time to tell the child what he must know—"

"And how do you know?" Estarion broke in.

She laughed. "Dear child, sweet child, I was old when your grandfather was born. I know what all the dead know."

"Mad," said Iburan.

Estarion's temper set in pure contrariness. If she knew—if, O impossible, it could be true— *"Is* she mad, priest? Or does she know something that none of us has known?"

"The Tower is halfway to the other side of the world," she said. "And that's a pity. You're half a Sunlord now, and half a Sunlord you remain, until you pass that door."

"It has no door," Iburan rumbled, but they took no notice of him.

"And what will I gain," Estarion asked, "when I come there?"

"Maybe nothing," she said. "Maybe all the power you think you've lost."

Estarion drew a knife-edged breath. All his power. All his magic. All his strength—to kill again. To slaughter souls. "I don't know if I want it," he said.

"Then you are an idiot," she said. She kicked her gelding into a gallop.

He watched her go. She was safe enough, he thought distantly: the scouts were well ahead, and the road was straight and clear.

"Sometimes," mused Iburan, "I wonder . . ."

"What?" Estarion snapped. Shock made him vicious; shock, and hope turned to gall. The woman knew nothing. No one, no power, even the Sunborn's own, could make him a mage again.

The priest shook off Estarion's temper. "She's no danger to you, whatever nonsense she babbles."

Estarion turned his back on all thought of Iburan or Sidani, hope or magic or the Tower that his firstfather had made. This was Asanion. Such things were nothing here.

The sun was dazzling on the snow. He narrowed his eyes against it. The others rode with heads down, trusting their mounts' sure feet, or wrapped veils about their eyes. They looked stiff with cold.

He felt it, but dimly. Half a Sunlord, was he? Then the whole of a Sunlord must burn like a torch.

"Quick now!" he called to the rest of them. "The faster we ride, the sooner we're in the warm."

"Warmer than any of us needs, maybe," Iburan muttered.

Estarion laughed at him. Somewhat to Estarion's surprise, he laughed in return. For a moment they were easy, as if there were no walls between them.

But even before this quarrel, there was the matter of the secret that Iburan had kept, worse betrayal than any trespass in an emperor's bed.

"If you had told me," Estarion said, "I could have forgiven you."

"Could you?"

"All of you," said Estarion with sudden heat, "every one of you—priests, princes, madwomen, all—never a one of you sees me as anything but a child or a ruined mage. When will I be a man? When my beard is grey? When I'm dead?"

"When you learn to forgive the unforgivable," said Iburan.

"Then there are no men," said Estarion. "Only saints and children."

"Even saints can err," said Iburan, "and I'm no saint. What I did, I did for love of you."

"No, priest. You did it for love of my mother."

"That too," Iburan said willingly. "But you were first. When your father brought you to me, and you hardly higher than his knee and hardly old enough to leave your mother's breast—all eyes and questions, and power shining out of you like light from a lamp—I knew that I would love you. Him I served gladly, for he was my emperor, but you I served with my heart."

Estarion drew a breath that caught on pain. "When I saw you I was terrified. You were the largest man I had ever seen. Mother's father was taller, and some of my uncles; but you were like a mountain looming over me. Then you smiled. And I loved you. Father was my father, soul and body both. You were my teacher, and my heart's friend."

"So am I still," said Iburan. "So shall I always be."

"Why, then? Why didn't you tell me?"

"Cowardice," Iburan said. "You never ask why I did it at all."

"What's to ask? She was beautiful and young, and widowed untimely; and you were thrown together in my incapacity. You'd be more than man if you hadn't warmed to her."

"I did try to resist," Iburan said. "For your father's honor. For your sake."

"And she?"

Iburan glanced back. Maybe he met the empress' glance; maybe he had no need.

"She wore you down," Estarion answered for him. "She's wise, and cold when she has to be. Her goddess isn't the bright burning god we worship, you and I. *She* would keep the secret, for her own purposes. But you should have told me."

"I feel," said Iburan after a pause, "quite properly rebuked." His expression was rueful, but there was something new in his eyes. Something, Estarion thought, like respect.

"I misread you," Iburan said. "And I misjudged you."

He had not. But Estarion was not about to confess to it. He bent his head stiffly. He did not say anything. Iburan bowed and wheeled his mount, returning to his place. It was not, Estarion took note, at the empress' side, but farther back, rearmost of the circle of mages.

Estarion's mind shifted itself away from little troubles; and it was little, this fret of his over his mother's choice of lovers in her widowhood. He was aware of Pri'nai like an ache in his own body, a wound that festered deep and would not heal. Whether it was that he was coming closer to it, or that his land-sense was growing keener, he did not know.

He was well in the lead now, with no memory of parting from his escort. Sidani waited ahead of him with Ulyai at her gelding's heels and the young ones tumbling over one another in the snow. When he came level, the two she-cubs sprang into their panniers on the gelding's saddle. The he-cub leaped, aiming for Umizan's rump. Estarion swept him out of the air. He settled purring on Estarion's saddlebow.

Sidani did not speak as they rode on side by side. Only a lingering shred of prudence kept Estarion from kicking Umizan into a flat gallop.

Pri'nai stood at a meeting of roads, where the great southward way met the traders' route into Keruvarion. Yet there was no one on the road. No travelers, no traders, no farmfolk walking to market. The houses they passed were silent, but not empty: they were full of eyes.

"They know we're coming," Sidani said. Her voice was startling after so long a silence. There was no other human sound, only the cold clash of metal in mail-ring or harness, the thudding of hoofs, the snort of a senel. No one was singing or talking. Hands were tensed on weapons; vanguard and rear-guard had drawn in, wary.

One of the scouts came back from beyond the hill. "Gates are open," he said. "Guarded, and heavily, and they're stopping people who come in or out. But there's no fighting."

"It's inside the city, then," Estarion said.

"I think, sire," the scout said, "maybe. There's a feel to it I don't like. Nobody out, and nothing moving outside the walls. It's brooding on something."

"I'll go in," said Estarion.

"Sire—"

"I'm going in."

He went in. Not slowly, not quickly after all his haste to come so far. He led his escort down from the hill toward the city of the crossroads. It stood in a ring of gardens, orchards and vineyards bleak in the snow, and the white mounds of tombs amid the bare branches.

The northward gate was open. Guards filled it. Troopers' bronze and officers' steel gleamed above it. If all the gates were so guarded, then Pri'nai was ringed with an army, and all of them in the black and bronze of the lord of Ansavaar.

And if Ansavaar itself was in revolt, then Estarion was well and truly destroyed; for this was the army which he had come to command.

He might have sent men ahead to prepare his coming, as he had done in every city he had entered since Induverran. But in this he had chosen to come unheralded. He knew better than to think that he was unexpected.

The wind caught his standard and unfurled it. Golden sun

flamed on scarlet, the war-banner that had not flown in the twofold empire since Varuyan was emperor. One of the Olenyai bore it. Not Korusan. The boy would not leave Estarion's shadow, or speak, or lift hands from swordhilts. He was ill, Estarion thought, or beset with some trouble. Estarion would put him to the question. Later.

Estarion wore mail and the scarlet war-cloak taken hastily out of the baggage, but his helmet rested on his knee. He did not intend to need it. He kept Umizan to a sedate canter, advancing lightly toward the gate and the guards. No one rode in front of him. He was a plain target, and so he meant to be.

A spear's length in front of the line of guards, he brought Umizan to a halt. They knew him: none would lift eyes to his face. "The emperor," he said, making no effort to shout, but knowing that they could hear him all along the wall, "would enter Pri'nai. Will the lord of the city admit him?"

There was a silence. Estarion sat calm in it. He heard behind him the soft snick of swords loosened in scabbards, and a seneldi snort. The cause of that came to stand at Umizan's shoulder, tail twitching, inspecting the guards as if to choose the tenderest for her prey.

"Every city," said a voice at last above the gate, "is the emperor's, and every lord is his servant."

Estarion looked up at the captain of the guards. The man did not look down. "Is it a quandary," Estarion inquired, "to stand above your emperor?"

He won no answer. Ulyai moved forward, growling at the nearness of the city, but unflinching. Umizan followed her. The guards melted before them.

After the quiet without, the clamor of the city was deafening. The walls contained it and sent it ringing back, a dance of echoes that made Ulyai snarl and the seneldi squeal and skitter. People fled the restless hoofs. Those who could, dropped down in homage; the rest vanished into doorways or darted down passages. No one lingered to watch the emperor ride by.

The clamor had a source, and Estarion sought it. Pri'nai's center was a broad open space, a court of temples and of the lord's palace, with a fountain in it, silent now in winter. Here were the people of the city, a milling, shouting, restless crowd, all turned to face the wide stair that mounted to the palace. Guards rimmed it. Further throngs filled the top of it and vanished through the open gates.

Estarion halted on the edge of the square and beckoned. His trumpeter edged forward, wary of Ulyai, who pressed close against Umizan's side. He passed Estarion with a glance half of boldness, half of panic. But boldness was stronger. He raised his trumpet to his lips and blew.

The crowd parted. Slowly, with much jostling, it opened a path to the dais. Silence spread as people went down in homage.

Estarion rode the length of that road of living bodies. His back tensed against an arrow that did not fly, a stone that was not flung. The desire was there, and the hostility, but it did not burst the bonds of fear, the power of a thousand years of emperors.

Estarion dismounted at the foot of the stair. The guards parted as they had in Pri'nai's gate. The press of people thrust and jostled and cursed itself aside.

The hall of the palace was dim after the brilliance of sun on snow, lamplit and windowlit, seething with lordly presences as the square had been with commoners. At the end of it stood a dais, and on the dais a tall chair, and in the chair, the lord of Ansavaar. There were others about him, a man before him with a scroll of the laws, and at his feet a huddle of men in chains.

They all stood frozen at the emperor's coming. He considered lingering in the doorway, but that was cruel. He did not pause or slow until he stood upon the dais and the lord of Ansavaar bowed down at his feet. "Up," he said, "my lord Shurichan."

Shurichan of Ansavaar rose with practiced grace, shying

from the ul-cat's shadow. Ulyai ignored him, taking station at the dais' foot.

He was a young man, taller than some and broader, and a rarity in an Asanian lord: a man who not only knew how to fight but evinced a fondness for it. He wore armor over his fivefold robes, and his princely coronet circled a helmet. "My lord emperor," he said. "Well come to Pri'nai."

"So one might think," Estarion said. He leaned against the chair in which Shurichan had been sitting, and folded his arms. "Now, my lord. Go on with your justice."

"Majesty," said Shurichan. "I can hardly—in your presence—"

Estarion tilted his head. He eyed the chair, and the man who had sat in it. Shurichan betrayed no expression.

Estarion looked about. There was a stool nearby, on which a scribe might have been sitting: he was on his face now, rusty black robe, rusty black hat. Estarion hooked the stool with a foot and drew it to him, and perched on it. "Now," he said. "Go on."

Shurichan was nicely shocked. He fell rather than sat in his high cushioned chair, and composed himself with visible effort.

Estarion watched him narrowly. Resentment, yes; his court of justice had been disrupted, his office lessened by the insouciant presence on the stool. But anger, no. And no move to protest.

Interesting. Estarion surveyed the men on the dais, the cat at its foot, the guards returned to their vigilance, the crowd of lords rising slowly from the edges inward but slow yet to resume their clamor. His escort had spread among the guards, ringing the dais, and his mages among them in a broad and broken circle. They were fully on guard; the wards had been raised about him since he left the hill above Pri'nai.

Within the wards, in the court of justice, men waited in chains. They were ragged, beaten and bruised, cowering in terror or glaring with defiance. Common malefactors, Asanians all, and nothing to mark them from any hundred of their like;

and yet Estarion's heart went still. Here, he thought. Here: not south of here, not in the siege of that lesser city, nor west where he had forborne to go. Here it came to the crux. He felt the force of it in his bones.

The men about him, lords, scribes, judges, rose one by one in order of precedence and returned to their places. The scribe whose stool Estarion had taken settled without apparent discomfort on the dais, set his tablets on his knees and raised his stylus, and waited.

The herald of the court glanced at his lord, and then swiftly, almost shyly, at Estarion. Estarion smiled. "Read the charges," he said, "if you will."

The man looked flustered, but he obeyed.

They were couched in the excess of Asanian ceremony, dense as weeds in a garden. Estarion was learning to find the flowers in the undergrowth, to pluck the essence of the charges from the knots of the law.

These were rebels. They had conspired against the imperial majesty; they had raised insurrection in Pri'nai and the towns about it; they had named themselves followers of one they called prophet and prince, lord of the Golden Empire, son of the Lion. And the one they followed, their prophet, their prince—he huddled among them in the wall of their bodies.

Estarion rose. The herald faltered, but Estarion's gesture bade him continue. His voice rang clear in the stillness as Estarion stepped down among the prisoners. They shrank from him. None sprang, though one looked as if he thought of it: a young one with a split cheekbone and an arm that dangled useless, and the eyes of a slave to dreamsmoke.

The one they sought even now to protect was a poor thing, a huddle of torn silk and tarnished cloth of gold, crouched with his arms over his head. Estarion lifted him by the wrists. He came as limply as a poppet made of rags, but once on his feet he stayed there, trembling. His hair was a brass-bright tangle, his face bruised ivory. His eyes were gold, and enormous. They were not lion-eyes, although to one who did not know, they might seem so, large-irised as they were. He was as beautiful as a girl, as delicate as girls in Asanion were supposed to be.

He looked remarkably, uncannily like Korusan. But Korusan was steel. This was silvered glass, so brittle that a breath would shatter it.

"Who are you?" Estarion asked him. His voice was gentle, and not through any will of his own; he should have been merciless. But it was difficult to be cruel to such a child.

The boy trembled until he nearly fell. Estarion held him, shook him. "I know what they say you are. You know as well as I, that that is a lie."

"I am," the boy whispered. "I am. Lion—prince—I prophesy—"

"But I am the Lion's heir," Estarion said. "There is no other."

"I am," the boy said. He was weeping, shuddering, sick with terror. "They said I was. They said!"

"What were you before they told you the lie?"

"I—" The boy swallowed. It must have hurt: his face twisted. "I was—he owned me. Kemuziran. He sold spices. And slaves. And—and—"

"And you," Estarion said. "You're a purebred, aren't you? The line they breed still, for the beauty and for the likeness to the Lion's brood. No Lion, you. You were bred to be a lady's lapcat."

A man, or even the beginning of a Lion's cub, would have stiffened at that and remembered his pride. This son of slaves flung himself weeping into Estarion's arms. "They made me! They said I'd die if I didn't do it!"

Estarion had hardly expected this armful of wriggling, howling child. He pushed the boy away, not roughly, not particularly gently. The boy stopped sobbing, raised great tear-stained eyes.

" 'They'?" Estarion pressed him.

"The others," the boy said, hiccoughing. "They bought me

and they taught me. They told me what to say. They said—they said—I could be—I could—"

Estarion held his burning hand under the boy's nose. "Would you want that?"

The boy shuddered and shrank away. It was not artifice, not the sleight of the courtesan. Estarion was sure of it.

"That is what they thought to give you," Estarion said. "Can you clasp the sun in your hand? Can you bear empires on your shoulders? Can you, little slave, sway the hearts of kings?"

"They told me," the boy said. "I would die if I refused them."

"You will die because you obeyed them."

"No," the boy said, weeping again. "Please, no."

The recitation of the charges had died away some time since. The boy locked arms about Estarion's waist and clung, burying his face in Estarion's cloak.

Estarion sighed and let him be. The rest of the prisoners watched, slack-jawed or frozen-faced. Guilt was as sharp as a stench, and hate with it, and fear.

"You," he said. The dreamer spat, aiming for Estarion's face, but the spittle flew wide. Estarion smiled, sweet and terrible. "I might forgive you your sedition, but this I do not forgive. A man will do anything at all, who stoops to the corruption of children."

"Such an innocent," the dreamer drawled. His patois was broad, his inflection an insult. "They say a king can be an idiot where you come from. Who set the coins in your eyes? The were-bear who follows you about?"

"No," said Estarion. "My father. And his father before him. And before them all, the Lion's cub, the Golden Emperor. I'm of his blood."

"Traitor's blood," the dreamer said. "No Lion's get, you, but liar's. Barbarian, outlander, stealer of thrones: you should have stayed in your own country."

"This is my own country," Estarion said. He gripped the

chain that locked the dreamer's collar, and hauled him up. "You are a fool and a teller of lies. Your dreams are the smoke's children. You know nothing of your own."

"And what are you?" the dreamer mocked him. "Not even a mage, and barely a king."

Estarion dropped him. He fell in a clatter of chains. Estarion faced the lord of Ansavaar and swept his arm round the huddle of prisoners. "Take these," he said. "Lock them in prison. In the morning, flog them. Then set them free."

"Majesty?" Shurichan frowned. "Majesty . . . free them?"

"They do not deserve death," Estarion said. "Death is for the great; for renegades, for traitors, for destroyers of thrones."

"And these are not traitors?" Shurichan demanded.

"These are fools and children. I will not ennoble them with death, or make them martyrs."

Shurichan blinked. He did not understand. His way was more direct: and there was irony in Asanion. Treason won death. Life in disgrace—that, Estarion thought, he had never heard of.

"That is . . . very cruel," Shurichan said at last, dubiously, as if he thought that he should approve, but could not bring himself to it.

"I call it justice," said Estarion.

"And that?" Shurichan asked.

Estarion looked down at the child who clung still, convulsively. "Him we keep. He's too great a temptation, with those big eyes of his. Ready a room for him. We'll keep him in comfort."

"But—"

That was great daring, to protest even so much. Estarion smiled at it. "Look at him, Shurichan. What can he do but seduce his guards? He won't want to be free. He'll welcome the safety of prison. No one forces him there; no one threatens him with thrones."

Shurichan bowed, veiling his eyes. Estarion pried the boy loose and gave him over to the Olenyai. He shrieked at sight of them, and struggled, till Estarion laid a hand on his head. "Hush, child. They won't hurt you, or let you be hurt. Go with them, let them protect you."

"I want to stay with you!" the boy wailed.

It was great pleasure to see the faces of the men who would have made this child their puppet: to know how perfectly they were nonplussed. "The next time you make an emperor," Estarion advised them, "choose a woolbeast in fleece. It will serve you better, and cover your backsides, too."

The prisoners were guarded as the emperor himself was, by both Varyani and Olenyai. Korusan did not find it difficult to take a turn of the watch, the one which happened to coincide with the nightmeal, nor did his companion object when he took charge of the feeding. That gained him the key to the cells, which he omitted to return.

Sentry-go with a Varyani could be interesting if the foreigner was hostile, or if he was inclined to chatter. Often he was both. This one, as luck would have it, was silent for one of his kind. He did not seem to object to the existence of Asanians, nor did he shy from Olenyai veils. He accepted the place of outer ward, granting Korusan the inner duty, which was to pace slowly along the passage, glancing at intervals into the cells.

The prisoners were kept apart lest they conspire to escape, and there were mage-bonds on them: Korusan's own wards itched in response. After several revolutions he glanced toward the corridor's end. The Varyani, a plainsman with a suggestion of Gileni red in his dark hair, stood facing outward, still as a stone. He glanced back when he heard the scrape of the key in a lock, but Korusan ignored him. Boldness, he had been taught, could be better concealment than stealth.

The plainsman did not protest as Korusan opened the door and slipped within. Nor did he leave his post.

Korusan stood in the dimness of the cell, waiting for his heart to cease hammering. The only light came from the cresset without, slanting through the bars onto the recumbent figure of the prisoner.

The man was asleep, twitching in the fashion of one too long forbidden dreamsmoke. He snapped awake as Korusan knelt by him. His eyes were bloodshot, blinking rapidly until he gained control of himself.

"You know me," said Korusan, soft and cold.

For once the dreamer was not smiling. He looked greener even than his condition might account for, as he stumbled up and then flung himself flat.

"Why did you lie?" Korusan asked him.

He raised his head, but kept his eyes fixed on the floor. He seemed to swell as he crouched there, gaining color and force. "For you, my lord. For you I did it."

"What? Found a slave's brat and called him emperor? Set him up to supplant me?"

"No!" the dreamer cried, but softly, as if he had sense enough not to rouse the Varyani's suspicions. "No, my lord, it wasn't like that at all! We needed a diversion, you see. A feint. A target for them to strike at, and be complacent, and think that that was all we had."

"None of them guessed," said Korusan, more to himself than to the fool on the floor.

The fool heard him nonetheless, and answered him. "They didn't, did they? I'm a good liar. I should be: I was a player before I became your servant."

Korusan curled his lip at the thought of this man as his servant. "You could have been the worst liar living, and still the mages would have shielded you. They would not wish their plots known to their enemies."

"But I lie well," the dreamer insisted. "I do. They said so. They hardly needed to put a magic on me. Just to keep me safe, they said. To free me to be your sacrifice."

Korusan recoiled. "I do not want a sacrifice."

"Why, bless you, my prince, of course you don't. But you shall have one. It's needed. The people will follow you all the more gladly once they've seen how we were willing to die for you."

This creature was unbearable. He actually shone, he was so full of his own glory.

"You are all idiots," Korusan said fiercely. "If you die, and I come to my throne, I will repudiate you. You lied in my name. You turned my honor to dust."

There was no quelling the dreamer. "Oh, yes, you have to deny me. I can't besmirch your brightness. But I die happy, knowing that my death helped to make you emperor."

"You are not going to die," snapped Korusan. "He will flog you and let you go. Fool, I thought him. Now I know him wise."

"I'll die," the dreamer said. "I'll make sure of it. Wait, my lord, and see."

Korusan restrained an urge to thrust him down and set foot on his neck. He would have welcomed the humiliation, and worshipped the one who did it to him. Korusan left him instead, shut and locked the door with taut-strung care, returned to his post and his silent companion.

To whom he said, "I thought I might get sense from him, once the drug had worn off. He utters nothing but lies and lunacy."

"His brain's well rotted," the Varyani agreed, "and the rest are witlings. It's a piss-poor excuse for a conspiracy, this one."

"But it suffices," said Korusan.

"It does, at that," the Varyani said. "And tomorrow we put an end to it."

Tomorrow, thought Korusan, it would hardly have begun.

"FULL OF YOURSELF, aren't you?"

Estarion paused. He was clean, warm, and about to be fed; he had rid himself of servants and won a few moments' solitude. The rebels' puppet was asleep, with one of Iburan's mages seeing to it that he stayed so. The rebels were in much less comfort, and under strong guard.

Sidani nudged a squalling ul-cub toward its mother. Ulyai, having laid claim to his lordship's bed, was amply content to nurse her young ones in it. She blinked lazily at Sidani, yawned, set to washing the he-cub's ears.

Sidani leaned against the doorframe, eyebrows cocked. "You think you did well in milord's court."

"I think I had no choice but to do what I did." Estarion scowled at the robes laid out for him, and looked longingly toward his baggage. The coat, maybe, embroidered with gold. Or—

"You should have killed them, and done it then. Not dragged it out till tomorrow."

"What, and made martyrs, but taught no lasting lesson?"

"Lessons are best taught quickly."

"Maybe." He pulled the coat from its wrappings and shook it out, and sighed. No. Not for this. He must be as Asanian as he could manage, however it galled him.

"Where's your shadow?" Sidani asked.

"Resting." Estarion dropped the robe he had been wrapped in and reached for the first of the ten.

"Are you sure of that?"

He whipped about, plait lashing his flanks. "What are you saying?"

She shrugged. "I wonder if you ever noticed whose face he wears."

"What, the Lion's mask? Yes, he has it. I'd be astonished if he weren't a cub of that litter."

"And it doesn't concern you that he might have ambitions?"

"Korusan?" Estarion laughed. "Korusan's ambition is to reach his twentieth year. If he manages that, he'll go for Master of Olenyai."

"Not emperor?"

Estarion went still. "He loves me."

"Do you love him?"

"Is that any affair of yours?"

"Do you?"

He thought of driving her out. But Sidani was not a tamed creature, nor one to yield to mere proprieties. He set his teeth and answered her. "If anyone holds my heart, it is one who does not want it. My Goldeneyes . . . have you ever been the half of a thing, and known that there was another, and it was nothing that you ever expected?"

Sidani's eyes closed. Her face was stark. "Yes," she whispered. "Yes."

Estarion stopped, drew a breath. He had not looked for that of all answers. "You don't call that anything as simple as love. It has no name. It is."

Her eyes snapped open. "You have no right to understand so much."

"Why? Because I'm young and a fool?"

"Because he isn't dead yet. You haven't had to live without him."

"I hope I never may."

"Then you'll be dead within the year."

Estarion shivered. He was naked and the room, though heated with braziers, was chill. "Are you prophesying?"

"I hope not." She moved toward one of the braziers and stood over it, warming her hands. "Go carefully, young emperor. Watch every shadow. There's death here, surer than ever it was in Kundri'j."

"Yes," he said. He put on the first of the robes. It was silk, and cold, till it warmed to his body. When he reached for the second, he found her hands on it, and her eyes behind that, daring him to refuse.

She helped him to dress, unplaited his hair and combed it and netted it in gold. Somewhere she had been a bodyservant, maybe, to have learned such lightness of hand. When the tenth robe was laid atop the rest, she turned him to face her. Her grim mood was gone. She smiled her old, wild smile. "Oh, you're a beauty, you are. If I weren't five times your age, I'd have you on the cushions in a heartbeat."

He was as reckless as she, when it came to it. He swept her backward and kissed her thoroughly, and set her on her feet again. She looked wonderfully startled. He left her so, walking lightly to the ordeal of the banquet, trailing robes and gold.

There were robes for Estarion again in the morning, and gold, but of Sidani there was no sign. Estarion wondered if he had frightened her into flight. That would hardly be like her; but who ever knew what she would do?

The night had been quiet. Korusan came in as Estarion readied for sleep, looking bruised about the eyes but protesting that he had slept. Estarion forbore to press him. It was not true, what Sidani had suggested. This was Olenyas only, whatever his face, and he lived to serve his lord. And if that was love, to see him so, and love was blind, then so be it. Estarion could not be other than he was; he could not learn to start at every shadow.

Korusan was in one of his muted moods, when he wanted rather to fold himself in Estarion's warmth than to dance the battle-dance that always ended in another dance altogether. Estarion was content to hold and to be held. He fell asleep so, though he thought that Korusan lay awake. The golden eyes were open, the last he remembered; and when he woke they had not changed, nor did the boy seem to have moved night-long.

They went out together, man and shadow, in a swelling crowd of attendants. The cold was less this morning but still keen enough to cut, the square of the palaces as crowded as it had been before, but its center, by the fountain, stood open. Lord Shurichan's men had raised a platform there and set the whipping-posts upon it, and ringed it with guards.

For Estarion there was a throne on the steps of the palace. The high ones waited there, muffled against the cold. He knew his mother's slender height in a cloak of ice-white fur, Iburan's massive solidity, the thickset golden-armored bulk of Lord Shurichan, the liveries of guards: Ansavaar's black and bronze, Keruvarion's scarlet and gold, plain Olenyai black.

When he came into the sun with Ulyai and her cubs at heel, all that throng bowed down like grain before a gale. All but his Varyani. He grinned at them. None of them smiled. The strain of dwelling in Asanion was taking its toll.

He sat in the tall chair. Ulyai stretched at his feet; her she-cubs, unwontedly subdued, crouched in the hollow of her side. The he-cub snarled at the press of people and sprang into Estarion's lap, where he settled, tensed as if on guard. Estarion rubbed his ears until he eased a little, but he would not relax his vigilance.

Merian came to stand beside and a little behind him. He slanted a glance at her. "Trouble?" he said.

"Possibly." She rested her hand on his shoulder. It would be a pretty picture: mother and son, empress and emperor, her white cloak and his scarlet against the gold of the throne. "Are you speaking to me again?" she inquired.

"Did I ever stop?"

"Often." She sounded more amused than not. "You could have forbidden me my pleasures."

"And made them sweeter? Pity I didn't think of that."

She laughed softly. She looked young this morning and beautiful in white and green, with gold in her hair. It was impossible to hold a grudge against her, however great her transgression. And what had she done but love a man worth loving?

She should have told me, whined the small mean thing that laired in Estarion's heart. But her laughter was too sweet, and she too much beloved, for all the sparks they struck from one another. He reached impulsively, caught her hand, set a kiss in the palm.

She smiled. "I think that you quarrel simply for the pleasure of forgiving me after."

His heart was too full, almost, for speech. But he found his famous insouciance and put it on. "What's life without a good fight?"

She leaned lightly against him, arm about his shoulders. He knew better than to think that any of it was uncalculated. She guarded him so, and claimed him for her own. But there was love in it, and pleasure in his nearness; a pleasure that warmed him even in the bitter wind.

A stirring on the crowd's edges marked the coming of the prisoners. The banners over them were Estarion's, and Shurichan's flying lower, as was fitting. Guards with spears opened the way before and behind. Of the captives there was little to see: a bobbing of bared heads, a pause and a flurry as one of them stumbled. The people were deathly silent. In Keruvarion they would have been roaring, surging like the sea. Here they were still. Watching. Almost, Estarion thought, like an ul-cat poised to spring.

Shurichan's troops were scattered through them, and his own who were not needed to guard his person, and on the roofs waited a line of archers with bows strung. If any in that throng either rose in revolt or sought to free the prisoners, he would meet with the point of a spear, or fall to an arrow from above.

The executioner mounted the block and readied his whips. One by one the prisoners ascended to face him. He was big for an Asanian, almost as tall as Estarion, and broad, and startlingly young, with the long gentle face of a woolbeast. He went about his work with peaceful deliberation, taking no notice of the struggling, cursing captives, or the cries of the cowards among them. They would believe, maybe, that Estarion mocked them with clemency, and meant to see them flogged until they died.

The last of them stumbled to his place with the aid of a guard's spearbutt. The executioner shook out the thongs of a many-headed whip, smoothed them, laid the whip carefully on the table beside the rest. He turned toward Estarion, bowing low.

"He is ready," Lord Shurichan said, "majesty."

Estarion hardly needed to be told. He raised his branded hand. The sun caught it, shot sparks from it. People flinched. His lips stretched back from his teeth, but not in pleasure. None of this was pleasure. But he would do it. He could do no less, and still be emperor.

Justice, he thought as the whip rose and fell. Some of the prisoners screamed. Some cried and pleaded to be let go. His stomach was a hard cold knot. His jaw ached with clenching. The ul-cub in his lap had dug claws into his thigh. He welcomed the pain.

They said that when the Sunborn wreaked summary justice, he opened his mind to the one who suffered it. Lest, he said, he grow too fond of exacting punishment, and too free of his power to do so. No one had ever pretended that he grew the softer for it, or the less implacable.

Estarion had no such greatness in him, and no such steel. But he would not put a stop to this. These were fools; and fools they must be seen to be.

The last was the dreamer, blue with cold and bleak with want of dreamsmoke. He kept his air of insolence for all that, shook off the guards who would have dragged him to his punishment, walked there on his own feet and in his own time, and held up his hands to be bound to the post. He managed as he walked to catch Estarion's eye and hold it. Estarion met the hard yellow stare with one as hard and, he hoped, as flat. The dreamer shrugged, turned his back, barely flinched as they stripped the robe from it. His shoulders were narrow and yellow-pale and thin, sharp-boned like a bird's. He did not seem to mind as the others had, that he was naked. He grinned over his shoulder and wriggled his bony backside.

He did not scream until the tenth stroke, and then in a strangled squawk, as if it had been startled out of him. It took the edge off his mockery. Still he walked away when it was over, though his back was laid open with weals that would turn to scars, branding his shame until he died.

Estarion rose with the ul-cub on his shoulders. The crowd was quiet. The guards were watchful but at ease. They did not like what he did; they had argued loud and long against it. But his mind was fixed. He would go to the scaffold and speak to the prisoners, and let it be known in Pri'nai that the emperor's justice was more than a cold word out of Kundri'j. It was here, present before them, and with his face behind it.

He began to descend the stair. His guards were ready for him, likewise his Olenyai, and his mother and his mages. They did not have his consent, but they defied him. If he would indulge this folly, their eyes said, he would go full guarded, or he would not go at all.

He could not quarrel with them now. And too well they knew it, as surely they knew what comfort they were, warding his back with power as with weapons.

Half of the way down, he paused. The prisoners stood on their scaffold, held upright if need be. Some were waking to awareness that this was all they would suffer; that they were alive, and would indeed walk free.

There was a stir behind Estarion. Ulyai growled. Estarion glanced back. One of the guards had stumbled. His fellows caught him. He steadied, muttering curses at his own clumsiness.

Estarion smiled thinly. He was all nerves and twitches. His captives stood waiting for him, their rebellion broken. He had not won in the south, nor yet in all Asanion, but he was lord in Pri'nai; that, he had proven.

The way was open as it always was, the people on their faces in homage. He would teach them to stand like men. But first he must show them a Sunlord's clemency.

He sprang lightly onto the scaffold, disdaining the steps that led up to it. He had caught his guards for once off guard. That made him laugh. Ulyai lofted herself up beside him and crouched, tail twitching, muzzle wrinkled in a snarl. Poor queen of cats; she hated Asanian cities with a deathless passion. Her son, riding on Estarion's shoulders, howled ul-cat glee.

No, Estarion realized too late. Rage. The cub dug in claws, reversed himself, and sprang. Estarion spun. The dreamer went down in a flurry of claws and teeth and steel.

Steel?

The air was full of wings, wind, knives. Ulyai roared.

"Starion!" Iburan's voice, great bull-bellow. "Starion! 'Ware mages! *'Ware mages!"*

Not mages, Estarion thought as the world slowed its turning and the wind died to a shriek. Not only mages. A Gate. And in the Gate, death.

They boiled out of the air, men in white, armed with knives. They sang as they came. They sang death, they sang oblivion, they sang numbing terror. All their eyes fixed on Estarion's face.

Claws hooked in Estarion's knee. He snatched up the he-cub, who was still snarling, bloody-mouthed but richly content. He did not spare a glance for the dreamer. Ul-cats, even as young as this, did not leave living prey. With the cub again on his shoulders, he leaped down into the roil that had been his escort. His throat was raw. He was shouting. Howling. "Here! I am here! Take me, fools. Take me if you can!"

He stumbled. Body. White. Assassin—but—

The world reeled. That was fur that hampered his feet, a great sweep of cloak spattered bright with blood. There was a body in it.

"No," he said. He said it very clearly. Battle raged about him. None of it touched him.

He knelt beside his mother. She breathing still. The knife in her breast pulsed with the beating of her heart. No blood flowed there; the blade stanched it. It was not the only wound, not by far. The rest were less clean, if less deadly.

Her head rested on Iburan's knee. The priest looked immeasurably weary; his head had fallen forward, his beard fanning on his breast. Her eyes wandered from his to Estarion's. "Take," she said, a bare breath of sound. "Take the knife."

"You'll die," Estarion protested.

"Yes," she said. "Take it."

Estarion tossed his head in furious refusal. "No! We'll get you out of this—call healers—mages—"

"I am mage," Iburan said, "and healer. I can do nothing."

"Of course you can." Estarion looked about. A wall of black and scarlet circled them. White pierced it briefly, but fell to the flash of a sword. Arrows were flying; one arced over him singing. And the people—the poor people—would be dying, trapped like cattle in a pen.

"Hold her," Estarion said to Iburan. "Keep her alive." He thrust himself to his feet. The scaffold was at his back. He gathered, leaped, half-fell to the splintered wood of the floor. He cast a glance about. The dreamer was dead. The rest were gone—alive, he hoped, and under guard.

The battle was not as fierce as he had feared. The knot of his guards was the worst of it. People fled the fighting, trampling one another, sounding at last like human beasts, yelling their terror.

He was calm. Perfectly, icily, immovably calm. His mother was dying. Mages had killed her. They thought maybe to deceive him, to feign their coming through the crowd of his people, his Asanians. But he had felt the Gate; he had known the wound it rent in the earth of his empire.

Something stirred in him; something shifted. It was not anger. No. Nor fear. Nor even irony. These rebels whom he had punished had been no more than a mask, their punishment a pretext. Now the enemy had shown his hand.

Mages.

Mages of the Gates.

He looked down. Iburan looked up, and deliberately, coolly, drew the knife from the wound in the empress' breast. She sighed. And her heart, her great wise heart, burst asunder.

Estarion's skull was beating like a heart, beating fit to burst. He clutched at it, rocking, dislodging the ul-cub. The cat fell yowling.

The empress was dead. Godri was dead. His father was dead. All dead, all slain. Because of him. Because of Estarion.

He howled. There were no words in it, only rage. And power. Raw, pulsing, blood-red power. He had driven it down deep and bound it with chains of guilt and terror, and sworn a vow beyond the limits of memory. Never to wield it again, never to take a life, never to destroy a soul.

He had done it, and done it surpassingly well: he had shut the door of memory, and made truth of the lie. Even mages had not seen the deception. They called him cripple, feeble, maimed and all but powerless. But his power lived, far down below his remembrance, waiting. Yearning to break free.

He was dizzy, reeling, stunned with the shock of magic reborn, but he was master of it still. He remembered the ways of it. He drew it like a sword, great gleaming deadly thing, and raised it, and poised.

Mages, yes. Gate: so. Land weeping with pain, people a knot of shadowy fear. He soothed them with blade turned to gentleness, calmed them, brought them under his shield. And turned then. Outward.

So it had been when his father was dead, before the dark came upon him. This clarity. This bright strength with its edge of blood. It was never as they had taught him, those who called themselves masters of mages. They feigned that it was difficult; that a mage must struggle to see what was as clear as sun in a glass, and as simple to encompass. Here were mages, little lights like candles in a wind, and the threads of their lives stretched spider-thin behind them. To cut, so, one had but to raise the sword. To snuff them out, one needed but a breath.

No. That too was memory, though dim. One should not wield the sword so; and never the breath that was the soul. There was a price—prices.

And what was the price of his mother's life, his father's, his friend and brother's?

Not so high. Not, again, so bitter. They had suffered death of the body. He would slay souls. And in that, be doomed and damned.

So simple. So very simple.

Starion.

Iburan. Again. And another.

"Mother?" Gladness; soaring, singing joy. "Mother! You live?"

No. Faint, that, but clear. *Starion, no. Never be tempted. Never for me.*

"Mother!" No answer. *"Mother!"*

She was gone. He raged and wept, but she would not come back for him, nor for any mortal pleading.

Mages bobbed and glimmered like corpselights. He caught the stink of them: self-delight and surety, and contempt for his frailty. They could not even see the light that was in him. They were too weak. He struck them blind, and they never knew.

He writhed in the darkness, twisting and coiling like a dragon of fire. A magelight darted at him, wielding what no doubt it reckoned deadly power. Estarion batted it aside. It reeled. He caught it. He considered the thread that spun from it, the light that flickered in it, and gently, most gently, plucked thread and minute guttering spark from the bubble of light, and pricked the bubble with a sharpened claw.

So simple. So precise. Body, soul, he left entire. Magery he took away. And when the last corpse-pale glimmer was gone, he drifted alone in the dark.

That too he had forgotten. What peace was here; what

quiet, where no storms came. He coiled, uncoiled. So supple, this shape, freed from the stiffness that was humanity. He had thought it madness to linger here. It had been madness to depart.

Now at last he would stay. The dark was sweet and deep, the silence blessed, and absolute. *Peace,* his soul sang. *Peace.*

VANYI HAD A few breaths' warning. She should have had more than that. Her Gate-sense had been uneasy for long days now, a broad sourceless uneasiness, but nothing on which she could set hand or mind. Estarion's insistence on making a spectacle of himself was purely Estarion, and no more foolish than anything else he might have taken it into his head to do. He was guarded with all the vigilance that any of them might muster; she was part of the wards, set among a faceless rank of Olenyai, weaving her strand of autumn-colored silk into the greater web.

The warding that the blackrobes wore was a hindrance, until realization came to her in a blaze of sudden light. Olenyai wards were made for shield and guard against attack. In the face of power that would weave with them and not oppose them, they yielded with astonishing ease. She was just finding the way of it, just beginning to know the pride of her accomplishment, when the web of the world began to fray.

She had never seen the opening of a Gate, never thought to see it. Yet there was no denying it; no hoping that it was something else, something less, something that did not pierce straight to the heart of the wards and shatter them. The breaking was not even deliberate. Estarion's mages had armed themselves against attack of steel or magery, but not against the forging of a Gate. It drained the power out of their working and wielded it for itself, drank deep of the resistance that some of them—fools, idiots, blind brave hopeless innocents—mustered against it.

But not Vanyi. The Olenyai shields protected her, woven with them as she was. She dropped out of the web half-stunned but conscious, and able to see with eyes of the body. She saw the battle begin, white-robed assassins against Guardsmen in scarlet, Queen's Guards in green. No Olenyai. The assassins veered aside from them. She saw the empress fall, and Iburan go down with her. She saw Estarion leap shouting to his mother's side. He wore a sword; he seemed to have forgotten it, or he was trusting his guards beyond life and hope. Or he had merely taken leave of his wits. When he struggled back to the scaffold, bright target for any assassin with a bow or a throwing knife, Vanyi remembered how to move.

She struggled within a suddenly solid wall of bodies. Yellow eyes fixed on her, hard and flat as stones. No lion-eyes; all of these were plain Asanian.

Even yet she had the key of their wards. She set it in its lock and turned it carefully, not too swift, not too slow. Beyond the circle the world was breaking—the empress dead, the mages fallen, blood feeding the Gate, and above them all, miraculously unharmed, the emperor.

She slid hands between two stone-still Olenyai and opened them like the leaves of a door. Beyond their circle was havoc. More magery; more Gate-work, taking its strength from the cattle-panic of the people as they fled the blood and the battle.

Estarion stood erect on the scaffold. His face was perfectly blank. His eyes were pure and burning gold.

"God," Vanyi said, her voice lost in the tumult. "Oh, goddess."

No one else seemed even to see him. His guards held off the assassins, taking bitter toll in blood and lives. He was no man to them then, no living, breathing, fallible human creature, but prize and victim of the battle. Those who fought to guard him, those who fought to kill him, were oblivious to him else. And mages, both his own and those others, knew that he had no power for the wielding.

She had heard his outcry in his riding: how he was nothing to anyone but a child or a ruined mage; a weak thing, a thing to be guarded and protected, with no strength of his own.

They were all going to regret that, she thought, remote and very clear. He was like a mountain asleep under the moons, motionless, lifeless, deep sunk in snow. But his heart was sun-bright fire. And soon, between one breath and the next, it was going to shatter.

Vanyi wrenched eyes and mind away from him. The ring of guards had widened. The assassins were falling back. The Varyani captain and the captain of Olenyai had matters well in hand; they had even, gods knew how, brought Lord Shurichan's men under their command. Within the ring, Estarion's mages were beginning to recover. But there were others among them, and that mountain of fire above them, and no knowledge in any of them that there was danger apart from steel or simple magery.

Down! she cried with her power. *My mages, my people—for your lives' sake, down! Shield!*

Oromin touched her with incomprehension, but shielded as if by instinct. Shaiyel and his little priestess were now clear in her awareness, now locked in walls. The others fled before the lash of Vanyi's urgency. But one resisted.

Iburan, Vanyi pleaded. *Shield yourself. He's going to—*

And where are your shields? Iburan lashed back. And when she wavered, struck so fiercely that she must shield or fall.

And the fire came down.

In the world of the living was nothing to see. A scattering of priests fallen on their faces. A battle that went on unheeding. A lone motionless figure on a scaffold, with the wind tugging at his scarlet cloak, and the sun in his eyes.

But in the world of power, even behind the strongest of shields, that figure was a tower of light. Corpse-candles danced and flickered about it. Mages, and none of Vanyi's kind, either. If they had heard her call to shield, they had chosen not to heed it. And they paid.

So would she have done if she had laid herself open to him.

He stripped the mages of their magery as easily as a child strips a sea-snail of its shell, but left them alive to know what he had done to them. He shut down the Gate without even thinking of it, healed the rent in the land and the air, and as an afterthought, in passing, herded the last of the assassins into the swords of his guard.

And then was silence.

Vanyi dragged herself to her feet. The fighting was ended. The people were fled, all but the dead. No one stood in all that wide and windy place but Estarion's Guard and Lord Shurichan's best, and a handful of stumbling, staggering priest-mages, and she.

Scarlet pooled on the scaffold. Not blood, thank god and goddess, but the emperor's cloak, blood-red for war. Estarion lay as if asleep. He did not wake when she touched him. His ul-cub crouched beside him, bristling, but did not snarl or threaten.

A shadow fell across her. She looked up into Olenyai veils, and eyes all amber-gold.

A great anger swelled in her. It was not reasonable, she knew it was not, but she was past reason. "You," she said. "Where were you when he needed you?"

"Fighting," the Olenyas said. His voice was as cool as always, but there was a tremor in it. "I could not come to him."

Yes, he was shaking, and trying not to. She had no pity to spare. "Look after him now, then. And by all gods there are, if you lay hand on him except to guard him, I'll flay your hide with a blunt knife."

"He is not," said the Olenyas, as if he struggled with the words. "He is not—he is not dead."

"We all may wish he were," Vanyi said, "before the day is out. See to him, damn you, and stop fluttering."

That stiffened his back for him. He called up others of his kind, and did as he was bidden.

She looked up. She was being stared at. Dark eyes, yellow

eyes, eyes of every shade between. No sea-grey or sea-green or sea-blue. That mattered suddenly, very much. They were all alien here. And they were all begging her to do their thinking for them.

The empress was dead. Estarion was worse than that, maybe. Iburan was alive, half kneeling, half sitting with the empress' body in his arms. But as Vanyi came down off the scaffold, he sighed and slid sidewise. She braced herself against the weight of him, and gasped. "You're hurt!"

"Assassins' knives," he said calmly, "as we know too well, are poisoned. Not that that need have stopped me, you understand, but it slowed me when I should have shielded. Do you know what I was to him? A stinging fly. He plucked the wings from me and let me fall."

"No," said Vanyi.

But that was her tongue, being a fool. She hardly needed power to know that his magery was gone. He was all dulled for lack of it, his great body shrunken. The eyes he raised to her were wry. "I always did misjudge him," he said. "Here I thought I could stop him, or at least slow him down, and he never even knew I tried. You're going to have your hands full with him, Vanyi."

"I?" She thrust the thought away. "I'm not anyone to deal with a Sunlord gone mad."

"Who else is there?"

"Oromin," she answered promptly. "Shaiyel."

"No," said Iburan. He sighed. It bubbled; he coughed. "They don't know—they can't master him. You have the power. No one—else—" He coughed again, a froth of bright blood, struggling to say more, all that there had been no time to say. That she had more magery than she would ever admit. That he had meant her to follow him—but not now. Not so soon. Not until he was ancient and august and tired, and she was fit to take his place.

"No," she said. But he only smiled, damn him; and the life pouring out of him as she watched. She must not weep, nor could she linger. She set the burliest of Estarion's northerners to work fashioning a litter, and the rest to taking up the dead and clearing away the flotsam of the battle. Iburan might have called that taking his place. She called it plain common sense. Someone had to make order of this chaos. It had nothing at all to do with magic, or with mastering emperors.

Somewhere in the midst of it Lord Shurichan appeared. There was not a mark on his armor, not a drop of blood on his prettily drawn sword. He had ambitions, Vanyi saw, to take matters in hand. He was the only great one left standing, and the only man of rank in that place.

Just as he drew breath to issue orders, she set herself in front of him. She was markedly smaller than he was, and markedly female, but he could hardly ignore the hand that plucked his sword from him and returned it to its sheath, or the voice that said with acid clarity, "My lord Shurichan. How convenient that you should appear. I was just about to send a messenger to inform you that the battle is over; it's safe to come out."

His mouth was open. He shut it.

"I commend your prudence," Vanyi said, "and I forbear to remark that a lord of a province who fails to stand at his emperor's back when that emperor is threatened, might find his loyalty called into question. You were taking the road of greater sense, I presume, and trusting to your men—who are as brave as a lord can wish for, and as faithful in defense—to guard his majesty. Since of course if he emerged alive, you would be present to aid him in your fullest capacity; and if he should, alas, fail to survive the consequences of his rashness, why then there would still be a lord in Ansavaar, and the empire's unity would be preserved." His face had gone crimson as she spoke; now it was vaguely green. She smiled sweetly. "Set your mind at rest, my lord. Everything has been seen to, and at no cost to your comfort. Surely now you are weary from so much excitement; you should rest. These gentlemen will assist you to your rooms."

A company of Estarion's Varyani took station about him. The smallest topped him by a head. He looked, she thought, like a gaffed fish. By the time he reached his chambers he would be bellowing; but that was no concern of hers. If Estarion came out of this alive, he would soothe the man's ruffled feathers. If he did not, then Vanyi would fret about it when she came to it. Estarion dead and his heir nine cycles in the womb, and no surety that the child would live to be born—

She would not think of that. Shock and the suddenness of attack kept order now, but once it had faded, there would be war.

Not if she could help it. She straightened her back and set her jaw and did what she had to do.

There was an ungodly lot of it, and no sleep till it was done. Somewhere amid the endless hours—it was dark beyond the window of the room in which she had taken station, but how long it had been so, she did not remember—some of Estarion's Guard came to her. Shaiyel was there. He had come ostensibly to tell her that Iburan lived still, but she could have ascertained that with a flick of magery. He thought to guard her; when the guardsmen entered, he was working his subtle western way round to coaxing her to sleep.

They were the young hellions she had always liked best, with redheaded Alidan in front. He looked tired and unwontedly grim, his fire banked for once, but no less fierce for that. He had a captive, a figure in soiled and bloodstained white, chained, gagged, and stumbling. The man behind him dragged another such. They flung both at Vanyi's feet.

The assassins lay unmoving, save that one of them twitched as he struck the tiled floor. Alidan kicked him. He jerked and went still.

"Do you need to be quite so emphatic?" Vanyi asked.

"With these," Alidan said, all but spitting, "yes." He hauled the man onto his back.

Man, no. The hair was cropped, the breasts were small, but

the face was too fine even for a boy's. The robe was torn. There was another under it, or a shift, neither blue nor purple but somewhere between. And the other, who was male, wore grey beneath the white.

Vanyi drew a long slow breath. She did not need the touch of power on minds that had been stripped naked and left to find their way unwarded; she did not need to sense here two of those who had threatened Estarion with magecraft. The robes were proof enough.

"Guildmages," she said. "They were to rise up in triumph, I suppose, and cast off their disguises, and proclaim the Guild's return."

The man was nigh dead; his life ebbed low. The woman opened bruised and swelling eyes. She did not speak. Her mind offered nothing but contempt.

"Half a mage I may be," Vanyi said, "but I'm more now than you. Is there another invasion coming? Should we look to be besieged?"

The answer flickered in the shallows of the ruined power, tangled in a weed-growth of nonsense. Vanyi swooped to pluck it out.

It fled darting-swift. She made a hedge of her power's fingers, and snapped it shut.

On nothing.

The woman's eyes stared up. Life faded from them; but even in death they gleamed with mockery.

The other was dead and growing cold. Vanyi straightened, swallowing bile. "See if you can find more of these. And quickly, before they're dead, too."

"There are no more," Alidan said. He sounded more angry than regretful. "These were the only two who lived. They waited, I think. To mock you."

"They were fools," she said. "Shaiyel, go with these men. Find what there is to find."

He was willing, but he hesitated. "And these?"

Her shoulders ached with keeping them level, her neck with holding up her head. "Search them. Then dispose of them."

There was nothing to find, of course. Their minds were wiped clean. That was a mage's trick, to leave no trace of themselves behind, even in the helplessness of death.

But she had learned enough. She had proof that the Guild yet lived, and ways, maybe, to track them down. They had built a Gate. It was fallen now—Estarion had seen to that. But she had memory of how it had come, and how it had stood, and how it had broken. She needed time, which she did not have, and leisure, which was forbidden her, but she would search out the truth. She swore a vow on it, alone in the dark before dawn, with the weight of empires on her shoulders, and the emperor clinging to life in a guarded chamber.

Haliya was with him. Vanyi had been aware of that from the first: how the little idiot crept through all the tumult, melted the guards with tears, and established herself at his bedside. She had not done anything foolhardy, and she did not make herself a nuisance. Now and then she bathed his brow, as if that little could bring down the fever that raged in him, or tried to coax water down his throat.

She was harmless enough where she was. If anyone ventured the chamber, he would be dead before he touched either, emperor or empress who would be. And if Estarion woke, he would not threaten her, Vanyi did not think. Even if he woke raging.

Vanyi need not approach him while Haliya was there. It was cowardice, she knew that, but she clung to it.

Of Korusan there was no sign. He had been with Estarion in the beginning. Now the Olenyai who stood guard were all strangers.

Vanyi might have pursued that, but her solitude was broken. There were disputes for her to settle, lordlings to placate, merchants of the city to soothe. All of them repeated the rumor that the emperor was dead, that he must be seen to be alive or they could not answer for the consequences. She put them off as best she could, but there were more behind them, always more, and no rest to be had.

And Estarion lived so his life long. Vanyi thanked the god that she was not born to it; that she could walk away from it. Soon. When there was someone to take the burden from her.

PEACE WAS BLESSED for half of an eternity, but then, in the way of things, it began to pall. Estarion knew first a glimmer of restlessness, an ache that might have been boredom. The dark that had been so sweet now seemed an unrelieved monotony. A single star, even the flicker of a candle, would vex less than this endless night.

He stretched, flexed. The darkness yielded, but still it conceived no light.

And should he wait for it? *Light,* he said, thought, willed. And there was light. One star, then another, then another. Once begun, they gave birth to one another, a blooming of stars like nightlilies in the fields beneath Mount Avaryan. All creation was stars, and all dark was turned to light.

And it was not enough. He floated in a sea of stars upon the breast of Mother Night, and it was only light, and he was only he, naked fish-sleek self whose heart was fire.

Beyond light, beyond dark—what was there, what could there be? All that was not light was dark; all that was not dark was light. And where they met, they wrought a wonder: a miracle of living flesh.

He was flesh. He lived. He breathed: great bellows-roaring, drumbeat of the blood along the white tracks of the bones. He counted each one; all those that were whole, the arm that had been broken long ago and set just perceptibly out of true, the ribs cracked and cracked again but healed the stronger for it. He traced their curve with fingers of the soul. And there, see, the chalice of the skull, a goblet full of fire, light within light, flame within flame, lightnings leaping from promontory to promontory. The Sun itself was in it, in what had been mere mortal brain.

Even that was insufficient. There was world beyond this world of the self. He opened his eyes to it.

And screamed.

"Hush, dear lord, hush. Hush."

The hands on him were agony, the voice a dagger in his skull. Everything—everything—

"Too much! *Too much!*"

"Hush," said the other. The Other. The half that was himself, but was outside himself. He struck it away; he clung with the strength of terror, till the creaking of bones, soft awful sound, brought him somewhat to his senses.

Korusan's face of flesh was a blur. Within was both darkness and flame, and pain, such pain—

"Peace," said the soft cool voice. Soft like velvet on the skin; cool like water, but with still the edge of agony.

Estarion lay gasping in his arms. The world was itself again, or near enough. It was Korusan who made it so, Korusan in his black robes with his veils laid aside.

Gently—Estarion would not have said cautiously—he laid his hand on Estarion's cheek. "My lord," he said.

Estarion closed his eyes and let that touch hold him to his body. "Oh, unmerciful gods."

"You wished to die?"

Estarion's eyes snapped open. "Better if I had!"

"My lord—"

Estarion spoke much more quietly, much more carefully. "I have the great-grandmother of headaches."

"That would indeed," Korusan said dryly, "make a man wish himself dead."

"How much wine did I—" Estarion broke off. "No. Oh, gods. I didn't dream it, did I? She's dead. My mother is dead."

"She is dead," said Korusan.

The storm of weeping swept over him, battered him, left him abandoned.

Korusan held him through all of it, saying nothing. When

even the dregs of it were gone, and Estarion lay exhausted, Korusan lowered his head and kissed him softly.

It was not meant for seduction. It was comfort; warmth of living flesh before the cold of the dead.

Korusan straightened. His cheeks were flushed, but his eyes were somber.

"Tell me," Estarion said. "Tell me everything."

Korusan frowned. Estarion saw himself in the boy's eyes: waked screaming from a sleep like death, shaken still, sweat-sodden, grey about the lips; but grim, and clearheaded enough, for the moment.

Korusan told him. Merian dead. Iburan alive but like to die—the mages sustained him with their magic, but he was failing. Assassins dead and burned; two mages caught, but dead before they could be questioned.

"Guildmages?"

Korusan frowned more darkly. "Yes." He went on with the rest, which was simple enough. "Your empire is secure, or no less so than before. Your priestess has it in hand. She does all that must be done."

"My—" Estarion struggled against a sudden thickening of wit. "Vanyi?"

"The Islander. The fisherman's daughter."

Estarion did not think that he would ever smile again. But warmth welled and spilled over, and maybe a little touched his face. "Ah, Vanyi. She'll be my empress yet."

Korusan did not say anything to that, but his grip tightened nigh to pain.

"But you," Estarion said, "are the half of myself."

The golden eyes closed. The face, the beautiful face, was as white as Estarion had ever seen it, but for the flush that stained the cheekbones. Fever again. Estarion uncoiled a tendril of the fire that was in him, took the fire of fever to himself. He was not even aware that he had done it until it was done. It was a shock, like cold water on the skin, or joy at the bottom of grief.

Korusan shivered.

"You are ill," Estarion said.

The boy laughed, breathless, bitter as always. "Am I ever not?"

"No longer," said Estarion.

"No," said Korusan. But what he meant by that, Estarion could not tell. He would have had to break the wards that were on the boy's thoughts, and that, he feared, would break the boy's mind. Later, when both of them were stronger, would be time enough to take down the wards, to heal the sickness, to put all fever to flight.

Now . . .

He sat up slowly. Korusan, at first resisting, suddenly let him go. He swayed. The ache in his head was blinding. Wind roared through his soul, wind of wrath, wind of grief.

He pulled himself to his feet. He did not remember this room, although it must be the one in which he had slept before this all began, the lord's bedchamber in Pri'nai. Memory of trifles was lost to him. But the great things, the grim things, the ranks of the dead—those he would never forget.

His hands were full of fire. It dripped from them, splashing on the floor. Each droplet congealed into gold, rayed like a sun.

He clenched his fists. The fire welled in them. He willed it to subside. It did not wish to. Its anger burned.

Korusan's eyes were wide and blank.

"Warrior child," Estarion said to him. "Lion's cub."

Korusan blinked, started, came to himself. The quick flash of temper was deeply comforting.

"Yelloweyes," Estarion said, "don't tell anyone."

"What?"

Estarion flexed his throbbing hands. They bled fire still, but more slowly. "This. It's not . . . it's nothing to be afraid of. But I'd rather you didn't tell anyone about it."

"Liar."

Estarion went stiff.

"Your magic," said Korusan. "It has mastered you. Has it not?"

Estarion set his teeth. "Not yet. Not, gods willing, ever."

"I heard the priests talking. They were afraid that it would be so. That the magic would be too strong and you too weak, and it would consume you."

"No," said Estarion. "I won't let it."

"Is it a matter for letting and not-letting?"

"Yes!" Estarion winced with the pain of his own outcry. And maybe it was a lie, maybe it was the feeble wishing of a fool, but he would not yield. Not while he had wits left to resist. "I will . . . not . . . give in. I will master it. It will be my servant. On my hand I swear it."

"Gods willing," said Korusan.

Korusan held the throngs at bay while Estarion drowned himself in drugged wine. Laughing, making light of it, but with a sharp edge of desperation. He had shown himself in the doorway of his chamber, smiling, upright, very much alive; he protested when his nursemaid coaxed him in again. But when the door was shut and barred, he downed the wine with rather too evident relief, and toppled headlong into sleep.

Once he was safely unconscious, his Vinicharyas crept out of hiding. She had fled there when he showed signs of waking, leaving the field to Korusan. As she had then, she said nothing, seemed not to know that the Olenyas was there. She sat where she had sat before, at the bed's side. What she thought she could do, Korusan did not know. He doubted that she did, either.

He left her to it. Tight-coiled terror had held him until he saw Estarion awake and speaking sense. Now it was gone.

He slipped out by the servants' way. In a corridor lit by a single guttering lamp, he leaned against the wall and shivered. Estarion had taken the fever, and with it the little warmth that was in Korusan's thin blood. He wrapped arms about ribs that stabbed with pain. Broken. Maybe. Who was to tell now, with sickness set deep in his bones?

His stomach spasmed. There was nothing for it to cast up: and that was well for his veils.

He pulled himself up, back flattened against the wall. The pain grew no less, but his will remembered its strength. He was the Lion's heir. He yielded to no master.

Plain obstinacy set him to walking. Training kept him erect, even lent him a semblance of grace. Between the two, he walked out of the palace as the Olenyas he was; and even, somewhat, convinced himself that he was strong.

He had the watchwords and the secret ways; they had been given him in Kundri'j Asan, for all the cities where the rebellion was strong. He did not think that he was expected here. The watchers admitted him unquestioned, as much on the strength of his eyes as on that of the words and the signs. They looked less wary than they ought.

The Master of Olenyai stood in a room like a guardroom, empty of any furnishings but a tier of lamps, but full of strangers. The Master of Mages faced him, looking unwontedly ruffled. The air had the thunder-reek of battle.

Korusan neither wavered nor hesitated. He was too angry to be afraid, too fevered to be cautious. He strode to the center of the circle, dropped his veils and faced them all.

He had shocked them properly. He raked them with his eyes: Master and Master, black veils of Olenyai, blank faces of mages, faces of strangers who were lords of the empire. He lashed them with his voice. "Who gave you leave to loose the attack?"

The lords stared openly at his face. Mages and Olenyai neither moved nor spoke.

Save the Master of the Mages. "It was time," he said. He granted Korusan no title, no mark of respect.

The Master of the Olenyai lowered his veil slowly. The lordlings flinched. "Your lives are mine," he said to them. "Remember it."

Korusan looked into that face which he had come to know

so well, with its nine thin parallel scars, the last of them still faintly livid. His own two ached as scars will in the cold, although it was warm here with the heat of bodies and braziers. "Did you countenance this?" Korusan asked.

"I did," said Asadi, "my prince."

"I did not," said Korusan, soft and still.

"It was time," the Master of Mages said again. "You were not within our reach, to consult. And," he said, "it was our thinking that you were best left untold, lest he or his mages discover our intent."

"You are saying," Korusan said very gently, "that you did not trust me."

There: that was a cause of the battle that had broken off with his coming. He saw the tightening of Olenyai hands on swordhilts, the tensing of mages' bodies.

"It is true," said the Master of Mages with calm that was either great arrogance or great folly, "that you appear to be entirely his putative majesty's creature. Could we endanger your semblance for the sake of a warning that, in the end, you did not need? You were not by his side when he fell."

"I was kept from him," said Korusan, "by my brothers." He glared at them, and at Marid most of all. "You knew!"

"We wanted to tell you," said Marid. "But when we were told, it was already too late; you were with him, and it wasn't safe."

Korusan turned back to the mage. "So. It was you who decided it. And it will be you who rule when I am emperor, yes?"

"If you are emperor," the mage said. "Is he dead, prince? You had him in your power—held him as he lay helpless. Did you finish what we began?"

Korusan's lungs were full of knives. He could not speak. There were blades in his throat, and his tongue was numb.

"He lives," the mage said. His voice was calm, expressionless, with an edge that might have been contempt. "You held his life in your hand, and you let it go."

"He has seduced you, prince," said another of the mages. It was a woman, a lightmage. He had not seen her before. "You are snared in his spell. For they do weave magery, those of his blood, all unknowing, and as they breathe, to make themselves beloved."

"When would you have given us leave to begin?" her master asked. "You forbade us in Kundri'j, before he had bound you. Now that you belong to him—"

"Koru-Asan is no one's slave," said the Master of the Olenyai, soft and deadly.

Master of Olenyai and Master of Mages stood poised on the edge of a new quarrel. Korusan found his voice somewhere and beat it into submission. "No, I did not kill him. If I am enslaved to him, then so is he to me. I will take him when and as I please, and ask no one's leave."

"So you said in Kundri'j," said the Master of the Guild. "And we gave him to you, laid him at your feet, and you pleased to let him live. There are good men dead because of him, strong mages destroyed, an empire in worse disarray than it has ever been."

"Blame him not for that," Korusan said, clipping the words off short. "You would not wait for me to take him from behind. You must open your Gate, proclaim your presence to every mage in every temple from westernmost Veyadzan to the Eastern Isles, declare open war upon the body of the empress mother, rouse the emperor's wrath and with it his magic—and you cry foul against him for your own immeasurable folly?"

"And how long would we wait?" the mage shot back. "Years, prince? Decades? While you wallow in his bed, come crawling at his bidding, weep tears of bliss when he permits you to kiss his fundament?"

Korusan could not kill him. That would be too simple. Marid would happily have done it for him. He restrained his swordbrother with a glance, and looked the mage up and down. "I had wondered," he said, "whether you were arrogant or a fool. Now I am certain. You are a perfect idiot." He drew his lesser sword, the left-handed blade, and stepped forward. The mage went grey-green. He held it before the man's eyes. "Your life is mine. Tempt me and I take it, magebound or no."

The blade flashed down, up. The mage gasped and clapped hand to brow. Blood dripped into his astonished eyes.

Korusan granted him a modicum of respect for keeping silence, though a blade as sharp as this wounded to the bone first and woke the pain long after.

The mage vanished in a flurry of light robes and dark. Korusan turned his back on them. The lordlings and the Olenyai waited in varying degrees of stillness. "You will wait," he said, "until the empress has had her death-rite. Then I promise you, we bring all of this to its end."

The Olenyai inclined their heads. The lordlings went down on their faces.

He swept his blade clean along the edge of his outer robe and sheathed it, and looped up the veils again. Some of the mages had left their master and faced him. He could not read them, whether they pondered threat or submission.

"You thought that you had simple enemies," he said to them: "a Sunlord who had slain his own magic and left himself open to your power, a son of the Lion so enfeebled by the failing of his blood that he would be your puppet, your creature and your slave. Long years you labored to create us both: he the weakling, easily destroyed; I the weakling, easily mastered. I will take what is mine, mages. Have you no least doubt of that. But I will take it as I will, and when I will, and where. You will serve me then. You will do as I bid."

He had no care for resentment or anger or thwarted pride. They gave him all of that. But they gave him also silence, and slowly, one by one, the lowering of proud eyes, the bending of stiff necks.

He turned on his heel. There had been bodies between himself and the door. They barred his way no longer.

* * *

Sheer white-hot will kept him on his feet through the maze that was that house, past the watchers and the guards, into the twilit street. People passed, scurrying from the shadow of him. His stride slowed. He stumbled, caught himself.

He would come to the palace again. He had willed it, therefore it must be. But it would be no easy journey. The knives in his lungs had sharpened. The ache in his bones was fiercer now, almost too much to ignore.

He was not dying. He would not allow it. He would walk, so, one foot before the other. Walls helped him; where they were not, he willed the air to hold him up.

It was no more difficult than the run through the mages' wood that had begun his initiation into the Olenyai, nor any more impossible than running from that ensorceled place into the test of wits and will against the mages' snares. Certainly it was no less simple than standing robed, veiled, two-sworded, Olenyas, and yet naked before a pair of golden eyes in a black eagle's face. All that, he had done. This too he would do.

He was aware of the shadow as it moved. Oh, he was feeble: he should have known it before ever he saw it, sensed it waiting, slipped round to catch it by surprise. He tried to leap aside, but his feet were leaden heavy. He stumbled and fell.

No blade swept his head from its neck. "Sweet Avaryan!" said the shadow in a voice he knew. He had not known how cordially he hated it, or even yet how weak he was, till he felt her hands on him, pulling him up, and no will in him to resist.

The Islander draped his arm about her neck. She was smaller than he but sturdy enough, no doubt from hauling nets since she was big enough to stand. One hand gripped his wrist. The other circled his middle and closed on his belt. So joined, like drunken lovers, they swayed and staggered homeward.

Such as home was, a palace sunk in the stillness of exhaustion, guards alert to every shadow, and its heart a dead empress, a dying priest, an emperor drugged into a stupor. Korusan was recovering somewhat, but Vanyi was too strong for him. She half-carried, half-dragged him into a chamber that must be her own, and lowered him to the narrow bed. She was gentler than she looked.

He struggled to sit up. "I cannot—I must—"

She held him down with one hand. He struck it aside and surged to his feet. Pain ripped through him. He gasped. The gasp caught on hooks and tore.

It was true, what they said. One could cough up one's lungs. One did it in racking agony, in bloody pieces.

His veils were gone. A basin hovered in front of him. Hands held it, and eyes behind that, eyes as grey as flints.

"Yes," she said. "Now you have to kill me. You can wait till you're done dying."

"I am not—" he said. Tried to say. His throat was raw, his voice scraped bare.

"Stop it," she said. Damnable arrogant peasant. "The blood's given out, hasn't it? It's a miracle you've lived as long as you have."

"Kill me, then," he whispered, since he could not say it louder. "Get it over."

"Oh, no," she said. "You belong to Estarion. He's the one to say whether you live or die."

"What? Is he your god?"

She smiled a blade-thin smile. "No. But I think he's yours."

That outrage laid him flat. The knives at least were not sunk so deep, the pain faded to a dull roar. He was weak beyond bearing, but he would live, he thought, for yet a while.

She laid the basin aside without apparent revulsion at its contents, and bent over him. Her hands ran down the length of him, not touching. His flesh quivered. Magery. Hers was less repellent than the others he had known, the pain of it sharper, but it was a clean pain.

"Goddess," she muttered. "You're a patchwork of ill-matched magics. What were they trying to do to you? Kill you quicker, or kill you more slowly? Or couldn't they make up their minds?"

He refused to answer. She took no notice. "That's half the

trouble. Look, there, that mending goes to war with this, and this—" She spat a word that must have been a curse. "Hedge-wizards! Why in the hells couldn't they have let you crumble away in peace?"

"Perhaps I wished to live," he said.

She paused. She seemed surprised that he could speak, even in a croak. But she did not know Olenyai hardihood.

"You are a pretty thing," she said. "That must be why he fancies you."

He bit his tongue. He was feeling stronger. More magery; but again it was different. He could, in a fashion, see through it into the mage herself: a tang that was jealousy, a white heat that must be her magic, a great bright singing thing that seemed to be part of Estarion, and yet was not.

It was for that that she healed him. Because she fancied that she saw it in him also, and because she thought that he had power, somehow, to guard the emperor. She, like the Guild-mages, believed that there had been a test; that Korusan had passed it, and proved himself bound to Estarion. And no one so bound could turn traitor. It was not possible.

Nor was this that she did. She could not make him whole. That was beyond any mage's power. But she could give him a few days' life—cycles, she was thinking, even years. But his bones knew better.

He rose carefully, drew a breath. It did not catch. He flexed his shoulders. They ached, but no more than they should.

She sat on her heels, watching him. He could kill her now. He had his swiftness back, and his strength. She was unarmed, unwary, bone-weary as mages were after a working. She would die before she mustered wits to move.

Estarion loved her. There was no accounting for it—she had neither beauty nor lineage nor sweetness of temper to endear her to any man, let alone an emperor—but Korusan could hardly escape the truth of it.

"I let you live," he said to her, "because I am not ungrateful. And because you belong to him."

"I do *not*—"

Her anger startled him; it made him laugh, which startled her. They stared at one another in sudden silence.

"I begin to understand," she said, "what else he sees in you."

Not until he was long away from her did it strike Korusan what she had done.

He was Olenyas. He was—or he thought he had been—warded against magic. And she had worked magic on him. Easily, potently, as if there had been no defenses on him at all.

He should be alarmed, but he was grimly delighted. Guild-mages scorned her for her common lineage, her lack of training in their arts of magic. And she made nothing of their magics on him; spat contempt at the weaving of them. She was more than they could imagine, greater danger than they might have anticipated.

It would be a pleasure to see their faces when they learned what this priestess-witch was. Even if he died thereafter, he would die in some measure of content.

45

WHEN ESTARION WOKE from his drugged sleep, he was alone. But there was a memory of presence—piercing to senses that, dulled for so long, were grown painfully keen. Haliya. As easily as he breathed, his magery followed the trail of her out of the room and through a maze of passages to the women's chambers. He did not track her within. She was safe there among his mother's guards.

Wild joy smote him. Mage—he was a mage again. But then with memory came the stab of grief, felling him even as he rose.

Merian was dead. He had quarreled with her endlessly, fretted the bonds of love, duty, honor, flown in the face of them all until surely she would learn to hate him. But she never had, no more than he had hated her for what she was: empress, priestess, mother of his body.

Robed as a priest but cloaked as a king, he went in to the hall where she lay. They had given her a bier worthy of her royalty, coverlets of silk, great pall of cloth of gold. She lay in the stillness of the dead, her beautiful hair woven into the many plaits of a northern queen. Gold was on her breast above the pall, and gold in her ears, and gold set with jewels on her arms, her wrists, her fingers.

Her panoply, she had always called that, like the armor that a king wore into battle. When she would be in comfort she wore an old threadbare robe, her hair loose or braided down her back, and no jewel but the armlet that her royal lover had given her before he made her his empress.

That she wore still, a plain thing amid the rest, copper that was much prized among her people, inlaid with golden wires shaping a skein of dancing women. She was the tall one, the one whose beauty shone even through the rough unskillful work. For her Sunlord had made it himself, given it to her in shyness that by all accounts was alien to him, and in accepting it, she had accepted all of him—not the man alone but the empire he ruled.

Now they danced together on the other side of the night. Their son knelt by her bier, hands fisted in the pall, and wept.

He wept hard, but he did not weep long. He raised his head. Her guards, tall women in bright armor, had averted their eyes. Tears glistened on their cheeks.

He scrubbed them from his own. His eyes had burned dry. He would not weep again.

Rage swelled where grief had been, rage as white and cold and pitiless as the sun that pierced the high windows of the hall.

It thrust him to his feet. It drove him through the palace in a train of startled people, animals, even a lone brainless bird that had escaped its cage.

The rebels who had begun it all were gone. He began to order out the hunt; then paused. They were but puppets. Whether they thought they acted of themselves, or knew that they were a feint, it did not matter. He knew. He had memory of the Gate, and of the powers that sustained it.

First he must look to the care of his mother's body. She would not be burned as priests of the Sun were; she was priestess of the goddess, and would be given to the dark and the silence. He did not know that he wished her entombed here, unless he made the whole city her tomb; and that was madder even than he was minded to be. A place waited for her in Endros Avaryan beside the body of her lord, in the tomb of the emperors beneath the Tower of the Sun. Yet that was far to go, and revolt between, that might swell to war. And there was the matter of revenge for her death.

Sunlords are above revenge. Her voice, his memory tricking him in a dart of sunlight.

Sunlords had never needed revenge; never, until Estarion, been the playthings of hidden enemies. Sarevadin who had been taken by mages and stripped of all but the raw self, had known by whom she was taken, and why. Hers had been open war, mage against mage and no quarter given.

He was prey to poison, treason, assassins. They had taken his father, his mother, his servant. They had robbed him of youth and strove now to rob him of manhood.

No more.

"My lord."

A priest, a mage in torque and braid, tawny head bent. Estarion stared at him, empty for the moment of speech.

"My lord, will you come?"

"To what?" Estarion asked him. "Treachery?"

The priest's head flew up. He was not pure Asanian: that pride was a plainsman's, and those eyes, yellow though they were, narrow above the high cheekbones. Power shimmered on him, bright with anger. "Yes, my lord, there has been treachery. The high priest of Avaryan in Endros is dying because of it. Will you deign to visit him on his deathbed?"

No, Estarion thought. There was no reason in it, no mortal sense.

The priest had no pity for him. "I would not have troubled you, sire. But he insisted."

How odd to be despised. How rare. He was loved or he was hated. Sometimes he was feared. But scorn—that was a new thing.

"Take me," he said.

They had laid Iburan in a room that must have been a servant's, with a bed as narrow as a northerner's, and no softening of silks or velvets. Braziers there were none. He did not need them. He had his priests and his priestesses, and the heat of their power.

He lay in the midst of them, burning with fever. His body could bear no touch of coverlet; his weight upon the bed was pain. The torque about his neck burned as if it had been molten, but none of them had dared to take it off.

He should have been dead long ago, but he clung to life with fierce persistence.

Estarion thrust through a wall of pain, and dropped to one knee beside the bed. The face that had been so beautiful was ravaged with poison. The body was grossly swollen, suppurating with sores. It stank.

Just so, he thought, remote and burning cold. Just so had his father been.

"They lack imagination, our enemies," he said.

Dark eyes opened in the ruined face. They warmed at sight of Estarion. The voice was a husk of itself, but there should have been no voice at all. "Starion. Still angry with me, then?"

"No," Estarion said. "Never again, foster-father."

Iburan's eyes filled with tears. They scalded as they overflowed. With infinite gentleness Estarion wiped them away. Even that cost Iburan pain.

"I took your power," Estarion said. He had not known till he said it. The horror came after; the bleak hatred of himself. "I have killed you."

"My own fault," said Iburan, "for getting in the way."

"Mine," cried Estarion. "My fault. Oh, Avaryan! It's I who should be dead, and not you."

"Stop that," said Iburan. "Time enough when we're all dead, to squabble over the bones. Now listen to me. While you were dealing with mages—and dealing surpassingly well, too; you were a marvel to watch—I happened to notice a thing or two. It slowed me down when I should have been getting out of your way, which was foolish of me, but I learned somewhat. Watch your Olenyai, Starion. If they aren't part of this, they know enough to damn them in any court of justice."

Estarion did not care. Iburan was dying, Merian was dead. What did anything matter but that?

But Iburan's intensity held him, and his hand, clasping Estarion's wrist with a shadow of its old strength. "Listen to me, Estarion. Watch them. The one they set to spy on you—the young one with the lion-eyes—"

"He's no spy," Estarion snapped, forgetting to be gentle.

Iburan paid no attention. "He'll kill you if he can. He's been ordered to do it."

"He loves me," Estarion said.

Iburan sighed. His breath rattled; he coughed. "No doubt he does. He hates you, too. Watch him, Estarion. Promise me."

The light in Iburan's eyes was fading, his grip weakening. It was only the mages' light, Estarion tried to tell himself, flickering as it was wont to do.

"Starion," said Iburan, "when you sing the death-rite for her—remember—how she loved best the hymn of the morning star. Sing that for her, for me."

"You'll sing it yourself," Estarion said with sudden fierceness. "You won't die. I won't let you."

He called his power. It was white fire, hot gold, sun's splendor. The priest-mages fell back, struck to fear. They remembered too well what that torrent of magery had done. Its consequence lay before them, dying powerless.

"No."

It was simple, barely to be heard, and it had no magic in it. But it checked the calling of Estarion's power. It held him motionless.

"Starion, don't. I'm too far gone. And, son of my heart, much as I love you, I think it's time I left you. I've guarded you, bound you, held you back till I nigh destroyed you. Better for you that I go. I've no fear of the dark land. She's waiting for me there, and her lord, my lord, whom I loved."

"You said you loved me more."

That was unworthy, but Iburan did not say so. He smiled, a stretching of cracked and bleeding lips. "Ah, child, that's why I leave you. The god never granted me a son of my body; and yet I never felt the lack."

Estarion's throat locked shut. He forced the words through it. "The god granted me a father twice over. Now he takes you from me as he took the other. Exactly—as—"

"That's merely justice," Iburan said. His fingers slipped from Estarion's wrist.

Estarion caught them, cradled them. "Foster-father—"

Iburan was still smiling.

So easily, after all, he went. Between one breath and the next: he lived, and then he did not. He slipped the flesh and all its torments as lightly as a lady sheds her garment, dropped it and rose winged, leaping into the light.

So could he have done at any time since he knew that he was dying. He had waited for Estarion. And Estarion had indulged himself in trifles. In sleep. In ramping about. In being a great roaring idiot.

So let him be for yet a while. He looked down at the empty, stinking thing that had been the greatest mage and priest in this age of the world. He kissed its brow, which already had begun to cool. He smoothed the beard, still beautiful on the ravaged breast, and folded the hands over it.

He straightened. The priests—his priests—returned his stare. Some were weeping. Some were angry. Some were both.

"I give him the Sun," he said. "By your leave."

"You have no need of that, Sunlord," said the proud one. Shaiyel, that was his name. He had not put himself forward before. In the clarity of grief, Estarion knew why. Anyone of Asanian blood in Keruvarion learned to walk softly round the emperor.

The taste in his mouth was bitter. He smiled through it. "And yet I ask your leave."

"Then you have it," said Shaiyel.

Estarion inclined his head. Shaiyel was not forsaking contempt for anything as simple as this, but he could grant justice where justice was due.

Estarion drew a breath. His power beat like a heart. He spread his hands above Iburan's body. The fire tried to bleed out of them; he held it back, though it burned and blistered.

The priests began to chant. It was not the death-chant but the sunrise-hymn, the song of praise to the god at his coming.

A shiver ran down Estarion's spine. The god was in him. Never so close before this, never so strong. It would master him; it would burn him to ash.

Then so be it.

He laid himself before the god. *As you will,* he thought, sang, was. *All, and only, as you will.*

He was the fountain and the source. He was the burning brand. He was the fire in the corn; he was the light on the spear. He was bright day in the dark land.

They were with him, all of them, not only the few who wrought the circle here. Priests and mages, servants in the temples, initiates on the world's roads, guardians at the Gates, attendants upon lords and princes—all gathered in the bright blaze that was his power. All knew what he wrought here; all wove themselves within it. He, their heart and their crown, took the body of the god's servant. He lifted it up, and it weighed no more than a breath. He filled it with light.

It burned like a lamp made of straw. Like a lamp it was beautiful, and like straw it was consumed. The shape of it lingered yet a while, a body of light. Then it too crumbled and sank into ash.

The light died. The circle withered and fell away. There was a great stillness.

Estarion looked down upon an empty bed. The impress of the body was in it still. "Great bear of the north," he said. "Great mage and priest. Dear god in heaven, dread goddess below, how I loved you."

The god's departing left him cold and ill and bleakly, grimly content. He did not remember what he said to the priests. He supposed that he had said something; they seemed a little comforted. One, the priestess who looked rather like Ziana, wept in his arms. He left her folded in Shaiyel's. They would all grieve together, once he had freed them from the vexation of his presence.

When he noticed again where he was, he was far from

them, surrounded by strangers. He blinked, clearing his sight to a frightened face, a voice babbling of something: "My lord, if you will eat, you have not touched a bite since yesterday, you should—"

Lord Shurichan, solicitous to silliness, transparently terrified lest he be found guilty of the empress' murder. He was guilty of much—Estarion could hardly approve of an agreement or three that he had made in the event of the emperor's death—but in that he had taken no part.

How simple to see the truth; how blinding the pain that came after it, the power swelling and pulsing, struggling to break free of encumbering flesh.

He was growing stronger, or more skilled. He swayed, but caught himself before anyone could wake to alarm. There was no mage near to recognize the hesitation for what it was. Only simple men, Asanians, who determined that he was weak with fasting, and herded him to a chamber and saw him plied with dainties until he ate simply to be rid of them. He drank considerably more than he ate. Korusan would have had something to say of that, but Korusan was nowhere about.

Dizzy with wine and wrath but steady on his feet, Estarion went in search of his guardsman.

He found the boy where he belonged, standing guard over Estarion's chambers. The sight of him woke something. It might have been rage. It might have been joy—black joy, that cried to Iburan's bright spirit: *See, he is mine. He loves me!*

Estarion pulled him within, shut the door on goggling faces, got rid of veils and robes and encumbrances and flung him down on the floor, as if he were the whole empire of Asanion and Estarion an army arrayed against it.

Korusan was not acquiescent. That weakness was not in his nature. But he allowed it. He did not struggle, though he could have fought free and felled Estarion if he had been so minded. He yielded because it was wise to yield, but, great dancer that he was, he yielded as it best pleased him, guiding where he seemed to be guided, leading where he might have been led.

And when they lay breathless, tangled in robes and rugs and one another, Estarion raised his head from Korusan's sweat-slicked breast. "Only you," he said, "could give me this."

"A fight?" asked Korusan.

"I'd have raped a woman," Estarion said.

"You would not." Korusan pulled him up and kissed him. "You are royally drunk. Who fed you so much wine? I will have his ballocks for it."

"You can't have them," Estarion said. "I need them. If not—for raping women—"

"You are incapable of any such thing. Now will you stop it before you grow maudlin? Tears are shameful enough. Tears soaked in wine are a disgrace."

"That too you give me," said Estarion, "brisk as a slap in the face. What would I be without you?"

"Dead," said Korusan. He wriggled free, sprang to his feet. But he did not move once he was up, standing half turned away, as if he did not know what to do next.

He had grown since first Estarion saw his face. He was a little taller, his shoulders visibly wider. He was less a boy, more the man that he was meant to be. But beautiful still. That would not change, however old he grew.

Estarion rose behind him, folded arms about him. "There now. I'm not going to die just yet."

Korusan was rigid. "And if I am? What will you do, my lord?"

"You aren't, either," Estarion said through the cold clenching in his middle. Not this one. Not this one, too. "See, you don't even have a fever. You're as well as I've ever seen you."

"Ask your priestess how that is. Ask her how much it cost her magic, to make me so."

Estarion started. "You went to Vanyi?"

He had not seen her with those about Iburan. She should have been there. She would tear herself with grief, that she had not.

"She came to me." Korusan's breath caught. It might have

been laughter. "Or I fell at her feet. I shall have to kill her, my lord. She saw my face."

"Kill her," said Estarion with deadly lightness, "and I kill you."

"And then, no doubt, yourself." Korusan sighed. His stiffness eased a little; he leaned back against Estarion. "She would almost be worthy of you, if she had any lineage to speak of."

"How perfectly Asanian," Estarion said.

"I am perfect Asanian," said Korusan.

THE SUN SET in a sky as lucent and as brittle as ice. The city was quiet, but it was the quiet of exhaustion. Where the rebellion would flare again, or when, no one knew. Not even Estarion.

He had begun that bleak day beside his mother's bier. He chose to end it there. In the morning he must sing her death-rite. Then she would go to the embalmers, who would prepare her for the long journey to her tomb.

Tonight she lay in peace. He dismissed the guards, who granted him that right, to keep the last vigil alone. His tears were all shed. He was as still as she was, and nigh as cold. His flesh felt little enough of it; the Sun's fire warmed it. But his heart was as hard as her cheek beneath his hand, and as icily chill.

Someone breathed close by. He whipped about.

Ulyai padded out of the shadows beyond the candles' light. Her cubs followed in a wary line, and behind them the woman whose name, after all, he did not know, nor anything of what she was. To his newborn mage-sight she was a dark glass, clear to the bottom and yet revealing nothing but a shadow of his own face.

The ul-queen stretched herself at the bier's foot. Her she-cubs pressed close. The he-cub sought the colder comfort of Estarion's knee. So high already. He would be tall, that one.

Sidani walked past Estarion as if he had not been there, round the bier, to bend over the figure that lay on it. Estarion had ceased to be astonished at anything she did, but this verged on impertinence. He opened his mouth to say so.

"She had Asanian blood, you know," the wanderer said, "and royal at that. Hirel never knew that he had a daughter among the tribes. It mattered little to them; it was carelessness in a chieftain's daughter, or willfulness, to bear the child of the one they called the little stallion. That's how you come by your eyes, youngling. She carried the Lion's blood, too—as much as your father did."

"When did Hirel ever—"

"On a time," she said, "when Sarevadin, proud idiot that he was, had slain a mage with power, and lost his own in return. It should have killed him. He found the Zhil'ari instead, and his companion found a diversion to sweeten the evenings. In the end they came to Endros and the Sunborn, and Sarevadin had healing, of a sort, though he hardly knew it then. He'd lost his magery beyond retrieving. He'd gained something that, once known, was more by far."

Estarion looked at her and knew that she was mad. But it was a seductive madness, of a most persuasive sort. It tempted a man to give himself up to it as if it were true. "Is that a secret, lady? That those who kill with magery become greater than mages?"

"Goddess forbid," said Sidani. "We'd have a world full of warring mages else, blasting one another to ash in the hope of becoming gods."

"You make no sense," Estarion said.

"I make perfect sense," she said. "You're a great killer of mages. Has it made you hungry for more?"

He could have killed her for that. He held himself rigid; smiled, even, wide and feral. "You can't imagine what it's made me."

"Oh, but I can." Her own smile was sweetly terrible. "You are a menace, child. You think that you have yourself in hand; you imagine that you can go on as you are now, a little colder maybe, a little harder, but shouldn't an emperor be cold and hard? That's pride too, and folly."

"You know nothing," he said, low in his throat. "You are a nameless gangrel woman with more addlement than wits."

"I had a name once," she said. She laid her hand on the

empress' cheek. "So beautiful," she said, "and so cold. How Mirain would have raged to see a priestess of the goddess upon the double throne, mother to its heir, regent of its empire. He was madder than any of us, and blinder. He could never see the dark for the blaze of the light."

"You speak treason," Estarion said.

She laughed long and free. "Oh, that word! So easy on the tongue; so deadly on the neck. I've spoken worse than that in my day, and to haughtier kings than you."

"How can anyone—"

He caught himself. She grinned, reading him as easily as she ever had. "You're nothing to some I've seen. You're a gentle one for all your fierceness; you wear another's skin too easily to be honestly cruel. Cruelty takes a certain lack of imagination, you see."

"I'd have thought it took the opposite."

"No," she said. "That's mere cleverness. True wit needs more."

"I have little enough of any of that," he said, neither wry nor precisely angry. He was tired suddenly, tired of everything. Even of what he knew she would say, that he was a master of self-pity.

But, being Sidani, she did not say it. "You were broken young, and you mended crooked. Surgeons know what to do when they see the like. They break again, then set anew, and this time set it straight."

"You'll break me?" Estarion asked. Humoring her, he told himself. Passing the long night in this strange painful amusement.

"You're broken already," she said. "Are your hands bleeding gold?"

He clenched them, pressing them to his thighs. "No!"

"You're a dreadful liar, child." She came round the bier again and took his hands. He mustered every scrap of will to resist her. None of it mattered in the least. Her fingers were cold, but there was heat within, a thread of fire. They pressed just so, and his hands unfolded.

The left hand was trembling; blisters had risen on it, grey against the dark skin. The right was all gold, roiling and flowing in the bed of the *Kasar*.

"Sages," she said as if to herself, "would set the seat of power in the loins, or in the heart, or behind the eyes. And so it is, in all of them and none. But in Sun-blood, wherever it begins, it ends in the hands. There's the god's wit for you. Where else is pain so intense, or so delicately modulated?"

Estarion had an answer for that. He bit his tongue, but she read it, perhaps in his branded palm.

She laughed. "Yes, there too. But the god set fire there long ago, and in every man—and in a woman it's not so easily got at, though it's hotter once it starts, and lasts longer. The hands it had to be. Do you think you're being brave, bearing pain that would lay strong warriors low?"

"It's no worse than it ever is," Estarion said.

"Liar," she said tenderly. "Ah, child, what a muddle they've made of you."

"Isn't that what we all are? Muddle and folly?"

"Everyone doesn't threaten empires with his muddlement." She touched the *Kasar* with a finger. He gasped: not that it cost pain, but that it cost none. A ripple of coolness spread outward from her touch.

"How—"

She was not listening. "And you are a threat, youngling. Never doubt it. You'll carry on for a while, and think yourself safe; but when you break again, you'll break past mending. A Sunlord broken is a terrible thing. Pure power, and pure mindlessness."

Yes, a deep part of him whispered, looking down into the sea of fire. "No," he said aloud. "What do you know of this? What do you know of anything?"

"What do you know, my lord emperor? Have you looked

on the face of the Sunborn in his sleep? Have you stood in the Tower that he made?"

"It has no door," Estarion said. "And if it did, what good would it do me?"

"Why," she said, "none, for all the use you'd have made of it. A door is a simple thing to make. It's what it opens on that matters. Mirain made that Tower of magery, and sealed it with the Sun's fire. His own fire, child. The same that burns in you and leaves trails of golden droplets wherever you go. It's not simple power such as mages know, that they draw from earth and air and wield through their bodies. It's a different thing, both stronger and stranger. Training alone doesn't master it. It needs more. It needs what is in the Tower."

"And what is that?"

"Strength," she said. "Knowledge. It's woven in the stones. It holds the Sunborn in his sleep, and guards the bones of his descendants. A night on the crag of Endros would drive a man mad; and so it still might, if anyone dared the Tower. But a man who is a Sunlord—he needs that madness, that snatching out of himself. It's the source of his power."

Estarion laughed, startling himself. "Oh, you are a master of talespinners! You almost had me believing you."

"I hope so," she said. "It's almost too late for you. And that 'almost' is more hope than surety."

"Oh, come," he said. "Now you're trying to scare me, as if I were a child with the night-terrors. I need lessoning in reining in my power, I admit it. But once this rebellion is put down and the empire is quiet, I'll withdraw to a temple; I'll submit myself to its mages; I'll learn to master myself."

"You have no time," said Sidani. "Even tomorrow's sunset might be too long. Look, you're bleeding again. That's blood, child: blood of power."

"Then I'll bleed dry, and be no worse than before."

For the first time she seemed impatient. *"Tcha!* You are the most exasperating infant. Power doesn't bleed like blood, not in Sunlords. It kills you, yes. But first it kills whatever else it lights on, and it grows stronger instead of weaker, the longer it bleeds, until there's no will left, only the power. What you were when it killed a mage's soul, what it was when it plucked mages free of their power as if they had been sea-spiders in their shells—that's the barest beginning. Your high priest is dead because you had no mind to notice that it was he and not a Guildmage standing in your path. What, when you begin to feed on your priests here, and after them, priests and mages wherever your power finds them? And when they are gone and your hunger still unsated, what's to do but seek the souls of simple men, and consume them?"

"No!" cried Estarion, struggling against her grip, trying to block his ears, his mind, his awareness that whispered, *Yes. Yes.* "It's all lies. You're raving. How can you know this? *Who are you?*"

"Sarevadin."

That was not her voice. It was colder by far, and somewhat deeper. It came out of the darkness, a shadow, golden-eyed. Another came behind it.

He almost wept at the sight of them—and no matter the riddle of their coming in together, priestess and Olenyas, and standing there as if they had been so for a long while, watching, listening, waiting for their moment. "Korusan! Vanyi. Thank the god and goddess. I've fallen prey to a madwoman."

Then the name that Korusan had spoken pierced through the veils of befuddlement. Korusan spoke it again. "I know what she is. I followed her here, and your priestess after me. She is Sarevadin. Look, take her hand."

She had let Estarion go. Instinct cried out to him to thrust himself as far away as he might, but something made him do as Korusan bade. She did not resist him, did not seem dismayed, stood smiling faintly as he seized her hand and turned it palm up.

Gold and ash. Gold—and—

He was not even awed. What struck him first was pity, and

horror of the quenched and twisted thing. "What did you do to yourself?"

"I tried to cut it out," she said.

He raised his eyes from the ruin of the *Kasar* to the ruin of her face.

No; not ruin. He had always thought her beautiful, with her proud bones under the age-thinned skin. "You look like your portraits," he said.

"Not much, any longer," she said.

"No," said Estarion. Obstinacy was a refuge. It kept him from having to think. "We all know you're dead, you see. And we look at the portraits and see the hair, like copper and fire, and take little enough notice of what's under it, except that it's a woman, and beautiful."

"You'd never hide as I did," she said.

"Why?"

She knew that he did not mean himself, or his eyes that could never be mistaken, not in such a face as his, but the fact of her abandoning it all, throne and empire and the power that she was born to hold. They had always understood one another. They were of the same blood.

"If you were given a chance at freedom," she asked him, "would you take it?"

"That would depend on the price," he said.

"I paid in my lord's life. I thought that I should die with him, and leave our son free to take the throne for which we bred him. I failed in courage once I'd taken the sword and set myself to fall on it; so I killed myself who was Sarevadin, but left the body alive. I became no one and nothing."

He looked at her. Something monstrous swelled in him, something that was not joy, nor terror, but a welter of both. "Then I have no right to any of this. It is yours. You are the empress who should be. You are the elder heir of the Sunborn."

"I think," she said after a long pause, "that this is your revenge on me for keeping my secret so long."

Estarion was too numb with shock to be appalled. "You don't want it?"

"Youngling," she said, "do you?"

He sucked in a breath. Her hand was still in his, forgotten. He laid his own over it, *Kasar* to *Kasar*. It was a perilous thing to do, but he was past caring. The lightnings jolted through him. He was fiercer than they. She stood like a rock in a tiderace, head tilted back, half glaring, half laughing in his face.

He had not stood face to face with living blood of his sun-born blood since his father was slain. He had forgotten, if he had ever known, what it was to know that whatever he was or willed to be, there was one who was his equal. Or—and that was stranger yet—his better.

"Now will you believe me?" she asked him.

He had almost forgotten what brought them to the quarrel. It was like her to remember.

"It is true, Starion." Vanyi, hard and clear. She stood behind Korusan still, her white robe like a shadow of his black one. "You will lose yourself in your power, unless you master it."

"And that needs the Tower in Endros?" Estarion spoke to them both, all, it hardly mattered. "If I ride out now, will I be alive when I come to it?"

"There is another way," said Sarevadin.

Estarion's glance leaped to Vanyi, caught on Korusan's veiled face. That the women had conspired to trap him—he could credit that. But he did not think that the Olenyas had had any part in it. The boy's eyes were wide, blank, astonished.

"Gates," Estarion said. "But the Mageguild wields them."

"Did I say it would be easy?" Vanyi was trembling as if with exhaustion, or with fury held rigidly in check. "You don't know what you look like to eyes that can see. The whole of the mage-realm pulses as you breathe. She"—she would not name the name, Estarion took note of that; had she perhaps not known until he himself did?—"says that there is a way to tame your power, to teach you what you have to know without the years that you don't have. You don't even have days."

"I may be stronger than any of you can guess," he said.

"You are a worse idiot than we could have imagined." Sarevadin slapped him lightly, just enough to sting. In the swift flare of his temper, she grinned her wild white grin. "There is a way, young one. Yon priestess says that she can raise a Gate. That's dangerous; I don't pretend it isn't. But if we move quickly, and if we move as I know how to move, we'll be there before the Guild knows what we've done."

"There," said Estarion, "but not back again."

"You'll take us back," she said. "Or we'll all die together."

"All?" Estarion asked.

"I'm going," Vanyi said. "I know Gates, and I can stand guard while you do—whatever you do."

"But you're not—"

"She's not Sun-blood," Sarevadin said. "She's not male, either. She'll not lose her wits in my father's Tower."

Her father. One forgot, or could not encompass it. This was Sidani the wanderer woman with her wild wit and her scurrilous tales, putting guardsmen to the blush with the songs she could sing. And it was Sarevadin the empress, great beauty of her age, great mage, great queen, great lover and priestess. This, standing by the bier of another empress, bidding Estarion do the maddest thing that he had ever done.

Walk through a Gate in defiance of the Guild that had risen against him. Enter the doorless Tower. Look on the sleeper who must not be waked, and mend his power that was broken, or die in the trying. With a priestess on Journey for defender, and a madwoman for a guide.

He spread his arms. "Well? Shall we go?"

"No," said Sarevadin.

His jaw had dropped. He picked it up again.

"It needs time," she said, "and your mother wants singing to her rest. And you should sleep. Tomorrow when the rite is sung and the feast is done, we go. Go light on the wine, youngling. You'll want your head clear for the working."

The hot flush crawled up his cheeks. He fought it with temper. "All this desperate urgency, and you'll dally at the end of it?"

"You will dally," she said. "We will labor long and hard to make ready. Gates aren't raised in a heartbeat; Gates warded with secrecy are slower yet."

"But I can—"

"You cannot," she said, flat and implacable. "You will sleep, if I have to lay a wishing on you, and you will play the emperor as your people require, and when it's over, you will find us waiting." She softened somewhat. "Don't worry, child. You'll have enough and more to do, once you're in the Tower."

KORUSAN ESCAPED IN Estarion's shadow. They all seemed to have forgotten him, the women caught up in the working that they must begin, Estarion in a temper at being sent to bed like a child. He went obediently enough, Korusan noticed, for all his snarling; he took the he-cub with him, which its dam did not appear to take amiss.

Korusan did not follow Estarion to his chambers. At first not caring where he went, then only seeking solitude, he found himself in what seemed to be an ancient portion of the palace, dank and dim and long untenanted. A torch was thrust into a wall at one of the turnings. Korusan lit it with a flint that he carried, with much else, secreted in his robes, and the steel blade of one of his lesser daggers. It caught sullenly, but burned bright enough for the purpose.

The cold was deep here, set in the stones. The walls were faded and peeling, the tiles of the floor broken or gone. The air was heavy with age and dust.

A stair presented itself. Korusan climbed it. His lips twitched in spite of themselves. Estarion, when vexed with the need to think, always climbed as high as he could, and perched there above the babble of the world; and then, as often as not, did no thinking at all, but simply basked in the sun.

No sun tonight, but stars like flecks of frost, and Brightmoon riding high. Her light was cold and pure and, Korusan thought, rather prim. She had no rival in the sky: Greatmoon would not rise until just before the dawn.

Korusan stood on a roof that ended in a crumbling parapet. It gave way behind him to a landscape of peaks and sudden valleys that was the newer palace, but before him was nothing but a stretch of winter-bare garden, a high wall, and the roofs of the city. Every so often a guard walked the wall. The man did not see the shadow on the roof, or else did not reckon it worth remarking on.

Korusan sank down, wrapped in his robes. He was shivering, the ache in his bones returning after its few hours' grace. He drew up his knees and clasped them, and rocked.

Now, he thought, was the time. Sarevadin had shown herself to her grandson's grandson. He had offered her his throne, and she had laughed him down. And given Korusan, at last, the key to what he must do.

He should go to the Master of the Olenyai. Once Estarion was gone on his wild hunt, the field would be free; the empire would be theirs, to win and to hold. And if Estarion came back, he would come back to a battle long since lost; and if he did not, then he was dead, and nothing that his people did could matter.

They would think so, Olenyai and mages both. The mages would find a way, no doubt, to trap Estarion in his Tower, or at the least to confine him to Keruvarion. Estarion in Endros would set Asanion free.

And yet. Korusan rocked, frowning at nothing.

Suppose, he thought. Suppose that there was a way . . .

The Sunborn was alive. The mages said so. Mages could lie, but in this they swore to truth. The great mage and traitor, the Red Prince of Han-Gilen, had laid a sleep on him within his own Tower, because he would not yield to the constraints of peace. That sleep preserved him, unaging and undying, until the end of days. Or, some said, until he was called anew to war. He was always a warrior king, was Mirain An-Sh'Endor.

And if he woke, what then?

He had been mad when he fell into his sleep. Mad as Sarevadin feared that Estarion would be: conquered by his magic. It seemed to be a hazard of Sun-blood, that the Sun overwhelmed the man.

Suppose . . .

Korusan counted the aches in his bones. The priestess had

given him days, who might have had but hours before he died. He dreamed no longer that he would live to wear the mask of the emperor. If his own frailty did not kill him, the mages would see to it that he died before he took thought for rebellion.

Then they would rule. Or not. He cared little. He did not have Estarion's soft heart for the people who lived outside of palaces. Veilless, swordless, halfwit multitudes; they were no kin of his. If he freed them from the barbarian yoke, then that was no more than his duty. He could not be expected to love them on top of it.

Mages of the Guild would be no worse for the empire than mages of the Temple. And Asanion would be Asanion again. Let Keruvarion have its conquerors. The Golden Empire would suffer no rule but its own.

Estarion could live, if that were so. Emperor of half an empire, to be sure; but so had he been before his mother pricked him into entering Asanion.

Korusan's arms tightened about his knees. Estarion alive, not dead. Estarion alive without Korusan. For Korusan would be dead, and soon. That was as certain as the cycles of the moons.

Korusan alive without Estarion was inconceivable. Estarion without Korusan . . .

"No," said Korusan, loud in the stillness. "He is mine. No one else shall have him. No woman, no man, no throne or empire. No one."

Estarion stalked snarling into his chambers, with the he-cub stalking at his heels. His vigil was broken, his mood ungodly. And it was barely midnight; long hours yet till dawn.

He had stripped, flinging garments and ornaments at anything that would stop them, before he knew that he was not alone. The ul-cub crouched in front of a small huddled person with eyes even yellower than the cub's. They watched one another with equal, wary intentness.

"Did he grow overnight?" Haliya asked, looking up into Estarion's face.

Estarion bit off sharp words. She looked cold sitting there, even wrapped in furs, white and amber and spotted gold. He, naked, was like a fire burning. He knelt and wrapped arms about her.

Haliya was tense in the circle of his embrace. "He has a name now, I think," she said. "Has he told you what it is?"

"No," Estarion said, startled. "You said you weren't a mage."

"I'm not," she said. "I'm a Vinicharyas, which is something different. He'll tell you when he's ready, I suppose. Do you have a fever? You're hot as iron in the forge."

"That's Sun-blood," he said. "The colder it is, the hotter I burn."

"And you're angry," said Haliya. "She got at you, didn't she? That horrible old woman. She says she's dead. Her body just hasn't admitted it yet."

"Her body has been failing to admit it for fifty years." Estarion shuddered in his skin. "I used to worship the memory of her. The reality . . . it's so much more. And so much less."

"That's usually the way of it." She eased a little, enough to stroke his face. "The dead should stay decently dead."

Her hand was small and cold and yet surprisingly strong. He turned his head, kissed her palm. There was no desire in him, not for her, not tonight, but he was not sorry, after all, that she was here. Friends had been simple for him once, and many, and since he came to this cursed half of his empire he had lost them all. But he had gained Haliya.

She was warming as he held her. Her shivering had stopped.

"You were with me," he said, "while I slept, and worse than slept. You kept running away before I could wake. Did I frighten you so much?"

"No," she said. It was not precisely a lie, but she could not meet his eyes while she said it. "I didn't want to trouble you."

"You could never do that," he said.

The he-cub thrust in between them. Haliya went rigid. The cub sprang into her lap. He filled the space between them. Her face was white beyond the cat's shadow-dark head. Estarion let her go, moved to thrust the beast away.

"No," she said, catching his hand. "No, don't."

"You're terrified of him."

Temper brought her eyes flashing up. "I will learn not to be. He's young, he's small. By the time he's grown I'll be as brave as you."

"By the time he's grown he'll be big enough to ride."

She put out a hand. It trembled, but it stroked the cub capably enough. He filled her lap and flowed over, lolling in her furs, butting against the curve of her belly.

Estarion was not terribly surprised. Not then. Not after all the rest. Ulyai's son traced the shape of her with remarkable clarity.

She must have conceived the first time Estarion went in to her, or the second. Unless—

No. She had been a maiden. She had known no man since. And he knew already how determined the Sun's arrows could be.

He laid his hand where the life in her was strongest, where it swam and rolled and dreamed.

It, no. He. Bright web of Sun-blood, its center a spark of fire. He would be mageborn; was mage already, waking to the touch of the *Kasar.* Her hand leaped to cover Estarion's. "He moved! He kicked me."

"He hasn't before?"

"Oh, yes," she said, "but never so hard. He knows you, my lord."

"Estarion."

"My lord Estarion."

She was laughing at him, crazy with relief. He narrowed his eyes. "That's why you were afraid. Why you hid. You didn't want me to know."

"I was afraid you'd send me back."

"So I would have," he said.

"You can't now," said Haliya. "It's safer here than anywhere out there."

"Gods," he said. "If my enemies knew . . ."

"They don't," said Haliya. Her face was hard, her voice was iron. "Nor shall they. I won't give them another target."

"You won't be able to hide it much longer," he said, "even wrapped in furs and hiding among the women."

"They guard me well," she said. "Especially your mother's armored women. And your priestess."

"Am I the only one who didn't know?"

She barely flinched. "Your priestess has known for a long time. The others either guessed, or I told them when your mother died. They had to know, to guard the heir."

"The heir." His tongue stumbled on the word. "You . . . really . . ."

"I won't lose him," said Haliya. "Vanyi has promised me that. He will be born alive, and he will be born strong."

"Vanyi knows." Estarion did not know what he felt. Pity, maybe. Fury, that she had tricked and trapped him, and never told him that it did not matter; that if he died, it was not ended. There was an heir. The line would go on. "She let me think that I was all there was."

"Maybe she thought it would be easier for you if you didn't know."

"Or easier for you," he said, "or for herself. She's a bitter, cruel creature sometimes, like the sea she comes from."

"And you love her," said Haliya.

She said it without pain, and without jealousy that he could perceive. "I love you," he said. He meant it. And not only for the child pressing against his hand, seeking the light of his presence.

"A man can love many women," said Haliya. "A woman finds it easier to love one man. I love you, I think. I like you more. Love's uncomfortable; it burns out. Liking is made to last."

"You'll teach him well, this son of ours," Estarion said.

"And you." She let fall her armor of furs and flung arms about his neck. The ul-cub spilled squalling to the floor. She did not notice.

His altered senses would have known her for a Vinicharyas even without the proof of her name. She made the world a clearer place while she held him in her arms. He was quiet there, at rest if not content.

Even his power was gentled, tamed and harnessed to his will. But this new clarity forbade him to dream that he might not after all be bound to seek his healing, or his death, in the Tower. There was no hope of escaping that.

He did not know that he wanted any. It was comforting in its bleak way, this knowledge that in two days, three at the utmost, he would most probably be dead.

She said nothing of it. She knew—he felt it in her. Vanyi had told her. Vanyi was not one to spare any creature pain, if she reckoned that pain necessary.

Haliya yawned, sighed, like the child she still in great part was. He carried her to bed. She would never be the singing fire that Vanyi was, or even Ziana; she did not need to be. Tonight she was content to hold and to be held, warm in his warmth, quiet in his quiet that she had made.

He closed his eyes, briefly as he thought. When he opened them, the air had changed to the chill that promises the dawn, and Haliya had left him. Servants were waiting with lamps and candles and the robes of the rite.

He was calm, greeting them. He submitted himself without protest; but it was not the empty passivity of his time in Kundri'j. He allowed this. He willed it. Tonight, by the god's mercy, he would end it.

The Tower of the Sun

48

DARKNESS WAS THE goddess' portion, and silence. But an empress must have the light and the singing for her honor's sake, now that she was dead.

Merian had never been one to shun the sunlight. She had mated with it, keeping the rites of the moon's dark, but when they were past, she stood in the sun when it was strongest, and loved it for its bright fire. Her child was the sun's child, but night's child too, with his dark face and his sun-gold eyes.

He gave her honor, and the music she had loved, singing the death-rite over her in the bitter-bright morning. The shell of her was cold under his hands, with ice in its still heart. He could have warmed her; burned her as he had her lover. But she would have the darker comfort of the tomb, and her emperor's bones beside her under the black Tower of Endros. Her cortege was chosen, her bier in the making. When the embalmers had done with her, she would go, across the long leagues of empire to the City of the Sun.

He would go before her. Tonight, at sunset and Greatmoonrise, god and goddess passing in the door of the night, the Gate would open. He would do what he must do. She might find him there when she came, laid on the stone beside his father.

He was calm now, empty even of grief. Some thought him numbed with wine, but he had touched none since before the death-vigil. He had not eaten, either, or drunk aught but a little water when he woke. There would be a feast after this rite. He would pretend to eat, although he did not need it. The sun was enough, and the cold clean air.

The hall was full of people, a glitter and shift of myriad

minds in his mage-sight. He was seeing almost wholly with it, had been since he left his chambers. It was a potent effort to see with eyes of the body, to look on dull flesh, mere stone, plain light of lamps and candles. So much simpler, so much more beautiful, to ignore the flesh and look on spirit bare.

And he had reckoned himself content without magery. It had come close to killing him, in soul if not in body. No spell of the Golden Palace, that, but a twisting in his own will.

And yet, he thought as the rite left him standing still and silent, and the choir of priests and priestesses sang the last of the great hymns: and yet it was an ill thing, what he had suffered this empire to become. He had not begun it, no, nor done more than continue what his fathers had done before him. But he had fostered it. There should have been one empire, one people, and there were two, eagle of the Sun and lion of Asanion yoked to the single chariot. They hated one another. They spoke of conquest and of conquerors. Keruvarion looked in scorn on fallen Asanion. Asanion turned on its Varyani emperor—not its own, never its own, always the barbarian, the alien, the foreigner—in murderous resentment.

They must be one. He might have said it aloud. No one heard him: the priestesses' descant soared high and piercing clear over the deep voices of the priests, drowning any lesser voice. He shaped the words again in the silence of his mind. *They must be one. Whatever comes of this that I do, whether I come back alive or lie dead in the Tower, the empires must be one empire. Or they break and fall, and shatter into warring shards.*

And if that would be so, then there could be no Golden Palace set apart, and no Palace of the Sun in the heart of the Hundred Realms. Kundri'j and Endros must not be separated. There must be a new city, a city that was of both and neither, set between the empires. And a new court, not Court of the Sun and Courts of the Lion but both together, Varyani, Asanian, and no distinction made between them.

And was he the Sunborn, to conceive such a purpose? He would be dead when the sun rose again, or worse than dead.

Nothing that he thought or willed or dreamed could be. He was a broken thing, a marred beginning. He would never come to more than that.

But his son might. He would give the child that, write it down when the rite was done, entrust it to the child's mother. Who would, god and goddess help her, be empress when he was gone.

The hymn soared to its crescendo and faded. He must sing the last words, the words that sealed the rite. For a terrible moment he had no words at all, no memory, only darkness and silence.

Then again he was full of light, and in the light, the music, and in the music, the words. "Dark lady, lady of the silence, Lady Night: come now, take your child, grant her rest. May the sun be gentle upon her. May the wind caress her. May the years tread light upon her bones."

Vanyi heard the singing from the heart of her own working. She was never there; there was always a duty to keep her away, always something to be done in Estarion's name. She should resent him profoundly. But she was not a reasonable creature when it came to Estarion. He knew what prices she paid—she had felt it when Iburan died, a tendril of thought that uncurled to touch her, then shrank away. He had expected her to be enraged.

That, not the necessity of her absence, roused her temper. So little he knew her. So ill he judged her.

And had she done anything to prove him false? What he had done in Asanion was as much her fault as anyone's. If she had not driven him away, he would not have gone to his yellow women. Haliya would not be huddled in her phalanx of guards, watching her emperor sing the empress mother to rest and reflecting in spite of herself upon the child she carried—how he too would sing these words, if the gods willed. She knew no sadness in the thought, and no fear that Vanyi could discern. She was not expecting to be empress as Merian had been.

Women in Asanion did not rule like men, with their faces naked to the world.

This would be empress-by-right if the night's working failed. This would rule, whether she willed it or no. This child, this innocent, this creature who was neither mage nor simple woman, but something between.

"She won't do badly," said Sarevadin, startling Vanyi back into herself. The walls of the palace chapel closed in once more, the wards set but not sealed, the substance of the Gate gathered but unformed. There was nothing to see with eyes of the body, and little with eyes of the mind but a mist of raw power under a shield and a ward. It was lumpen to the touch of her senses, inert.

Sarevadin crouched in front of it as if beside a wanderer's fire, arms resting on knees, eyes fixed on Vanyi. The angle of the light caught the scars on her neck, brands of the torque that she had worn as priest and priestess, until she cast it away. "She's a child," she went on, "but she's wiser than she knows, and stronger than she thinks. He chose her with his temper, true enough; but a Sunlord always judges best when he's not trying to think."

"Are you saying," Vanyi asked, "that Sun-blood is better brainless?"

"Often," said the Sunborn's child, "yes. If the god exists—if he's not the dream of a mage afraid of his own power—then I think we may be one of his more splendid failures. Or maybe we're the joke he plays on the world's fools. My father honestly believed that he was sent to bind the goddess in chains and raise up an imperishable empire. I learned what folly that was; I lost my magery to it, and my very self. But I had my own idiocy. I thought that I was to make one empire of two, I and my lord. I thought that I had done it; or close enough, once my lord was dead and I had killed my name. When I left, I meant to leave forever—to become nothing, a nameless thing, a leaf on the wind.

"And I did, priestess. For a lifetime of simple men, I did.

Then I wandered back through the empire I had forsaken and by then nearly forgotten. I paused by a river, and saw a young man fishing. He looked like any other princely idiot with a line and a hook and a bag of Islander tricks, which made me smug, because I had brought the Isles into the empire.

"Then he turned his eyes on me. I had no name yet. I refused to have one. But he forced me into his orbit. He made me remember. He spelled me as my father spelled the princes he would conquer, or as I would trap my lords of the warring empires. I was the biter bit, priestess. I was a Sunlord's slave."

"What are you trying to do?" Vanyi asked her mildly enough, all things considered. "You don't need to snare me in lies. You won't snare him. He's past that."

"Well," said Sarevadin, unruffled. "It's not untrue. He did startle me. He did remind me of what I'd been. And he's lethally charming when he wants to be."

"So are you," Vanyi said. "I don't suppose you'll tell me how you got in here. There are wards. Or didn't you notice?"

"Isn't it a little late to wonder?"

"You aren't a mage. I think that much is true. But you're something else." Vanyi's eyes narrowed. "You *are* magic. That's it, isn't it? That's what the mages did to you. They shattered you and made you anew; but when they did that, they made you a new thing: a human shape, a human soul, but sealed with power. I could sever myself from my magic, if I were driven to it; or Estarion could, as he did to the mages who fought him. You can't do that. Every part of you is woven with magery."

Sarevadin shrugged. Perhaps she truly did not care; perhaps she had known it for so long that it no longer seemed to her a wonder.

"And," said Vanyi as the truth unfolded in her, "that's why you didn't die when Hirel did. You can't, can you? Not while the power is in you. You made yourself age, for a disguise. Left to yourself, you'd still be as you were when you left Endros. And that wasn't as a woman of threescore years should be. In yourself, in truth, you haven't aged since the mages made you anew. Have you?"

Sarevadin smiled. "Are you going to remake yourself, priestess, and be immortal?"

Vanyi shuddered. "Gods, no. I've earned the scars the years have given me. I want to die when my time comes, and go where the dead go."

"If that is anywhere," said Sarevadin, "and not to oblivion."

"Oblivion would be pleasant enough," Vanyi said. "You're barred from it, yes? You tried to enter it, and it refused you. And Hirel went without you. Will you ever forgive him for that?"

"No," said Sarevadin. She was no longer smiling. "You should be less wise. You'll live longer."

"Are you going to kill me, and kill Estarion, and take back your throne?"

Sarevadin shuddered precisely as Vanyi had. "I'm going to keep you children alive. We made a royal mess of things, my father and I; we need you to patch it together. Estarion will, you know, if he doesn't shatter before morning. And you, if you don't do something ridiculous."

"And if we do," said Vanyi, "you'll live. You'll do what must be done. Promise me that."

"I promise nothing," said Sarevadin.

"Then I give you nothing," Vanyi said. She stretched out her hand, limbered her power. "No Gate. No help. No defense against the mages."

She would do it. She was angry enough, and tired enough of all of it. She was not royal, not even noble. She cared nothing for honor or duty or any such foolishness.

Sarevadin sighed. She was looking younger; or maybe it was the light. There was a faint coppery sheen in the frost of her hair. "Avaryan defend us from stiff-necked commoners. If we're trading threats, then shall I threaten to separate you from your magic?"

"Then I'll be no good to you," Vanyi said. "And Estarion might object. He's stronger than you."

"But younger," said Sarevadin, "and completely without guile. I learned trickery from the greatest of masters."

"So do it," Vanyi said. "What difference does it make whether he destroys himself now or later?"

"There now," said Sarevadin. "Where's your insouciance? We're going to win this game, priestess. Win it or lose it splendidly."

"I'm not a Sunlord's get," Vanyi said. "I don't know about bravura. All I know is stubbornness."

"That will do," said Sarevadin.

Korusan waited for Estarion. He seemed to do a great deal of that, some of it voluntary, some not. Korusan could not tell which this was. He could have been at the death-rite. Should have, perhaps. But he chose to stand guard on the empty chambers. They echoed without Estarion to fill them. He wandered through them, pausing to touch a vase that Estarion had liked, a cup that he had used, a cushion on which he had sat.

When he had walked the circle of rooms, an Olenyas stood waiting for him. Marid. He was almost still. In him that was ominous. His eyes held no malice, his stance no danger; but no friendship, either. None of the warmth that should be between brothers. He said, "The Masters summon you."

"Do they?" Korusan almost laughed. It was not mirth. "Tell them that I shall come to them."

"Now?"

"After sunset."

"They said now."

"I am in trouble, then?"

Marid's eyes widened in honest surprise. "Of course not. How can you be?"

Easily, thought Korusan. Aloud he said, "I shall come to them after the sun has set."

He thought that Marid would protest. But his swordbrother

sighed, shrugged. "He's to die tonight. I heard them say it. With or without you, they said. Some are wondering if you really are the Lion's cub."

"That," said Korusan, "I am. Have no doubt of it."

"They say he has you bewitched. Is he such a master of the high art as that?"

"No." Korusan leaned against the wall. It was not that he had grown weaker; he was past that. He should sleep, maybe, if the pain would let him. "He has no art. He is all instinct."

"I had a northerner once, for curiosity. It was like coupling with a panther."

"So it is." Korusan considered Marid slantwise; thought of killing him. Thought of dying, and of taking Estarion with him. "Tell them. After sunset."

"You're ill again," said Marid.

"Go," said Korusan, "or I drink your blood."

Marid stiffened. If he had reminded Korusan of the bond that had been between them, Korusan would indeed have slain him. But Marid was wise, or too angry to speak. He bowed with precision that came close to insult, and did as he was bidden.

When he was gone, Korusan let himself slide down the wall until he crouched on the floor. His veils stifled him. He flung them off. The air was cold on his cheeks. The brands of his rank stung like fire. They had magic in them, maybe, to discern his treason.

He was no longer Olenyas. Son of the Lion he was born, Son of the Lion he would die. But the brotherhood of the sword that had bred and trained him, kept him alive when he should have died, shaped him for their ends—they had never been his, nor he theirs.

He should have known it long ago. It was written in his face, branded in his eyes. His kin was the one whom he was sworn to destroy. No one else bound him. No one else could command him.

He drew a breath. It stabbed, but it would do, for a while. He felt light; free. He had no masters. He had no brothers but the one, who was his lover, whose life belonged to him. But for that one he was alone.

He would keep the robes, because they were warm; and the swords, because he would have need of them. He moved to rend the veils to shreds, but paused. They too might serve a purpose. He thrust them into his belt and settled to wait.

The feast of the dead would go on till dawn, with wine and singing and merriment that increased as the feasters undertook to forget the death that had brought them here. Estarion left them long before the sun went down. If any noticed, he did not know of it. They would expect him to grieve in solitude. And so he had, and would again, if he came back a living man.

They were building the Gate: Vanyi, the priests and priestesses who had been Iburan's and were now, in default of another, hers, and a strangeness that he knew was Sarevadin. He felt their working in his bones, as he felt that his presence would be no help to them. His power burned too fiercely. It would seize them all and wield them, and in the end destroy them. Wiser to keep apart and bind his magery, and pray that it would not burst its bonds before he came to the Tower.

Korusan waited for him with the patience of a child or an animal. The boy had taken off his veils. There was meaning in that; but he gave Estarion no chance to ask what it was. "Dance with me," he said before Estarion was fairly past the door.

Yes, thought Estarion. In the dance was forgetfulness. He should worry, maybe, that they danced with swords, and Korusan an Olenyas, a spy, possibly a traitor, against whom he had been warned. But Korusan was his, heart and soul. He knew that as he knew his own name.

They danced as they always danced, without rest, without quarter. Estarion was stronger, and longer of arm. Korusan was swifter. Deadly swift now, with death in his eyes.

Estarion matched him stroke for stroke. He laughed as he did it, because if he died it did not matter, and if he lived, he would die soon enough.

They locked blades. Korusan's eyes held fast on Estarion's. His wrist wavered a fraction. Estarion's sword sprang free, flashed round, halted a hair's breadth from the boy's throat.

Korusan smiled. "Yes," he said, a mere breath of sound. "Slay me now."

Estarion let fall the sword and pulled him in. "Idiot child," he said. "I'll never kill you. I'll keep you alive till you grow old with me."

"That will never happen," said Korusan against his breast.

Estarion bent his head over the yellow curls. They were damp with exertion, scented with something faintly sweet: spices, or the ghosts of flowers. "You're growing tall," he said. "Look, your shoulders are nigh as wide as mine."

"Never," said Korusan, "as tall as you."

"That's the northerner in me. I'm small among my kin, as you are tall among yours. That makes us even."

Korusan tilted his head back. "Do you love me?"

"You know I do."

"Do I?" Korusan looked hard into his eyes. Estarion did not look away. He had no shame to hide, no lie to dissemble. "Do I know that, my lord? You are all the world to me. To you I am an afternoon's diversion. If I died, you would mourn, and raise your beautiful voice in the rite for me, and lay me in my tomb; and then you would forget me."

Estarion recoiled, wounded. "Do you think so little of me?"

"I think that you are greater than I. My heart has room only for you. Yours contains a world."

"You're calling me a whore," Estarion said, lightly he thought, but Korusan lashed out with temper.

"Always you laugh at me. Always you reckon me a child. If I were a man grown, would you cast me off as men do their boys who are boys no longer?"

"Are you trying to make me hate you?" Estarion asked. "You can't do that."

"No? Even if I told you that I have been sent to slay you?"

"I knew that already," Estarion said. "You haven't killed me yet. I don't think you will."

"I will," said Korusan. "I have sworn it. I hate you, beloved. I scorn you. I spurn your name beneath my feet."

Yet as he said it he clung with fever-passion, pulling Estarion's head down, kissing him until he gasped. Estarion laughed. "You're eating me alive."

"I hate you," said Korusan. "I hate you with all my heart. I will slay you, and mount my throne above your grave."

"I love you, too, dear lunatic," said Estarion.

Korusan thrust back, furious. "You do not believe me! I am your enemy. I am the Lion's son. I was bred to destroy you."

"And I am the Sun's child," Estarion said, "and the other half of you. The throne is mine, and shall be till I die. Not even you can take it from me."

"Mad," said Korusan in despair. "Mad, mad, mad."

"Hush," said Estarion. "Love me."

He had not been certain that Korusan would obey. But the boy was his, whatever the blood he claimed. He yielded as all men must, to the will of the Sun's son.

Sun and Greatmoon sat face to face on each horizon, winter-gold and blood-red, the sun its wonted fiery disk, the moon a shield of blood. One could, if one blurred one's eyes just so, see how the sun reached across the arc of heaven to embrace the moon, god embracing goddess, light bending to its will the power of the dark.

There was none of that here where no windows were. Estarion's power had taken flight of itself to look on sun and moon and open sky; he dragged it back to the walls and the wards and the circle of watchful faces. Vanyi had brought in everyone whom she thought she could trust, who had power to sustain her Gate. It was a surprising number. Her priests and priestesses, of course, and some from Estarion's Guard, and a handful from the guard that had been his mother's and must now be Haliya's. But also the dark-robed priestesses who had walked soft in his mother's shadow, and a pair of nervous, darting-eyed Asanians in Lord Shurichan's livery. One wore the robe of a tame mage. He looked even less at ease than the other, who was a servant of rank, with a spark of magery that burned low but steady.

When Estarion came to the circle, Vanyi had already begun to draw them together, to make them one mingled skein of magic. His coming nearly shattered it, but she seemed to have expected that; she pulled him into the center with hand and power and held him there, willing him to be still. He did not resist her. He had never stood beside her in a great working, or even in a lesser one. He had never been mage enough to venture it.

Here, closed in the circle, he could see with both eyes and

power, with no fear of losing the capacity for either. She had done as he had, dressed for comfort rather than for state; like him she had chosen well-worn riding garb and plaited her hair behind her, and worn no ornament but the torque of her priesthood. She seemed at ease in the midst of her magic, frowning slightly, oblivious to him except as a force to be constrained lest it shatter the circle. She was something more here than she was elsewhere, and something less, ageless, sexless, almost pure power.

Strange then to realize who, and what, stood a little apart from them though still within the circle. Sarevadin truly had no age, no sex; if Vanyi seemed made of power, this was the truth of it. She was calm, neither helping nor hindering, watching Vanyi with a flicker of amusement and a glimmer of approbation, as a mother watches a child, or a master her pupil.

Estarion had had training, however Sarevadin disparaged it. He knew that this should be one mage's working, that the rest were there simply to provide Vanyi with strength as she needed it. Therefore he did not do as he longed to do, seize the power that Vanyi had gathered and shape it more swiftly, and raise the Gate in his own time and not in hers, that seemed so crawling slow.

He could have done it more quickly, and more enduringly too. But this was not his working. He lacked Vanyi's affinity for Gates, her sense of the moment when at last all the power was gathered, the wards at their strongest, and no force beyond them could know, or knowing hinder.

That moment sang in his blood, when sun and moon poised in the last movement of their dance, before the sun sank beneath the rim of the world and the moon sprang into the sky. Greatmoon was a cry like trumpets, the sun a ringing of bronze upon bronze. Vanyi smote her hands together, and the earth shook. What had been raw shapeless power rose up taller than a man and broader, looming over the lone small woman who presumed to master it. She raised her hands joined palm to palm. Estarion moved on instinct, laid his branded hand upon her shoulder. In the same instant Sarevadin did the same. Vanyi buckled under the weight of twin suns, but she was stronger than they. Slowly, as if she parted the leaves of a great door, she spread her hands apart.

Wind howled. It rocked her, but the others held her, and her hands never wavered. Lightnings cracked. None of them touched her. The force of the Gate plucked at her. She braced against it, even when it strove to coil about her, grip her, suck her into itself. Estarion's hand was white pain, her shoulder under it rigid. The Gate, half opened, was a cauldron of twisting, seething, boiling fires. It blinded him; it roiled in the pit of his stomach. His throat burned with bile.

Her hands were at their farthest extent, flattened as if against the posts of a door. Her will snapped out. *Help me!* Estarion raised his free hand, fighting against sudden, leaden weight, and gripped what felt, as it looked, much like a doorpost. He set his teeth and pushed. It pushed back. It tempted him to let go her shoulder; but that, he must not do. Holding to her with his right hand, with his left he thrust the gate wider, past the stretch of her shorter arm. When his arm was straight, trembling with strain, he glanced at her. The Gatefires had died down a little. Her face was a shifting pattern of lights and colors, but it was discernibly a face, tight-lipped, intent. "Now," she said.

He hesitated a fraction of a breath. Then he let go.

The Gate pulsed. His arm snapped up again, but stopped half-extended.

Vanyi sagged briefly under his hand, leaning against him, before she remembered to be prickly-proud. "It's done," she said. Her voice was crisp. "Best we move quickly. This is a warded Gate, and therefore secret, but even that may not be proof against the mages who first mastered Gates."

The circle shifted. One of them, the priest Shaiyel, came out of it to face Vanyi. "I'll keep the watch. The others should rest. If you need them later . . ."

"You'll know." She smiled. "You did well, all of you. Places are prepared for you, with wards to keep you safe until we come back."

Not if, Estarion noticed. Until. She had her own degree of arrogance, and no little penchant for acting the empress.

She waited until the last of the circle, but for Shaiyel, had retreated slowly, with many glances back at the wards, at the Gate, at the three who stood before it. Shaiyel withdrew to the edge of the wards, shaping the words and the gesture that would seal them anew.

A shadow slipped past him. Two shadows. One, feline, flung himself on Estarion, purring raucously. The other, robed but unveiled, turned a defiant face upon him.

"Yelloweyes," Estarion said, "you can't—"

"Wherever you go," said Korusan, "I go."

"Even to my death?"

"There above all else."

Estarion glanced at the women. Sarevadin had her blank blind look, as if she had forgotten where she was, or when, or why. Vanyi seemed merely interested; but that too was a mask.

"I don't trust him at all," she said, "but he belongs to you. You bear the burden of him."

Estarion wondered where she had learned to be so hard and cold. Not, he prayed, from him. He brushed the boy's cheek with a finger. It was fevered as it so often was, but the eyes were clear, unwavering. "Damn you," Estarion said. "If you kill me, you'll die a grimmer death than you ever dealt me."

"I would not wish to live if you were dead," Korusan said.

Estarion looked from him to the Gate. Death was in it. He saw the flicker and shift that was its shadow. Sudden joy filled him; a fierce, reckless, heedless delight. "Come then," he said. "Come with me and die."

"Not," said Vanyi, "if I can help it."

Estarion barely heard her. He seized Korusan's hand, caught another—Sarevadin's, fire-hot, fire-strong—and sprang.

"You blazing *idiot!*" Vanyi's voice, stripped to raw panic. Her hand, locking on his belt. They plunged into the maelstrom that was the new-made Gate.

He was drowning. Stones dragged him down—Korusan, Sarevadin, Vanyi, the ul-cub with claws sunk in his leg. He struck out with the one leg that was free, and with arms—wings—something—some untrammeled part of him that beat against the surging of the flood.

Wings, then, improbable as they were. And if he was winged, then this was not sea but storm-wild air, this turmoil the boiling of clouds, this tumult the thunder rolling in his blood. The winds that tore at him were worldwinds, sweeping him through the chaos of the Gates.

Small things rode him, clinging like grim death. He roared laughter, soared, swooped, soared again, riding the storm. It was mighty, but only in resistance. It was terrible, but only in battle. If he eased to it, yielded to its buffeting, it lost its power to destroy. It bore up his wings. It carried him from cloud to cloud, each cloud a world, each levin-bolt the fire of a Gate.

One of those who rode him crawled to his ear, shrieking into it. He would not have heeded anything so shrill, but the words forced themselves through the exultation of his flight. "Stop! Damn you, stop! You'll lose us in the worldwinds!"

He would not. But he had let himself forget why he flew here.

While he paused, struck with remembrance, Vanyi flung a bridle on him. He reared against it, but the bit was burning cold in his mouth, the reins implacable, drawing him about. Like a rebellious stallion he fought her; like a strong rider she turned his battle upon itself. And still the worldwinds bore them all.

A new hand took the reins. A new voice spoke in his ear. "Such a senel you make; and such wit, to gift yourself with wings. Tame yourself now and fly."

Sarevadin wore a new shape here, one that he had known in portraits since he was a child: northern face, copper-bright hair. But whether it was she or he, woman or man, he could not tell. Now it was the one, now the other. But the smile was the same in both, white and wild, and the bright dark eyes. "I know the way," said the Twiceborn, shifting, woman to man to woman. "Gates wrought me. Power is woven in me. I'll bring us to the Heart of the World."

Not the Tower of the Sun? Estarion wondered. But he did not speak. The bit forbade him, and the grip upon the reins, and the legs clamped to his sides, driving him on.

The storm was above him. Road rang beneath his feet—his sharp cloven hoofs, for he had willed this shape, and it was so. Worlds sped past him, but the road was outside of them. Magic quivered in it, on it. Magic rode him, nor could he turn aside.

He was pursued. How he knew it, at first he was not certain. Then his ears, straining back, caught the sound of feet; his nostrils, flaring, caught a scent like blood and burning.

"Mages," said Sarevadin, settling briefly to woman's shape.

And Vanyi behind her, holding to her, turning to peer past a pair of golden-eyed shadows: "We're warded against them."

"Not here," Sarevadin said. "Wards are no use on the mageroad." She—he—dug heels into Estarion's sides. "On, young one. On!"

He ran. Four legs were swifter far than two. Wings, he had lost or forgotten; no time now to win them back again. The burden he bore was light, though there were three of it; the fourth ran at his heels, darkness golden-eyed. It had been born amid the worldwinds, in the silence between Gates. It had come from Gates with the child of the Sunborn, to bind its soul to the Sunborn's heir. Here it was not so young as it seemed in the world beyond the Gates, nor so small, but it remained an ul-cat, with magic in its blood.

He stretched his stride. The ul-cub matched it; danced, even, laughing as a cat will, batting at his heels with half-sheathed claws. He started, bucked, learned at last what swiftness was.

* * *

Vanyi clung for dear life to an impossibility: a senel who was Estarion, and a shifting shape that was indubitably Sarevadin. The Olenyas clung to her with the rigidity of perfect terror. The worlds whirled past. Some were dark and some were light, some green and some bleakly brown, some full of water and some full of air, and all strange, all alien.

She had lost control of this venture before it was fairly begun. It was different to be in a Gate than to be outside of it, standing guard upon it. Here all laws were broken, all sureties undone.

Yet, once she had looked fear in the face and given it its name, she knew a strange delight. She was here, riding the mageroad. She was alive to know it, and strong in her power, and the Gate that had brought them here was hers.

Pursuit was gaining, though Estarion outran the worldwind. The watchers wore any shape they chose, but now, as if to honor Estarion's own choice of shape, they ran as direwolves. Magelore had it that they were empty of intelligence; they existed simply to catch trespassers upon the worldroad and dispose of them. But the eyes in the lean grey heads were bright with malice, and the teeth were bared in wide wolf-grins. They were hungry for manflesh, senelflesh, even—maybe—catflesh.

The first of the watchers drew level with the ul-cub. He slashed sidewise with dagger-fangs, and raked with claws. The watcher howled and tumbled from the road, bleeding fire. The others neither wavered nor slowed.

One of the arms deathlocked about Vanyi's waist let go. Steel hissed from sheath. Korusan held the longer of his swords poised along his thigh. She undertook not to shrink from that keen-honed blade hovering a handspan from her leg. If he was truly a traitor, he would plunge it into Estarion's straining flank and kill them all. And she would not be able to stop him.

A watcher sprang. The sword swept down.

Sarevadin bent forward over Estarion's neck, pulling Vanyi with her—him—both, neither. Hair the color of new copper lashed Vanyi's face. She gasped, blinded, and felt teeth close on her foot. There was no pain at first, simply the knowledge that pain would come, and the thought, dim and almost wry, that if Estarion bucked at the slash of teeth in his heels, Korusan's sword might cut off her foot. Would she bleed power then, or plain blood?

She kicked as hard as she could. The teeth tore free. She would not feel the pain. She must focus on holding to her rocking, heaving seat and keeping out of the way of the Olenyas' sword. He was an artist with it. He wasted no movement, indulged in no flourishes. Every cut found flesh, or what passed for flesh.

If these had been true wolves, they would have given up the chase long ago, even if they were starving. These would not pause until they downed their prey. Were there more of them? Or did each that fell give space to another, so that their number never varied?

Sarevadin muttered a curse. There was a long rent in the trousers, blood bright against dark skin. The face that half-turned was as male as Estarion's when Estarion was not wearing a stallion's horns, and as keenly carved, red-bearded, black-eyed, furious. "This will get us killed," he said. She. Shifting again, impervious to her own strangeness. She flung herself from Estarion's back, so sudden that Vanyi toppled bruisingly forward, locking arms about the straining neck. She struggled to look back. The watchers had paused, but not to devour Sarevadin. She—he—ran in the midst of them, slapping them with a bare and burning hand, kicking those that lunged to snap at his unprotected throat.

Vanyi hauled back on the reins. Estarion jibbed. "I'll be polite later," she snapped at him. "Slow *down,* damn you!"

He plunged to a halt that nearly flung her over his head. Before she was properly settled, he wheeled. And changed.

The road was hard. She got up stiffly, nursing a bruised tailbone. Estarion took no notice of her. He was running in his own shape toward the pack of direwolves, dagger in hand, shouting something indistinct.

Sarevadin shouted back. In man-form he was a little smaller than Estarion, a little narrower, and no less hot-tempered.

"Gods," said the Olenyas. "How like they are."

So they were, even when, again, Sarevadin was a woman, shoulder-high to Estarion, glaring down her nose at him. The watchers crouched whining at her feet. She laid her hand on the head of the one that had led the pack, and said distinctly, echoing in that eerie place, "What did you stop for? We're almost there."

"What in the hells did *you* stop for?" Estarion shot back.

Her direwolf leered at Estarion's ul-cat. The cub crouched low and snarled.

Sarevadin quelled them both with a glance. "This was getting out of hand. It's one thing to teach you how to run. It's entirely another to kill more watchers than can restore themselves."

"But these—things—the mages—"

"These are watchers," she said with taut-strung patience. "They won't harm you; they're only here to guard the road."

"But—"

"Watchers watch and guard, and keep young idiots moving. Guildmages close in ahead and behind, from the thresholds of their Gates. You have to be in control of yourself when you meet them, or they'll devour you whole."

"You've led us into a trap," Estarion said, flat and cold.

"It's easy to think so, isn't it? You can't stay here. You can't go back—the watchers will stop you. Now will you run?"

Estarion looked as if he would have argued, but the ul-cub had his wrist in its jaws and was pulling him about. One of the watchers nipped at his heels. He kicked like the senel he had briefly been, spat a curse, and bolted.

He swept Vanyi in his wake, and Korusan with not-blood dripping still from his sword. The pack ran behind, and Sarevadin among them.

They were warding, Vanyi realized almost too late. Protecting their erstwhile prey from enemies behind and, as some of them edged ahead, from danger before.

The worlds spun faster. Too fast. She struggled to stop, but the road had her. She could not slow or turn, or alter any moment of it.

Estarion veered. She cried out. And fell.

Quiet.

She half-sat, half-lay on stone. Stone arched over her. Fire burned, blessed warmth after cold she had not even known she suffered.

"The Heart of the World." Sarevadin's voice, no longer shifting, and her face as Vanyi had known it in Asanion, pared clean with age. She stood by the fire that seemed so simple and was so great a mystery, for it was no mortal flame but the light of power that ruled the worlds. She warmed her hands above it.

Estarion circled the wide bare hall with its walls that seemed painted or hung with tapestries, until they shifted and changed and showed themselves for Worldgates. They, like the fire, were simplicity to the eye, mystery to the mind. He made as if to touch one that showed a place of water and green things; it changed to a hell of fire. He drew back carefully and turned. "Why are we here? Is this a betrayal?"

"All who would master the Gates must begin here," said Sarevadin. "All roads of the Gates lead to this place."

"That may be true," said a cool bitter voice, "but I smell death here." The Olenyas had found himself a shadow to be part of, and the ul-cub to share it. He had sheathed his sword but kept his hand upon it. He moved from his chosen shadow into Estarion's. "If you have led us ill, you will answer to my sword."

"Gladly," said Sarevadin. She beckoned with her scarred hand. "Come, children. We're dead if we linger. They know we're here; they'll be moving to close the Gates."

Vanyi, stretching her bruised power, gasped. The quiet

here was illusion, the stillness a mask. Below that frail semblance was naked chaos.

The Heart of the World, that core of magic in all the myriad worlds, hung on the thin edge of ruin. Was it their coming that had done it?

Even as she shaped the thought, the Heartfire roared to the ceiling, then sank almost to embers; blinding bright, then blind dark. "Swiftly!" cried Sarevadin. "Take my hands!"

Estarion had her right hand, the Olenyas her left. Vanyi, slowest to move, hesitated between Estarion and his guardsman, yearning toward the one, shrinking from the other. Hating herself for both.

That moment cost her dearly. The fire roared up again. The worldwalls throbbed, flickering dizzily from world to world. She lunged toward Estarion, just as he sprang into the fire. Her hand caught his; tore loose.

She stumbled and fell to her knees. The floor heaved and rocked. Worldwind howled over her. Mages were in it. Watching. Waiting. Listening. They wanted—something. The Tower. The magic that was in it. The advantage that they reckoned to gain, somehow, from Estarion's healing. Or, and more likely, his death.

She clung to stones that surged like the flesh of a living thing. Shadows danced in the fire. One of them had a voice. "Can't move us through. Can't—move—"

Sarevadin. And Estarion, breathless, tight with what might have been pain. "Can't move back, either. You may be made of fire, but I'm half flesh. And my guardsman is all human. Get us out of here. It's killing him!"

Vanyi crawled across a floor turned treacherous, clinging where she could cling, slipping where it fluxed and slid. Her power was as bruised as she, and as helpless. She set her teeth and struggled on.

The fire was a sheet of blinding heat from floor to heaving, quivering vault of roof. Vanyi, well outside of it still, felt the heat of it on her face, searing her hair, crisping the flesh on her bones.

She had walked into this fire when first she mastered Gates. It held no power to harm a mage. Yet now it was worse than deadly, and they were in it, trapped in it. She could just discern their shapes: Sarevadin still unscathed but seeming helpless, Estarion clutching a writhing body to his breast, crying, *"Get us out of here!"*

Vanyi thrust a dart of power at the fire's heart. It sprang back, piercing her with agony.

"No one can get us out," said Sarevadin to Estarion. "Except you."

"I can't," he gasped. "I don't know how."

"What does knowing have to do with it? Open the Gate!"

"What Gate?"

"This!" The shadow that was Sarevadin wrenched his shadow-hand from the shadow-Olenyas and held it up. Vanyi shielded her eyes against a blaze that made the fire seem a dim and lifeless thing. "This, that opens all doors. That is itself a door."

"Open your own!"

"Mine is broken." She hauled him about within the fire. *"Open it!"*

"I don't—I can't—"

Vanyi touched the fire. Her fingers blistered and charred. She bit her lip until it bled, and pushed against the pain.

She could see them through the veil of it. Estarion held Korusan as if he had been a child; the boy's head was buried in the hollow of his shoulder. He raised his branded hand. His power flared more wildly even than the fire in which he stood. He must control it. Master it. And when he had done that, walk through the Gate that he had made.

She could do nothing. The fire was too strong. He was bred of it, and he could scarcely endure it. She could not imagine what torments racked the Olenyas.

She raged until she wept, beat on the fire with fists of power, gained nothing but blistered hands.

He raised the *Kasar* above his head. His hand trembled; he steadied it. He drew it down the fiery air.

The fire parted, folded away before that fire which was hotter than it could ever be, shrank and cooled and dimmed until it was simple Heartfire once more. A Gate opened in the midst of it, and Sarevadin set foot on the threshold. Estarion paused. "Vanyi!"

"Go!" she screamed at him in anger that came from everywhere and nowhere. "You don't need me now. Go!"

"Vanyi—"

She would have plunged into the fire, whatever it did to her, and pushed him through the Gate. But Sarevadin, poised in the Gate, caught hold of him and flung him through.

Vanyi was lost. Korusan was unconscious or worse, a slack weight upon Estarion's shoulder. And where they stood was nothing like the worldroad. It seemed a perfect void, save that something held him up beneath his feet, and something else tugged him onward.

Sight grew slowly. There was little to see but the shape that led him. Its hair was copper-bright again, its gender indistinct. That maybe was the truth of the Twiceborn; what she—he—was in the world of the flesh, was but a shadow.

Warmth pressed against his leg. The ul-cub had followed him yet again, moving easily through these Gates that racked human flesh and drove human minds mad. So led, so guided, he passed out of the darkness and into light.

He stood inside of a vast jewel: flat beneath his feet, faceted about and above him, everywhere netted and veined with splendor. No lamp had ever burned here, nor ever would. The stone burned with its own white light.

Carefully he lowered Korusan to the floor. The boy struggled suddenly, all but oversetting him. He found himself crouching and Korusan standing over him, gripping his shoulders with terrible strength. White rimmed the golden eyes. The face was the color of bone.

Korusan let go. Estarion straightened slowly. The boy seemed to have forgotten him, sliding through the shadowless light, veering wide round the ul-cub and the motionless, voiceless Sarevadin, toward what lay in the jewel's heart.

Black stone like an altar, or like the slab of a tomb. A sweep of white and gold: cloak of leather and fur undimmed by the years. And laid upon it, clad as a northern king, the sleeper.

He was asleep, truly, not dead. The fire of his life was banked low, the pulse of his heart slowed to the beat of the ages, the wind of his breath stilled to the faintest of whispers. And yet he lived, and living, dreamed.

Estarion knew that face. It met him in every mirror. Though all the portraits showed Mirain clean-shaven, his beard had grown with the slowness of his sleep. It was a little longer than Estarion's, curling in the same fashion. His hair was plaited along his side, his hands folded on his breast. He would not be a tall man, standing; somewhat taller than Korusan, maybe, compact and smooth-muscled, with a warrior's strength, perceptible even as he slept.

He seemed harmless as any sleeper was. And yet this Tower was his, this light that beat in it, this mighty stillness. Estarion's power touched the edge of his dreams and leaped back startled, stung as if with fire.

"Yes," said Sarevadin. "He's angry still. It's been a long night's sleep for him, and memory as keen as if it were yesterday. I'd wager little on the life of anyone who woke him now."

"Can he be waked?"

Estarion did not mean to ask it, but his tongue was as befuddled as the rest of him. She answered as calmly as ever. "Of course. He'd wake raging, and he'd sear you to ash in doing it, but wake he would. It's easy enough to do. Just command the spell to break."

Estarion bit his tongue. "Is he . . . supposed to . . . calm down while he sleeps?"

"After an age or two," she said, "maybe. Mages drove him to the edge before he was brought here. I doubt there's much left of him by now but anger. The Red Prince hoped that he'd dream his way back to sanity in this place that was built of his own best magics, and then, if there was a world left to wake to, go out to do the god's will."

"So he thought he did," said Korusan. He had drawn back from the sleeper, swaying on his feet. "Who is to teach him that the god is a lie and a dream?"

"You can say that here?" Estarion asked him.

"Here above all." Korusan stopped swaying and drew himself erect. "Is this not a place for learning the truth?"

"Such as," said Sarevadin, "that you are sworn to destroy all that the Sun has made?"

"My lord knows," said Korusan. "I told him."

"Does he truly, cubling? Truly and surely, in his bones?"

"I know," Estarion said.

They paid no heed to him, standing face to face beside the bier of the Sunborn. Estarion saw a memory, or perhaps a dream: this same two, this same battle of wills, but Sarevadin was young, as young as he, and heavy with the child who would be his grandfather's father.

"You are not my lord," she said, "and yet, young lion, you are. You love as he loved. But your Sunchild can never be yours entirely. We ended that, you and I, when you lived in that other body. We made a new thing. We wrought—"

"Failure," said Korusan, too cold for contempt. "And now he has brought me here. Is he a fool, do you think? Or merely eager to die?"

Estarion would not hear the flatness in those words, the hate that burned beneath them. He would remember the love that had been no lie, the despair that would lighten once he had his power again, his strength, his throne.

He felt the rising of the power that was in this place. It was part of the sleeper, and yet apart from him. It was all that he was not: coolness in fire, stillness in rage, darkness in light. It flowed softly over Estarion's rent and ruined magic. It soothed like a healer's touch. It guided him through the intricacies of his self. It began to make him whole, as he was meant to be.

He would have lain down beside the Sunborn and let the Tower work its healing. But Korusan stood between, and Sarevadin now old, now young, laughing in the boy's face. "Ask yourself, cubling. Are you the fool? Are you looking to die at your lover's hand?"

"Together," said Korusan. "We die together."

"Korusan," said Estarion through the mist of power. "Koru-Asan. What is this talk of death? You'll live while I live."

"And die when you die." Korusan drew his swords. They glittered in the strange light, but never as bright as his eyes. "I am dead, my lord. The fire in the cold place—it lodged in me. It consumes me."

"You're raving," Estarion said. Moving here was like swimming through light. He reached, paused as blades flashed into guard. "Here, stop that. What you're feeling is that you're whole. You've never known what that is."

"No," said Korusan. "I die." He slapped the left-hand blade into sheath, shook back the sleeve. His arm was a patchwork of bruises, wrist and elbow blackened, swollen.

Estarion caught his breath. He reached again. This time no sword prevented him. He laid hand on Korusan's arm.

Pain rocked him. So much broken, so much mended, and broken, and mended again.

Korusan smiled, bright and bitter. Bruises had begun to shadow his face. His blood was breaking its bonds. His bones were crumbling.

"No," Estarion said.

"Yes," said Korusan. He sheathed his right-hand sword and spread his arms. "Come, my love. No need to weep."

Estarion's eyes burned and stung, but not with tears. He stepped into his lover's embrace.

Iron hands flung him back. Sarevadin sprang on Korusan, impossible, shifting, young-old creature shouting words in no tongue Estarion knew.

She had hurled him into a corner of the Sunborn's bier, knocking the wind from him. He gasped and wheezed, struggling to breathe, to straighten, to stagger to his guardsman's defense. Steel flashed. A knife. The hand that wielded it was black with bruises, but ivory-white about them.

"No," said Estarion very softly. He knew the trick. Who did not? A sweet word, a proffered embrace, a dagger in the back. It was perfect Asanian.

Not Korusan. Not his gold-and-ivory princeling, his dancer with swords. He had slept in those arms for nights out of count, stood naked within reach of Olenyai steel, offered his life to it again and yet again. And Korusan had never harmed him.

They battled like brawlers in a tavern, black robes, dun leathers, long-limbed alike, wily-vicious alike, wielding teeth and nails when steel had failed. Estarion, though still gasping, found that he could move. He waded in.

They turned on him. But he had fought such battles before Asanion made an emperor of him; memory was swift and clear, here in his own Tower, in his own city, in this half of the empire that was truly his. The one who was armed was more immediately dangerous. The one who was not seemed confused that he eluded and would not strike her. He kept the corner of his eye on her, closing in on Korusan.

Korusan's eyes did not know Estarion at all. Maybe they were blind. His face was patched blue-black and ivory. His breath rattled as he drew it in. He coughed. Estarion tasted blood on his own tongue.

His power was slipping its bonds again—even here, where no Sunlord's power should be aught but mastered.

Korusan slashed. His hand was clawed with steel. Estarion darted in past it. Too slow, too slow. Burning pain seared his arm.

The second thrust aimed for the heart. Estarion reeled back. "Korusan. *Korusan!*"

No use. There was death in those eyes.

Sarevadin sprang again between them. She was as mad as the Asanian, and as murderous.

She at least was unarmed. He clamped arms about her and held grimly. She was strong, but not strong enough. She was a shield against the Olenyas: he hesitated, lowering his blade a fraction, seeming to come a little to himself.

"Put me down," said Sarevadin. She was breathing hard, but she sounded like herself again.

Estarion did not loosen his grip. "Give me your word you won't kill him."

"Only if he swears he won't kill you."

"That's between the two of us," Estarion said.

"Not with you it isn't. You've an empire waiting for you. Or have you forgotten?"

"Would to the gods I could."

She twisted in his arms. For a woman so ancient she was wonderfully supple. She slid down a handspan. He shifted his grip. She drove an elbow backward into his belly and tumbled free.

She did nothing at first but stand just out of his reach. While they struggled, Korusan had drawn back to the Sunborn's bier. He stood over it, knife in hand still, held loose at his side. He seemed rapt in contemplation of the sleeper's face.

As they watched, Estarion working pain out of his middle, Sarevadin immobile and seemingly empty of will, Korusan touched the still brow. Estarion gasped. But the spell did not break. The sleeper did not wake. His dreams quivered with anger, but so had they done since his haven was invaded.

This Estarion would become, if he did not master his power. He traced in pain the line of the wound in his arm. The Tower had driven Korusan out of his wits. It was no more than that, but no less. And Estarion had brought him here. Estarion bore the guilt of it.

Korusan bent. His whisper was clear in the stillness. "How like my beloved you are, and how unlike. He is a soft thing, for all his strength. You . . ." He laughed, low and surprisingly deep. "You are steel in the forge. Would you rule again, great king and liar? Would you conquer all that is?"

"He'll kill you," Sarevadin said.

Korusan set a kiss on the Sunborn's lips, mocking yet also, in its strange way, reverent. "May every man be given such a death. And maybe," he said, "I would draw blood before I died."

"Maybe not," she said. "Try it and see."

Estarion was beginning to understand.

She was farther away, and seemed for the moment disinclined to move. Korusan had laid his hand on the Sunborn's heart. Was it beating stronger? The air had a strange taste, like the moment before thunder. The light had dimmed by a fraction.

"Yes," said Korusan. "A son of the Lion stands in your own stronghold. He would set you free, that all may fall. All of it, O bandit king. Sun, dark, Keruvarion, Asanion, lion and black eagle—all that is. And look!" he said. "There is a stranger on your throne. He bears the Lion's eyes. He was born of the night's priestess. All that he is, you fought to avert. They have betrayed you, your son and your son's sons."

There was a singing in the air, faint and eerily clear, like shaken crystal.

Estarion's bones were glass. One stroke and they would shatter.

Was this what it was to be Korusan? This exquisite pain, this perfect despair? To know that he would never be more than he was now; that before he could be fully a man, he would die.

"I am the last," said Korusan. "No son can be born of my seed. When I am dead, the Lion is gone, and you are victorious.

"And yet," he said, "I too shall have my triumph. I take with me the son of your sons. When the Lion falls, so shall the Sun."

But, thought Estarion, it would not. Haliya in Pri'nai, walled in guards, made sure of that. He almost said it, almost betrayed the one secret that Korusan must not know. Not now. Not until he was sane again. For if he knew—if he found a Gate—

One could love what one most feared. One could even love what one hated. He had learned that in Asanion.

He moved softly. He knew better than to hope that he could take an Olenyas by surprise. But that he might come close while that Olenyas was absorbed in rousing what must not be roused—that, he could pray for.

His power strove to rage out of its bounds. Only the Tower constrained it now. He was as vast as the crag, his body a tiny brittle thing, creeping over the shimmering floor toward the man on the bier and the shadow above him. He willed himself down into the feeble flesh, his sight to narrow to the compass of his eyes, his awareness to focus upon this one, deadly moment.

Steel came to his hand. Olenyai dagger. He nearly cast it off in revulsion, but his fingers clenched, holding fast. He thrust it into his belt beside his own sheathed blade. The sound did not bring Korusan about. He had spread his hands over the sleeper, tracing the shape of the body.

"He knows," Sarevadin said, the shadow of a whisper. "They taught him well."

She had not moved, nor would she. She would let it happen. She would watch, and when the time came she would die; and she would have the rest that had eluded her so long.

Estarion did not want rest. He wanted—he did not know what. But not this.

He gathered himself and sprang.

Korusan wheeled. Estarion fell on him. He twisted. In the last possible instant, Estarion saw what he did. No need of spells or chanting if they fell full on the body of the Sunborn, and Estarion bleeding power in a spray of molten gold.

Estarion wrenched, heaved. They crashed to a floor that seemed harder than stone, smoother than glass. Light pulsed in it. Korusan lay still. Stunned? Dead?

Estarion shifted atop him. He surged, hands clawed, springing for the throat.

Estarion caught them. Pause, again. Blood rimmed the golden eyes. A bruise spread across the curve of the cheekbone, swollen, nigh as dark as Estarion's own hand. "Korusan," Estarion said. His voice caught, for all that he could do. "Yelloweyes. It's I. Wake; see. I've healing for you."

"You do not." Korusan arched his back. The pain tore at Estarion's bones. "Let me die," Korusan said.

Estarion's eyes blurred. He was not seeing with them, not truly, nor feeling with the heart that beat in his body. No.

"If you do not kill me," Korusan said, "I will wake him."

Estarion tossed his head from side to side. It ached, ah, it ached. He was breaking, mind, heart, power, all at once. "Wake yourself. You're dreaming, youngling. Wake and let me heal you."

"Will you let me kill you?"

"Would it comfort you?"

"No," Korusan said. He twisted, thrust sidewise, broke free. He had drawn his swords. One flew gleaming from his hand. Estarion caught it unthinking. It was the longer, the right-hand sword.

He dropped it at his feet. "Come here, Yelloweyes."

Korusan lunged.

Estarion did not believe it, even seeing it, even knowing the track of that blade. Even with the sting of the older wound, even in the face of all that he had seen, heard, suffered, he could not believe that this of all men intended his death.

Straight to the heart. No pause. No wavering. And worst and most terrible, no regret.

Unarmed, unable to move, Estarion looked into the face of his death.

And knew himself a coward. He dropped. The sword flashed over his head. He surged up. His hands locked about Korusan's throat. "Yield," he pleaded. "My dear love, give it up."

The sword shortened, stabbing. It slid on the toughened leather of Estarion's coat. He pressed his thumbs against Korusan's windpipe.

"Don't," he said. "Don't make me do this."

The golden eyes neither wavered nor fell. Korusan was smiling. He let go the sword. It clattered to the floor. His hands fell to his sides. Estarion began to ease his grip.

A claw raked his side. He gasped.

Korusan's smile was wide and sweet and quite empty of reason. He struck again with the dagger that had been hidden in his sleeve. His lips shaped words. *Hate you,* he said. *Love—*

Blood trickled down Estarion's ribs. If there was poison on that blade . . .

He was sobbing. For breath. Of course. His cheeks were wet. With sweat: naught else. "Stop it," he whispered. "Oh, my love, stop it."

Korusan slashed, caught Estarion's cheek so swift there was no pain at all, stabbed downward. *Die with me. Beloved, die—with—*

Estarion's fingers flexed on the boy's throat. He could not, oh, merciless goddess, he could not. Korusan thrashed. One hand dropped. Estarion felt—could not see, had no need to see—the narrow deadly blade like a needle, angled to pierce his heart.

And it would. So much Korusan loved, so much he hated, that he would die, and take his lover with him.

"No," Estarion wept.

They were body to body as they had been so often, locked like the lovers they had been, would always be. Korusan tensed against Estarion. His smile widened. His blade thrust again for the heart.

Estarion's body chose for him. It twisted, arched, took the needle in the meat of the breast—pain no greater than any that had come before, and no less. His thumbs thrust inward with terrible ease. And snapped the boy's neck.

51

VANYI STOOD ALONE in the Heart of the World. She was thirsty. That was so small a thing, and so absurd, that she laughed, a bark in her dry throat.

The Gate that Estarion had made had closed when he passed it. The Heartfire burned like simple fire, with even the illusion of wood beneath it. The worldwalls had returned to their slow cycling, shifting now one, now another, in a stately dance.

She could walk through any or all of them and find herself anywhere. She was tempted. To forget duty, honor, pain, priesthood, to become nothing and no one in a world empty of humanity . . . there was a dream for a black night.

She should have been prostrate with exhaustion from the raising of the Gate and the running of the worldroad. In any other place perhaps she might have been. Here, where all power had its center, she felt as she might in the midst of a long day's working, with much completed, but much still to do.

The way to the Tower was shut but not barred. It should have been locked against any but Sun-blood. Had the Olenyas done that? Or had Estarion left it so, to let her through?

Idiot. She called in her power to secure the Gate. It flooded her, nearly drowned her. She gasped and struggled.

It slowed. She shut herself off from it, willing her heart to stop pounding, her hands to stop trembling. Everything was stronger here, with the Heartfire to feed it. Even a mage sure to arrogance of her own mastery, could be taken by surprise.

She opened a sliver of gate to let the power trickle in. With it came awareness, and widening of senses that had focused on herself and her troubles.

Watchers. Not the wolves of the worldroad that had proved themselves loyal to the Sunchild. These were wolves of another sort, two-legged, skilled in magery. They were eager, like wolves on the hunt; hungry, yearning toward sweetness. What that sweetness was . . .

They were swift to shield, but not swift enough. Sealed behind her own strong walls, she studied what she had brought in with her, snatched swift and secret from the mages who watched: a web of greed woven with malice and old ranklings, and in it surety. The emperor had taken the Olenyas with him into the Tower. Through that one they would enter, slay the Sunlord, gain mastery over the one who slept. Even enspelled, Mirain was a mighty power. The mage who mastered him was master of aught that he desired. And if that desire was the Mageguild's power, its strength reborn, its puppet on the throne—then so might it be.

"You do lack imagination," Vanyi said. She did not trouble to keep it to herself. "You tried that once, and failed resoundingly. What makes you think you'll win it now?"

The Heartfire flared. Power beat on her shields. She rocked before it but did not fall.

"You are cowards," she said, "and always were: working through slaves and servants, hiding behind walls, lurking in Gates. Now you leave everything to a dying child, while you shiver in shadows."

They beat harder. She would crack, but not, she prayed, too soon.

"You're afraid of the Tower and the sleeper. You think that you can rule both—but no one can do that, unless he bears the *Kasar*. You haven't found a way to counterfeit that, have you? And you never will. You are small men, cravens and fools. True bravura would have attacked the Tower long ago. Maybe no mortal man can master it, but who's to say it can't be broken, and the sleeper taken in its fall? He may be a mage and he may be mad beyond recovery, but he's no more than a man."

"And would you do better?"

He came out of a Gate, one that had shown a mountain against stars and a constellation of moons, blood-red, sea-green, foam-white. He looked like a merchant grown discontented with prosperity. He fostered that impression: well-fed, well-clad, sleek, yet petulant about the eyes. There was a new and livid scar upon his brow.

To a mage who could see, he was both more and less than his body's seeming. He walked in power as in a cloak, as one who is master of it, and certain of that mastery. Yet he was not content with it. He was one who wanted. It almost did not matter what, or why, only that what he did not have, he wished to possess.

That too might be a mask, a temptation to contempt. Vanyi armored herself as she might. She would not be anything to incite the admiration of an Asanian with pretensions to rank: undersized Islander woman in clothes that, though serviceable, were near enough to rags. Of her power, little showed itself that might not be reflected glory of the Sun's blood.

Behind the mage who must have been the Guildmaster, came others robed in violet or in grey. They were all Asanian. She did not find that surprising. The Guild had been born in the Nine Cities, but those had given themselves to the temple. Asanion never had.

They spread in a circle about her, but not, she noticed, between her and the fire. Maybe they feared it. Maybe they thought that she did.

She did indeed. But she feared more what they might do if they seized the Tower and the king who slept in it.

She was a very poor guardian of this Gate. Her strength was not for battle. Her knowledge was in making, not in breaking.

She remembered the tale as it had been sung in Shon'ai by a eunuch singer. His clear voice rang in her memory. Mages in the Heart of the World, battle of power that turned to battle of steel and fist, and ended in the Tower of the Sun.

This was the same battle. They had won a truce only,

Sarevadin and her lion's cub. Now it was broken. Now it would end.

Vanyi shook herself free of despair that was a working of mages, even through her shields. The mages' Master shrugged slightly. "Our slave will do what must be done in the Tower," he said. "Do you think that you can stop him?"

"He's not your slave," she said.

"He serves us," said the Master.

"I think not." Her feet ached with standing. She sat cross-legged in as much comfort as she could feign. "You shouldn't trust the emperor's Olenyai. They serve the throne, and nothing less."

"The throne belongs by right to the one who serves us."

"The water-blooded offspring of a female line? A man whose seed has failed, who will sire no get? What, after him? The bastard of a slave?"

She had pricked his temper. Good: it weakened his magery, eased its grip upon her. "He is the emperor."

"Then he cannot serve you," she said reasonably. "Quite the opposite."

They were closing in behind. No doubt they had knives. They could not even live their own tale; they must thieve from another.

She had a dagger, but it was small, good for little but cutting meat. She had her power, which was no greater than it should be. Her best weapon, her tongue, would not be useful much longer. They would see that she was delaying them, and ride over her.

Unless . . .

She rose slowly, with as much grace as she could muster. She opened her mind by degrees, touching the Gates one by one. Her Gate-sense was overwhelmed here, where all Gates began and ended. She thrust blindly with her power.

The worldwalls stilled. The Heartfire burned steady.

The mages glanced at one another. She felt the leaping of thoughts, the forging of the web that bound mage to mage.

Now, she thought, while the web was still half-woven. A dart—there, where the web was not weakest but strongest. And in the instant of confusion, mind and body gathered, leaped.

Pain.

She shut it out.

Agony.

She willed it away.

Torment.

She flung herself through it.

Estarion fell to his knees. Korusan writhed in his arms. Death-throes; no life, no sense left, only the broken, witless shell. He clutched it to him and wept.

A body tumbled out of air, spun, righted itself. It had come through a Gate. The Gate slammed shut, bolted with power.

He stared blankly. The body had a name. Vanyi. And a voice, grating in his ears. "What in the hells—"

She was not looking at him, or at the death that he had made. He followed the line of her gaze, because it was less pain than that dead face.

Sarevadin stood where Korusan had been standing, bent over the body of her father. She seemed intent, almost curious, tracing the lines of his face, murmuring something that had the cadence of a chant.

Vanyi's breath hissed between her teeth. "He's waking."

And Sarevadin was singing him out of his sleep.

If a woman wanted to die so much that she did not care what died with her own death—if she were years gone in madness—might she not turn on all that she had been? Might she not undo the magics that she had wrought at such great cost, and rouse the power that she had sung to sleep? Would she even know what she did, save that she saw her death, and moved to embrace it?

The Tower healed the wounds of Sunchildren. If life was a wound, and healing was death, and death came only through the sleeper's waking, then the Tower itself would feed Sarevadin's will. It would do as it was wrought to do—even if it destroyed itself in the doing.

Vanyi was moving, trailing tatters of light. She gathered it in her hands, knotting swiftly. Sarevadin's hands lowered over the sleeper. If she touched, if she spoke his name, he would wake. Wake angry. Wake in a torrent of fire.

Vanyi flung her net of magic.

It fell short and shattered on the floor. Its strands of broken light blurred into the shifting, pulsing patterns of the stone.

Estarion laid Korusan aside gently, without haste but with speed enough. He was moving as he moved in the dance, slow to his own senses, swift to those of the world without. The flames were rising. The sleeper breathed in time with them. His fingers flexed on his breast. The faint line of a frown creased his brow.

Estarion glided forward. Vanyi had fallen. She had put all of herself into the net; she had no strength left to stand. She stirred, but feebly.

Sarevadin swayed. Her face was rapt.

Estarion closed arms about her and gasped. She was wise, and wily in her madness. She was shielded against his power.

He set his teeth. His body convulsed, but he held. His power fluxed. His blood was boiling. His brain was like to burst from his skull.

And he held. She could not finish her working while he killed himself on her shield. She poured power into it. He poured it away. It roared through blood and bone. It battered the barrier of his skin. It found exit in the *Kasar.*

He barred it. He did not know how. He did not care. He shut the gate that would have saved him.

"Stop it!" she shrieked at him. "You'll burn alive!"

And he would not when the Sunborn woke?

She raked nails across his face.

So low she had sunk, she who had been both prince and princess, Sunlord and Sunborn empress. He counted the sting of those small wounds with all the rest, and laughed. It was pain, not mirth. His throat was full of fire. He could hold no more of it.

And more came. He would break, he would die.

Or he would grow to hold it.

As a flower grows, or a child, because it must; because its nature is to become greater than it is. Swiftly, of necessity; slowly, in the order of things, little by little, each small part of it full and complete before the next began. One could lose oneself in the wonder of it.

His body was healing. His soul would not. Grief was nothing that even mages could mend, except with forgetfulness.

And still the power came. She was draining it out of herself, and out of the working she had made, and—dear god—into the spell that bound the Sunborn.

She had not been waking the sleeper at all. She had been fighting him. Estarion, mistaking her, had come deathly close to breaking the spell himself.

The flow of power had stopped. Sarevadin was not empty; she could not be while she lived. But she was weakened, and sorely.

Vanyi was weaving her web again. She took its strands from her own substance, plaiting it with threads of stonelight. She murmured to herself as she wove. It sounded less like a spell than like a string of curses.

"Help her."

He glanced down startled.

Sarevadin's eyes were open, no anger in them, no scorn of his idiocy. "She's not strong enough to do it alone. Help her."

Estarion tossed his aching head. "What can I do? What if I go wrong again? What if I finish what I began, and wake the Sunborn?"

Her brows drew together as if with temper, but she sighed. "I don't suppose I should expect you to trust your power, after all you've done to it. But you have to learn, and quickly. She thinks she's enough. She's not. With you she may be."

"What can I—"

"Shut up and do it."

He could not. He did not know how.

Sarevadin climbed the ladder of his body. He tensed to thrust her away. She caught at his arms. Her hands were burning cold. "Do it," she gritted. "Do it, damn you."

He loosed a thread of power. It met Vanyi's shields and snapped back.

Sarevadin shook him, nearly oversetting them both. *"Do it!"*

He could not. His touch was too strong. Even the brush of it frayed the web.

"Fool of a boy," muttered Sarevadin. She closed her eyes. He clutched her before she fell. But she was firm enough on her feet, with him for a prop. Power hissed and crackled about her. It stung. He was caught; he could not let go.

Her power seized his with ruthless strength and wielded it. Full in the heart of the weaving. Darting through the knots and plaiting, needle-thin, needle-sharp. Drawing them in. Making them strong. Plucking the net from the hands that had made it, and casting it over the man on the bier.

He tossed beneath it, raising hands that clawed to rend it to rags. He was not awake, not yet, but his anger was roused, and it ruled him.

Sarevadin crooned: to herself, it might have been, or to the web that strained and tore. Estarion's power was in her hands still. She poured her own through it, taking from it what she needed: youth, strength, raw unshaped will. She gave it shape. She wove the web anew, and herself into it, as Vanyi had.

Vanyi had kept her soul apart from the making. Sarevadin's soul was the making. Her life was her power. Her body was wrought of it. She shifted as she had on the worldroad, a woman to man to maiden to youth to shape of both and neither. And still she wove, singing her wordless song.

The sleeper fought her with mindless rage. His dream had turned to fire.

She sang it down. She cooled it with water of the soul, sweet spring of light, soft rain on parched earth. She sang calm; she sang sleep. She sang a soft green stillness into which his wrath subsided. She bound it there. She gave it dreams; dreams of peace.

The Sunborn lay still under the pall of power. He was not all resigned to it: one hand had fallen to his side, clenched into a fist. But he was bound. He would learn perforce the ways of peace, who had ever been a man of war.

Sarevadin sighed in Estarion's arms. She was herself again, fragile with great age, and her eyes were calm, almost happy. More truly so, maybe, than they had been since Hirel died.

She smiled. Her voice was a thread, almost too thin to bear the weight of words. "That will keep him for a while. Do you trust me now, a little?"

"I always trusted you," Estarion said.

"Don't lie. It makes you twitch." She shifted; he settled her more comfortably. She weighed no more than a child. "You'd better lay me here. It's a long way down to the tombs, and I'll be dust before you come there."

"You're not dying," said Estarion, but his heart clenched. She was withering as he watched.

"They said I couldn't die. They didn't think I'd strip myself of power. They didn't know I could. No more," she admitted, "did I, until I did it." She smiled. "I'm not sorry I tried. It gave you yourself. And it gave me . . . it gave me . . ."

"Death," Vanyi said. She was white and shaking, but she was alive. She stretched out a hand, not quite daring to touch the cheek that was thin skin stretched over bone. "Wouldn't a simple cliff have done as well, with rocks at the foot of it, and the sea to sweep you away?"

Sarevadin was beyond answering, but her eyes laughed.

The Sunborn's bier was broad enough for two. Estarion laid her on it, gently, and straightened her limbs. He had nothing to cover her with, but she was too frail to bear the weight of cloak or pall, even if it were made of light. Her life was ebbing softly, slowly, like water from a broken cup.

Her body sank with it. Flesh melted from bone. Bone crumbled to dust. No pain went with her dying, no fear, no thought but joy. And that was a splendid, soaring, bright-winged thing, casting off the memory of flesh, leaping into the light.

THE SUNBORN DREAMED again his long dream. Beside him on his bier lay a shape of ash that fell in upon itself and scattered in the wind from the Gate.

Estarion whirled. There had been no Gate, once Vanyi was in the Tower. Yet the wall behind him was open, and beyond it the Heart of the World. Mages stood there, one in robes that mingled dark and light, and those behind him like guards, some in violet, some in grey; and in a half-circle about them the black shadows of Olenyai. One Olenyas stood beside and a little behind the master of the mages, hands on swordhilts, so like Korusan that Estarion almost cried his name. But Korusan lay beyond the bier, crumpled, twisted, dead.

Vanyi's voice shocked Estarion into his senses. It was clear, hard, and perfectly fearless. "I forbid you to trespass here."

"Are you Sun-blood," demanded the Master of the mages, "to permit or forbid?"

"Are you Sun-blood," she countered, "to set foot in this place? Men go mad here, mage. Men die."

"Old jests," said the mage. "Old nonsense."

"Then come," she said. "We killed your spy. Our own madwoman is dead. The Sunborn is not likely to wake in this age of the world; and no thanks to your plotting for that."

The mage's eyes widened slightly. He seemed for the first time to see the bier, the Sunlord beside it, the body of the Lion's cub with the ul-cub crouching over it as if on guard.

The Olenyas had seen it long since. His eyes were on Estarion, level, betraying no emotion.

"Yes, I killed him," Estarion said. "It was my right. His life was mine, as mine was his."

The Olenyas inclined his head. "Majesty," he said.

Estarion stiffened. He was being given—something. He did not dare to hope, yet, that it was acceptance. "Do you serve me, Olenyas?"

"I serve the emperor," said the Olenyas.

"You," said Estarion as knowledge came clear, voice and eyes and set of the body in the robes, "are the captain of Olenyai in the Golden Palace."

"I am the Master of the Olenyai," said the Olenyas, "majesty."

Estarion drew a breath. "Am I the emperor?"

The Olenyas paused. Estarion did not breathe, did not move. Nor, he noticed with distant clarity, did the mages. Their Master looked as if he would have spoken, but did not dare.

"Yes," said the Olenyas. "You are the emperor."

They won their veils in battle and their rank in combat, man to man. In slaying their prince and champion, Estarion had won their service. He even bore their brand: the sting and throb of the long cut in his cheek, that Korusan had made before he died.

It gave him no joy. "If you are mine," he said, "then serve me now. Take these traitors to my throne. Kill any who resists."

The mages seemed unable to believe what they had heard. Even after their allies closed in upon them, taking them captive; even, some of them, when they broke and ran, and swift steel cut them down.

The Master of mages was quicker than his fellows, and closer to the Gate. As the Olenyai closed in, he bolted for what he thought was safety.

Estarion sprang to seize Vanyi and fling her out of the mage's path. She ducked, slid, broke free. The mage hung in the Gate. Her power pulsed, holding him there. He raised lightnings against her.

She hurled them back at him, reckless, in a blind fury, as if all of it were seething out of her—grief, rage, guilt, fear, hate, love that had bent awry and turned to pain.

The mage seized on that pain and twisted. She lunged into the Gate, went for his throat. He laughed in his bonds. He had trapped her.

He caught her in midleap. She kicked and flailed. He held her just out of reach of eyes and throat, and while she raged, forgetful of power, he smote her with his magery.

She sagged. He drew her in. He would kill her with his hands, bind her with his power, seal her to his will—any or all of them. Estarion, helpless on the far side of the Gate, barred from it by magewalls, could only watch and rage.

The mage clasped her tightly. His power uncoiled.

She erupted, body and power. He toppled astonished. She bound him as he lay, her movements swift, furious, and heaved him up.

He hung again in the void of power that was the Gate, wound in cords like a spider's prey. And like a spider's prey, he looked living on the face of his death. Shadows gathered about him. Watchers: dim shapes like wolves, grinning wide wolf-grins.

The ul-cub yowled and sprang. The watchers scattered. The cub in the Gate was larger than they, black beast sun-eyed. He bared his fangs at the mage. The mage began to struggle.

Vanyi stood back, watching, saying nothing.

The mage spoke with remarkable steadiness under the circumstances, but there was no mistaking the desperation in his voice. "Let me go," he said. "Lady, priestess, whatever you wish, whatever I can give—"

"What have you given us," she asked him coldly, "but death and betrayal?"

"I erred, I confess it. I'll serve you faithfully. Only let me go."

"No," said Vanyi.

He offered her gold. He offered her slaves. He offered her empires—and what right, Estarion wondered, had he to do that? She ignored him. He offered her magic. She clapped hands over her ears. He offered her the Gates and all that was in them, if she would set him free.

"Take him," she said to the ul-cub.

The cat flowed toward him. He began to scream.

"Goddess," she said in disgust. "Nothing's even touched him."

Nothing, Estarion thought, but terror.

The ul-cub circled the mage, tailtip twitching. He fought harder against his bonds.

They snapped. He dropped, still screaming. The ul-cub sprang.

It was a clean kill. One spring, one snap of jaws in the neck. The ul-cub stood atop the body, treading it with half-flexed claws, as if to ask it why it jerked and twitched.

Slowly it stilled. He sniffed it. His nose wrinkled. He stepped away fastidiously, shaking a paw that had drawn blood, pausing to lick it clean. The watchers had stood back in respect, but once he had retreated they closed in, surrounding the body. Their chieftain sniffed the blood on it, tasted it. He barked once. The pack fell yelping on the feast.

The ul-cub ignored them. He sprang out of the Gate and flung himself at Estarion's feet, and set to washing himself thoroughly, with much snarling and sneezing at the stink of mageblood.

Vanyi followed the cat, walking steadily. Only Estarion, maybe, saw how pale she was, how pinched her face. He yearned to clasp her to him, to stroke her pain away. But he had grown wise: he did not touch her.

When she turned again to the Gate, she was calm. She said to the Olenyai, "By your emperor's leave, take the prisoners back to Pri'nai. He will follow when he is finished here."

The Olenyai glanced at Estarion. He hesitated. The Gate sang faintly to itself. The watchers were still feeding.

Below the Tower was the crag of Endros and the river, and

his own city. He had but to find the door to that doorless place, and walk out of it, into his palace.

Or he could pass the Gate, enter the Heart of the World, walk from it to Pri'nai and Asanion and rebellion that was not ended for that its prophet was dead.

His heart shrank from facing Asanion again. Even Haliya, even his ladies in Kundri'j—he was duty to them, no more. Asanion would never be his, would never learn to love an outland conqueror.

He knelt beside Korusan's body. He had straightened it when he laid it down, so that the head did not hang awry on its broken neck. The face was quieter than it had ever been in life. Not at peace, no. Peace was alien to emperors, or to princes of the Lion's brood.

Estarion was the last of that blood, but for the child in Haliya's womb: he with his dark hands, his alien face. He was the Son of the Lion.

He kissed the cold lips. "I loved you," he said. "Not enough. Not as you loved me. No one can love like that and live. But as a Sunlord can love—so I loved you." He lifted the body, cradling it. Already it had begun to stiffen.

He could not lay it on the bier. It was not fitting. Yet he did not wish to take it from the Tower.

His power was in him, filling him like wine in a cup. It flexed a tendril of itself. The Tower responded. Where had been blank luminous wall, a niche stood open, like the tombs of the kings in the crag below. Estarion laid Korusan in it. It fit him precisely.

As Estarion drew back, the wall closed again. Through it as in a glass he could see the shadow that had been his lover, his enemy, his kinsman. He kissed his burning palm and laid it against the stone. He did not speak. All that he could say was said. There was nothing left but silence.

They were waiting still, Olenyai and mages beyond the Gate, Vanyi and the cat on this side of it.

He spoke to the Olenyai. "Let your prisoners go."

The Olenyai did not wish to obey, but he was their emperor. The mages responded variously to freedom. Some stood still, as if they did not dare to move. Some shook themselves like ruffled birds. A few stepped apart from their erstwhile jailers and faced Estarion through the Gate. Those would be the strongest of them, or the most determined in rebellion.

"The battle is mine," he said to them.

"But the war may not be," said a woman in grey. Her shadow-brother stood behind her, hands on her shoulders, and fixed Estarion with a cold stare.

He gave them fire-heat. "You have a custom, yes? Whoever defeats your master in battle of magecraft, becomes master in his stead."

The lightmage was not pleased to answer, but answer she did. "That is so."

"Then by your law," said Estarion, sweeping his hand toward Vanyi, "this woman is your master."

Vanyi opened her mouth. The lightmage spoke before she could begin. "That is none of ours. She belongs to the temple."

"She is a mage," said Estarion, "and a master of Gates."

"Estarion—" said Vanyi. She sounded as if she could not decide whether to kill him quickly or let him die slowly, in the most exquisite agony she could devise.

"She defeated your master in combat," Estarion said to the mages. "Fair, I would hardly call it, but there is no question as to the victor."

Some of the mages looked as if they would have argued, but the lightmage, who seemed to hold rank among them, silenced them with a slash of the hand. "What are you proposing, Sunlord?"

Another merchant, this one, and settling in to haggle. He was in no mood to indulge her. "This is your trial, mage. I judge you guilty. You have earned death, but I am weary of killing. I give you all to this priestess-mage. Your Guild is hers, to break or to keep. But if she breaks it, then you die."

"And if I won't kill them?" Vanyi demanded.

"Then I will." There was iron in his voice, the taste of it in his throat like blood. "Let them live, and be master of them. Refuse to master them, and they die."

She looked long at him, studying him as if he were a stranger. Maybe he was. He was not the fragile young thing that had come to this place. He was not whole, either, not surely, not yet. But he was beginning to be what he was born to be: mage, priest, emperor.

"If I do this," she said, "you'll lose all hope of making me your empress."

His belly knotted. He had been going to command her in that, too; to name her empress in despite of the woman in Pri'nai. No one else was more fit to rule.

"Haliya might surprise you," she said, reading his thoughts as she always could, even when he was shielded; as he had been able to read hers even when he had no power to speak of. It was not magery. It was love.

"Yes, I love you," she said. "I always have. I always will."

"And your price is the Guild—the deaths of its mages?"

She flinched. He had not meant to say that. It had come out of him, out of the high cold thing that he was becoming, here in the Tower of his fathers. She seized his hands. "You won't let them live? Even for me?"

He looked down at her. He never remembered how small she was. Not much taller than Haliya, but tall in the soul, and great in power. Very great. She made so little of it that even mages failed to see the truth.

"You don't want me," he said, reading it in the eyes that lifted to meet his. "Not except for yourself; not for what I am or the titles I bear. You were never made for empire. But power and the Gates—there you are mistress and queen."

"Not queen," she said.

"No," he said. "But Master of the Guild, yes. It won't be easy. There are more mages, maybe, than any of us imagines. I wager you'll find them on all the worlds of the Gates, or near enough. And they're mostly Asanians. They hate foreigners, and they despise the lowborn."

She was shaking as if with cold. She was no fool, to be fearless of what he wished on her.

Wished, no. He wanted her at his side, sharing his throne, his bed, his heart.

Wisdom was a bitter thing.

"If you don't lead them," he said, "and keep them rigidly in hand, they have to die. I can't trust them. They contrived the death of my father; they nearly killed me. I won't leave them free to destroy my son."

He had startled the mages and brought the Olenyai quivering to attention. He would have laughed, if he had remembered how.

Vanyi took no notice. Her eyes were full of tears, but they were as hard as his own, and as clear. "You've changed," she said.

"For the worse, I'm sure." She caught his irony; her lips twitched. She still held his hands. He turned them to clasp hers. "I envy you. I have my empire, and my power is mine again. You have the high magic. The Gates are yours, and all the worlds they command."

"If I can master them."

"You doubt it?"

Her lip curled. "I'm not a prince's get. I don't know what I can do until I do it."

"Nor do I," he said, "and I'm a Sunlord's get."

"You don't leave me much choice, do you? Empress or Guildmaster. What if I want to be a simple priestess on Journey?"

"The mages die," he said.

She drew her breath in sharply. "And you? What are you going to do? Hide in Endros? Hope your troubles go away?"

She thought she had him. It was fair, he supposed. "I . . . thought I might rest. For a while."

"While your empire falls about your ears? That's wise, yes."

"Of course," he said, "before I can rest, there's a little matter of civil war. And a pair of empires that must be one. And two cities that will submit to the mastery of another that is neither Asanian nor Varyani, but both. Once that's built, then I'll sleep for a cycle, and go hunting for a season, and forget that I was ever born to rule this monstrosity of an empire."

She gaped. She would never forgive him, he thought, for mocking her. Then she laughed. There was pain in it, but it was real enough for that. "Confess, Estarion. You didn't know you'd say that until you said it."

"I didn't," he said.

"We know each other well," she said. She let go his hands, ran hers up his arms, stroking them, as if she could not help herself. "If I take the Guild, you've lost me. I won't come to your bed. I won't be your lover. What I will be . . . I'll be your friend, Meruvan Estarion, but not your servant. I'll serve you as I can, as the needs of the Guild allow. But if I see that your commands will serve the Guild ill, I'll oppose you."

"Even to death?" he asked her.

"If I must."

Her hands rose to his shoulders, crossed his breast, came to rest over his heart. It was beating hard. "I can't promise you," he said, "that I'll always do what's best for the Guild. If breaking the Guild will serve my empire, I'll do it. Even if it kills you."

She bowed her head, raised it again. This was no easier for her than it was for him. But she had courage at least to match his, and will as strong. She took his face in her hands, pulled it down and kissed him. "For remembrance," she said.

If he had had tears left, he would have wept. She let him go, turned, walked toward the Gate. She stepped through it. The watchers watched but did not move. She stood before the mages. "You heard," she said. "Now heed. You saw what came of your Master. Remember it."

They would remember. Estarion would never forget.

The ul-cub rose from his crouch by Estarion's feet,

stretched from nose to tail, and eyed the Gate. He was thinking of his mother and his sisters, of milk and meat and sleep.

Yes, Estarion thought. Sleep. The long night was past; the dawn had come. He looked about, to remember: black bier, bright walls, shadow in the stone.

Beyond the walls the sun was rising. It brought light into this place of all places, great tides and torrents of it, flowing over him, singing in his blood. He filled his hands with it, and bore it with him through the Gate, and in that cold hall of all suns and none, poured it out upon the stone.

The mages did not understand. The Olenyai, maybe, did. Vanyi looked ready to strike him. "This is not your place," she said.

"All places are mine," he said, "and none, as they are for any man. I'm lord of a world. May I not bear tribute from it to the Heart of all worlds that are?"

She did not trust him. That was pain, but it was just. She was his equal now; and that both pricked and pleased his pride.

He met her glare with the flicker of a smile. "Welcome me to the heart of your realm, mistress of mages."

Her glare did not abate. He would not have been surprised if she had flung him back where he came from, cat and guards and all. "You have nerve," she said as if to herself, and not kindly either.

His smile widened. He did not mean it to. With all the grief on him, the guilt, the blood on his hands, he should never smile again. But there was a pool of sunlight between them, here where sunlight never came, and she was wonderful to watch, mantled in her magic, wrestling with her temper.

She mastered it. Sparks still flew from it, but when she spoke she was civil, if not precisely gracious. "Welcome," she said, "to the Heart of the World." And after a pause, in which no one seemed to breathe: "My lord emperor."

That would do. For a beginning.